STAR DESCENDANT CHRONICLES

THE
DRACONIAN CONSPIRACY

M.G. PRICE

Copyright © 2020 Adrian Price

ISBN: 978-1-925442-56-4

Published by Vivid Publishing
P.O. Box 948, Fremantle
Western Australia 6959
www.vividpublishing.com.au

Cataloguing-in-Publication data is available from the National Library
of Australia

STAR DESCENDANT CHRONICLES

PART 1:
THE DRACONIAN CONSPIRACY

1.

Terra; better known to Oil Man as "Earth". No matter how many times Sorjana told herself they were her ancestors, she could only see monkeys. From her vantage point on the Athena, the view of their antics was boundless. It was as if she was standing on the planet; intelligence Sentinels manifesting their view on the surface to the ship. Trying not to be distracted from the amusing things they bickered over; the colour of one's skin. The way one tribe ran their people, upsetting another tribe. My Deity is better than yours. It was amusing the first ten times or so, like watching someone else's child throw a tantrum. Now it was just irritating.

The blue and green planet was also visible as a sphere. It did look beautiful. In Sorjana's time it will be a dead rock with a ring orbiting weakly, where its moon once was. Its sun will still be fine, but its giant gas planet neighbour will be exhausted of her gases, permitting asteroids to wander freely throughout the solar system. The outer gas giants, thankfully, were too far away to make their plundering practical. A voice inside her head abruptly cut her off from her daydream. She turned to see the person who startled her. A scarred, battle hardened man approaching middle age glowered at her. He had cropped hair military short, a traditional hairstyle for his profession millennia after millennia. Discipline was discipline no matter what aeon you lived in. Gunnery Sergeant Klaan O'Brien was muscular, much more so than the average man in the Arcturian Commonwealth.

'The Admiral wishes to see you, Ma'am.' O'Brien hissed. It was a telepathic whisper, intended only for her mind. 'He wants to know, discreetly, the ramifications of yesterdays' Draconian victory. Do not even bother with that Einstein's jargon.'

Sorjana considered this, taking for granted the fact that telepathy isn't the same as reading minds. Chronophysical ramifications were measured in Einsteins, in honour of the ancient father of Chronophysics. One unit is the equivalent of one future event changing. From a certain individual not being born, to an object not being invented. Scowling, she reminded herself she was under Arcturian sovereignty. She took in Klaan's facial features as she did this; ruddy skin, black pupils within black irises and an up-turned pig-like nose. Plieadians and Arcturians, although sharing the same common ancestor, had different colour skin, facial features, and stature; shorter than Pleiadians by three or four inches on average. Countless generations on their respective home planets have guided them on different evolutionary paths. Arcturians and Pleiadians are now different species, though descended from the Terran humans who were still engaged in their primitive, petty antics on the console in front of them. Now a dominant one was scheming how he could exploit his subordinates just for the sake of more luxurious possessions. He was at a market where they trade craft concerning their primary methods of transport. Small, primitive ground faring craft, powered by early forms of combustion. It was only last year that they introduced something called a catalytic converter, an early, if feeble attempt to make them less toxic so as not to destroy the planet in view.

'I assume the sooner the better,' she turned and replied. It was not a question.

'He is in his quarters, as usual, when we're waiting for another Draconian or Zeta fleet to emerge from Shrink-space.' His voice inside her head even carried a slight accent, certain sounds being exaggerated. 'You don't have to rub it in, Gunnery Sergeant, or can I just call you Gunny? My fellow Pleiadians are working fastidiously to protect our ancestors from Chronophysical warfare, but its next to impossible to guard every point in time, and as you know the Draconians have the strategic advantage of having civilisation sixty-five million years old, making a counter-attack ridiculously impractical.'

To go back to the origins of the Draconians, evolved from the Terran Dinosaurs, would take hundreds of years of real time. Early man being perhaps one million, but only in the last two hundred thousand or so years were they even remotely becoming a threat to the ancient Draconian empire. Hence, two hundred thousand years "only" takes about two hundred thousand minutes, or about eight months, plus calibrating time to line up your fleet towards the intended time and place, often doubling the time faring phase.

'Only if I can call you Ms. Hoolde.' O'Brien retorted. *Surnames were always the most subtle way to prevent inbreeding*, he thought.

The Admiral was close to retirement. He carried himself with authority and charisma, with chiseled features and grey cropped hair. He wore only half his military uniform, his coat with all the baubles of office hanging behind him. He sat at his desk wearing khaki leotards. Opposite his coat the Arcturian Commonwealth flag hung limp. It looked as tired as he was. Aside from the coat, the flag and his desk, the room was sparsely furnished. Generations upon generations of Socialism in the Arcturian commonwealth meant that practically no one surrounded themselves with burdening, uncomfortable and cluttering possessions. Terran plants were placed strategically at each corner in pots, more for making the Athena seem less clinical than purely for decoration.

He looked up from his work when Sorjana came in. On his desk were hard copies of authorisation requests only for his approval. Upon approval, they would automatically be synchronised with the ships network, and those wanting to be discharged or transferred, the homesick and the ill alike, would receive notification. The ships' Quartermaster wanted approval for various goods, weapons, equipment and food, but this will have to be on the next shuttle out. Its destination would be well over two hundred thousand years from now, on a planet not yet discovered, let alone colonised, by humanity. Hopefully the next time faring shuttle in will have his golfclubs, Arcturian whiskey and his collection of Space Opera data. Luxury by Arcturian standards. His wife gave Sorjana a little nod, a truly timeless form of communication in the age of Telepathy. She was short and willowy, with greying dark hair. She knew the importance of why the Director of Chronophysical Intelligence for the Athena would see her husband personally. She retreated through a door to the side of the office, to the Admiral's apartment. Their two daughters had left the Athena to start their own professions, one only last year on the last shuttle out. Their son was also an officer in the Arcturian Marines, but, in the interest of avoiding accusations of nepotism, he was on New Terra "now", i.e. thousands of years from now, on the capital of the Arcturian Commonwealth.

'So it seems that the Draconians have planted a new religion. And these monkeys that we are supposed to watch over bought it. A religion intended to be science's arch enemy. That means our technology could be adversely affected, right?' The Admiral looked bored.

Sorjana should have seen it coming, and chided herself. A Draconian disguised himself as a Terran primitive, showed these superstitious apes a few tricks, and now they hail him as a prophet. Millions could pledge their allegiance to a misogynistic or sociopathic (or both) Deity. But only Benevolence for the good of all, and altruism, could lead to spiritual enlightenment. Organised religion will not be forsaken for another few thousand years. The Draconians certainly were not hastening it.

They were everywhere on the planet in front of them. Many were disguised as tribal leaders. Some became prophets. One prophet undid a Fellow Pleiadian missionaries' hard work, one called Jmanuel, to educate the primitives about how benevolence and altruism can make them all happy, and thus bring spiritual enlightenment and peace. Of course, the primitives did not understand Jmanuel, and misunderstood his teachings. Oh how frustrating and tiring it would have been! And when he left, the legend goes, that he was born in a trough to a virgin mother, and he was executed on two staves perpendicular to each other. Its funny what ignorance spawns. Now what was that Draconians' alias? Constant? Consonant? Constantine? It didn't matter. She had bigger worries.

'That is correct, Admiral. Every organised religion that begets worship through fear and unconditional servitude to a deity can only be the work of the Draconian Empire. Apparently, our ape-like ancestors you see before you are either too commercially viable in their livestock trade, or it seems that they *want* those animals,' she gestured towards the general direction of Terra, 'to evolve, eventually, to create the United Commonwealth. Perhaps we are in a cold war, or it's in their best interest to have established worlds to conquer.'

'Ahh I know that tactic, or strategy,' the Admiral mused. 'It was first conceived around about the time we are in, right *now*. An ancient leader called Stalin, decided it would be vastly more efficient to invade a country subtly, using diplomacy as a weapon, rather than send in war machines to annihilate the infrastructure, so if the would be conquerors succeed, a regime change will suffice; rather than the costly rebuilding of all the destroyed dwellings, infrastructure and such. Communism, slightly similar to our political system, but far more aggressive.' The Admiral was almost reciting a history lesson.

Speak of the Devil.

'You know our ancestors are in a cold war right now. Civil war by galactic standards. Two great tribes, one capitalist, one communist. Right now each tribe is calling on their allies. The skirmish is over primitive but destructive nuclear weapons, which work on the same principle as Draconian's Pyrokinesis'. In the United Commonwealth, the main use of thermonuclear energy was for Draconium metallurgy, which is one of the reasons Draconium was over fifty times more expensive than titanium. Now would be a perfect time to instigate a war. Sorjana knew her job was going to get a lot harder now. Humanity never had Organised Religion, or Nuclear Weapons. Now the draconians have changed history for humanity not just through psychological warfare now.

'Which is why we need you down there, among them,' the Admiral replied. 'You are, no offence, shorter than the average female Pleiadian, and you have the features of a creature from their superstitions, one representing benevolence and love; an angel. Just like most in your species,' The Admiral gestured over her whole body. 'That is why the Commonwealth of Arcturia employs your kind.' The admiral was clearly trying to take the alienation out of his words.

The Admiral let the words hang for a moment.

Presently he said, 'How have you been anyway? I know it's coming up to a standard year since...' He searched for the right words, 'the loss of your late husband.'

Sorjana's husband was involved in a Star Mining accident; he and his fellow crewmen were too close to the event horizon of the centre of the galaxy, whom the Commonwealth own a twenty three per cent dependency of the super massive black hole, and in that dependency the suns that came too close were also theirs for the taking. Sorjana cared for only the basics of star mining; a star is elongated into the event horizon, crushing its hydrogen or helium or whatever atoms under very dense gravity, producing the element Draconium, which is then collected via particle accelerators to the mining vessels........or something like that.

'My husband is with me......always, Admiral.'

He understood. Everyone in the Commonwealth was spiritual, but that was the extent of humanity's superstitions now.

And it was like that. Sorjana was going to be with the primitives tomorrow. They did not have telepathy, they communicated with sounds, something called a language, like the Draconians' bird song languages and the improvised varieties made by the Simians and the Neo-Terriers. She had to make contact with them, but her first priority, along with the other few thousand Pleiadians on Terra, was to thwart any Draconian attempts to instigate a nuclear war. Or, at least gather intelligence to find out if they would resort to that.

Her personal ship was shaped like any other small ship in the galaxy; either disc shaped or bell shaped. In space, friction is not an issue, so the need for streamlined, bird-shaped craft was redundant. Besides, their design was symmetrical, so they could change direction quickly. Its door was open. The back of the door doubled as a step. Three jack legs supported the ten-metre-diameter craft as it was being prepared by engineers. The cargo hold of the Athena was eight stories high, with ceilings as white as snow. It was spacious wherever you turned. The walls were grey and distant, their details barely visible, a blur.

Presently a bell-shaped craft came in through the entrance. It approached at over two hundred kilometres an hour then came to an abrupt stop. It deployed its jacks and settled on the deck. A door opened. The inside of the door also served as steps. *What a science fiction cliché*, Sorjana thought. The man that emerged from the shadows and hunkered down the steps wore the baby-blue one-piece leotards that served as a uniform of the Pleiadian effort on Oil-Age Terra. His wavy blonde hair was to his shoulders. He had hard blue eyes, and a very chiseled face with a hawkish nose. He reminded Sorjana of an ancient barbarian. His muscular body was revealing in the leotards, but there was no vanity behind the Pleiadian dress code. He towered over Sonja by more than a head. At nearly seven feet tall, above the average height, large, slightly slanted eyes, high cheekbones, all the image of a model male Pleiadian; he would otherwise terrify those poor primitives on Terra. Thus, Obron Altemeus kept a low profile there. Being a senior field agent meant he knew all the tricks in the book, both Pleiadian, and how the Draconians disguised themselves among Terrans. So far, in his thirty Standard Years of service, He had only encountered a handful of the dragon-like higher castes. The rest had been soldier caste Draconians. He looked pleased with himself.

'Director, that underground base of those Lizard Men,' the derogatory term for Alpha Draconians, 'Won't give us any trouble no more.' He scratched his stubble. "They wouldn't let us take any prisoners, I have to hand it to them. Same old story. They don't value their own life it seems. They know we are a people who would never stoop to torture, so I'm guessing it must be their pride.'

Pleiadians have not used violence in anger for countless centuries. It is as if those traits are no longer in their genes. Everyone in the Commonwealth shared a common ancestry with the higher caste of humans, whom survived the last Terran ice age, roughly one hundred thousand years after the Oil Age. At that time, the higher caste began a vast space exodus to far away planets, leaving the lower castes at the mercy of the harsh dry, cold planet, as well as the massive meteorite soon after. Thus, new human species evolved respective of their particular new planets' environmental conditions; The Arcturians with their ruddy skin and raven hair, the Hyadeans with their dark skin, the Lyrans with yellow-olive skin and dark hair (like the Arcturians but with more cherubic features) and of course the Nordic-like Pleiadians.

'That is music to my ears, Obron. It's just what we need for morale. You may call me Sorjana or Sorj now that you are my brother-in-law, but only in private. How's my big sister doing down there? You had better be taking care of her and treating her right!'

'Ahh a fine woman at that! She's the one who's protecting me from them Reptoid bastards, this Damede of ours. Speaking of which, they're getting smarter, and harder to spot. Both castes that is. They're even hiding their cloaking devices they wear at there belts, which makes it even harder.'

The Draconians have perfectly mimicked Primitive Terrans for millennia. They provided them with technology, likely showed them how to produce nuclear weapons, and have infiltrated their hierarchy right from under the Terran's hairless-monkey noses. It is making life hard for humanity now, as if their ancestor have betrayed them. *Well they made their own bed doing business with the Draconians. We just have to make the best of it now.* Sorjana thought.

Presently another bell shaped craft entered the hold, but this time half the speed. It settled a few hundred metres away. Three half-spherical shapes adorned underneath. They served to negate magnetic fields. Transparent circles circled the craft near the top. Rudimentary and robust, its design made it an ideal terrestrial scout craft, but it was relatively handicapped at space travel. It was coated with a layer of Draconium, so was heavy, clumsy and unagile. Its Arcturium powered anti-matter propulsion engines hummed as if warming down. A door opened a few seconds later, and a man trotted down the steps and diagonally towards the nearest restroom, towards Sorjana and Obron. As he came nearer, his features could be recognised, and Obron gave the man a wave.

'Darius, my man! How goes it? I hear you had a run in with a Ciakar?' Obron projected his telepathy towards his friend's general direction.

'I will fill you in later, my friend. Right now, well you know.' Darius replied in his nasally accent.

Darius was Tau Cetan. He had thick brown curly hair, brown skin and dark eyes. His nose ran from forehead to tip in a straight line, with no curve when looked a side-on, like a roman statue. Almost-*almost* a mix of Mediterranean and Polynesian.

Might be called handsome, Sorjana thought, *If he wasn't a different species from myself*. Although sharing the same primitive common ancestor, Terran *Homo sapiens*, the various species of humans under the United Commonwealth can no longer interbreed. Hundreds of millennia of being isolated on separate worlds mean that the descendants of Terran humans have now diversified into several species, just like the ancestors of *Homo sapiens* had, in turn. Anthropology does seem to repeat itself.

'I hear the primitives keep mispronouncing your name,' Obron teased. 'And some crap about you being three-hundred standard years old. Maybe its one of those trans-sentient language barriers, like when an animal misunderstands your command, or maybe its your accent.' Another feeble attempt at a joke. Though the Arcturian Archive Command have the majority of every word spoken in humanity's past on tap, telepathy was one of those mysteries where beings could communicate regardless of the language they spoke.

But Sorjana paid little attention. Ciakars. That was bad. Even the most seasoned fighter of humanity knows fear only when faced against the dragon-like royal caste. Not simply because they were as tall as nearly three men. They are extremely aggressive, and outsmarting them is out of the question. But it was their pyrokinetic abilities that made them truly resemble, or most certainly were, the Dragons of Terran Primitives' myths.

This pyrokinetic ability was not magic, but pure science. It was achieved through accelerating and then combusting hydrogen and nitrogen atoms in the air, through and unknown form of psychokinesis. Because the atoms combusted in the direction of the Ciakars' mental concentration: in front of their forehead, it was often misinterpreted as "breathing fire". Surprisingly little is known about their origins, why the Draconian Super-species had even evolved that awe-inspiring Caste, but Parapaleontologists from both sides of the curtain have their theories.

Presently she said, 'I will be leaving the Athena shortly, and if there are Ciakars as you say, well I'm certainly not trained to deal with them. I'm an Intelligence officer after all, and not a Marine with Amplifiers.'

Amplifiers are ungainly looking headsets that act to heighten the Alpha, Gamma and/or Beta waves, maximizing Psychokinetic energy. Arcturian Marines are issued them prior to entering most battles. Nevertheless, more "primitive" methods of combat are also at a Marines' disposal; from various energy projectile firearms to explosives, to small arms with caseless projectiles, even shotguns. Going back even further to humanity's martial roots, simple melee weapons and unarmed combat; modified and (dare they claim) improved forms of truly ancient Martial Arts of Terra.

And every Marine spends long days for months, sometimes even Standard Years, training to be far more than competent in dealing with anything their career throws at them.

'Regardless, we all have a job to do, if not for yourself, then for the Pleiadian Sub- Commonwealth, or the United Commonwealth of Humanity.' Obron listed, not conscious of how far the human Superspecies has progressed some two hundred and thirty thousand Standard Years from the present. "So cheer up, Sorj, as most would kill, well do anyway, to be in your shoes.'

'Hmm, if I didn't know any better I'd say you've picked up an ancient cliché on there.' Sorjana replied. 'And to use another cliché', She mimed quotation marks, '"For the record", *Surganna* was my Commontown. Have you forgotten everything Damede has told you? Men will always be men, I suppose. How many more millennia do you need to evolve the ability to listen to the "fairer sex"?!'

Yes, some things never change. And that could be interpreted both ways. He thought to himself, taking for granted that Telepathy and reading minds are two different things.

Obron could only nod and grin.

2.

He chided himself for his xenophobia. He was better than this.

But Ambassador Xankyu kept looking to his left, and across the table at an empty seat. A female should be sitting there. Though not of his own species, a genetic cousin would have done. Everyone else in the room were aliens. They certainly were nothing to look at.

The absent female had her own reasons. And the aliens took advantage of her absence.

And Xankyu was torn between too philosophies. What philosophy should he recommend to his people? To pledge their allegiance to? And possibly forever. Whatever decision they made would likely be final.

Now the time for pleasantries. But there was a third option; to remain neutral, and his people stay in their comfort zone. Until the Draconians see a neutral party a belligerent party. Or they decide neutrality is betraying your genetic cousins, where your loyalties should lie, and being too cowardly to "officially" side with the weak and sycophantic United Commonwealth.

So what's it to be Sirians? Blood or morality?

He looked down at the table before the diplomatic conference was about to start. He still had time. He could see his reflection on the polished titanium surface. His eyes, like all Sirians, carried a false impression of ferociousness. Practically identical to that of Draconians; black vertical slit pupils surrounded by nothing but inferno red irises, with no whites whatsoever.

Now those eyes looked up at that empty chair again. Each respective seat had each respective dignitary's flag, or insignia.

This one had a winged serpent, that formed in the same shape as the constellation Draco, when viewed from Terra. Of course, the symbol, being tens of millennia unchanged, is now out of date; for the constellations move over tens of millennia.

Behold. The Draconian Empire.

Practically everything about the Draconians was warring. Even the chair was a psychological weapon, smuggled into an otherwise peaceful room devoted to diplomacy. It resembled a demonic throne, straight out of these aliens' ancient myths about a place called Hell. In turn Hell was a machination of Draconian Propaganda, an attack against humanity sent back hundreds of Standard Millennia from the present. The sheer irony amused Xankyu.

He still had two Standard Minutes before the meeting was scheduled. A representative from Zeta-Reticuli, nestled itself in, obviously waiting till the last minute, as the Greys generally felt out of place on a chair. Their spinal system was not conditioned to them. All around Xankyu most other dignitaries were already seated, either preparing themselves or simply killing time completely.

Standard Minutes, Standard Hours, Standard Years. It was funny how each life form in the Galaxy, except the insentient, as well as The Indigenous of Planet Yngkhazh, synchronised their clocks with their common Mother Planet.

At last the speaker entered, and sat down gracefully without any ostentation to announce her presence, no cheesy music or confetti, no sycophantic chamberlain. In the United Commonwealth of Humanity, politicians seldom received more perks than a humble labourer. They have learned from their ancestors' mistakes, and spend practically none of the taxpayer's hard earned money on pampering politicians. All menial tasks to do with governing were done by computers and other machines, including counting the taxes. Less for administration, more for schools, or healthcare, or housing. And regrettably, defense.

Well it was in their best interest anyway. If the taxpayer found out taxes were being squandered on the same hypocritical politicians, who preached the joy of socialism?! Well! They certainly would be more proactive about protesting than their gullible or unassertive Oil-Age ancestors have been.

The Speaker, a middle-aged Lyran who wore her dark hair in a spartan and clinical bun, and had a habit that was at first irritating. Even with telepathy some Sapients needed to orchestrate communication with hand gestures.

But this woman was worse than most. Xankyu even now still found that habit irritating as she began with;

'Welcome here, all who could attend. Firstly let us welcome and congratulate the representative of the Star Miners' Workers Union...oh, for the Commonwealth's share of the Great Centre anyway. Chancellor vam Rees of the Vegan System, whom recently left his career as a titanium orbit-ore maintenance superintendant, of over twenty Standard Years, to his aforementioned current position. We wish him the best, and are sure he will do a impeccable job.'

The dark skinned mustachioed man presently nodded and smiled sheepishly around the room at everybody who applauded. Obviously, a quiet achiever who felt un-comfortable being put on a pedestal. The Great Centre was the backbone of the economy in the galaxy, and every governing faction; The Commonwealth, The Empire, and Xankyu's Sirian Republic. And, only in the last few millennia in the aftermath of the Grey Liberation, Zetas and Bellatrixians also acquired a fifteen percent stake in the profits in Atomic Mining. The other three factions gave up five percent each, due to either benign or more "assertive" treaties, either willingly or not. The Great Centre of the galaxy is essentially the mother tree of Atomic Mining, with the exception of the odd scattered black hole. This is where vast numbers of mining vessels harvest the fruit of what is Draconium and Arcturium.

The Vegan System's chief export is titanium ore that orbits their Capital planet, the remains of an ancient moon, in the guise of a ring. It is considerably cheaper to harvest than Draconium, and half of the ring is now depleted. The former superintendant's job was in fact a redundancy, after titanium had to start being recycled, and orbit-ore mining minimalised.

'Now as you all have most likely of noticed, the Draconian Representative is absent, for reasons that are confidential,' the speaker continued as the applause died down. 'Now then,' she made an audible. Audible! Sigh as she continued, 'Anyone want to raise any matters they wish to address on their Factions' behalf?'

Even Xankyu, a genetic cousin, had difficulty pronouncing the Draconian representative's name, Koowotah. Her name was more onomatopoeia than word, more bird-like call than anything.

The Daconians were the only Sapient species, barring the Neo Terriers and Ascended Simians, to still use audible communication. Most of humanity's Christian and surnames are translated from ancient names, or are ancient names completely. Sirian and Grey names are chosen at a young age, by their own choice. Xankyu literally means, "One who fights hardship with defiance." Not that meant anything, now that he was supposed to be a well-behaved diplomat. He lifted his cone-shaped head and discreetly stood, slowly, to communicate and be noticed. It was then his sleek-but-by-no-means puny frame manifested itself, reinforced by an iridescent gunmetal grey skin.

'On Behalf of the Sirian Republic, we either are delighted or regret, whatever applicable, to inform the following.' He paused for affect. 'The Commonwealth and all other present Factions hereby are informed that the notion to be assimilated into the Commonwealth is...' 'He again paused to buy his Faction more clout...' Denied. Although we share a similar common goal with humanity, we are deep-down also obligated to compromise a relationship with our Draconian cousins. Thus it is decided that we shall remain neutral and unallied. We sincerely hope that the Commonwealth understands and look forward to continue trade as usual. That is all.'

As humbly as he stood up, Xankyu took his seat again. There. It was done.

The Lyran nodded and said, 'Noted is the official decision of The Republic in the Assimilation Proposal. I will not however, comment on the decision as it is not my place.' She then looked around and brightened robotically, smiling commercially with slightly-too-large white teeth. 'Now I hope that's the last unpleasantry we have to attend. Now unless anyone has anything else, let's discuss how we can make hydrogen powered automobiles commercially viable, so as to become less dependant on Biobrids. Anyone?'

Ambassador Koowotah slipped into her throne at the conference nonchalantly, showing not even a hint of remorse for arriving halfway through. She nestled into her seat with a haughty sneer. After the brief attention was divided again from her, she leaned forward and steepled her talons. Turning up late with an indifferent attitude not only suggested Draconian dominance, but also suited her own convenience. Besides, she was still a lower caste of her species, even if her position is about the most esteemed a lower caste could ascend in Draconian society. And more importantly, her caste lacked telepathy, so she had to hear using a sophisticated console that picked up alpha waves and translated them into her audible bird language, like an ancient analogue receiver. Furthermore, this was a pointless meeting, and she knew the Commonwealth had little currency in Draconian interests.

And she only had to endure half of this pointless meeting.

She looked at the Lyran woman and almost cackled out loud when it occurred to her. The only habitable planet of the Lyran system, Ryclonius iii, was destroyed in the Lyran civil war tens of millennia ago. So every Lyran was therefore a refugee, and a bleeding-heart Liberal's dream. The survivors were scattered throughout the Commonwealth, and still remain a minority, but nonetheless more than tolerated.

Aww, would you just look at the hard-bitten poor refugee. So let's give he a job as a speaker for the Galactic Trade Conference. Won't that appease the God of political correctness!

The Speaker concluded the meeting with, 'Would the Draconian Ambassador care to put in her input on behalf of her faction?'

'There is nothing to report,' Koowotah replied stoically via a dome-shaped translating device sitting in front of her with a smooth, silky-voiced speaker. 'My race has been economically independent for well over fifty million Standard Years. The only crisis we have ever faced was the

Cretaceous nuclear civil war on Terra, sixty five million years ago. Almost every Draconian ancestor was either killed directly or by radiation, famine and the ensuing anarchy that followed. Only a small minority made it to the Draconian system as refugees to the then fledgling terraformed planet, what is now known as Ki'iria (pronounced ("Ki," as in "high", ee-ree-ah), translated into Common as "Draconia Prime", our Capital. The Sirian Ambassador knows this. Our common ancestors also came to the then frontier planet now known as Planet Selonabus.'

Xankyu, in his resplendent lime-green robe with gold trim and matching sash, glowered at her as if to say, "don't bring *me* into this!" but he was reminded of his home, the swampy, humid world with astounding floating metropolises. Vast spaceports floated tens of miles above the surface, practically in its stratosphere. Selonabus was also "only" roughly ten light-years from Terra, orbiting Sirius B, and making it the closest habitable exoplanet in relation to Terra.

Nevertheless after a moments silence, Koowotah continued, 'So as you humans also faced a similar though not nearly as severe, predicament, one hundred and thirty millennia ago, I will say no more about that. I will however, emphasise that although the Commonwealth has little currency in our interests, we will consider negotiating concessions and trade agreements, in exchange for a certain embargo being lifted.' She paused for another moment to let the Commonwealth jog its memory and rack its small brain, which unfairly had the telekinetic ability that was envied by the Draconian Empire.

Here it comes, The Vegan Chancellor realised. He did not bother to hide the disgust on his face, although the others did not seem to realise.

As if to say "give up?" Koowotah concluded over her speaker, first her bird language said these next crucial words, and there was a slight split-second-out-of-sync as the machine calculated bird song into Common. This was the universal written and audible language of the United Commonwealth, when telepathy did not suffice.

'The Draconian Empire wishes only for the United Commonwealth to permit, without any interference, and unconditionally, the gathering and farming of pre-historic *Homo sapien*. This includes purposes for but not limited to: the consumption of meat for food, a eugenics programme for efficient breeding of stock and the culling of underperforming specimens, and finally, the administration of growth hormones for faster production. It has long been common knowledge that these prehistoric creatures are considered a delicacy in Draconian culinary culture.'

Perhaps it was the fact she so pragmatically described the concept of treating humans as cattle, or the thought of human flesh being cut up, then bitten and ripped off the bone, without even being spared the dignity of being masticated before swallowed, but the outrage that followed was surprisingly quiet. Or at least it was to a caste that was utterly isolated to telepathy. Even so, the ones that remembered to push the button to activate their translator retorted in a trembling voice, not even lost in mechanical translation. Koowotah found it amusing, obviously they were doing their best to remember their diplomatic obligations and keep their offence, and perhaps even anger, in check. After objections upon objections were bombarded from all directions, she still sat there smirking, as if she were some class clown who made a wisecrack that appalled the teacher, but made all the class peers burst out laughing. She looked pleased with herself, and Xankyu noticed, though the others could not read *Saurosapienia* body language.

Finally, Kowohtaar had enough and shot up out of her throne. She arrogantly clapped her hands, which were talons on muscular scaly green forearms, if one did not want to be too anthropomorphistic. She now boomed over her machine, but the bird song was, surprisingly, hardly any louder than normal.

'Oh come, come on now, time to choke on humble pie and then you die!' The Zeta-Reticulans, however, seemed to widen their already too large black bug eyes. If they played their cards right, it would mean getting the leftovers, at the very least. Though not for food, but precious genetic material. Zetas and Bellatrixians were partial to Terran cattle. Soon enough, the Commonwealth representatives, however, and indeed even the speaker who had also joined the half hearted angry mob, had now hushed and paid her full attention.

'You really think you are any better!? Do I need to remind you that you have done the same to animals you call cows, and pigs, and sheep and whatever else for countless millennia. Do you consider yourselves evil for doing this? No? Then why is it considered evil for us Draconians? Furthermore, must I bring up chickens? They are indeed relatively close genetic relatives of ours, so I will let you make your own conclusion on that'.

The representatives had indeed been humbled. How could they argue with logic like that? Koowotah added insult to injury by continuing, 'And you had once, when you were all,' She circled her arm around the room and her entire body followed as she emphasised "all", '*Homo sapiens*, assumed you were the first and only sapient life form to have ever evolved on your planet.' She now deliberately sounded sad and disappointed, though humans were completely unfamiliar with the tone and context, the way Draconians mix with their language to convey emotion.

At that, without being dismissed or even waiting for the speaker to comment, she turned and strode out of the room wordlessly. Her gait was nothing like anything human, her anatomical proportions being so different. With each stride, her bare feet clenched in mid-step, and opened up again before resting on the ground, rather like that of a chicken.

Even though most were expecting it, merely because they looked alike, Xankyu decided it would be for the best if he stayed seated and not follow her out.

3.

Two adolescents were about to enter the real world. They were on their way to adulthood.

And today was the first day of being what they wanted to be when they grew up.

A Pleiadian girl tagged along behind her new mentor. He was short for a man, this mentor, barely taller than she was. At eighteen standard years and one hundred and seventy five centimetres tall, she would be like all girls her age. With another fifteen centimetres to grow in another seven Standard Years she had left before she legally became an adult in the Commonwealth. Like all modern humans, newborn infants are born with the same sized brain, even compared to ancient *Homo sapiens*-the maximum size that could be birthed. But the extra seven years to reach maturity gave the brain time to grow considerably larger and more developed than *Homo cras Pleiades*' primitive ancestors. Thus at eighteen Standard Years, Magne Mimee was the equivalent of a fourteen and a half year old *Homo sapien* child. Her purple eyes and even rarer raven hair made her popular with the boys at her school. She will be starting her internship next year, and those purple eyes took in every detail a civilian could muster.

The other lagged behind a few paces. He was an unremarkable Pleiadian boy about the same age, but from a different academy on Ptaah, the only habitable planet in the Pleiades system besides planet Erra. He only had blond hair and blue eyes, and was average height for a boy his age, also just under six feet tall. But his name was the most boring thing about him by far. Skyler, an oil-age and therefore old fashioned name which was more suited to an ancient and bookish librarian or accountant than a teen whose main priority was blending in with peers. If that wasn't bad enough, then a surname like Tjeons certainly was. It was the Plieadian translation of "Jones."

In spite of all this, he made the best of his fate by at least making an effort to not conform. His blonde hair was nothing like what was fashionable in Plieadian culture; long hair that was generally worn loose for both sexes. That custom had stagnated for uncounted millennia. No, his hair was short and spiky that he gelled fastidiously twice a day. Whenever in mufti, he always chose a one-piece black vinyl outfit and all-too-large black boots. Sometimes he even wore black makeup on his lips and eyelids. Of course he was not the only adolescent on Ptaah who dressed like an ancient punk or goth, and indeed he had congregated many times in his little gang of punks back in his Commontown in his free time. Their pastimes included, but not limited to, general loitering, listening to unwholesome music and generally being "esoteric-and-proud-of-it".

The mentor finally turned around with his hands behind his back, and smiled a benevolent grimace. His long blonde hair, shoulder length, was tied in a ponytail, and Skyler thought he resembled an ancient male pornographic movie star. He grinned in spite of himself, which his mentor interpreted as politely returning the gesture. The mentor was relatively puny, a small man by today's standards, in the age of supereugenics and designer, custom-made offspring. But his burgundy loose fitting one-piece robe with long sleeves, black belt and matching shoes made him somewhat sophisticated looking. An intellectual after all, smarter than most. He had to be. He was one of the few chief Chronophysicists of Shrinktime Enterprises, a state owned space and time faring transportation company, though now partially privatised as the Commonwealth tentatively flirted with capitalism.

'Good to see you could make it, my prospective Chronophysicists. I am Master Pteru Hoolde.' Pteru nowadays loosely meant the ancient name, "Peter". He had led them to a small, white and clinical training room. He walked over to the door, a simple swinging type, practically unchanged in hundreds of thousands of years. Well a door is a door after all. He turned the handle and opened it.

'Please, take a seat.' He gestured towards the also simple desk and chairs, proffering out his hand in stereo with the telepathy. As the two interns took their seats, and sheepishly avoided eye contact with each other like teens should, Pteru wandered over to the simple whiteboard and picked up a temporary marker. He scrawled, "What is

Chronophysics?" messily in a writing that was essentially a hybrid between calligraphy and gregorian.

'Anyone?' He projected mentally to the whole room out of habit, looked around, then down when he realised the only others present were sitting front centre. Magne, who had previously formed a bipod with her arms and hands to rest her head straightened and put her hand up. Then stood from her chair almost instinctively and recited:

'Chronophysics is the science concerning the relationship between time and the laws of physics, i.e. how physics affects time or vice versa.'

'Good. Now don't forget that space and time are synonymous. That is the most elementary thing you must know. This is where your job comes in. Your task, should you be successful, will be to mate distance with time. Sounds simple, yes, but don't forget that every lightyear of distance shrunk will still cause a year to elapse in real-time, regardless of the fact it only physically takes about a minute to travel through a lightyear worth of shrinkspace. Unless, of course, you remember to give the order to launch Sentinels, but more about that later. First we need to inform you of your rights and responsibilities as an employee at Shrinktime.' He then droned on about some public liabilities and litigations and the like for over fifteen minutes. Skyler did his best not to look uninterested. He would be, he hoped, the first time-travelling punk. Maybe even one day he would blend in with his ancestors at the dawn of his credence and listen and headbang to the music back then. But for now this is just one of many hoops he would have to jump through.

* * *

'Skye-lehr Tay-ohns.' He offered his hand at recess and shook when she grasped it. It felt limp as if her parents had never taught her how to properly execute this truly ancient custom, originating from when warriors offered their empty hand that would normally carry a weapon as a gesture of peace or camaraderie.

'Mag-nay Mime-ee', she replied.

There was awkward silence as they were both novices of interacting with the opposite sex. To make matters worse, they were clearly from different clicks, with different taste in music. Skyler could not get his head around cheesy techno-pop, about having boys buy you everything or whatever (he could not hear the words over the monotonous electronic beat) and she thought ancient anti-establishment rock was redundant and crude. But she had no trouble fitting in with her peers either, so could not comprehend the personal glory of being different and defiant.

'You...errr, I mean what's it like to grow up on Erra'?

Magne's purple eyes widened at the thought that Skyler had never been off Ptaah. Well the climate is certainly less temperate, she realised after taking in Skyler's more tanned skin.

'Erra, well its uh, more cooler, it snows during winter. I hear it never snows on Ptaah? That during winter its still slightly tropical. Well this planet is a bit closer to its sun'.

Ptaah's sun had not been affectionately named with a layman's title, but still had its astronomical serial number.

The Pleidians of Ptaah even had a distinctive accent, exaggerating their w's and pronouncing "ooh" sounds with an annoying drawl. On Erra you could always tell a Ptaahian. Even when their tan fades.

'Here," she fished out a device called a Holotab, in this case the latest model, femininely customised in pink and fake diamonds. She frowned as she calculated why there was poor signal, and moved around while holding the prissy thing to the sky.

'Aww,' she said as she placed a finger on the screen. A holographic menu manifested before their eyes, and she selected the "search" icon, then entered "Erran landscape" on her search engine.

An audible high pitch noise, not unpleasant by any means, preceded a new scenery, crackling in manifestation for a second. Skyler looked around, at the temperate landscape with lush greenery and overcast with mountains in the distance. Only half the mountains were visible under the low, moist clouds. He turned around and had the view of an beautiful, but icy fjord. Skyler realised he was on top of a canyon. Plovers could be seen and heard down below. Or at least that was what his eyes told him.

As if reading the fact that Skyler had had enough, Magne swiped her fingers over her Holotab.

'Looks cold', Skyler was trying to be nice, despite the fact his demeanour was obnoxious and angry. After all there is no else his age to talk to today.

'You...have your Biobrid licence yet? Oh.' He jerked his forehead back at the epiphany. 'This is mine.'

This time a scratched and slightly battered black

Holotab came out. Skyler opened his menu and grabbed the "album" icon that seemed to levitate in the air. He missed, nearly grabbing another holographic icon, but his second attempt came true. Finally a rustic looking machine appeared. Like all biobrids, it resembled a lovechild of a shoe and a beetle. Unlike their ancient pre-decessors, they had no wheels. Instead they had stubby looking pods made of Draconium, where the wheels used to be. When the biodiesel or ethanol-hybrid engine roars to life, all the electrical energy goes to the four pods, making the Draconium glow lightning coloured. One property of this metal is when it is conducted with elec-tricity it becomes anti-magnetic, and enables the vehicle to glide a metre or so above the ground. This method of locomotion is nearly a dozen times more efficient than pneumatic tyres alone.

Skyler's menacing looking Biobrid even had a primitive looking supercharger, mated with biodiesel for "torque" over power. The body also had slightly faded black paint, as if to match his rugged Holotab.

Magne did her best to look interested, let alone impressed.

"Was my fathers. He is a Biobrid mechanic and engi-neer. Runs his own repair business with my older brother the other side of Ptaah, that way.' He pointed to the east.

Magne simply replied, 'Back on Erra you are only eligible for your licence at sixteen Sy's.'

Sy's were the colloquialism for Standard Year, partic-ularly among adolescents. She continued a moment later, 'But in the Commonpolis, or city, where I was raised most people use the Hycoaches, or those Gyrons if they prefer to commute in solitude.'

Even two hundred and thirty thousand years into the future of the Oil Age, hydrogen was still an expensive element to harness and turn into a source to power vehicles; only coaches carrying dozens of people made it economically viable. But Hydrocoaches were little more than a giant hydrogen powered Biobrid.

As for solar powered vehicles, that was completely out of the question. Solar power had reached its efficiency pinnacle about a hundred standard years after the end of the Second Terran Oil Age Civil War. Even covered end to end every square inch, in solar panels, a groundcar stuggled to exceed more than a dozen kilowatts, not nearly enough to electrify four Draconium pods.

Gyrons were glorified bicycles that had Draconium pods where pneumatic tyres should be; the electricity was produced through pedal power. A cyclist can easily attain eighty kilometres per hour, barely getting a raised heart rate. But the Draconium made them weigh as much as two men, so they could not be carried up stairs. They seldom broke down, however.

Skyler sipped his coffee, a habit nowadays frowned upon. He changed the subject by saying,

'So, have you ever wondered what the future would be like? Why has no one travelled to the future? Don't tell me, time travel in the future cannot exceed natural chronology. That will be in the test. Why? Something about the fact that the universe say, a thousand Sy's from now doesn't exist. Exactly why, like the scientific reason,

I'm having trouble with.

'Just the main handicap of Sentinels, can only travel through artificial space-time, which is the space-time that has already happened. Probably just put that down for now.' Magne gave a dismissive gesture. Smart, pretty and popular. And now pragmatic. She pointed to the cup in Skyler's hand. 'You, ahh, about done with that coffee? We only get fifteen minutes. We should be heading back soon.' Magne only drank, like most good Plieadians, water and green tea.

4.

Rion Murphy. Capo in the Annunaki. Feared and respected on Planet Nibiru.

His seven-foot frame stooped to look into the side mirror. Though corpulent, his strength was surpassed only by his telekinetic ability. The Arcturian outcast was scruffy with his wild black beard and his black leather jumpsuit and matching long stiff overcoat, which he wore open to expose his hairy barrel chest. The chest was adorned by a medallion and chain made of pirated gold, when the Anunnaki went back through time to ancient Babylon, where they made sure the Babylonians feared them as deities, and enslaved them, made them mine for gold. The name Annunaki, however, was mistranslated by the Babylonians as "ones who came from the sky." Satisfied, he sneered at his reflection, then turned.

Despite being born into a species and society that endeavoured to prevent the birth of sociopaths, Rion was one of the few that slipped through the cracks. The bad apple of the barrel could no longer return to his birthplace on New Terra. His exile was instead spent on Nibiru and quickly ascending rank in the Mafia of Space and Time, which was what the Sirian word "Annunaki" actually translated into. The name stuck for millennia, in both the Commonwealth and his organisation based on the smugglers' wasteland exoplanet, Nibiru. He looked around at the bleak sepia sky, perpetually covering its sun. The only sound was a cold howling breeze that complimented the cold, sandy, rocky landscape of mountain crags and gorges. Nibiru was from an old Sirian dialect meaning "graveyard."

He then mounted his ethanol-powered motorcycle. As soon as the menacing looking chopper fired its engine, the two Draconium power pods electrified and slowly levitated him in the air. Rion gunned the throttle. It was intentionally too loud, especially since the good people of the Commonwealth saw no need for the ancient, primal roar of a combustion engine.

Whatever empathy and respect that remained of his character was spent on his beloved motorcycle; anyone else's vehicle he would have thrashed it without first warming it up. In fact he had little respect for others and their property. Satisfied it was warmed up, he kicked the motorcycle in gear, and thundered down the dirt path that eventually descended down a barren mountain range.

He wore no helmet, and could feel the wind on his bald scalp. It was already midday. The days on Nibiru seldom lasted more than ten hours.

At last, at the foot of the mountain range, he came to a frontier style smugglers town, devoted to practically every vice of the underworld. He slowed right down when he reached the heart of the town, his motorcycle now purring quietly. He parked across the road from a brothel, and as the Draconium pods lost charge he sank to the ground with a quiet thud. He killed the engine, then dismounted gracefully, his leathers creaking and his boots stomping. He then swaggered down the street, where others going about their business wisely kept out of his way. A Hyadean prostitute straightened, then melted into the shadows, and avoided eye contact. Others chastened themselves as he strode past the various businesses; a gambling den here, narcotics manufacturing building there. Past another brothel, and he rounded a corner where there was a freight yard piled with caches of stolen goods. Two men were opening a crate with a primitive crowbar; this was a spoil when they commandeered a Lyran zionist vessel. The two men scowled at the relatively invaluable items within: foodstuffs and a few electronic goods, likely obsolete Holotabs and movies (not even pornographic which would at least have value on the black market!)

Never mind. He thought to himself. *There are still plenty of crates to open. Well what do you expect from a Lyran vessel? Narcotics? Draconium and Arcturium bonds? Gold? A deed to a private Terraformed moon perhaps?* He scoffed out loud. But he was not here to inspect a pirate's booty. The Gaadyu, or head of the Annunaki, was an ancient Ciakar, well over three hundred Sy's old. Rion was summoned perhaps, as a possible successor, as the Gaadyu was getting too old to even fight to the death to defend his position. Fortunately for the Gaadyu, he was the only Ciakar in the Organisation, so for over a century he had no rival. Until he became senile and forgets what he was fighting to the death for.

At the back of the freight yard was a large chop shop where stolen luxury Biobrids and even a limousine hijacked from a diplomatic vessel were being cannibalised. The other half or so remaining biobrids were being illegitimately recommissioned if they had buyers waiting. Indifferent to the angle grinders, noise and sparks, Rion told a greasy Vegan engineer the Gaadyu was expecting him. The engineer escorted him to the back of the chop shop, ducking his head under a suspended Biobrid, with Rion going around. They came to a set of steel stairs leading to a mezzanine office block. The Vegan climbed the stairs and turned his head around halfway up to see if Rion was still following.

'In here sir,' was all the engineer said as he slipped past Rion timidly and down the stairs to return to his work. Rion faced two burly lower caste Draconian thugs, obviously bodyguards. They both stood with their arms crossed at their wrists, and regarded Rion haughtily. Not many, besides the Gaadyu, can make eye contact with Rion at eye level.

'Gaadyu summoned me. Rion Murphy. Stand aside. Now.'

Rion was never reprimanded for talking to other sapients in such a way and as such has made quite the habit of it. The thugs eventually moved to one side, but not without glaring at him. One even held the door open for Rion. It was dark inside, but Rions' black eyes, which the visual spectrum was down to the infra-red, made out different shades of grey and shapes immediately. He was glad he wasn't an ultraviolet-seeing Pleiadian.

The Gaadyu was lounging on an enormous sofa, five metres or so by three metres wide. Even then the Ciakar had little room to toss and turn. He sleepily propped his head up and leaned on his scaly forearm, like a dragon awakening from its slumber to shoo a gnat away. Even laying down on the sofa like he was, he could nearly look eye to eye with Rion. A titanium alloy suit of armour adorned his torso, painted gloss black. For Ciakars, it was indeed fashionable to wear armour. Unlike the lower caste Draconians, his snout was long and protruding. The snout revealed decaying, yellowing carnivorous teeth as the Gaadyu smiled at Rion.

The Gaadyu made the first move at conversation. His bird song language was clearly raspy, and the translating console built into the wall mimicked his raspy voice. He sounded almost exactly like an Italian mafia don from ancient Terra.

'Reeyonne, my boy. You make your Gaadyu proud. How are a you?'

'Considering I'm the only Arcturian on Nibiru, and that I will face an execution should I ever return? Fine. How are you my Lord Gaadyu?'

The Gaadyu saw that Rion was subtly hinting at his imminent retirement, and cut straight to the chase. '

As you know my time has come. I will be gone in one Sy at a the most. Indeed, you know exactly why I summoned you here. You have a worked hard for this organisation for a long time, and have done so much.'

Rion nodded and smiled at the praise, he was a lot of things, but however, a sycophant was not one of them. The old Ciakar Let the words hang for a moment, then;

'However, I am a sorry for my favouritism, but, after much a consideration, I must pass the a torch on to one of my kind.'

As if on cue, one of the burly Draconiam body guards came in from outside the mezzanine office. Anthropomorphism or not, the gloating, satisfied smirk on the reptilian's face was unmistakable.

The Ciakar continued, 'Meet your new Gaadyu, effective from my imminent death. Rion, this is Oohkee. Oohkee, this is the Arcturian you have seen a few times but have never a formally met, Rion. Rion ahh. Ahh Murphy that's right.'

It took every ounce of strength in his large, powerful body for Rion's face to be impassive. It took all his self discipline, which required the requisite empathy a sociopath lacked greatly, not to burst out in a juvenile tantrum, as he often did when things did not go his way. And in the dark mezzanine office, no one could see Rion tremble with fury.

5.

Sorjana found much solace on Terra. Especially a thousand or so years before the Oil Age.

The Hopi people were probably one of her ancestors, going back nearly a quarter of an eon. Sorjana went back on the next available Timeliner to the medieval times, at a time humanity had not yet began to cross-colonise other continents on Terra. In this case, the indigenous peoples of the new world were enjoying their lives, unmolested by European colonialism. Sorjana was however, strictly forbidden to warn the Hopi of their fate in five hundred or so Standard Years time. That would undoubtedly merit capital punishment in the United Commonwealth. At least they would give her a proper burial, unlike any sociopaths that seem to be discovered occasionally.

Her Nordic features flickered in the firelight and she smiled benignly. It was nighttime and the Hopi were chanting and dancing. The song and drumbeat was over and everyone dancing took their seats around the fire.

Sorjana was accepted by the Hopi almost as a deity. She told them it wasn't necessary, but they took in her saucer-shaped spacecraft, her sky blue jump suit, white boots and blonde hair, and refused to be convinced otherwise. She always made time to return to her beloved *Homo sapien* tribe every six months or so in her possible, and hopefully only, future.

The primitive ancestors were sharing their innocent attempts at science, using myths and deities in an attempt to understand the world around them. Sorjana's Holotab at her belt translated for her into Commonish. There was no longer a word in commonish for words such as "water-spirit" and "treegod", so the context was mistranslated a little. A shaman-like *Homo sapien*, all liveried in animal cloaks, bones, and other remains, was being drowned out by the translating console at her belt. What was being translated, she only paid cursory attention to, in case the Hopi would quiz her later on as if to test if she had been paying attention.

An animal carcass was being slowly roasted over another fire in the background. It was almost ready. Sorjana would have to politely turn down a helping. Any diseases in the meat she would have no resistance to, and it would take a substantial amount of time to return to a time when there was adequate medical science, plus the medical staff would need time to diagnose and treat the disease. This would likely involve digging into an archive of long-cured pathogens. And secondly, *Homo cras Plieades* have such an underpowered digestive system, accustomed to millennia of processed foods. It would likely cause digestive problems. Plieadians especially had difficulty digesting red meat.

The moon of Terra was full, and Sorjana could not help anthropomorphising a melacholy face on it. Just as her ancestors around her would have done the same. *There is no escaping instinct, regardless of evolution and selective breeding. And no doubt that even our ancestors before Homo sapiens did the same.* Sorjana mused. Her thoughts were interrupted by the leader yelling at some youngsters about to climb into Sorjana's saucer shaped craft, landed ten or so metres in the background. Glistening in the firelight, it had almost a sinister tinge to it, as it flickered orange in a black background. She got up and calmly strode over to her vessel, and projected in a forgotten language from here holotab.

'It is quite alright, Sakacheezweah.' The chief slowly sat down, with the aid of a decorated staff, but his painted-black face and black eyes did not dare look away from the ship and the children. Sorjana was now at the foot of the stair of her craft, where three children whose age Sorjana did not bother to calculate in Pleiadian terms giggled and stood at attention. She squatted down at eye level to the *Homo sapien* youngsters and gave them a beatific smile, with glistening blue eyes that gave the youngsters an impression of child-like mischief.

'Children, who would like to fly with me, like a great eagle, in my craft? Just be patient, and after you have all eaten, I will take you in my craft.' The holotab spoke for her, and she never stopped smiling as it spoke their language. Presently, she proffered her pinky, not recalling where she got the custom from, but the children each linked with her pinky. It was a gesture to confirm a verbal contract.

The cooks trumpeted on a bison horn, and the steaming animal carcass was shouldered by two *Homo sapien* adults, slung underneath a staff. They placed the carcass on a tarpaulin of large, lush leaves, then twisted the staff away from the bonds, sliding it out. When they were gone, the chief of the tribe stalked up to the feast, his staff practically never leaving the ground. Slowly, he turned around, and his black painted face looked at Sorjana imploringly. Sorjana refused politely, like every time, but the chief's disappointment was, as usual, plain on his painted black face and matching black eyes.

The *Homo sapien* youngsters disembarked Sorjana's craft nothing short of astonished. Sorjana could see their primitive legs trembling as they stepped on solid ground again. It was getting late, some four standard hours after sunset, and Sorjana thought it was time for them to unwind and call it a night. Even she was starting to feel fatigue. She would be gone by morning. Even hundreds of Standard Years before the Oil Age, there could well likely be Draconian agents on Terra. Her stomach sank at the thought of those unscrupulous, vile reptilians, with their sinister discus-like black craft. And staying here too long would increase the probability of them finding her. Alas it was about another seven hours to return to the Oil Age. Back to work tomorrow on the Athena. She thought of the Admiral, some ten times more stoic than her. Klaan O'Brien, the battle damaged veteran Marine. She would be replacing the dashing Darius from the Tau Cetan system. Honourably discharged, not long before Sorjana left to visit the Hopi, after having the lower half of his left leg disfigured by a Ciakar.

She closed the steps to her craft, which folded up like a door. She needn't worry about being alert for intruders while she slept; *Homo sapiens* lacked the knowledge or technology to break into her craft. The interior lighting to her craft flickered and hummed to life; an ultraviolet teal colour. Pleidians found this ambience soothing. An Oil Age *Homo sapien* would liken the lighting to a nightclub or disco. She reached her sleeping pod. It was a plain, sterile, reasonably firm white mattress. There were no blankets or pillows; she preferred a straight spine, and the ambient temperature was practically perfect. She stripped off her one-piece blue leotards, boots, and finally gloves. There was no ablution facilities in her craft. Besides, a primitive hot shower, which Sorjana preferred, would only make her alert. A few paces from her cot she stood, and somberly pushed a stainless steel button. A whooshing sound preceded a special dry-ice-like substance, used to sterilize space and time-fairing travellers with soulless efficiency. It took less than a minute.

A nearby cabinet, she found a virginal looking one piece satin night gown, beige coloured and long sleeved, it did not stain as easily as white. It was comforting against her voluptuous yet muscular and genetically engineered, body. The soothing, intimate feel of satin against her skin made her realise how tired she was. On cue, Sorjana's joints and muscles ached. She sat down on the edge of her mattress, and took a final tally of the integrity of her craft. At the other end of the ship was the pilots console; either flown by a human or entirely with automata. At the very centre of the saucer shaped craft was the hydrogen powerplant. The red pilot light could be seen from where Sorjana sat; contrasting with the ultraviolet teal lighting. Satisfied it the craft would maintain its integrity as she slept, Sorjana wearily swung her lugs over the edge of the cot and lay down. The mattress in unquestioning servitude molded to shape and conform to her skeletal and spinal system swiftly. Sorjana, sighing, shot a telepathic command to the automata, and the teal lighting faded to black. Only the red pilot light illuminated the interior, But Sorjana was not bothered by it.

About four Standard Hours before the automata would give her a wake up call. Four hours for an Ascended human was considered a good night sleep. Part of the designer offspring doctrine was to select the genes that enabled the subject to require minimal sleep, giving the offspring an advantage of more waking hours available. As she lay there thinking of the other species of human she would be united with tomorrow, the thousands on the Athena. Some she liked, some she didn't. The majority she has only seen, and never met. Sorjana had more than enough companions nonetheless. What really mattered in numbers was the amount of enemies. *Tomorrow will be a new day. When you are accustomed to time travel, however, "tomorrow" is teeming with irony.* It was the last thought in Sorjana's three-litre brain, as that brain seized its well-earned slumber.

6.

For Pteru, the breathing apparatus was uncomfortable. It was, however, a necessary evil, as the air on planet Yngkazh was primarily sulphur dioxide. Water, if you were a Terran-pedigree lifeform, had to be sourced offworld; the liquid on Yngkazh was essentially the same found in a lead-acid battery.

He was here to bid a farewell to an old friend, a scholar like himself. The Imperial Parapaleontologist was a lower-caste Draconian who suffered the affliction of kindness and empathy. By Draconian standards this constituted him, like a mere human, as eccentric, by the very least. He usually worked in solitude as Imperial psychologists have even gone as far as to diagnose him with a personality disorder. Pteru approached his friend silently from behind, and slipped in beside him, joining him in therapeutic observation of a bizarre extraterrestrial. The indigenous life of Yngkazh was the holy grail of parapaleontologists of both Empire and Commonwealth. This particular creature, as with the organism it was feeding on, still as yet was a taxonomical mystery. Neither the reptile nor the mammal standing next to him knew, or could decide, if it were a herbivore feeding on a plant, or a carnivore eating another animal alive. Presently, the reptile kept his eyes and head forward, not daring to take his eyes off his scientific quarry when he began.

'Yngkazhian Mastodon, seen here feeding, or perhaps grazing, on an Umbrella Fungus. My old friend Pteru, I had not expected to see you here. It is a delight to see you indeed.' The translating console at his belt spoke for him. Being held up by this belt was a one piece wrinkled white set of overalls, with black trim at both the top and bottom cuffs, the strip along the centreline of the body that unzipped and unbutton was also as matching black. He even wore boots, which was rare for a Draconian, but served to protect him. Like his mammalian confidante, he also wore a breathing apparatus. The console, amazingly, was not handicapped by the fact his bird song language was muffled by the apparatus. But his reptilian face was not spared from being hidden. All that could be seen when he turned to face Pteru, finally, was a yellow-and-silver tinged faceless head. He could quite easily pass for human, except for the slightly longer forearms and much longer legs in proportion to torso, and green hands with black talons. Like Pteru, he was short-statured and slight for his species, at just two metres tall, not a centimetre more; the average height for a human nowadays.

'This is my first time on Yngkazh.' Pteru replied. 'Meerkah, although this place is fascinating, I regret to say goodbye. In three days Standard, I will be on the next Timeliner to Oil-Age Terra, to where my primitive ancestors reside. As with the current diplomatic relations between the Empire and Commonwealth, it may be the last time you will ever see me. I cannot promise you will see meet again, I'm afraid. There may not be a Commonwealth, a humanity to return to.'

Meerkah turned forward again, nodded solmenly. An oddly human gesture, Pteru did not know where or how he found the habit, as itt certainly was not a Draconian or even Sirian custom. But instead the reptile continued to commentate on the zoology.

'Truly enigmatic organisms we see here. Imagine no sight, hearing, smell or maybe even taste. All senses sacrificed to acutely detect anomalies in magnetic fields. Because all life is anaerobic, no cells have nuclei. Therefore a brain could not evolve. With no nuclei, sexual reproduction is also out of the question. You will notice the pool of liquid the Umbrella Fungi is growing in; about two parts water to one part sulphuric acid. As a natural battery, it is reasonable to assume the fungi receives some nutrients with a thing called Electrosynthesis. As the weather on Yngkazh is primarily acid rain and electrical storms, with the sulphur dioxide atmosphere blocking most of Yngkaxh's sunlight, photosynthesis would be unheard of.'

And Pteru saw what Professor Meerkah was seeing in this inhospitable, hellish planet. The days had a perpetual sepia tone. The ground was a purple-brown formation of smooth flat rock, smooth as well-used asphalt. Only the occasional puddle of battery acid with an equally again occasional fungi gave the landscape any character. No mountains or hills to be seen. The gravity fluctuated several times a day, from less to more than Terras'. It must be Yngkazh's odd shape playing the devil's advocate; actually two planets fused together like a fifty-thousand kilometre Siamese twin. Like the foetal twins it emulated, two molten fledgling planets had collided during the formation of its solar system, and millions of years later had hardened into a solid. Because one twin was bigger than the other, Ynkazh, when seen in space, was an irregular helix shape, where a sphere should have been. Its moon was however, a gaseous sphere of primarily sulphur dioxide. There was no other place like it. It could be called a true alien world, and not the faux Terraformed commonplace variety.

'A misnomer, these Mastodons.' This time Pteru was the one to speak. 'They resemble nothing of the Pleistocene Terran pachyderms. Look! They have wheels! And two legs!

The strange, green and white dome shape took locomotion. Roughly the size of an elephant, it proceeded to skate off on its free spinning wheels, like an ancient mechanic surfing on his gurney, pushing himself with his feet whilst laying down.

'Evolution, it seems, had beat us to inventing the wheel.' Pteru continued as the creature grew smaller and smaller. 'As it had beat us to inventing wings and flight. Tell me about the Mastodons' wheels.'

'What we do know, the science of Parapaleontology, is this.' Meerkah's translator dutifully relayed his bird language like a fastidious secretary. 'Carbon dating has shown that planet Yngkazh is roughly a billion years younger than Terra. Life appeared two billion years ago. Unlike on Terra, evolution has found a few short-cuts; cut out the proverbial middleman here, skip a stage there. Microorganisms did not need to ascend from simple bacteria to relatively complicated cells. And when Life in the Yngkazhian ocean did become complex and migrated onto the land, organs required to sustain life was different to the standards of Terra. Evolution itself is not the pro-verbial arms race both our genuses are familiar with. It is reasonable to assume it is fairly stagnant and uncom-petitive, with a very elementary ecosystem. Why I'll bet that that Mastodon was practically unchanged for five hundred million Standard Years.

Meerkah paused as if to chide himself for digressing, and eventually changed the subject and continued. Presently he returned to lecturing;

'The wheels, we think, had evolved as a energy-con-serving organ. Think about it; Yngkazh is flat and smooth. Legs have the advantage of stepping over things such as logs and rocks, effectively going where a wheel cannot. But on Yngkazh, the landscape is like a natural ancient tar-seal road; perfect for wheels. The joint where the Mastodons' wheel fuses to, is a three sixty degree cartilage organ, effectively a natural bearing and shaft. The wheel itself is a round, wheel shaped bone of mainly carbon. Remember there is acid everywhere. Calcium cannot exist here.'

It was at that moment when a pack came over the horizon towards the east. Meerkah knew they were headed towards where the Mastodon had been. Pteru, who did not bother to hide his apprehension and nervousness about what was going on in front of him, wondered why the famed Maglev Slugs have never been known to attack visitors from another planet. They have likely never seen a carbon-based lifeform before. If they could see that is. About half a dozen or so crocodile-sized gastropods glided only fifty metres away, straight past a reptile and a mammal. Meerkah had once told him Yngkazhian life was phosphorous-based. So alien this world, it might have been another dimension, and not a planet only a couple of thousand lightyears from the Pleiades system.

'Locomotion through magnetic levitation, thus we do know. What we do not know his how they store so much electricity, how they have come to have a high concentration of iron in their underbelly and still have plenty of charge left to discharge copious amounts of electricity for attack and defence.' Meerkah said.

'How do they know where they're going?' Asked Pteru.

'Hormones, mainly.' This puzzled Pteru. Meerkah soon continued,

'And feel. They cannot see, taste, smell or hear. They are however, very sensitive to electromagnetic anomalies and communicate these anomalies with one another through pheromones. And the Mastodon took off from eating the fungi because it too, detected the Slugs *electricity*.'

The disorganised, dark purple pack with no hierarchy whatsoever were oblivious to the two scientists whose ancestry was Terran. Before long, they disappeared over a crest the Pteru and Meerkah's left. Hills and crests were few and far between here. The two scientists practically held their breath waiting to find out what would happen next. Just as they were getting short of breath, and conscious of it, a flash emitted from the direction where the Slugs and Mastodon would have been. Pteru expected a moan of pain from the Mastodon as it was fed upon by the Maglev pack. But no sounds came from there.

'How does the Umbrella Fungi reproduce? How do any of them reproduce, for that matter?' Asked Pteru, his disgust vaguely betraying in his tone, which was most likely missed by the *Saurosapien*.

'That, we don't know, but that is why we are here, and have set up a massive research station, a joint venture between the Empire and Commonwealth, at a time when we all got on as well as you and I do.' Meerkahs reply was sad and musing, and even the mammal heard it in the reply.

It was nearly two standard hours back to the only settle-ment of civilisation on Yngkazh, like a research station on Oil Age Antarctica, it was strictly frontier themed and spartan. In the cafeteria, Meerkah ordered a plump, juicy *Xenotitanosaur* steak, while Pteru fumbled absent-mind-edly with his plate of vegetables and scrambled fish. The cafeteria catered to nearly twenty species of sapients, and indeed, there was a multiculture of other diners in an otherwise clinical restaurant.

'Where are you off to next? After you're done with studying the wierd and wonderful creatures of this planet?' Pteru inquired.

'I am of to the Sirian system, planet Selonabus, to

study *Xenospinosuchus*, which is the apex predator on there. From there, the Empress demanded that I study *Titanosuchus*, which are the biological war machines of the Empire. I assume this has something to do with the Empire's military.'

Xenospinosuchus evolved from the Spinosaurs captured from Cretaceous Terra and bought to Selonabus. Left to evolution, it is now a cold-blooded semi-aquatic creature, twelve metres long by three high, and resembling a hybrid of an eel and an otter. It still retained its ubiquitous sail on its back, which kept its blood warm and metabolism high, giving it an edge over its crocodilian rivals.

Titanosuchus was a crocodile twice as massive and designed more of a psychological weapon by the Empire than the deadly war machine that is the *Ciakars*. Not found on Selonabus, they fed mainly on the *Xenotitanosaur* that browsed on vegetation in ranches on Empire worlds. *Xenotitanosaurs* were massive, about as large as a land animal could theoretically get. Instead of resembling the long necked and tailed dinosaurs from which it evolved from, it now had a short stubby neck and larger head in proportion to its body. Its brain was much larger than its Cretaceous ancestors, due to the fact draconians bred genetically modified vegetation designed for very easy digestion. *Xenotitanosaurs* stomach thus shrank and its brain and muscles grew.

At last, the steak was bought in front of Meerkah, by an android who served it on a simple plate, already diced up as Meerkah had ordered. Meerkah did not hesitate to tuck in; he was evidently hungry. Pteru watched, could only watch, as his friend pecked at his plate of meat, cooked to perfection, and tossed his head back and swallowed, like a bird. Pteru even watched the meat slide down his esophagus, and Meerkah did not use his clawed talons that served as hands even once while he ate. When Meerkah had finished only a few standard minutes later, his reptilian eyes locked on his mammalian friend. Pteru could only now tuck into his meal, almost shamefully.

7.

The gust of heat hit him as he stepped out of the air-conditioned comfort of the spaceport for the first time in years. It was certainly the humidity, rather than the temperature, only twenty-nine degrees centigrade. The lone habitable planet orbiting a star in the Tau Cetan system, translating to the people of Planet Tsorra being a small sub-commonwealth of the Commonwealth Of Humanity. Tsorra was only marginally bigger than Terra, and most of the pastoral land was devoted to growing tropical harvests. Practically everything inedible had to be imported offworld. In return Tau Cetans provided the other species of human with the finest wine and Biobrids available, particularly from a non-belligerent source.

Darius hobbled, to be charitable, about how he now walked. Still he had to admit to himself, a simple, primitive crutch was invaluable in his current situation. He didn't bother to take the scenery in; there would be plenty of time for that later, as it would be another standard year before another lower leg for him was grown. And another three months after that on the waiting list to have an automata surgeon to attach it to where his stub now was. Darius had stopped feeling sorry for himself on the Timeliner back. He had five and a half months from when he left Oil Age Terra to return to his home and in his time. He reflected in all that time he had only himself to blame, how hubris had made him stand up to that Ciakar and not run and hide. *Next time lizard man, I will be armed with a Psionic Amplifier on my head. I'm no Arcturian Marine, but I can hold my own with any reptoid worker. I did not know how to deal with a Mothman at the time, but now I have them figured out. Next time, will be different.*

It was over five standard Years in real time since he last visited the family farm. Darius broke the legacy of his father by enlisting with the Intelligence wing of humanity's defence. He would have been a twelfth-generation biodiesel farmer. Still he hobbled on his crutches. He felt like some mechanical insect as he let the crutches lead and his one good leg follow. *Clip, hop. Clip, hop.* The onomatopoeia was hard to get out of his mind. It came natural now. *Clip, hop. Clip, hop.* Was the only sound he heard now. The shuttle that bought him down from the Timeliner was now resting. The spaceport was a quiet one this time of day, almost deserted, and it was a weekday. There were only a dozen or so others outside the spaceport, either walking to or from. He could see the driver of the coach he was about to board, and the primitive clipboard that held the passenger manifest, tucked in his armpit. The driver was standing with his arms in his pockets next to the entry door to the coach, which looked like a silver, blinding bullet-beetle in the early afternoon sun. Six stout

Draconium pods rested underneath it, all evenly spaced underneath the craft. Darius was now squinting his eyes as the sun glare from the coach stung him. When he finally got there he stopped a pace away from the driver, and his duffle bag slung over his shoulder swung forward with the momentum. He held himself tall on the crutches while he gave his name to the driver, how presently ticked off his name and grabbed Darius's bag unsympathetically. Darius soon found himself skipping awkwardly up the stairs and onto the coach, and felt twice as awkward when he discovered his fellow passengers were staring at him. There was ostracism in the air. His seventh sense told him so. He now could empathise with the Vietnam veterans of Oil Age Terra where he had recently come from, most who had looked as dispossessed and swindled as he now did. When disguised as a *Homo sapien* ancestor back then, riding on their primitive public transportation (which he realised just now, the interior of the coach he was presently on looked very similar to the interior of an Oil Age Bus), he came across scores of them in his years spent some two hundred and thirty thousand Standard years ago. But Darius could not console those veterans even if he had wanted to. He was mute and decided was best not to attempt fraternisation and interact with his ape-like ancestors.

The isle was narrow but he managed to find two empty seats side-by-side halfway down. He was forced to fold his shoulders inward to fit through, all the while avoiding eye contact with his fellow species of human, with the exception of about half a dozen offworld tourists whose origins he did not care about. It was only the Tau Cetan humans, with their distinguishing roman-statue nose and olive skin and curly blonde hair, who had ostracism in their eyes. The war with the Draconian Empire was evidently unpopular with the insular people of Tsorra.

He took his seat. It was a slow, painful, clumsy process. No one offered to help. He did not want it anyway. Darius either faced forward or looked out of the one-way window on the sides of the coach, which conformed to the arc of the bullet shape. This was the only direction his head would face for the rest of the journey to the old farm.

Another final passenger boarded, another Tau Cetan, and finally the coach operator. Computers and automata were still incapable of replacing a human operator on this planet. Or they wanted to protect jobs. Presently the hydroelectric engine of the coach roared to life, which powered the six draconium pods. Darius took this as a cue to settle back and nestle in his seat. It was only a few moments later when he felt himself being levitated, at first jerkily, and then smoothly. A slight, almost imperceptible feeling of blood rushing to the back of his skull and he was moving forward. The palm trees and blue sky was all that could be viewed out of his window now. Tsorra was Terraformed in the likeness of a tropical paradise over two hundred millennia ago. To Darius, he knew, this planet would be anything but a paradise from now on.

The coach was now travelling incredibly fast, how fast Darius did not know, only that the landscape was blurring past him so fast his eyes could not focus on and object outside and identify said object. He was told it was another three standard hours to the farm, which conveniently was situated off a main road which this coach passed through, and only about half a kilometre from a bus stop from there. He had nothing to entertain himself; his holopad was destroyed with the Ciakars' pyrokinetic attack. He had no ancient paperback novel, newspaper, nothing. All Darius could do to pass the time, was sleep. He grabbed his crutches and wedged them in the gap between himself and the window; he assumed the other Tau Cetan passengers would take them out of sheer spite, but now they could not do so without waking him. Leaning into his crutches, he tucked his head snuggly in the crook between the window and headrest of the seat. Darius reluctantly closed his eyes slowly. He did not know how long he lay awake with his eyes closed, maybe quarter of an hour? But Darius was indeed asleep a moment later, lullabied by the hum of the hydrogen-powered power plant.

Darius look around and could see nothing but off-white surrounding, even the ground was off-white. He was alone in his one-piece blue leotard that was the uniform of the Chronophysical Corps. *I am on the Athena*. It occurred to him eventually after standing there for a time that seemed like years and yet simultaneously, seconds. Slowly other objects at random manifested themselves; An automated gurney here, a person there. Darius felt in his mind a faceless material handling vehicle whizz past behind him. But the background still retained its off white form. He felt himself floating involuntarily, and found he had no will to resist. He was going where his irrational subconscious mind took him. Part of him knew it was the start of a bad dream but he felt powerless to wake himself, and lacked the motivation. It was like gawking at a terrible accident. He found he could not help himself, and demanded to find out how the story would play out. His eyes twitched and a door was in front of him. It came out of nowhere, was not there a moment ago. The door did not open by himself. Instead it was gone and he found that he had teleported into the room that was behind the door. Only a face was in this room, the room of plain off-white. The face seemed both simultaneously near and far, big and small. His subconscious could not comprehend dimension. It was agonisingly slow for him to compute that the face was in fact that of an Arcturian human. Eventually he realised the Arcturian was old, with silver cropped hair in the classic military fashion. *The Admiral!* Darius realised. The old Arcturian's face was emotionless. It was hazy, barely recognisable, only half detailed. Darius had only met The Admiral a few times, the last time when he was discharged, and The Admiral was disappointed, if anything then. Disappointed at Darius' hubris for taking on a Ciakar without an Amplifier.

Just as Darius felt a wave of guilt wash over him even while asleep, and assuming his subconscious mind was making him re-live his charges, the surroundings changed. The office was now almost a perfect replica as it was in reality. Darius found his eyes and head dart involuntarily around the room, and when he face The Admiral once more, a Draconian had took his place. This was no ordinary Draconian. A black Titanium chest plate covered its immense muscles, giving it a look of a sentient, wise, and deceptively angelic, medieval dragon-knight in some ancient fairytale. Green, seemingly vestigial wings flanked its shoulders, folded down but still making it seem even bigger. Even though Darius's mind still had no concept of dimensions, he knew it was many times bigger than he was. A Ciakar! The same Ciakar Darius had fought and lost against. The huge thing did not move or talk, just stood there motionless.

At once Darius found himself moving again, as if his dream were some mere ancient theme park ride. Presently he was on the deck of the *Athena* again. And again the deck was only sparsely, partially detailed. A bell-shaped Draconiumcraft, fuselage blew past him on his flank, the same robust, tank-like model he favoured. All around him detail manifested itself agonisingly slow. Human shapes, all faceless were walking every which way past Darius, none of them paying attention to his dream avatar. However still hazy, his avatar discerned a myriad of objects; things such as metal plates bordered by fasteners beneath him. His avatar turned around, and Darius found he was standing less than a metre away from the edge of the entrance to the cargo hold, a massive mouth of a thing, enough for ten of Darius's bell-shaped craft to fit through simultaneously. Beyond the entrance to the hold was the vacuum of space, and the brilliant spectacle of stars in the galaxy, with no light pollution. His subconscious mind left out one scientific detail; that if the mouth were indeed open to space, everything should be sucked out of the *Athena*. Except in reality there was a transparent, one-way Arcturium energy field, that acted like a check-valve, allowing only objects of significant mass to pass. Objects large enough such as the myriad of saucer-shaped craft in Darius's universe.

Finally his avatar focused on the human shapes again, and he was abruptly in the centre of the hold again. He did not remember teleporting, he was just there. Once again, the faceless human shapes were bombarding him from every possible direction, and in his dream Darius grew more and more irritated. The other people did not move out of his way, and he was constantly sidestepping, changing direction, and turning his body side on. He did not know how long he was doing this, or where he was walking to. He did not even know how long it was before he noticed that the human shapes had now indeed had a face. And they had changed colour. His avatar focused on one face, finally. Inferno-red irises with black-slit of pupils looked down at him contemptuously. Sharp teeth protruded downward from its mouth. The head looked reptilian, but it moved around in a bird-like fashion with speed and metabolism impossible for a conventional cold-blooded reptile. But what was the most frightening part that Darius realised, was what it was wearing. A tight-fitting one-piece blue jumpsuit with white boots, its inhuman body now ill-fitting with different anatomical proportions. Presently the boots now were gone, and were replaced by bare green, scaly feet that resembled that of an ostrich. The feet were now walking, and pointed their toes daintily forward as it took each step, only to land heel-first like that of a human. Darius felt his dream avatar look all around him simultaneously, as if eyes were all around his head. Draconians were swarming the *Athena*, where humans should be. His avatar looked to the left, looked to the right, it did not make any difference, every human was now a disguised Draconian. He was the only human on a ship with thousands of Draconians! But the reptilians were paying him no attention. Was he invisible? Darius felt his sleeping body jolt as his mind tried desperately to leave this place. It did not want to know what was next now, but still Darius felt powerless. He jerked again involuntarily, his body sitting on the coach seat. Darius blacked out. He did not know how long for.

When Darius came to, he was on the hydrogen-powered coach once again. The same bland, spartan interior, that was barely different from Oil-Age Public transportation vehicles. Darius lifted his head warily. His neck protested and felt stiff. The Tau Cetans sitting around him paid him no attention. The coach went over a bump. Their heads bobbed with the bump, including Darius's. He felt his neck *click*. The heads returned to their upright position, and Darius recovered from the unexpected discomfort. Only this time the heads in the seats in front of him had changed as well to the eerily familiar snake-like scaled dome. Darius looked to the side, to the seat next to him, across the aisle, and found inferno red irises and black cold slits of the fellow passenger staring back at him irritably. He looked behind him, and on the seats to his rear, found only Draconians in human clothing. Some ignoring him, most glowering at him. Even the off world tourists, which Darius remembered there was a Sirian among them, were Draconians.

Darius did not remember getting off the coach, and how he was now inside the old family dwelling on the old biodiesel farm. But here he was, in a simple dome shaped three-bedroom house. He found himself seated in a dim, stuffy room at the kitchen table, the simple wooden type build for function and durability above all else. The chairs were matching, practically unchanged since ancient Terra. The kitchen was primitive even by Oil-Age standards. Not a speck of technology could be found, no electric appliances except a high efficiency refrigerator. Automata, now found in most modern kitchens, controlled by a computer which could prepare a meal from scratch, was out of the question here. The oven and stove unit was biodiesel. Naked flames would burn underneath pots and kettles. There was a small container next to it, which siphoned the biodiesel. A bench and sink used for menial food preparation and washing up looked centuries out of fashion.

Abruptly Darius heard loud cloppy footsteps beyond the kitchen door to his left flank. A few steps later, the sound stopped. Shadows where the feet now were visible under the door. The shadows simply remained stationary under the door for what seemed like an eternity. Only the sound of Darius's heart could be heard. *Father? Why is he waiting behind the door!? Is he still upset at me after all these years?* Darius knew it was only a matter of time until the door would swing open and he would know if the salty old Tau Cetan would be pleased to see him.

Abruptly, it occurred to Darius that what was behind

the door would be yet another Draconian. Just as his mind, however, began to debate the subject, he blacked out again.

A hand was on his shoulder, shaking him. Telepathy could be discerned in his mind now. '... your destination, sir. Can you hear me? Time to wake up.'

Darius sleepily opened his eyes. His mouth tasted like phlegm gone rotten. He willed his mouth to summon saliva at once. His neck was indeed as stiff as his dream avatar's had been. He sat upright as reality told him the coach was on a tight schedule and could not wait for him to enjoy breakfast in bed. As he began to rise from his seat, he felt his leg protest. He half slumped again toward the window, and realised it was because balance was the problem. His eyes focused on the crutches tucked in between the seat and window. The affirmation of his affliction returned to him now. His heart sank.

Painfully, he swooped up the crutches and tucked one under each armpit carefully. His seventh sense, all the while, could feel the coach drivers eyes locked on to him. Impatience was growing in that piercing stare. Darius ignored him, did not even look at the coach driver. On autopilot he skipped to the aisle. He was now aware of the idling hydrogen engine droning from the back, vibrations echoing from random places in the coach. Muscle memory now intruded on his senses. He remembered how to use his crutches. *Clop, skip. Clop skip*, Darius chimed in his mind absently. He was now negotiating the stairs of the coach. It was sunset now, and most of the days heat had gone as his remaining foot hit the ground of his homeworld once again. His duffle bag was now a pace away, dumped on the ground disrespectfully. He turned to face the coach driver accusingly, but found the doors had already slammed close behind him. By the time he tripodded himself and twisted his body, a blur was all he had to protest against, as the coach was now already moving off again.

8.

There were two warring tribes in the mid Oil Age, after the second Terran Civil war. The capitalist tribe, which bore a symbol of a distant relative of the Draconians, the eagle. Their archenemies, which bore the symbol of a beast called a bear, were the direct opposite.

Unkaalah was charged by the Empire with giving one of these tribes a new technology ten standard years after the Civil War. *Homo sapiens* liked their environment too cold. He shivered, despite being wrapped in warm clothing in his disguised form. As a low ranking field agent in the Draconian Chronophysical Warfare effort, it was only natural his superiors gave him such an unpleasant task. He was briefed only with need-to-know basics of why the two tribes were fighting. The irony of it was twofold; he was giving technology and information to an ape who also fancied himself an agent in a war that the Empire was fabricating. The ape would think their tribe was at an advantage over the other, only failing to realise the bigger picture. Espionage within espionage.

And second, this ape he was supposed to meet any minute now was likely an ancestor of a sworn enemy of his, and yet Unkaalah was seemingly helping them out. Espionage within espionage.

His superior, a Ciakar general based in an undiscovered underground fortress of Oil-Age Terra, had mercifully waited until the summer to give Unkaalah this task. If it were winter, Unkaalah would have died of hypothermia in minutes, regardless of how he wrapped up. Where this tribe lived, winters were harsh even for most mammals. A reptilian would not be so lucky. Unkaalah lurked in the shadows of what the *Homo sapiens* called *Gorkiy Park*. It was nighttime here, and the curfew imposed by the strict regime of this tribe, and the fact that they were too overworked and downtrodden not to be sleeping now, meant that there were no *Homo sapiens* here. Still Unkaalah retained his human form. This level of caution had served him well. Ten Sy's as an agent gave proof to the fact he was doing something right.

It was at this thought that Unkaalah heard the groan of an amusingly pathetic black groundcar, coming down a service road that groundskeepers typically used. That must be his contact. He eased out of the shadows wearily carrying a briefcase that primitive spies of Terra favoured, to rendezvous with the groundcar as it ground to a halt. A red rectangle with a golden hammer and sickle was on the side of the vulgar thing. Unkaalah saw that symbol everywhere here. A *Homo sapien* climbed out, dressed in a snug black winter outfit. Another ape on the other side of the groundcar did the same a few seconds later.

They were walking over to Unkaalah expectantly, like animals in a zoo during feeding time. He looked around for witnesses as they approached. It was odd to be at eye level with a human less than two metres tall. Unkaalah almost forgot that he was in the form of an average *Homo sapien*. He handed them the briefcase, and put all his faith in the translating console he carried under his tongue. It should speak decent Russian with an American accent. He would open his mouth to sing his birdcall Draconian language, only to have it intercepted in a microsecond and translated by the indispensable gadget. At last one of the apes spoke, but Unkaalah could not see its face in the dim lighting of Gorkiy Park. That would also work in his advantage. The primary shortcoming of the translating device was that he had to hold his mouth open for it to project sound. Other agents had opted to actually learn the languages of *Homo sapiens* and speak it, but it was generally anatomically impossible for them.

'The Party thanks you, comrade, for your generous gift', the ape said in the language called Russian while it took Unkaalah's briefcase. 'But we have to ask, what is it you expect in return?'

Unkaalah did not anticipate this. The apes should have took their new toy eagerly and not even thanked him, as was planned. Thinking fast, however, he replied, also in Russian,

'Having thwarted the capitalist system that wronged me is its own reward, comrade. That and knowledge the People's Party would put what I have given you to good use. There is the matter of my defection, of course, *Nyet*?'

At that, the ape beamed wolfishly, and Unkaalah was trained thoroughly on reading *Homo sapien* body language and facial expressions. The animal was evidently pleased at the sycophantic answer. Presently the other one walked quickly back to the groundcar, opened a door in the rear of the ugly thing.

Climbing into the beast Unkaalah realised what happened to him from hereafter was meaningless. He congratulated himself for being so professional. Most Daconians would have killed a *Homo sapien* for its meat. Or at least gawked at the delicacies hungrily with watering mouths. It took discipline to be a field agent with the Imperial war effort, above all. Certainly not intelligence, with these dumb animals. Unkaalah climbed into the backseat, and the animal closed the door. Where they were taking him, and what was going to happen to him, Unkaalah did not care. He could easily overpower these animals if things turned ugly. The groundcar lurched off painfully slow down the service road and gained speed, scarcely faster than a cart pulled by beasts of burden. The two *Homo sapiens* in front kept facing forward, focused on the illuminated road ahead. Unkaalah nestled in the cold, spartan corinthian seat and realised keeping warm was the most of his worries now. His mission was accomplished. He had given them what the Empire had wanted now, and the proverbial wheels were in motion, the proverbial chess pieces have been played. Unkaalah tried to remember the *Homo sapien* name for what was in the briefcase. The groundcar bounced and moaned on poor suspension over rough roads when the he recalled the name. Yes. The briefcase contained plans and blueprints, everything this tribe would need, to make, primitive by Draconian standards, but nevertheless destructive, weapon. It worked on a similar scientific principle to the exalted Ciakars' Pyrokinetic abilities. Nuclear fission of hydrogen atoms into helium, creating searing heat and incredible energy. Unkaalah had heard the rival tribe name it the *hydrogen bomb*. Not that it mattered. The real weapon was the ramifications caused by both tribes now having this *hydrogen bomb*, and not knowing they were playing right into the Draconians' powerful, taloned hands, an enemy *Homo sapiens* did not even know existed, and not so for years to come.

9.

A titanium putting club brushed against a golf ball for the first time on the *Athena*. An aged and stout pair of hands fidgeted over the high quality handle. Moments later, the white ball disappeared into the first hole. The pair of hands triumphantly twirled the putting club and slid it into the golf bag. The Admiral was not as rusty at the Arcturian official pastime as he expected himself to be; he reflected this as he fished the golf ball from the hole. Scooping up his golf bag, he strode toward the lift that would take him and O'Brien up to the next level, where the next hole would be played. The *Athena* was so immense that a multiple-storey golf course took less than two percent of the internal space on the city-sized ship. It was odd to have a golf course on a military ship, but it generally doubled as a common park and playing fields for other ancient sports on most days. But not today.

Gunnery Sergeant O'Brien walked beside the shorter Admiral in silence. It was also his day off. The Admiral had boasted they had both earned it. O'Brien had to agree. He was the one who had rescued an insubordinate and arrogant Tau Cetan from that Ciakar. Even armed to the teeth with a Psionic Amplifier on his head, a light but hardy suit of armour and an automatic Anti-Rifle, the Ciakar proved to be no pushover. Nearly half a dozen Marines had perished that day in the effort to terminate the Ciakar and thus rescue that Tau Cetan. It was O'Brien's eighth Ciakar he had now on his record. It was well above average for twenty Sy's of service with the Arcturian Marines. Most didn't even have one.

The Admiral had wished now not to forsake a simple electric golf cart, practically unchanged from their Oil Age predecessors. Not because he was lazy or tired, but because time was getting on. He picked up his pace at that thought. The nearest service elevator was still a few hundred yards away. It was O'Brien's turn when they got off the elevator to the next level, ten metres up; each had to alternate turns with every level. That equated to nine holes each. The admiral found his heart rate had increased when they reached the lift. This pace, however, was O'Brien's regular walking pace. The two veterans of humanity's cold war with the Draconian Empire boarded the lift with their shared golf bag and clubs. It was the transparent type, with clear sidewalls but a Draconium platform. An electric generator somewhere within the *Athena* charged the platform with copious amounts of electricity. A moment later, and the charged Draconium levitated the admiral and the Gunnery Sergeant up to the next level in seconds.

O'Brien was irritated when they got their first look at the second hole, just as the platform slipped up though the ground like a mole. The door opened, complimented by an audible chime, and the Admiral huffed when he saw what O'Brien did a moment before. This level was polluted with a dozen or so other golfers using the *Athena's* only recreational facility. O'Brien would simply have to work around the three other Arcturians presently teeing off. The Admiral had scored a birdie on the previous hole. O'Brien, not being a passionate and devoted golfer as his superior officer, would be lucky to achieve a bogey.

'Remember that you only have a limited height on this course,' the Admiral's telepathic voice finally intruded in O'Brien's mind. 'Indoor courses are always so challenging compared to the outdoor variety.'

'Duly noted, Sir.' O'Brien plopped the golf ball on the ground. He did not bother with a tee. His mind was on other things, and he never took this game seriously at the best of times. He swooped up the longest driving club from the communal bag. With no ostentation, he positioned his body next to the ball, lined up the club, and prepared mentally to swing. An audible *whotisch!* was heard only a moment later as O'Brien teed off. The ball arced in the air for eighty yards, then bounced off the ceiling ten metres above them. The ball ricocheted to the left, and plopped on the green a further ten metres from that. Which happened to work in O'Brien's favour. If he actually really cared about winning that is. It was after all an informal, if not friendly, game. And he felt vaguely obligated to tag along with his superior officer. One did not refuse an offer from the Admiral of the *Athena* after all. The Admiral grimaced patronisingly.

'... Or not, Gunny. Next time may not be so lucky. It may ricochet into an ace in the hole next time!' The Admiral did not bother to hide his sneer.

'You are a sly, witty man, Sir. Perhaps you could be a part time comedian when you finally retire.' O'Brien replied in half-hearted telepathy.

They strolled towards the Gunnery Sergeant's ball in silence, taking in the sights. The artificial park that doubled as a golf course was, internally and superficially, a strange mix of a greenhouse and an ancient multiple-storey shopping mall. The ceiling which the golf ball had recently bounced off was a metallic black dotted evenly with spotlights. The paradise-implying presence of palm tree leaves and branches were the only things to break up the mechanical monotony. On this floor alone, dozens of palm trees dotted the golf course in random places, accompanied by the occasional sandy bunker pit or small lake. There were no birds, of course, although most would expect them in a scene like this, along with a clear blue sky. In the distance, to the left, right and ahead, was a solid white wall with the occasional emergency exit. It was only a little over one standard minute before they got there, where the ball was perched on the green. O'Brien still had over forty-five yards till the hole. And he was a mediocre putter at best. It took him an average of three attempts to get the ball in the hole with a putting club. Only once, ever, in his whole life did he sink the ball on the first attempt. He put down the communal golf bag and chose a random iron without even looking. It was one size too long for the range, but O'Brien didn't care.

Presently, he lined himself up with the ball, his shoulders perpendicular, and swung. He was good enough to hit the ball with almost every swing. But only just. The ball sailed in the air, almost on a forty-five degree angle from the hole. And it overshot the hole by nearly ten yards. O'Brien didn't care about that either. He just wanted this game to be over. He almost loathed the game of golf. Not that he had told a living soul. The Admiral and Gunnery Sergeant walked to this ball in under a minute this time, in silence also. O'Brien lined up his body begrudgingly and swung again. It was a bunker this time. It landed almost perfectly centre in a large sand pit that guarded the flat, well-tended green immediately sur-rounding the hole. The flag could be seen about twenty-five yards from where they stood. The Admiral's aged face doubled in wrinkles as he patronisingly flinched and audibly whistled. He was unconsciously leaning on the club he held, which made him look even older.

'Well well, Gunny.' The Admiral almost boasted with his telepathy at the Gunnery Sergeant. 'Looks like you need to go on a sand-wedge diet, huh?'

'Once again, Sir, your military prowess is surpassed only by your unparalleled wit.' O'Brien did not bother to hide his sarcasm, to which the Admiral did not care. He knew the joke was probably old and over-used even on Oil-Age Terra that orbited the other side of the star from where the *Athena* was now drifting aimlessly.

The Admiral won the game, of course. O'Brien was lounging in his barracks on the *Athena*, glad the game was over. Glad the Admiral ended the game quickly, in fact. Even though he was fit enough to be a seasoned member of the Arcturian Marines, which required the highest fitness level of any occupation in the Commonwealth, except perhaps professional athletes, he found that last game of golf surprisingly tiring. Maybe it was because he walked at the Admirals' slow pace for hours. Or maybe it was because pretending to look interested in activity your heart was not into was tiring work. It didn't matter now. O'Brien unwound by watching a film on the screen. The film was set in a time on Terra even more ancient than the Oil Age. It comprised of men in wide-brimmed hats riding horses in a desert. The men were currently, in the film, shooting at each other with nearly stone-age rifles and six-shot revolver pistols. The western themed films were currently popular. The latest fashion on Oil Age Terra, on the other side of the nearest star. This western film was O'Brien's first, dubbed over the original English by Commonish. The mouths moving as the men talked no longer synchronised. English was a needlessly complicated ancient language, so O'Brien had heard. Unlike Latin, even more ancient, from which English was now often compared. Needless to say, O'Brien was not impressed, and wondered what all the fuss was about. He had, until now, never even heard of the western days, or the renaissance, or the dark ages, and had assumed the transition from stone age to Oil Age a seamless, automatic and above all trivial, process. At least his mind was taken away from golf. Or that idiot Tau Cetan Darius, whom O'Brien had never really liked from the start. And did not know why.

His thoughts and woolgathering interrupted suddenly, O'Brien was now running to the loading dock, as is. The Incredibly large spaceport inside the *Athena* where dozens, sometimes hundreds of saucer-shaped spacecraft landed and mothballed, so large and vast, you could seldom see when it ended. The ceiling was high overhead, about fifteen storeys, and one had to squint their eyes at the beams and rafters and such, to assure themselves it actually *was* a ceiling. In emergencies such as this, It also served as a muster point for every crew member on board, up to and including ones already fast asleep. Claxons sounded in his ears, drowning out his footsteps bashing the metal decking. The claxons had begun to imprint an unintended melody in his mind. He was beginning to labour for breaths when he reached one of many service elevators that would take him to the bowel of the *Athena*. He reflected that perhaps he should not use the elevator if claxons were sounding, and use one of the many flights of stairs instead. The elevator was the same transparent type he had used earlier that day on the makeshift golf course with the admiral, the transparent walls and Draconium base. It took him down over forty levels with a smooth, transitional speed. Much faster, and better, than stumbling down forty-three flights of stairs.

The transparent doors opened, and he ran in his combat boots to the nearest crowd, a few hundred metres away. The entire crew had orderly formed themselves in squares of a hundred or so each, and formed ranks, like the legionnaires of Rome, ancient even for the Oil Age. O'Brien was among the stragglers. He had barely caught his breath, about half a minute later, when the claxons cut out. There were of course, so many on the *Athena* that a role call would be hopelessly impractical. It was something that should be reviewed and amended in the future. No one was grabbing their battle gear, complete with Amplifiers, or heading to the ships larger Artillery-Amps, which helped the user destroy entire asteroids with their telekinesis. Or to the rotary Anti-Cannons, or any other fixed armaments on the *Athena*, so O'Brien knew it wasn't about a Draconian attack or meteor shower (the latter which the *Athena* could easily withstand.) He would just have to be patient and wait, like all the others.

Presently, the Admiral appeared on large screens scattered throughout the spaceport at every convenient location. The fact he was still in his spartan office, with the lone potted tree and desk, with the Arcturian and Commonwealth of Humanity's respective flags flanking his shoulders, drooping down their poles restfully, supported the idea that it was not a Draconian attack from the depths of Shrinkspace. *What can all this be about, then?* O'Brien wondered to himself, as he was lost in the crowd, another face among thousands, even though the Admiral knew him well. '

My fellow Citizens. Do not be alarmed. The nature of this assembly is bought about through dire actions of our primitive ancestors, the *Homo sapiens*. Recently, especially in the past decade, humanity has began its first steps in leaving its Motherplanet, Terra, on the other side of that star in front of us.' The *Athena* had always assumed itself safe from primitive Terran telescopes by stalking and creeping about the largest planet in the Terran system, Jupiter. That ancient name was still being used in the age of Shrinkspace (even though it now refers to a dead gas giant with only a rocky core to its name.) Now however, with the recent launch of an ancient spacefaring probe, that was about to change. The *Athena* and her crew could be discovered by this nosey, annoying piece of junk. That nosey mechanical monstrosity was now heading for Jupiter. The *Athena's* scanners and other automata warned her crew that it will be here in less than a day.

'We are about to be discovered, the *Athena*, by an early Terran spacefaring probe. It will be here, in Jupiter's orbit, at around oh nine hundred. Unless we move where the probe won't discover us, The Terrans will find the *Athena*, which will have grave Chronophysical ramifications. So far we have ascertained that this probe is setting off towards each of the outer planets in this system, in order of distance from this star. What is worse, we have recently confirmed the ancient Terrans have launched an identical, second automated probe. This probe will have us on the run. We will be on the receiving end of a proverbial hide-and-go seek game with our ancient ancestors,' the Admiral concluded gravely. He added latently, 'Don't you all worry. Running out into Shrinkspace to avoid detection, thereby abandoning your fellow citizens, our Chronophysical field agents, on Terra, is not an option. We can't afford to leave them behind. They themselves could, if discovered or captured, bring Chronophysical consequences regardless. Heed my words, good Citizens of The Commonwealth. WE ARE NOT GOING TO

ABANDON THEM. We will do everything we can to let them know our new position, or better yet, get them all back here. That is all. Dismissed, and back to your posts.'

It was a well known rule, that once a craft travelled through time, it could not return to the exact same time, where that said craft was entering or has entered Shrink-space. To do otherwise, would mean a pseudo-like copy of the *Athena* would return instead. Not really existing, and not not existing. Essentially it would be stuck in a surreal limbo of paradoxical existence, almost like a kind of parallel universe. Hence, the hundred or so saucer-shaped craft, along with their loyal field agents, would return to a phantom *Athena*, attempting to dock on a mothership in another dimension. And they would be marooned in the time of Oil Age Terra, until another timefaring mothership came, two hundred and thirty thousand Standard Years from now.

The Commonwealth's timefaring doctrine went something like, "Once a time faring craft emerges from Shrinkspace into any point in the past, it must not enter Shrinkspace again until all personnel, equipment, Biobrids, spacecraft, etc is returned and accounted for. Timefaring craft, by definition, include, but not limited to; 1) Timeliners 2) Warships of the Navy, and 3) small, privately owned miscellaneous craft capable of time faring.

Presently, the Admiral terminated signal, and every screen within the spaceport went blank. The ranks of disciplined Marines, Sailors, cooks, cleaners, freight handlers and field agents, who were all distinguishable wearing their trademark blue tight-fitting jumpsuit and white boots, began to at-ease. They quickly became a crowd, among many crowds, losing ranks, and became human again. An orchestra of telepathic chatting of thousands of simultaneous conversations flooded O'Brien's mind. Even he now shifted around uneasily to face other members of the crowd. It was a motley hotchpotch of six different species of human in different clothing and uniforms. Even so, they understood and communed with each other, almost as one, bridging their differences. They might as well have been clones of the same human. O'Brien turned to a hulking Plieadian with long wavy blonde hair, rugged facial features, and the Blue jumpsuit that pegged him a field agent. O'Brien was large for his species, but even so had to look up to match his gaze.

'Damn straight we're not leaving.' The Pleiadian grizzled to the Arcturian. 'I have a sister in law somewhere on Terra. If I come back without her, my wife and her father will have my hide.' Obron Altmeus half joked, half complained with a smirk.

10.

Magne Mimee's hands gently grasped the control wheel of the Timeliner simulator for the first time. She beamed in spite of herself. The console that would guide a ship that would send people and freight not only through space but also through time, felt so good in her young hands. So right. Magne did not even have her biobrid licence, had not even yet thought of getting it, and here she was, about to control something that was infinitely more capable than a mere Biobrid. *A simulator!* She reminded herself.

Magne looked up and forward out towards the observation screen in the flight deck. It was redundant to refer to it as a windscreen. How she had never seen so many stars!

This is what space must look like from the cockpit! She told herself. It was beautiful. Until she had begun her internship recently, she had never been offworld, ever. She was the daughter of an average mother and father, average citizens of the Commonwealth. Thus her family had no reason to leave Erra; had no relatives offworld, and no acquaintances from another species of human that made their home on other Terraformed planets throughout the galaxy.

'Good Magne,' Pteru's voice was telepathically transmitted on the earphones she was wearing. The room was dark. She could barely see anything except the glowing controls.

'Give it more thrust, but not too much. Pull back slowly but with confidence. Pulling back tentatively will only make the Timeliner jerk.' Pteru again. 'There is nothing ahead for at least one astronomical unit. Do not worry about any collisions. That is the least of your worries.' Magne did her best to follow her tutor's instructions, but the simulated Timeliner, although massive, was surprisingly twitchy. It took her a full ten minutes to become familiar with the ship, how it accelerated, and how it handled.

'This is far different from a primitive groundcar or even a Biobrid. You are in the vacuum of space. Unlike on land, there is practically no friction. You are doing fine. Just remember-smooth, gradual manoeuvres.'

Magne was now virtually-travelling incredibly fast. She looked at an instrument that measured velocity. Zero point zero-two-one. Just over two percent the speed of light. However, in deep space, there is nothing, no planet, no star, not even a tiny asteroid, for light years. One-fiftieth and one-tenth the speed of light looked the same. The beatific gas clouds, nebulae and constellations in Magne's vision did not change, did not become larger or smaller. Nevertheless, the synthesised Timeliner was accelerating rapidly. In the ten or so seconds that had passed since, the instrument now read zero point two-nine. In another ninety seconds, the ship would reach almost the maximum theoretical limit to the speed a solid object could attain; about one tenth the speed of light.

'Allright, Magne. I assume you have been keeping an eye on the instrument to your left that measures your current velocity? Yes? Let me know when you reach zero point four-zero.'

'It's at point oh three-eight now. Close enough?' Magne ventured into her earphone receiver telepathically.

'Yes, okay. Doing good. To your right is a touch screen console with red button and a green. The green launches conventional Sentinels. The red will send the Arcturium Displacers that launch Chrono-Reversal type of Sentinels. For now push the Green one. We don't want to go time travelling just yet. Not for a while, I am afraid.'

Magne reluctantly pushed the green button as was instructed. The simulator tremored slightly as three kidney-shaped probes shot forward in the deep space before her. Their Arcturium anti-matter propulsion method meant that they were invisible; the colour of Arcturium in its anti-matter form was black as deep space. Of course it was only a simulation, and the Sentinels were fake. In reality, as they were made of primarily Draconium, each of the kidney-shaped drones cost as much as a cheap Biobrid. The Sentinels that enabled time travel backwards, and not just nullified time, were over three times even more costly. Hence one of the many reasons Magne was sitting in the chair of a simulator.

Presently the three probes ahead of the virtual

Timeliner were now one-fifth an astronomical unit ahead. Although Magne could no longer see them, they had formed a triangle formation, evenly spaced. The drones oscillated in sync and faced the inside of the triangle. Magne could soon make out a faint crimson triangle ahead. She checked her instruments diligently, and noted she was travelling at a velocity of point zero six-eight. Six point eight percent the speed of light. Incredibly fast by Oil Age standards, but puny and therefore painfully slow if one would wish to travel to another star system.

'That is, I think fast enough, Magne. Now push the control wheel in. That leads directly to the valve that fuels the propulsion system. In reality you will now travel at this speed for several lightyears, as again, no friction. But I digress. The Sentinels are now slowing down and will match your speed.'

Indeed Magne looked up and was astounded to witness the crimson triangle was over twice as large, and was doubling in size every half a minute or so. Again, Magne checked her instruments diligently, as if trying to impress or appease an imaginary tutor sitting next to her in the dark cockpit. Zero point seven-one now, and staying there, as she hoped. The triangle was now roughly eight times bigger than when she first witnessed it. And still it was growing.

'The Sentinels are now about one-twentieth an astronomical unit ahead. They will gain velocity and match your speed soon, when you are only a million or so kilometres ahead. They are, in real life fully automated and synchronise with the Timeliner's speed, so there is no need to worry about them. Just concentrate on the 'Liner. Make sure you get it through shrinkspace in one piece.'

A few standard minutes passed and the crimson triangle indeed grew larger no more. It was at this relatively close distance that Magne could appreciate how big it really was. An average moon could fit inside the triangle. *Why does it need to be so big!?* She wailed to herself.

'Okay Master Hoolde, what now!?'

'Just relax. The timeliner's automata will do most of the work. When the triangle ahead of you no longer grows any larger, and a "ready" light blinks on the touchscreen console, above the green button you pressed earlier. When you find it, push it. This will give the command for the sentinels to increase the anti-matter particles within the triangle. Not enough to reverse the polarity of space-time, only nullify it. Again we only want to travel in real time, And not time-travel to the past. Neither of you will be ready for that for a while.'

Magne found the panel easily, waited for Pteru to stop his telepathic windbagging before she executed the command. The "ready" icon disappeared at her touch. Seconds later, and the crimson triangle a million kilometres ahead of her dimmed. And went darker. As if some supergiant space deity had snuffed it out like a mere candle flame. It dimmed to a flicker, and then Magne could only see bright spots in her vision where the triangle had burned a temporary photograph into her retina.

"Master Hoolde, I think I broke it.' She projected telepathically over her two-way earphones. Her voice betrayed her increased guilt and nervousness. She was expecting to be reprimanded next. Though what Magne did wrong was anyone's guess.

'No, you didn't. It is just the sentinels increasing the amount of anti-matter, which is black. Blacker than any black you would find on Erra or any known planet. Don't worry, this is perfectly normal.'

And indeed, when a relieved and calmed Magne looked ahead of her again, out of the cockpit observation window, a large chunk of the beautific stars had disappeared. It was only recently that the night sky was absolutely covered densely in them. Now a whole section was missing. The section was a triangle shape! It wasn't her imagination. It was as if someone had stuck a jet-black handkerchief to the window, blocking her vision. Even now, the moon-sized triangle turned an even darker colour than pitch black. This shade had a hint of purple tinge. Magne had previously assumed there was no colour blacker than black.

'That's it now, the Sentinels are ready. In real life they are shrinking space in that dark patch you see before you, with Arcturium. Now pull the control wheel out again, slowly but steadily. Leave it out until you reach around zero point zero seven-five. Any more can cause hazardous levels of stress on the anti-matter propulsion system. An Arcturium meltdown makes a conventional nuclear one look like an ancient molotov cocktail in comparison! Don't worry, the Sentinels will take care of themselves. The default simulation is ten lightyears of space shrunk. That equates to about fifteen standard minutes to travel through, even though it would take say, two hundred and fifty Standard Years without the Sentinels. But again I digress. Magne, now simply steer into that dark triangle. You are doing great so far.'

Once more, Magne did as was instructed, her school-girl hands unaccustomed to being in the workforce trembling slightly to pull at the precise speed. The simulated Timeliner increased acceleration immediately, with every passing second the instrument to her left increasing. Less than ten seconds later, it had reached zero point zero seven-three and Magne, using her discretion, decided that would be the right time to push the control wheel in again. She did her best to push back in again halfway with the same precision, only at the start she was slightly too fast. The jerk was barely perceptible. Her discretion came true; it settled exactly on zero point zero seven-five. Returning her gaze over her other instruments diligently again, she realized steering into the massive triangle was deceptively difficult. Most movements she made had to be overcompensated the opposite way. By the time she was satisfied with the way the 'Liner was travelling, The triangle was frighteningly close. It nearly covered the whole cockpit screen in front of her. And was doubling every few seconds. Now she was so close, that she had to crane her neck up and to the side to see the edge of the triangle. Any second now she would hit the ominous, sinister thing.

She had thought she had finally made contact, but still another two seconds before she actually did seemed like an eternity. The Timeliner shuddered like an Oil Age airliner suffering turbulence as she entered Shrinkspace for the first time. She had been told the energy produced from shrinking the fabric of a lightyear of space meant it would be incredibly hot in reality. Many times hotter than a star, Pteru had told her. She pondered if her Timeliner could possibly maintain its integrity in such incredible conditions, when she reminded herself, *It's only a simulator. It's only a simulator.*

As if at that mantra, the synthesised automata took control of the turbulence and the shuddering stopped. Magne now had the luxury of looking out the cockpit, but only saw pitch black, not a star could be seen. The anti-matter had forsaken any light from getting in. Magne squinted her violet eyes. Not pitch black. But dynamic shades of purple-on-black. All she could do was listen. Magne held her breath.

Is that howling or moaning I can hear outside the 'Liner? she wondered. Her heart rate increased, but not from the stress she now placed on her body by denying it oxygen. She listened more closely, still held her breath. The howling wasn't like that of the wind around a building. It was organic. But far from human. For her to decribe the sound as eerie was an understatement. The sub-human hell-howling continued.

'That's enough for today, Magne. Well done.' Pteru's sudden telepathic intrusion over the earphones made her jump.

'Are you sure, Master Hoolde?' She struggled to find her telepathic voice.

'Quite sure. A standard minute in synthesized Shrink-space is enough to get the idea. Any longer, and I was afraid you would fall asleep with boredom.' Pteru half joked.

Only a minute passed? Magne wondered. It seemed like an eternity. The lights inside the simulated cockpit came on at Pteru's command, illuminating the room. This was an unspoken visual cue to get out of the seat and exit. It was as ancient as the Oil Age. When the operators of an ancient cinema that played films inside a theatre would light up the room at the conclusion of the film.

And every moviegoer would get up and exit the theatre like sheep as the credits were rolling. Only to go outside and forget where they were, who they were and what they were doing next.

Magne opened the door of the exit. Her legs felt weak, and she did not bother to hide it. Her violet eyes had to adjust to a brighter room. Pteru was a few paces away, waiting with his arms casually crossed. Skyler Tjeons was right behind him, obviously weary with the waiting.

'Was that fun? How was it?' Magne did not respond to Skyler, just walked past him and sat down at a nearby desk. She stared down at the desk, while messing her raven hair with her hands absently. Skyler called over to her with his telepathy.

'Well, you better not have broken it.' He laughed flirtatiously. 'It's my turn next.'

11.

Nordic Alien Encounter? Sorjana was reading an Oil Age newspaper. She had been trained to speak and read fluent English, as one of the requirement to be a field agent. To most others in the Commonwealth, however, English was a long forgotten language like Latin. Only those with an aptitude for classical studies had a real interest in romance such as English and Latin. *Should I be offended?* She chuckled to herself. She was waiting for a primitive electric train that ferried people around the city underground. She was leaning against a sign that read *"Valid ticket must be in possession to ride."* Sorjana was dressed as a *Homo sapien*. She wore her hair up and in a bun, which covered her enlarged, powerful, evolved brain. For good measure, a large pair of tinted eyeglasses to hide her larger eyes. Now she blended perfectly among her genetic ancestors from hundreds of millennia ago. None gave her a second thought or glance.

Presently, the incredibly ancient multiple-carriage coach on rails could be heard from deep within the bowels of the underground subway. A cacophony of metal-on-metal grew louder, its two headlights now visible. A few seconds later, the laughably primitive box was screeching to a halt. Sorjana began folding up her newspaper and took a cursory, if inconspicuous, look at the other *Homo sapiens* who were about to board with her. A near even mix of male and female, Sorjana noted. She walked casually to where the doors would open, blending with her genetic Terran ancestors in the process. When the doors finally opened, agonisingly slow, Sorjana was one of the first on, stepping on tentatively at first, surveying the inside. It was relatively empty for the trams in this ancient commoncity, and she had no trouble finding an empty seat. *Homo sapiens*, she noted, had a habit of travelling to their occupation at the start of every day, and away from their ancient cities near the end. Hence, that was when the ancient trams would be highly congested. She had timed it well.

The tram rumbled through the underground after taking what seemed like forever to Sorjana to gain speed. She sat on her seat illuminated by the artificial lighting, and pretended to be interested in the paper, like a typical *Homo sapien* would. What these primitive ancestors had failed to realise that, there were reptilians everywhere, and Sorjana was here to protect them, by any means necessary. She was the only human on the whole train who could spot a disguised Draconian, from the way that they had that distinctive smell and thousand-yard-stare. The only Modern Human on this carriage; unless, of course there were deserters that had formerly fought on Sorjana's side. Whom might come to her aid if she were to be ganged-up on by the vile reptiles. She knew not to rely on that option however, if things turned dire the hard way. They were called deserters and therefore cowards for a reason. Fortunately right now, however, on this carriage there were also no Draconians. But that did not let her lower her vigilance. She continued to stay seated, swaying and bobbing on the carriage, disguised as a *Homo sapien*, feigning interest in the trivial Terran newspaper.

Before long, the carriage began slowing, and a ticket-inspector-come-chamberlain, announced the present station. It wasn't Sorjana's. She did not look up at her male genetic ancestor at the other end of the carriage, as most trained in the art of Oil Age apathy wouldn't. Presently the tram ground to a halt, and she swayed in her seat with the sudden inertia, retuned upright, all while holding the newspaper up. Her sunglasses, she had faith in, hid not only her larger, oval eyes, enabling her to blend in. No one noticed her eyes, but more importantly, what they were doing. She was not in fact reading the newspaper, but scanning her surroundings constantly, looking for characteristics in these *Homo sapiens* that betrayed them as members of her archenemy species. Right now, as the people about to board the train came into clear view, her ultraviolet eyes locked onto the impending fellow passengers. The carriage door opened agonisingly slow once again, and a dozen contemporary humans shuffled on.

None of them Draconians. So far. Sorjana learned quickly that there would be days, weeks even, not a single reptoid could be found, and sometimes three or four in a single day. Today would likely be one of the former.

Satisfied they were typical *Homo sapiens*, Sorjana finally relaxed. Allowing herself the luxury of actually reading her newspaper, and thus letting her guard down, and returned to the slanderous article about Pleidians.

Stanley Crompton, 41, a local tractor salesman and mechanic, was driving home late at night to his fourth generation family farm after working extended hours and visiting bar for a late meal. Not deviating from his regular commute, it was about 9:45 pm when he noticed strange lights ahead. Crompton initially assumed it was the scene of an accident, so naturally reduced speed and proceeded with caution. It was not long that he noticed the lights were in fact in the air, approximately thirty feet above the ground-

Damn the ancient Imperial measurements! How high is thirty feet?! Sorjana mused. She looked up and around from the paper again, not to keep watch, but as an involuntary reaction to the digressing thought. She realised it was not, after all important. Returning to the article a few moments later, she sniffed as she found her place again.

.... and realised that a helicopter, if it was one, would be heard for miles.

"This aircraft in fact was silent", Crumton later told the reporter. " I knew an aircraft was loud but this (one) was whisper quiet. As I drove closer I realised that this could not be a plane or helicopter. It was then I noticed it was a UFO. It had that distinctive disc shape, three balls underneath it, everything."

The bell shaped, three-sphere configuration is a common factor in many alleged UFO sightings to date. Other types include the plain discus style, 'That would be the Greys,'

Sorjana realised, *the hamburger shaped, and least common, the sinister black symbol-shaped UFO.* That sent a surge of vehement disdain down Sorjana's spine. That could only be Draconian. The article continued with the interview.

"It was then that I found my car had died. The engine was off and (I) couldn't start it again. That was when the UFO landed. It was nothing like a helicopter landing. It sank like a stone and hit the ground without a sound. Not long after that people came out. Not little green men or Martians, this made Sorjana smirk contemptuously. Too many science fiction movies for this little ape. *"But actual humans. White people. Tall and muscly, I remember. Oh and they had long blond hair. They looked like pro wrestlers on TV, kind of. And they all wore blue tight-fitting leotards."*

The "people" Mr Crompton described resembled other eyewitness accounts of alleged contactees, often referred to as Nordic Aliens or very rarely, Pleiadians.

"That's the scariest part," Mr Crompton continues, *"That you know in the back of your mind that they're aliens from another planet, like a zillion (sic) miles away, and (you) expect purple blobs with three eyes, green men with four arms, anything but humans with blonde hair. How is it possible that they look so much like us?"* Take a guess my ape-like friend.

Surprisingly, the occupants of the UFO could speak English. Mr Crompton described them actually talking to him, in a voice that sounds like what Mr Crompton describes as "almost generic electronic." One of the occupants, what appeared to be a male, told Mr Crompton that they were not after him but a stowaway in his vehicle.

"The men, (there were three of them) walked right past me as i got out of my truck and walked around the back (of the truck). It was then a guy jumped out of the back of my truck and took off. One of the three men in the UFO put something that looked like a bicycle helmet on his head and stopped the poor guy dead in his tracks. But it was dark, and I couldn't see much. Then they just walked past me and back to their flying saucer. The poor guy was floating above the "Man" (Mr Crompton makes the quotation mark gesture with his hands) with the helmet thingy, I remember that bit. I didn't get a look at him but he looked Chinese or Japanese or something like that."

The helmet that this *Homo sapien* referred to was undoubtedly an Amplifier. But an Asian looking man? That could be a Hyadean defector being reacquired to stand Court Martial before the Admiral. Or it could be a disguised Draconian. It couldn't be the Greys, as they had no significant interest in Chronophysical Warfare. At least Sorjana hoped.

"Then they carried the man into their flying saucer. Badda-bing! And then it just up and took off. It rose so fast it was just a blur. And it didn't even make a sound as it left. It was gone, not a trace, seconds later."

At that moment, a sleazy *Homo sapien* male sat next to Sorjana. It reached over cavalierly and started playing with Sorjana's blonde hair. Sorjana put down her paper and stared straight ahead. Annoyance was clearly on her face now. Still the oversexed *Homo sapien* was fondling her hair. By this time a few members of the animal's gang sat on the other side of Sorjana, clearly offering support to the man on Sorjana's other side. They began jeering at her, echoing the leader's propositions sycophantically. Sorjana's eyes now moved to the other passengers. They either pretended not to notice or were gawking dumbly. Either way none of these animals, in their typical bahavioural apathy, would come to her aid. Sorjana now knew she would have to simply help herself. She was outnumbered three to one. But Sorjana reminded herself she would be more than a match even if every *Homo sapien* on the whole carriage turned on her.

Where was that ticket inspector? She reminded herself. But he was simply gawking too, Afraid to take on three low class but streetwise ruffians. Don't make me take *the law into my own hands. That would be bad. That could blow my cover. This is the last thing I need now!*

Sorjana, *irritated*, not intimidated now waited for the opportune moment. If she lashed out to grab the man's arm, from this side-on angle, the ape will simply pull away and jeer even louder. At that moment, however, as if playing right into Sorjana's hands, the leader threw an arm around Sorjana's shoulder in a gesture of psuedo-compassion. Sorjana turned to face the *Homo sapien*, Her Nordic features and dark sunglasses working in stereo to give an impression of aloofness. Her face, a moment later, formed an amused sneer plagued with contempt. The man hesitated just a fraction of a second at the unexpected reaction from his next intended victim.

Sojana knew it would do to get on her feet, drag the man up with her and toss him over her shoulder. He would anticipate and resist. Instead she grabbed the animal's paw with her hand, reaching across her body. Twisting her head around the other side of the animal's arm, whilst simultaneously throwing the arm upwards and over, she gracefully gained the upper hand in less than a second. Now the man was astounded as she tightened her grip, for what should have been a petite and not-so-strong delicate *Homo sapien* woman, actually had surprising strength. And a lot of it, for the man was subdued by an opponent with the strength of a gym junkie. Sorjana's brute strength alone had the animal whimpering now in pain.

Designer genes for brute strength, She thought. Humans were now many times stronger than their *Homo sapien* ancestors, reversing the trend of swapping *brawn for brains* as humans evolved. When designer genes had became popular among human breeding, millennia beyond the Oil Age, people feared the human body would shrivel up to a puny blasphemy of its former self. It could even put the Greys to shame. So humans of Sorjana's age, and indeed Sorjana herself, opted to have their offspring to become the pinnacle of human athleticism, developing the body as well as the mind to advance as much as possible. As a result, Sorjana alone had the strength of three to four Oil Age men. Pleiadian men were typically twice as strong as the smaller statured Sorjana, small and willowy for her kind.

By now the other two members of the Oil Age gang were upon poor Sorjana. The first one grabbed her in a primitive headlock, attempting to pull her off the leader and loosen her grip.

Things are getting worse. I'm trying to be inconspicuous

here. Don't need this little scene to draw attention. The headlock was inefficient, with the *Homo sapien* clearly relying on strength for it to be effective. Fortunately, Sorjana could easily still breathe; this animal clearly did not know how to crush a windpipe like that. Or maybe he wasn't trying to. Regardless, he remained tense and stiff, while trying to wrestle Sorjana away. She released her hydraulic grip on the first man, with the third one now coming around to face her.

Inefficient fighting system, relies on brute strength and intimidation. Just plain old street fighters. Well Sorjana Certainly was not intimidated, even now. Although she could not use her telekinetic powers, not here. *I am gonna have to fight them off myself the old fashioned way.*

By now the third man was in front of her, with the first one recovering from the pain of the crushed hand. *I tried to be diplomatic. Here goes.*

Sighing, Sorjana speared the attacker in the armpit, resumed her signature titanic squeeze on the man's pectoral muscle. Wincing, the ape's arm relaxed around Sorjana's neck effectively going numb. Without hesitation, Sorjana seized the opening. In a sudden motion with practiced efficiency, she dropped to one knee, grabbed her attackers' arm, and tossed him over. He went sprawling, was catapulted over, as if he were a plastic mannequin. His heel caught the first man true in the solar plexus, knocking the wind out of him. This surprised even Sorjana, for she knew she did not plan that move. By accident, luck had come to her defence then. The leader collapsed and lay gasping, as Sorjana went on the offensive, and despatched the third attacker with a crippling palm strike to the right ear. With a ringing ear, he struggled to withstand the pain, and shakily took a step towards Sorjana, rage clear on his face. Not waiting for the third man to make a move, she intercepted his next step with a sweep to the ankle before it even touched the ground. With his balance distorted with the ringing, throbbing ear, the attacker toppled easily, landing head first. Sorjana did not bother to check if his neck was broken or his skull split; the attacker she threw a few moments ago had gotten to his feet again, with the other man whom his foot landed into breaking most of his fall. This time however, after surveying how easily she took care of the other two, in a matter of under five seconds, now had doubts in his eyes. Sorjana saw that he wished he had bought a weapon. After hesitating for a second, he reluctantly started forward to attacker her, this time he ducked to tackle her with as much speed as he could muster. Sorjana instinctively skipped backwards, without thinking, but only managed to clear one leg before the Terran grabbed one and sank his body weight in. Sorjana struggled irritably for a moment, almost insulted by such a clumsy, unsportsmanlike but often effective, move. Unable to get free, but still able to keep her balance as the Terran tried to take her to the ground, she again dropped her grappled knee, using the momentum of a sudden slight loss of balance to her advantage. The Terran had a vulnerable, exposed, back of the neck, which Sorjana struck with a stiff, hard blow. With what the Oil Age Terrans colloquially called a *Karate chop*, the hapless *Homo sapien* was instantly dead; his own neck vertebrae crushing his spinal cord. Sorjana head a dull *thud* when her hand hit the solid tissue.

Barely a raised heartbeat, Sorjana wearily got to her feet as if she were trying to recover as much dignity as possible. Still the other Terrans on the tram did nothing, although the whole battle had lasted around ten seconds. None had even given her the effort to get up off their seats. Nothing. *Are these things really my ancestor? They are revolting. Not that I needed their help, but I have never experienced such cold apathy.* Sorjana looked at these animals in a new light. She glowered back at them with deadly contempt, and realised that their body language displayed shock and awe, barely different to that of modern humans. Abruptly, she realised that the room was brighter now. Her sunglasses had fallen off in the struggle, and now they could see her overlarge, more oval eyes.

Presently, the tram had neared its next station, and was slowing down. Without that useless ticket inspector announcing the station, Sorjana did not know where she was about to get off, and did not care. Recovering her sunglasses and donning them again almost redundantly, she fumbled for the door-open button, and pressed it absently. A few moments later, when the tram had finally stopped, the doors open, and Sorjana slipped out.

She found herself walking briskly in her cumbersome Oil Age clothing. She kept her eyes forward, not daring to look, as the tram began its clumsy rumble past her. She came to a flight of stairs just as the tram disappeared from view, and immediately took them two at a time. Beyond the flight of stairs, she could resume melting into the crowd of ape-like ancestors and become inconspicuous.

I should look behind to see if I am being followed, was the last chiding thought she had before she fainted. Or fell asleep. It didn't matter which now.

12.

'What is your name my Sirian Friend?' The comic read the nametag erected on the desk in front of the Ambassador. 'Xankyu? You're Welcome!'

That bought only a few chuckles in the audience, as the pun would be esoteric to anyone who did not know ancient English. Only the Vegan stand-up comedian actually found it significantly amusing. But Ambassador Xankyu remained unimpressed at this fancy dinner. His face remained neutral, unamused. He did not understand, speak a single word of, one of the ancestor language's of modern humans. Certainly, he had no reason to ever learn.

'It is pronounced "Zan-kigh-you", Vegan.' Was all the Sirian Ambassador replied, emphasising the phonetics patronisingly. As if he were a more mature classmate chiding another for making a genitalia-related pun out of his name.

After seeing Xankyu's unamused, neutral expression, and the lack of interest from the rest of the crowd, the comic broke off. Presently he spun around, and, changing the subject, addressed the audience again.

'Thank you all for coming,' he telepathised into the Amp that converted brainwaves into sound that boomed out of speakers scattered about the hall. 'So good to be back on New Terra with the Arcturians. One thing I have noticed about this place, is that you people can't drive for shit.' That promply bought boo's and hisses of telepathy, unapproving, from most of the audience. A few even laughed reluctantly. When the noise had finally died down, the comic continued, 'Like, take the other day, when I was driving my Luxury Tsorran Biobrid. Beautiful thing. Anyway, like I said I was just driving like us Vegans do. Do-de-do-do.' The comic made a pantomime of a Vegan driving a groundcar. More laughs from most of those humans. Xankyu maintained his sour demeanour at the dry humour. When the laughter had died down once again, the comic continued.

'Anyway, I was driving my Biobrid, when this fool up and pulled out in front of me. And then he waved after I had to stop. Can you believe it? Actually waved at me, thanking me! Aww yeah you're welcome, but I had to stop, idiot, or we would have had a collision!' The comic's telepathic tone went from neutral to condescending as he delivered the punch line. With the exception of Xankyu, the entire audience immediately burst out laughing. When the laughing stopped, almost ten seconds, *ten seconds!* later, the comic continued onto the next joke.

'That's not all. You Arcturians are always so busy-like. You just rush, rush, rush everywhere you go. I was walking out yesterday, and this dude came up behind me, walking faster than I was, and I was like, "to hell with you fool."

So I started walking faster. Anyway, the guy behind me was no longer gaining, so I kept up the pace. But after a few minutes I started daydreaming and forgot what I was walking quickly about, and resumed my normal pace. By the time the guy was beside me, I remembered, "shit, I supposed to not let him pass." But if I walked fast again, I would just look pathetic, so I just let him pass anyway.'

The comic made obscene gestures to where the faster walking man would be, as if to indicate the punch line was delivered, but the audience were in hysterics now, regardless. An Arcturian man, middle aged and nondescript, who sat at the table next to Xankyu, turned and chuckled to the ambassador. 'Its funny, because its so true.' Xankyu simply gave the man his trademark unamused expression, not so different to the one he gave the comic only moments earlier.

The Arcturian man, in a huff, as if to say "Sirians just have no sense of humour," faced forward abruptly.

This is going to be a long night, Xankyu thought, *If this is what the human Genus regards as entertainment.*

Nearby to the Sirian ambassador, sat Koowohtah, the Draconian. Her elegant fuchsia toga-like robe served her not to suggest femininity, but frustration and aggression. A male Draconian sat at a table nearby, eyeing the attractive female reptile-bird. Meerkah was invited to the fancy dinner, because he had a relative in the Draconian embassy, whom he visited on the way back to the Empire. The Timeliner had berthed in orbit over the Arcturian Capital, and will not shrink space bound for the Empire until over one week from now. Very few travelled from the Commonwealth to the Empire, and Shrinktime Enterprises spared almost no Timeliners bound there. Meerkah had so much time to kill. So he came along to this event. When he laid eyes on the Draconian ambassador for the first time, he was glad he came.

Meerkah leaned over and asked his cousin, quietly as the Draconian bird song language would permit, 'Who is *she?*'

'The Draconian Ambassador to the humans. Forget about it, Meerkah. She's both out of your league, and bad news. You wouldn't want a diplomat as a Mate. They're Mated to the Empire first, as should every good and loyal Draconian. Next, they are Mated to their career. Third, comes their mate that bears them offspring. Trust me,' she sang, then paused for effect. 'I should know. Take it from me, my dear cousin.'

Meerkah could only sit there, chastened, and ask, 'Why do you think she is out of my league, cousin? I am very intelligent, well-mannered and considerate after all.'

'Now, listen, Meerkah. And you listen good. Those 'qualities' are actually flaws to many Females of our species. Particularly Ambassador Koowohtah. Her ideal mate would be a Ciakar trapped in a Standard-Caste's body. A real proactive go-getter who knows what he wants and takes it. That counts you out for sure.' Meerkah's cousin, like all female Draconians, tended to be larger than the males, and Meerkah, who was a runt of a Reptiod was all but dwarfed by her. She tossed her head back, rolled her eyes, and sighed, taking a few moments to think of how to say what she meant. 'Second, now I am only going to say this once, I think you have been hanging around humans for too long. You have forgotten how to be a Draconian. The qualities you have just described sounds exactly what a *human* female would choose in a mate. Not a female Draconian. Are you really listening to me?!'

Meerkah had forgotten to ogle the Ambassador. He looked away, from his cousin. He knew she was right. Female Draconians find scientists an unattractive profession, like humans would find rubbish collectors or septic tank emptiers. That alone had almost made her less attractive to him. As if his low self esteem was a defence mechanism. Still It would not hurt to try. Or at least dream. The previously sank-hearted Meerkah straightened up again.

'I don't care. You know her better than anyone here. You have to introduce me to her, at least.'

'Forget it, cousin.'

'Come now! At least tell me if she doesn't already have a Male. She doesn't, does she?'

'So what if she does? You wouldn't stand a chance against him. Besides, we don't fight over Mates, remember? You have been studying to many animals at that juvenile Time Zoo. And again, she wouldn't consider you for all the Draconium in the galaxy, like I said. Move on, cousin, and stick to playing with your animals. Maybe a Female zookeeper there would chose you as a Mate instead.' Meerkah's cousin concluded with a sneer, in the most condescending tone.

Meerkah typically worked at the communal Time

Zoo, built by the Empire a forgotten millennia ago, under the reign of one of the more benevolent Empresses, on the outskirts of the Empire. Many animals from Terra's prehistoric past were either abducted from millions of years in the past, or brought over during the Great Draconian Exodus of the late Cretaceous, and unchanged for millions of years, isolated in their glorified zoo pens. Juveniles both human and reptilian loved to go there, and was also where Meerkah's discipline, Parapaleontology, was in its element.

Presently, a stand up comic came over to a table near the two related Draconians, causing a significant distraction. It was the same comic that made fun of the Sirian Ambassador, about five Standard minutes ago.

'What have we here, folks? We have two Lizard Dudes from the Alpha Draconis system. Everyone give them a round of applause.' The crowed clapped and cheered like sheep, but to a Draconian, who lacked telepathic ability, only the sound of clapping could be heard. The two Reptilians raised their heads, stretching their neck in a bird-like fashion. The diminished, near vestigial crests on their heads fanned out, and they both blinked incessantly, cocking their heads to one side. At that, with the audience watching Meerkah and his cousins' reaction, the audience chuckled. The resemblance to a two-metre chicken was surprisingly uncanny. The two Draconians however, were wounded by both the alienation and being made a spectacle of. Meerkah was merely humiliated. His cousin, however, only like a Draconian could and should be, was clearly outraged. But only to the Draconian Ambassador, who looked behind her at her aide, reading the humiliation and other body language, began to share the outrage. The laughing soon died down, however.

The Comic mercifully knew better than to push the issue and potentially enrage the wrath of the Draconian Empire. Wisely, carrying his hand-held portable Amp that served also as a prop, he moved further back down the large, cavernous hall. He stopped a few tables back to a Lyran delegation, whom would be better suited to his taste in comedy. *As long he does not mention the Lyran Wars, the destruction of the Lyran homewolrd and the tragic and regrettable exodus*, Meerkah thought. He switched off the Vegan comedian's preachings and rants, stories and gags. He began to think about that attractive female ambassador, diagonally front and to his right. He resigned to the fact his cousin may be right. She was always right. Meerkah sighed. He was a scientist, and knew nothing about politics. *Perhaps I too, am Mated to my occupation, after the Empire. I have never even thought about settling down and finding a Mate. I am nearly halfway through my life expectancy now. My dear cousin is right, of course. I have been too preoccupied with my animals, and Parapaleontology. But at least science does not reject me, because I am not aggressive or ruthless or wealthy enough*, Meerkah thought bitterly.

Later, when a serving automaton came to his and his cousin's table, and as a gesture of defiance to The Empire, and indeed his species Meerkah ordered a succulent roast chicken. Nothing else. The sacrilegious dish was a delicacy to humans, but a faux pas for Reptilians. His

Cousin could only give him an offended, shocked, and disappointed look, as Meerkah savoured the Terran bird and genetic relative of the Draconians, in only the eerily bird-like way they ate.

13.

The Starmining crew was in a jubilant mood. From the sanctuary of a significant distance from a black hole, Captain Razmal Hoolde watched as a star approached the event horizon. A typical star would yield vast quantities of Draconium. Millions of standard tonnes, potentially. Now, however, this was no ordinary star. The white dwarf star was getting closer moment by moment. He gave the order for his crew to be more than ready. It will be less than five Standard minutes now. He could not afford any errors. His Starmining vessel, roughly half the size of the *Athena* that his estranged wife served on-thousands of years ago-would be laden with priceless Arcturium. Not that he or his crew would see any of that fortune. The state-owned behemoth would provide The Commonwealth with years, perhaps decades, of the element necessary for time travel. His crew would therefore be well commended and rewarded.

Presently, the white dwarf showed signs of elongating. Razmal asked the particle accelerator crew over the two-way telepathy Amp if indeed the thing was working and ready. Affirmation came the reply. Less than three standard minutes now. The white dwarf had elongated quite noticeably now. He addressed his crew over the Amp, on an open channel so all the four-thousand crew could hear. Cheers came the reply, for he promised them early leave with a decent bonus of Draconium Bonds. Because Draconium was so heavy, and Arcturium so radioactive, trade was conducted by bonds representing the respective elements in Standard tonnes. This psuedo-money was surprisingly stable and relatively immune to economic recessions, rather like gold retained or increased its value predictably on ancient Terra.

Two standard minutes now. The white dwarf now showed signs of swirling, with a tail forming, bee-lining to the maw of the black hole. The faded, used-up or collapsed hydrogen atoms were about to brake away. It would take less than half a standard minute for the atoms to travel from the star to event horizon, and be gone forever. His crew had little margin of error, but they were well trained and paid to ensure the atoms travel into the ships hold; teleported there via a powerful particle accelerator. And quickly too. For uncountable-trillions of crushed, refined-by-nature atoms passed through the machine every second. Razmal telepathically gave orders via the Amp for the particle accelerator crew to be ready and fire on his command. He eyeballed the white dwarf. Not daring to woolgather. The white dwarf's tail was clearly prominent now. It was beginning its stretch into the event horizon of the black hole. This is where his crew came in. *Not yet*, he told himself.

As Razmal watched the tail, now approximately a quarter of the way to the black hole, his eyes narrowed as he painfully synchronised his crew's response time with the passage of the atoms. Seconds passed and his eyes widened as he issued the command on the Amp for the particle accelerator crew to fire their beam. A couple of seconds passed before the beam was catapulted out of the ship at light speed. Captain Hoolde watched as tracers built into the beam intercepted the elongated white dwarfs' hydrogen atoms just as they had been crushed and refined at the event horizon. The beam took twelve seconds to reach the black hole. Only a second after the first atoms were lost. He had timed it almost perfectly. His knowledge of physics told him that what he was seeing in fact was twelve seconds old news.

The reverse-cycle method of the particle accelerator meant that the heavier, now-Arcturium atoms would be automatically transported to his ship. They would accumulate in the ore body behind him, well behind the bridge of the Starmining vessel. The area reserved for Arcturium-ore occupied four-fifths of the ship. If it were fully laden with Draconium, the vessel would weigh as much as a moon. But Arcturium was different, less dense, more powdery, but dozens of times more valuable. Presently, The ore body superintendant reported dutifully yet excitedly over the Amp the first standard tonne had now materialised in the vast hold. The powerful particle accelerator had now successfully "teleported" the first Arcturium atoms onto his ship. Fifty more standard tonnes of Arcturium ore would be transferred to his ship every second, like money transferred electronically into an ancient bank account. Razmal smiled as he stared at the white dwarf star being sucked into a black hole, tail end first, and The Commonwealth of Humanity would reap the rewards of the hapless, elderly stars' fate. By now, as he watched the green tracers built into the beam, and the violet tracers that signified the returning, atom filled beam, one thousand standard tonnes would be in his ship by now. The beam itself was invisible; the tracers were what gave the beam its twin colour of green and purple. Travelling at the speed of light, the spacers set kilometres apart were a blur, which gave the beams their colours, like food colouring in an ancient blender.

Abruptly, claxons sounded inside the bridge, followed by automata informing the captains of other ships that have come under detection range. The vessel's computer had already, faithfully, identified the ships as enemies for him, like a fastidious secretary. *Space Dinosaurs*, he corrected the official identification of *Draconian* on his console to the left and before him. It resembled an ancient radar. There were dozens of Draconian ships, varying in size, gradually getting closer to the position that marked his Starmining vessel. In the centre of the cluster of enemy ships, was an irregular shaped vessel, many times bigger than the half dozen or so that immediately surrounded it. Small blips representing the black, symbol shaped Draconian fighters were scattered around the outside serving as escorts. Razmal counted over thirty before he conceded the unarmed vessel would not stand a chance. He considered fleeing through Shrinkspace, but the ship had a safety system that prevented moving whilst the particle accelerator was operating. It would take nearly thirty seconds to shut it down. Razmal had no time to think of the irony of the safety system being their unsafe downfall. He knew it would take a further two and a half minutes for the clunky mining vessel to finally disappear in the refuge of Shrinkspace, to another place in space and time. He estimated the Draconian fleet was three minutes away the very best, realistically two, two and a half, tops.

He had two options; flee or surrender. He knew in his mind the Draconian privateers would kill he and his crew anyway, and take the Arcturium whilst use their own fleets to mine the white dwarf. He decided immediately to cut his losses with the small amount of harvested Arcturium and flee. On the Amp, he gave the order for the particle accelerator operating crew to terminate the task immediately, without an explanation. They complied as ordered but it would still be another thirty seconds before he could even turn the vessel's engines and controls on; the vessel was now uselessly floating in space as automata packed up the particle accelerator. Captain Razmal Hoolde could do nothing for half a minute.

Spending that thirty seconds generating regrets in his mind, he cursed the various Treaties that prevented Starminers and their equipment getting involved in the cold war between the Empire and Commonwealth. These Treaties, separating Starmining from State, had the hidden affliction of preventing, in turn, Starmining vessels from being armed or being escorted by armed fighters. The Draconians, have, evidently for the first time, finally broken those Treaties. Everyone in the Starmining industry, however, knew it was only a matter of time.

Razmal looked again at the console. His Pleiadian eyes widened at an epiphany. That irregular ship in the centre, dwarfing all others, resembled very strongly an asteroid. *That's no ship! They are transporting an asteroid. But why?* Razmal felt a moment of relief. *Perhaps it was a mineral-rich asteroid. But everybody knows this is an uneconomical and unviable method of acquiring worthless iron ore! Even it were pure titanium the Reptoids would only just break even.*

On cue, the superintendant of the particle accelerator confirmed it was ready over the Amp. Not wasting time in affirmation, Razmal frantically fired up the engines, controls, and told his entire crew over the open Amp to brace for hard acceleration, to hold onto something solid. Seconds later the anti-matter engines roared and shuddered under abrupt, hard throttle. Razmal looked at the console once more while the cumbersome vessel of Draconium and Titanium began its sluggish acceleration, twice as slow as the average Timeliner. *These things are just not built for speed, period*, he thought as he squinted at the radar-like screen in front of him. To make matters worse, he had received not an ounce of training in military tactics and evasive manoeuvres against belligerent ships. Such a thing has never happened before. But if the Draconian fleet were indeed merely passing through with their captured asteroid........

The Asteroid! They have lost it! No it's ahead of them! What's going on?! He silently demanded. The asteroid was almost now halfway between the Draconian fleet and his vessel.

The old reliable girl kept accelerating with everything she had, but the asteroid was getting closer, was gaining regardless. Suddenly he realised, *They are using the asteroid as a battering ram! They intend to destroy my ship with it and hence make it look like an accident! As if my ship had collided with a neutral astreroid.* He knew there would be no time to enter this into the ships log and transmit to New Terra. He had to evade this thing. At that moment he pulled the controls to a sharp left, the first thing that came into his mind, without thinking. After all it mattered little which way he turned, the Draconian Fleet would likely go to plan B and finish him off regardless. Unless he could completely dodge the asteroid and enter Shrinkspace on time............

The vessel lazily pitched left while sluggishly accelerating. Razmal looked again at the console; the asteroid was now about three quarters of the way from the Draconian fleet. Range was just under a million kilometres; not far in terms of objects that travel at twenty thousand kilometres a second. He looked forward again, to the beautiful view of millions of distant stars, and noted his mouth had begun to dry. Licking his lips absently, Captain Razmal Hoolde returned to the console screen. His theory had been correct; the six larger ships on the screen were diverting towards the black hole and the poor white dwarf star, now at the southwest corner of the radar. They must have been Draconian Starmining vessels that have been modified to carry city-sized asteroids. The thirty or so Draconian fighters were tailing the asteroid at a safe distance. Razmal knew exactly why; to confirm a kill and finish the job if necessary. His own vessel was finally facing forty-five degrees from the path of the trailing asteroid. It was going to miss. He felt a surge of relief once more. Now all that was left was to launch his only Sentinels and escape into Shrinkspace. If he could manage that, the Draconian fighters will also be a thing of the past. Of course he needn't worry about the Draconians following him into the wormhole of condensed space-time; Sentinels typically permitted only one large object through and out the other side before expanding space to its original form once again.

His relief was short lived, however, when he returned to the console. Not the fact that it was barely half a million kilometres away, but to his amazement, the asteroid itself had changed direction, with the Draconian fighters following suit. They were all on a collision course once again. Captain Hoolde swerved the control wheel in the opposite direction. It was an agonising five seconds before the sluggish Starminer complied. He checked the range; four hundred thousand kilometres and dropping over ten thousand a second. The asteroid was still gaining though not as quickly. At this rate, with the rate his Starminer accelerated, he had little more than a minute, he estimated roughly. His blip at the centre of the radar had pitched forty-five degrees in the opposite direction, ten seconds after it first changed direction. He saw the asteroid had now done the same, and was now facing the same bearing only a few seconds later.

How can an asteroid change direction like that?! Captain Hoolde wondered in silent despair.

The damn reptoids must've rigged up an asteroid with automata and propulsion engines, and made a self-propelled kamikaze drone. In his mind he pictured a rock floating in space with propulsion engines protruding in all directions, as if many ships had crashed into the thing, with their rocket-like engines sticking out, still intact. *Someone tell Sorjana I love her.* He conceded. In his last resort abandon, Captain Hoolde fired the "Launch" button for his sentinals, whilst simultaneously straightening his Starminer. Three probes shot forward at one-tenth the speed of light, about four times his vessels' current speed. It was still a few seconds premature; The Sentinels cannot hold the door of Shrinkspace open for too long for his slow ship to finally catch up. He doubted he would beat the asteroid anyway at this rate. It was fifty-fifty at best. He double-checked that the throttle was indeed pushed to its maximum.

At just under two-fifty-thousand kilometres, the asteroid was gaining at only eight thousand kilometres per second. The Sentinels were still half a minute before they were ready. No point in changing direction again; even if the asteroid did not follow, the fighters would do the job, and the meagre four thousand standard tonnes of Arcturium he had on board would be salvaged later by a Draconian Starminer. Arcturium ore was virtually indestructible, could easily survive an explosion from an ill-fated Starminer. Also, The option to enter Shrinkspace would expire; the Sentinels could not follow in the change of direction. They were mindless drones and hence were not designed or programmed for that. Captain Razmal had only enough probes to Shrinkspace once and return to The Commonwealth. He decided to push forward and continue to where the Sentinels would work their magic. He spent the time now to address his entire crew over the Amp. He could do nothing else.

'Ladies and Gentleman of The Commonwealth, this is Captain Razmal Hoolde. As you have likely guessed by now, we are under attack. I repeat, an unarmed commercial mining vessel is likely the victim of the first Starmining privateering raid in a very long time. Thus, the time has finally come, where Starminers are going to be casualties of war. The time for relying on Treaties is over. There is a large asteroid converted into a sacrificial drone on our bow, ahhhh, two hundred and five thousand kilometres and down six thousand a second. I have launched our only Sentinels; they are pre-programmed to return us to New Terra in real time. If we can reach the Sentinels in time, we can escape into Shrinkspace and cut our losses. The Commonwealth will forgive us for returning practically empty when we make it to the other end of Shrinkspace. I promise you, it with be the reptoids who will have some explaining to do. Trust me. But that's a big "if."'

Captain Hoolde looked at the console; the gap between his vessel and the asteroid was now barely discernable. He checked the range; under one hundred and fifty thousand kilometres. His current velocity was a smidgeon under eight thousand a second. The asteroid was travelling at twelve thousand, give or take. They may just make it.

'I have done everything I can to evade our attackers, but as you know this is no warship. You have probably guessed surrender is not an option. We will either be killed after this vessel is commandeered, or we won't reach the safety of Shrinkspace in time.'

The Sentinels signified they were ready on the control panel to his right. Razmal hit to confirm without hesitation. The Crimson triangle, under duress, was stationary only one hundred thousand kilometres ahead. They had allocated that a Starminer was twice as slow as the average timeliner as well. Presently the crimson triangle, blocking the stars in its shape, performed its trademark fade and flicker. It would go out like a candle in a few moments. Then the darkness would turn even darker as anti-matter was being manifested.

'Whatever happens, the reptoids will not take us alive. Remember that we have served The Commonwealth well, have done our bit for the cause of humanity.'

He checked the status of the pursuit; Asteroid was one hunded and five thousand and pursuing, Shrinkspace eighty-five. He could not think of much else to say to his crew.

He continued by concluding,

'Together, we will make it to Shrinkspace. Or we will die trying.'

Captain Razmal Hoolde tragically replaced the mouthpiece to the Amp on its receiver.

With nothing else to do, he checked his throttle was pushed to its maximum once more. It did not matter if it wasn't anyway. His Starminer was now going as fast as it ever did; just over nine thousand kilometres a second. With his skills and options exhausted he gripped the controls, steering his vessel to the safety of the blacker-than-black triangle. Satisfied that his ship was surely aimed correctly, without any doubt, he checked the console one last time. It read thirty thousand kilometres ahead, ten thousand behind.

With only a few seconds before fate decided the outcome, Captain Razmal Hoolde could only hug the controls and close his eyes.

14.

Darius found himself less than welcome when he returned to his family biodiesel farm for the first time in five standard years. As he sat in the same rustic, spartan kitchen in his dreams and his childhood, he could only stare at his mug of hot green tea. His mother sat opposite him with her green tea, his father, however, could not settle. He paced around the kitchen like a caged lion in an ancient zoo. His dungarees bobbed up and down as he walked. Complimented with his wellington boots and well-loved fisherman's hat, he looked strictly speaking, unchanged from a farmer two hundred and thirty thousand standard years ago.

'What made you think you could come back, boy? What makes you assume you are welcome here?' Darius' father's telepathic voice was gruff and corroded, which betrayed his age and lifestyle. Decades of hard work on the farm, cut off from social interaction with the exception of his underappreciated wife. She sternly pacified her husband by saying,

'Do not be so hard on your eldest son. What he did

was the right thing. Tsorra can't bury their head in the sand forever with the Reptilian Menace out there in our past, attempting to erase us from existence. Why, if it were not for people such as our son here, you wouldn't have a biodiesel farm to reign over.' Chronophysical Warfare was not a household name on the Tau Cetan planet of Tsorra. Not many things regarding galactic politics and current events in fact, were. Presently his father, not a man of words and hence no retort, simply pulled up a wooden chair and sat down at the table. He did not have a mug of green tea. Evidently he was too upset to eat or drink. Darius's younger brother was currently attending tertiary education. Darius had lost track of what he was studying this time; Xerxes tended to be flighty and indecisive.

"To make matters worse,' his father continued, 'is that you're now a mongol, boy. A cripple. You're no good on the farm. Can't even drive machinery.' In the commonwealth, straight biodiesel farming, construction and mining machinery, with primitive pneumatic tyres, were still being used, particularly on planets such as Tsorra. After all, the Biobrid configuration on a tractor would be useless as a plough or bulldozer. The oil Age Terrans had farming equipment similar to that of present day. After all, if a design works and does the job well, why change or replace it?

'Thank you for making me feel worse than I already do, father. Just when I though I have hit rock bottom, you have shown me I can sink even lower. After all, it's what you do best. Oh and my affliction, if you can call it that, is temporary only. The military looks after its wounded;

the laboratories will soon grow me a new leg from stem cells and attach it, in a year at worse.' Darius seldom stood up to his pugilist father like that. In a telepathic voice that was quiet and calm but ultimately carried more venom, his father simply retorted,

'You had better hope that precious, great, army of yours will look after you, that your pension is enough for you to live off. Because you won't see a penny from us! If you can't work for a living, boy, you go hungry.' His father still used an ancient expression, surviving tens of millennia, even though pennies were taken out of circulation and were no longer legal tender at the end of the Oil Age. Darius doubted his father even knew what a penny even was. Darius simply took a sip of his green tea when he replied,

'I don't know why the war against the Empire is so unpopular on Tsorra. Remember that without the Arcturians, there would be no Terraformed Tsorra.'

'And also if The Commonwealth falls, who would we then sell our wines, biodiesel and Biobrids to?' His wife interjected. Tsorra built the finest sports and luxury Biobrids in The Commonwealth, if not the galaxy, although very few could afford them, in a mainly-socialist Commonwealth. Sorjana had once told Darius that his people make good sportscars. She had picked up the term from Oil Age Terra, which were the forerunners of biobrids.

'Tsorra, and us Tau Cetans are self-sufficient. Remember the ancient Terrans that you, boy, had a wonderful time visiting a million years ago, or whatever? They had everything they needed. Correct me if I'm wrong, but were not our ape-like ancestors that you visited while everyone on Tsorra was doing things that are now so obviously beneath you, confined to their only planet? From what I can remember, they had farms, and metal, and food, and everything else they needed to survive? So what makes you think us Tau Cetans need help from outside planets? So the Vegans have heaps of Titanium? The Sirians and Arcturians build the best Timeliners? You can forget the Hyadeans with their so-called cutting edge robots and computers. They have no place on Tsorra. No we will do just fine without The Commonwealth, thank you very much. All The Commonwealth is to us is a hole in the taxpayers' pocket! What do we care if we have pig-looking Arcturians or the Reptiles raping and pillaging our hard-earned money!?'

Darius took another sip of his green tea. It was getting cold, and he found he could now almost skull it. He looked around the kitchen, at the sheer primitiveness of it, the evidence of a technophobic lifestyle of Tsorrans, and had to concede, that perhaps his father had a valid point. But that did not, for an instant, not now, not ever, make Darius regret fighting with his Brothers and Sisters from other species of human. He rather liked the Pleiadian humans, with their light skin and long blonde hair, their selfless, benevolent temperament. Even the Arcturians, with their upturned nose and ruddy complexion, their assertive, "Don't-take-no-crap" attitude. The other three remaining species of human, the zion-esque Lyrans with their no-longer-existent planet, the outspoken and dark-skinned Vegans, and finally The Hyadeans, with their vaguely mongoloid features and fastidious approach to life. He suddenly realised he really had not had much to do with them, had not really gotten to know these genetic cousins that came from planets lightyears away. Presently he replied only with,

'I chose to join the human war effort. I will not regret my decision. I have the rest of my life to farm biodiesel and culture wine. This, however, is my meaning of life. It is sad you cannot support me. If you don't want to support me, father, that's fine! But then don't antagonise me!'

'Because I love and respect your mother, I have agreed to let you stay here for as long as you want. Remember though, who I am doing it for. Its fortunate, and I'm grateful that I don't have to face the folks in the common-towns who know I fathered a black sheep. It matters very little whether you were killed fighting Space Dinosaurs or not. You are dead to me, as you were when you left here five Sy's ago.'

That earned him a glower from his wife. But she could only say, 'It is your duty to support your son, as I have and always will. Sooner or later you will have to forgive him. He has done nothing to harm our species. He is, and always will be, Tau Cetan. To Hell with the public opinion against the war.'

Darius could only down his now-warm tea. After placing the primitive ceramic mug on the table, he reached across for his crutches. After awkwardly pushing back the chair and replacing it, he rigged himself onto his crutches and got to his one-remaining foot. Presently he telepathically spoke, 'Thank you for the tea, and the offer of hospitality, but you misunderstand me. I will find my own accommodation in a day or so, the next coach out of here. I am not here for charity; only because I had assumed you all had missed me.'

Tears began to well up in his eyes and his telepathic voice cracked with grief as he said "missed me." Darius said nothing else, and avoided eye contact with his father and even his mother, who must have been giving his father a deathly glare. With his now well-practiced and familiar tripod walk, Darius silently and tragically left the kitchen. A few seconds later, his parents must have heard the front door slam.

Darius did not look back at the dome-shaped dwelling, at the only blue Biobrid parked next to it, the same from his childhood, battered and well used. It must be, by now, about two generations old. The design went out of fashion decades ago. He recalled on ancient Terra farmers also favoured old groundcars and had little incentive to upgrade them. Presently, a sleek but old and decrepit shape intruded in his eyesight. Darius soon skipped around a carcass of an old, biodiesel-powered tractor, much older than the family Biobrid. It even had pneumatic tyres; most modern machinery had the non-pneumatic type, with high tensile springy spokes, which were state of the art in the Oil Age; Terrans used them on their terrestrial exploration drones on neighbouring planets and moons. What was left of the rubber had deteriorated into mere flakes, only the rubber around the rim was still attached.

The rusted rims had sunk into the ground years ago. Cobwebs had capitalised on the gaps between the chassis and axles. It reminded Darius of a discarded shoe, for some strange reason.

Darius soon realised was hobbling around aimlessly down a dirt track; he was miles from the nearest Commontown, with no transportation available. Although he was simply pacing around the old farm, he just needed to get out and clear his head. At least it was a beautiful tropical day, with clear blue skies typical of Tsorra. To his left and right were inedible crops as far as the eye can see. In a week or two they will be harvested and refined into biodiesel. Cicadas, who chirped their typical tune that only signified it was a humid day to humans, were the only sound that intruded upon his Tau-Cetan ears. Just as he began to woolgather and lose track of time, he came to a familiar titanium windmill from his childhood. Its design was ancient; it resembled an Oil Age airplane fuselage on a stick. This provided the farm with electricity. Another, even more ancient windmill, with about twenty, twisted rotors was seen in the distance. This spun to pump water directly out of an underwater bore. Darius had also seen this design on Oil Age ranches, to provide cattle with a water source, especially in arid areas. As he passed the first windmill, a vineyard could be seen in a nearby valley. To his right, and opposite the vineyard, was a maroon shack that served as the wine distillery. Darius decided to change direction towards the distillery. Before long, the comforting stench, or aroma to Darius, of fermented grapes invaded his nostrils. He came to the entrance of the dark, damp distillery, and realised how much effort that took on crutches. The winery was at the opposite end of the farm from the Dome-shaped homestead. He remembered it taking the better part of an hour to trot there in his childhood. *Must have hopped over four kilometres on these things.*

Darius wearily opened the door and skipped through. It was pitch black inside, so Darius held the door open as he fumbled for the dusty light switch. He let the door close behind him as the primitive halogen globe fired to life. *Humanity still uses lightbulbs, huh.*

At a nearby basin used for washing, Daruis scavenged a semi-clean cup. He turned the ancient style tap on and rinsed the cup. Behind him was the reservoir where raw wine accumulated. He awkwardly, wearily turned around and opened the tap to help himself to a cup. He did not hesitate to down the cup, rather than savour it, as tradition dictated. He simply drank it as if it were water. It was moments before the vinegar taste in his mouth, the burning of his nostrils, invaded his senses. He filled his cup again without hesitation or thinking. Pulling up a nearby crate to use as a makeshift seat, he collapsed awkwardly with his crutches. He held the cup in his teeth as he did this. Letting his crutches fall to the floor beside him, he downed the next cup unceremoniously. The only sound in the distillery was his now heavy breathing.

Well, humans have been doing what I am doing now for hundreds of thousands of years. So what's the harm of doing it now. I have earned it, anyway, have I not?

He began to feel the effects of the fermented grapes on his evolved, psionic brain. Just as his primitive ancestors had for hundreds of millennia. His head began to swirl he felt his body go limp, but that did not stop Darius from twisting around and filling his cup with raw red wine again. He did not care how long he was going to be here, especially not now. All that mattered was the calming aroma of fermented grapes everywhere.

15.

Sorjana kept reliving the nightmare of her late husband's murder. It could not be referred to as anything else. She awoke with a hardened psyche of a familiar, if not mundane, fear. It was many moments before she realised she had no idea where she was. Lying in her cot, a hard, stretcher of a thing, made of primitive fabrics. It was then Sorjana realised that the room she was in was some sort of cell. *A cell!* Sorjana abruptly remembered the trainline incident, the brawl with the three male *Homo sapiens*, how the primitive animals that were likely an indirect ancestor of modern humans assumed she was also a *Homo sapien* female. She had probably looked attractive to them after all.

Perhaps I should not have killed the Homo sapien, possibly two of them, Sorjana mused. *But then again, they would only have lived to sire lower caste humans in the long run, who would have perished in the last Ice Age of Terra, millennia from now. Thus their deaths would bring no real Chronophysical ramifications.*

She surveyed her room, as she realised she was

fortunately not bound or gagged. She could therefore move freely about the room. At one corner of the room, a typical ancient CCTV camera, typical of the Oil Age, glared at her disapprovingly. At an adjacent wall, directly beneath the camera, was a silver-glass panel. Sorjana instantly recognised this as a one-way mirror. The bare concrete walls, ceiling and floor gave the mirror a polarised, silver tinge, especially to the ultraviolet spectrum of Sorjana's eyes. Rolling over reluctantly, as if not wanting to know what was on the other side of the cell, she found only more colourless grey decor. With the exception of another cot across the room, this part of the room was also bare, even by spartan standards. Sorjana's eyes rolled over the concrete walls, even though she knew there would be no flaws in the construction. When she came to the cot again, she realised there was something strapped to the cot. Her ultraviolet eyes squinted in the dim light; an Arcturian would have no trouble seeing in here, with the only illumination coming from a light beneath the solid steel cell door. It was nearly ten seconds for her eyes to finally adjust, but finally a slender grey-skinned figure in a thick black, jumpsuit was obviously laying there. The skin was not only grey, but also rubbery looking and had a smooth, almost slimy sheen. The eyes were the same black as the jumpsuit, only incredibly large in proportion to the body; nearly accounting for a third of its face. Sorjana's heart skipped a beat. *A Grey from the Bellatrix system! It looks like it can't move. Not that that disgusting abomination could best me.*

Although not direct enemies of The Commonwealth,

and although they despise Draconians even more than humans (generally) did, they were still not to be trusted. An analogy Sorjana once heard from a subordinate Agent summed it up perfectly. If the Commonwealth were NATO, the Draconians the Eastern Bloc, then the Orion Grey, a small empire in its own right, would be the Chinese. In the distant past, millions of standard years ago, The Draconians created they Greys as a servant race, from splicing cetan DNA until a human shaped, upright abomination, incapable of reproducing, like the abomination before her. They served their Draconian masters for millions of Standard Years, before some revolt long before even *Homo sapiens* were on Terra had made the Greys an independent republic in the Orion System. Why they could not reproduce, and the details of the revolt, that Sorjana did not know and did not care to find out. She only cared about that, right now, that the Grey was likely to be comatose, and that she had to get out of this cell. Greys typically had a distinctive odour. This specimen, either dead or comatose, would soon smell unbearable.

Sorjana wearily sat upright and rubbed the back of her neck. *The Pain!* Her Terran clothes were soiled, as if she had been dragged through dirt. She did not know how long she had been in them, how long she had been unconscious. She gave her body a cursory check over; other than the stiff, aching neck, and a petty graze on her right elbow, she was unharmed and intact. She could move her legs now with ease. She remained seated on her cot, and surveyed the cell for a weakness. The one-way mirror would undoubtedly be reinforced, possibly able to withstand an ancient fifty-calibre bullet with ease. That was out. There was no telling how much concrete was in the walls, but it would obviously be impenetrable to anything short of artillery fire. *The Door!* It was solid steel, but it would have to do. Sorjana took a deep breath for good measure, opened her eyes and focused her mental powers. She pictured the steel door, and instantly, concentrated alpha waves, labouring the midriff part of her highly evolved brain. A moment later, space-time rippled in front of her, invisible to all but those with ultraviolet eyes. To Sorjana, mirage-like heat ripples crashed in front of her in an incredibly fast and powerful concussion, like an air pocket or bubble. The Telekinetic ripples crashed against the steel door like a crashing wave. It moaned audibly, but held true. Sorjana tried again, the door rattled and creaked, even slightly warping out of shape, but nevertheless held true. Sorjana knew she could not break it down with brute, physical strength either. Her psionic powers, even without an Amplifier, were many times more powerful than her body.

Remembering ancient Terran doors had hinges, Sorjana aimed her psychokinetic might; everything she had, and attacked the integrity of the hinges. This time the pins even visibly moved and the door bobbed up and down, with the same moans and rattles. After a few seconds Sorjana realised that not only would it not break, but by now she had probably caught the attention of the *Homo sapien* guards.

'They know you have Psionic powers. So don't waste your time. You are here for good.'

A shrill, annoying voice of telepathy, almost elf-like and lilting intruded into her mind. It came from the cot accross the cell. The half human-whale abomination lifted its overlarge head. The voice was sexless, as was its source. Its black bug-eyes stared at Sorjana intently. '

'What's it to you Grey? Youre welcome to come with me once I break this door down. If you can break free of your bonds that is. What is your name Bellatrixian?'

The Grey hesitated, as was expected. Its weak facial muscles flexed and twitched as the overlarge, blug bug-eyes were obviously darting around the room nervously. If it had a tail, it almost should be between its legs. Sorjana had never known these abominations to be so mischievous, then be so timid, almost childlike. A surge and pang of sympathy had suddenly sunk in her heart. And a guilt for letting her prejudice get the better of her, and how she was so sneering and rude to this creature only moments before.

'I am called Mishta. That was the name I have chosen for myself, as all Bellatrixians do.'

'Mishta.' Sorjana both mused and replied. 'Do you not have a last name? It can't hurt to tell. I don't know what the *Homo sapiens* have planned for you, but you probably don't have long to live, you know.'

'True, your genetic ancestors are not above vivisecting individuals who they capure offworld. A Pleiadian like yourself would probably not be immune to the same fate,' Mishta retorted. 'But to answer your question. We........... simply don't have surnames, like humans. Millenia upon millenia of asexual breeding has made genetic lines and interbreeding regimes, that sort of thing, well, beyond obsolete.'

'I am Sorjana Hoolde,' is all she simply replied.

At that moment, the door could be heard clicking and clanking. Sorjana initially thought it was latent telekinetic powers acting upon the door. It was when the primitive bolt on the other side of the door slid open, and shadows could be made out behind the door at the narrow slit of light underneath, that she realised the door was going to open. And open the natural way that it was intended. By their *Homo sapien* maker's skilled hands. Beyond that door was a guard, perhaps two, or three or more. Sorjana got to her bare feet whilst vaulting upwards from the cot. When she landed the floor was surprisingly cold. She had no shoes. The *Homo sapiens* had confiscated them. *But why?* She wondered, as she trotted for the door barefoot. *Is this one of the ways These animals dehumanised their captives? They intent to interrogate me then! So be it. They bought what I'm about to to them on themselves.*

At this thought Sorjana had reached the door as it was being swung open, inside towards the cell. Being light on her feet, however, Sorjana side stepped easily upon the open side of the doorframe. Without a trace of hesitation she shot out of the gap, under the cover of a shadowy, lightless cell to surprise and confound the ape-like men. The first *Homo sapien* she faced indeed was surprised and over-whelmed for a split second. Sorjana only shoved him hard out of the way with her surprising brute strength. She knew there would be more armed guards immediately nearby, escorting the man who opened the door. She did not dare change direction; only bursting with speed with the momentum of her push, ready to fight any *Homo sapiens* that would block her escape. She did not know where she was. She only heard the cries of the primitive humans in dismay. She did not see any in her peripheral vision, so they must be behind her. She did not dare look behind her to see how many.

Turning a corner now, after only a few strides from her cell, she bolted at full speed. Her designer genes propelled her at speeds that were beyond the extreme limits of mere *Homo sapien* anatomy. The guards behind her should have opened fire on her by now with their relatively stone age weapons. Instead, claxons sounded. Red strobe lights flashed and rotated. It would have been better if they had fired. Now every guard was alert in the complex, and with her not even knowing the way to the exit. Only sprinting blindly, hoping for the best. She could be running in circles for all she knew. She took the next left corner, having to take the risk of slowing.

Another straight corridor. This one stretched so far, she could not see the end. Perhaps it was an underground tunnel? What these primitives called their idea of a sewer. It did not matter. What mattered is the claxons were now going for twenty Standard Seconds. Every guard would certainly be armed and on alert by now, hunting her. She sprinted once more straight ahead. Her heart rate was now beating rapidly, and she found her breathing was beginning to become laboured. She never did enjoy long distance running. Certainly did not do it voluntarily. Being short statured for her species did not help. She certainly wasn't the fittest Pleiadian in the Common-wealth either. But still she pressed on, half on adrenaline. She had been sprinting for over Two Standard minutes by now, well over one of it down this long corridor alone. Still there was no end to this tunnel.

Her ultraviolet eyes scanned the shadows for an ambush prudently. It was by now she had time to take in her surroundings, perhaps get her bearings. Her three-litre brain was doing it whether she liked it or not. Without being told. *Its just concrete floors and walls with steel pipes running along the ceiling, with a primitive lightglobe every ten or so paces. Much like my cell. My former cell.* Sorjana reassured herself. *Where am I?* She wondered as the claxions rang in her ears. By now the echoes of their screech had formed a secondary tempo, and had intruded into her mind as music. Her mind was quickly becoming addicted to this music that drowned out her laboured breaths. Sorjana felt her feet harden at being stamped against cold concrete thousands of times. They would only take the luxury of stinging when the adrenaline wore off. *If* it wore off.

At last the corridor ended. Only this time the corridor did not end; guards ahead of her narrowed the gap galloping towards her. They were too far ahead to discern their freatures, but Sorjana knew they were armed, and there was at least half a dozen of them. At least. They would have plenty of time to aim and fire their weapons too. She should have to use her psionic powers to get past them, but she would have to slow and concentrate. Furthermore, telekinesis was not in eternal supply to a

Pleiadian, or any modern human species. Already she had noticed a slight mental fatigue after she tried to break the cell door with her powers. Perhaps it was best to save it until she was really cornered. So Sorjana stumbled to a stop, and turned around instead. She was probably going the wrong way in any case. The *Homo sapiens* could be heard wailing in their rudimentry verbal communication that all prehistoric humans shared. And their ancestors before them, with their primitive tongues, voiceboxes and vocal cords. Their ape-like hoots became quieter and further away as she clearly was outrunning them already, leaving them behind. They were now firing loosely at her, deliberately missing, wanting her alive for interrogation. There were no side corridors either. Just the straight and narrow back towards where she came. Her breathing was now significantly laboured, and her throat and lungs began to burn. Her throat was gathering phlegm by now. She pressed on, sprinting foward desperately.

Not one minute later, she found she had returned to what is now a T-junction. The left turn she had taken a few minutes ago on a nothing-to-lose gamble was now dead ahead. She slowed and came to a stop a few paces before the junction, her breathing drowned out by claxons. Listening for running footsteps was out of the question. Her chest heaving, she poked her head around the T-junction, knowing they were an Achilles heel in urban warfare. Anyone who faced the apex of the T was prone to an attack sumultaneously from both sides. Even the primitive *Homo sapiens* would have known this, and used to their advantage. She hugged a wall with her back, side-stepping. She was surprised when she quickly peered over the wall in front, only the contrary was found. Nothing but another empty corridor. *They must be on the other end, then, with weapons poised*, Sorjana empirically deduced. She faced the front once more, where she was going, and leered to her right with the closest eyeball. The wall slowly uncovered more corridor. It seemed to take hours as more and more of the corridor was revealed. Even though Sorjana knew the *Homo sapiens* she had most recently fled from were less than half a minute behind.

Within seconds, the entire corridor was revealed. How could it be? There was no one. This place should be crawling with *Homo sapiens*. It was just Sorjana and the monotonous claxon. She slipped around the corner and trotted cautiously, eyes scanning the shadows once again. She realised she was heading back towards her cell. Perhaps she could slip back into there, the last place they would expect her to go there? And wait awhile, for the guards to disperse, assuming she was making for the exit. Well these *Homo sapiens* should be easy to outwit in any case. It was only a matter of locating her cell once again. As she trotted past a different cell, she realised hers would have an ajar door. She rounded that corner. It should be the first open, unlocked door on Sorjana's left. It shouldn't be too far now. She passed a locked door to her right, scanning the shadows whilst blocking out the droning claxon. That, combined with her laboured breath, her brain grasping for oxygen, she found it difficult to think.

There it is! She cheered to herself. It was only twenty or so paces from the previous cell on her right. Still no *Homo sapien* guards in sight, either. She came to her door, still half open, and slipped inside again.

'Mishta!' She shouted telepathically so the Grey could her her over the claxon that would be thumping inside its head. 'Mishta, it's Sorjana again. Did you manage to escape? Where are you?' Her ultraviolet eyes took agonising seconds to adjust to the darker cell and as she darted her head around desperately, searching. 'Keep quiet if you are! I'm taking you with'-

Her telepathy was cut off simultaneously as one after the other, human figures formed inside the cell as her eyes finally adjusted to the shadows. A *Homo sapien* guard in the shadows to her right, behind the door, shot a primitive electric projectile, Sorjana felt herself crash to the floor and writhe and shudder with the high voltage stunner weapon, incapacitated with sheer agony. The guards that had ambushed her were closing in, as if they had just killed an animal and intended to eat it, starving.

I have clearly underestimated the cunning of my primitive ancestors, was sadly Sorjana's last thought as one of the guards rendered her unconscious once again.

16.

Rion Murphy was still seething about his rejection on his expected promotion to Gaadyu recently. Piloting a stolen Draconian fighter amongst a pack of motley other saucer-shaped small ships, stolen from Commonwealth and Empire alike, Murphy rushed forward at nearly one-tenth the speed of light. The Annunaki's target was a hapless, unarmed Timeliner on the outskirts of the Hyadean system. Murphy intended to take his anger out on the hundred thousand or so tourists of time. He did not care where in time the upper-middle-class and above citizens of the Commonwealth were heading. All that mattered was the fact that his party would intercept them with ease, before they could escape into Shrinkspace. The passengers would be hostages which the Annunaki would release only upon payment of at least a hundred Sentinels, but Rion Murphy would push for one hundred and fifty. The Timeliner itself would have at least half a dozen, for a return trip into the past. And right now, the Timeliner had no idea what was about to happen. The pilots in the cigar-shaped craft were accelerating casually, without any sign of duress. It would be only a matter of time before they noticed however, and raised a distress call, while rushing for the safety of Shrinkspace. Murphy looked behind him, sizing up the Annunaki Enforcers who now acted as makeshift pirates. Each saucer ship carried over two dozen of them; his ship had mostly Reptilians, with half a dozen humans of varying species from different star systems. There were even a couple of Bellatrix Greys, armed to the teeth with Anti-Rifles, as were the rest of his tough-guy soldiers of the Annunaki. Rion calculated that once they boarded the ship, they would be outnumbered four to one, if there were indeed one hundred thousand aboard the Timeliner. Although unarmed, a substantial proportion of the tourists would be able to fight back with psychokinetic powers. Murphy and his band would have to rely on old-fashioned storm-tactics and ruth-lessness and surprise. He had no doubt he would lose a few good men in the seige. Possibly himself. The Gaadyu should have spared more enforcers, to guarantee that the Annunaki's losses would be minimal. Not that would have happened. Besides, Commonwealth citizens seldom had the stones to use their powers. Unless they were an Arcturian marine...... Rion Murphy pushed aside such thoughts. There would be no Marines here.

He did not dare to utter a war cry until the Timeliner made a break for it. It was best to maintain radio silence. His fleet of about a thousand saucer-shaped ships stayed in formation silently, as if by telepathy. Murphy looked out and behind him, out of a viewing port of his stolen fighter. Scores of saucer shaped craft glittered against the fuchsia background of a beatific nebula, reflected off the light of the nearest star, the last of the Hyadean system, dozens of astronomical units away. The formation was not military perfect, but it was strong and well spaced. None would certainly collide.

Murphy faced forward once again. The cigar-shaped craft was now faintly in view, glistening of the light from a distant sun in a gorgeous ivory colour. It was the size of a small asteroid, thirty kilometres long. At this distance it looked the size of a grain of sand. Murphy estimated they were less than half an astronomical unit away, and still the Timeliner was unaware. This was almost too good to be true. Maybe it was a trap, set up by Arcturian marines, a civil Timeliner full of soldiers? It doesn't seem likely. The Annunaki was low on the list of priorities of the Marine Corp. Besides, even if they did manage to annihalate the Annunaki, an even worse Mafioso would simply usurp the empty niche. No, the Annunaki was certainly the less of all evils, despite how ruthless and malicious Rion Murphy was.

Now, the distant Timeliner had almost doubled in size, but was still very small. As Murphy estimated the distance again, and reflected on their luck, the distant ivory cylinder abruptly began to increase speed. *So, they have finally noticed us. That's too bad, too late. It will be another five minutes at least before they can enter Shrinkspace. We will be there in three, unless my calculations are way out.* Murphy let an on-board computer check his estimations. One eighth of an astronomical unit away, and dropping dramatically; the Timeliner was about eleven o'clock from his fleet, practically head on. It was also slightly below his fleet. Murphy now realised his eyes were slowly being cast downward as they came nearer and nearer. *The fools! Increasing speed only makes the possibility of escape ever more slim. My fleet should alter trajectory soon, so we don't whizz past them, if that is their plan? And they escape into Shrinkspace as we swing around and catch up? Do they really think we were born yesterday?!* Murphy had picked up the ancient expression some time ago. So long ago, he did not remember where. And the expression seemed to stick in his habits. Murphy chose this moment to utter a primal warcry over the Amp within his fleet, which helped kickstart his band into a fighting mood. Primitive in the age of faster-than-light space travel.

As the ranged dropped from one eighth to one sixteenth of an astronomical unit away, however, the Timeliner seemed to launch three missiles in self defence. Murphy squinted at the indigo tails of Arcturium propulsion they left; not the missiles themselves, which would be invisible at this distance. *Those are not warheads! They are only Sentinels. Isn't it a little too early for that?* At that epiphany, however, a distress cry came over the Amp as another pilot in his fleet, one who had also saw the Sentinels and mistook them for warheads of some kind. Immediately, at the conclusion of the cry, a few of the Annunaki fleet scrambled and broke off formation, veering off at random trajectories. Murphy cursed silently and fisted a sturdy part of the controls to his right, not doing any damage. At least now he knew who the weak links in his band were, pilots who cracked under pressure.

After a brief swivelling of his head to perform a cursory tally of the scrambled craft-Murphy lost count after about a dozen-he grabbed the Amp mouthpiece to his left and barked. Even though he was not appointed leader of the raid by the Gaadyu. He realised there *was* no leader as he howled with his telepathy over the waveband. Raids seldom needed leaders to work effectively regardless. But not this time however. Murphy would have to be the unwritten, unelected leader of twenty five thousand.

'Get back in formation, all you idiots! Those are Sentinels only! You should know that! And look, they're in range! We will destroy them now, so they can't escape into Shrinkspace. Get ready to fire.' Murphy could not wait the few precious seconds for his stragglers to return into formation. 'Fire! Now!' Murphy removed the safety from the trigger and instantly opened up without even bothering to aim. He did not expect to destroy the Sentinels; even if his aim were perfect, they would take anything his fleet threw at them with ease. Pure Draconium was indestructible to everything except thermonuclear temperatures. No, the Anti-Cannon fire was designed to aim in *between* the Sentinels and Timeliner. This should, at least in theory, force the pilot to abort his escape into Shrinkspace. To reduce weight and cost, a peaceful Timeliner was only made of steel, ceramic and titanium alloy. The pilot would have to slow frantically and bank away from the path into Shrinkspace, to safety, lest the anti-matter projectiles would cut through the Timeliner. As if the thing were made of ancient cardboard. That would also be bad for the Annunaki. A destroyed

Timeliner with no survivors to take ransom was simply worthless.

A few seconds later, the scattered potshots, colour of the same indigo Arcturium anti-matter as the Sentinels" tails, bombarded the space between the Timeliner and Sentinels. A few of the sphere-shaped projectiles even hit the Sentinels, being absorbed uselessly. What really mattered is none of the projectiles even came close to the Timeliner. At least his motley band had enough sense to not aim at the valuable 'Liner, without needing to even be told. As expected, the Timeliner had already panicked, slowed, but did not change direction. The pilot is tougher than he expected. He would still try for the refuge of Shrinkspace. Murphy picked up the Amp mouthpiece and shrieked 'Fire!' once again. A moment later, and thousands of fireballs spewed forward like transparent volcanic rocks. This was the last ballista of projectiles his fleet could unleash without risking damaging or destroying the precious Timeliner. His window of opportunity was closing. This had never happened before in the few-and-far-between raids on civil spacecraft. The Timeliner's pilots are obviously calling the Annunaki's bluff, knowing they do not wish to destroy the Timeliner. The pilot might even be laughing, mocking Rion and his band of cutthroats. That is unless the next barrage, rocketing forward at the speed of light, does what it was supposed to. By this time, the craft that had broken formation about a minute ago returned to complete the spearhead of flying saucers. They latently, almost sheepishly and humbly, opened fire a second or two later. In the ten seconds or so it took the first projectiles to cut through the path of the Timeliner, now close enough for details to be discerned, Murphy knew they were now barely a minute from reaching their prize. They were now about the same distance as the average planet was from its moons. Again a handful of projectiles hit the indifferent Sentinels indiscriminately. Murphy narrowed his eyes and squinted at the growing Timeliner. The last of the anti-matter missiles disappeared in the vast distance and into the black void of deep space.

Now was the crucial moment. Murphy was now holding his breath. If the Timeliner powered forward towards Shrinkspace in defiance, he would have to lead the other ships in his new contingency plan. This has never happened before. Every Timeliner surrendered at the first barrage and hoped the Arcturian Navy would save them in time. They would be over half an hour away at this distance from the Hyadean system. It would make more sense to escape into Shrinkspace. Murphy watched and waited and hoped for either the ship to surrender or to bank away and try to outrun them.

Rion Murphy cursed again as the Timeliner did not change course, but increased speed again, heading for the Sentinels. *The Sentinels! They're changing!* The fact they were now in their triangle formation removed all doubt. Already the indigo triangle net was now starting to illuminate slowly, like a giant ancient floodlight. It took up a decent percentage of the view in front. Murphy snatched the mouthpiece to the Amp once again.

'They're heading for Shrinkspace. Don't worry, we

will get to them first.' The Timeliner would take at least another two minutes to escape into the surreal triangle. The Annunaki needed less than one. 'We will reach them in seconds. Alter trajectory about now, and intercept the thing.' They were indeed less than half a minute away now. The ivory 'Liner was now the size of an insect. Murphy tilted his controls and banked his flying saucer to where the 'Liner would be, bisecting its location twenty seconds or so from now. The spearhead formation of the other Annunaki fighters followed suit. The spearhead changed direction and reformed in a few seconds, like a flock of seabirds only twice the agility.

By now the moon-sized triangle was dimming, the anti-matter process turning over. The 'Liner obscured from view momentarily, and peeked over the crest of the triangle a moment later. When it did it was twice as large. The instrument that measures range was now changing so quickly most of the numbers were indiscernible. It had already dropped to a smaller scale; kilometres. *Six hundred and something......no five hundred and something thousand.*

'Ten seconds, people,' Murphy spoke evenly on the reciever with his telepathy. The Liner was now increasing in size as if it were being inflated by an unseen giant's lungs. It was now at ever increasing angles to the attacking fleet, which Murphy and the entire Annunaki expertly compensated. Presently it was directly in front, and then slightly to the left, all the while increasing in size.

'We should be slowing down now.' A Draconian accented voice replied over the Amp.

Murphy complied absently, grateful for the reply. He actually forgot to! *Five seconds*. The fleet immediately slowed to half their pace within a second. The liner had now monopolised everyone's viewing port ahead of them, blocking out most stars. It was the size of a dog by now. His fleet was now down to a quarter of their original velocity.

'Brace for impact!' Murphy hissed over the Amp. Barely a Standard Second later, and the 'Liner was pelted, was bombarded by saucer-shaped fighters, like ancient shurikens in a giant white whale. The Draconium of the Annunaki pirate craft penetrated the mere titanium hull of the liner with ease. Murphy hardly felt the collision; in relative terms, it was like an ancient tank penetrating an equally ancient blimp. The disc shaped projectile that was like Murphy's craft simply cut through titanium like bullets through cardboard. After a split second of flinching he was slowing his craft at near-fatal deceleration; Murphy felt blood surge to the front of his head like a crashing red wave. His ears rang and he felt his nose bleed whilst simultaneously losing most of his consciousness, his vision gone, yet he still gripped the controls with nothing but mere defiance. He was still partially conscious. It was like being half drowned in a massive, crashing, wave that swept you under the ocean, with one being spun and flipped helplessly.

Murphy did not know how long it was that his vision had gone, how long he was half conscious, but memory told him that most small spacefaring craft can come to a complete halt from hundreds of kilomtetres a second in a few blinks of an eye. And his craft, as well as dozens of others, had scores of solid metal barriers that were the rooms and compartments to help slow them. It was only one second, two at most, before his vision began to return and he regained full consciousness. Outside his craft; he could be anywhere inside the liner, would be nothing but smoke and metal fires caused by the phenomenal friction, caused by the improvised manoeuvre he and his fellow Annunaki Enforcers had just performed. The 'Liner would be severely damaged, would resemble a smoking, pockmarked, mechanical whale. Already, automata should be repairing the dozens of holes, sealing the ships' crew and passengers from the vacuum of space. Murphy knew the 'Liner would recover in seconds, and be space-worthy once more; The Commonwealth had anticipated the calamity of a 'Liner caught in a meteor shower, solar flares and the like.

Murphy glanced behind him, his ears still ringing, and checked on his passengers. All but two of the quick thinking Annunaki had lain on their back. The human, Draconian and even Grey anatomies were almost infinitely more capable of withstanding over a hundred times more, than the standard gravitational force-what ancient fighter pilots referred to as "G's"-this way. About two dozen Annunaki wearily, painfully, sat up and got to their feet, coughing and moaning in the process. The two that were not so lucky, did not follow suit of their comrades, were either dead or comatose. Fluid of yellow for the Grey, and the familiar red for the human, had erupted from any orifice available, including the eyes. Murphy would do what he did best, among many things. Coldly, callously write those two off. Besides, it was a miracle that he was alive. He had hoped the Annunaki on the other ships had had the sense to do the same lest their numbers would be too few to follow up on their illegal mission. No doubt most of the other pilots would be dead. It will be a while before he regained his hearing. No matter. He could still "hear" telepathy. That would have to do.

With his legs all but limp, Murphy heaved himself out of the pilot's spartan seat, pushing himself up with both arms. When he finally got to his feet, it was valuable seconds before his legs would permit him to walk. It was as if his legs themselves were automata; they were running on sheer willpower alone. A subordinate handed him an Anti-Rifle. Most were waiting for him patiently, for him to lead. Two dozen sets of eyes watched him with antici-pation. Murphy was in no real hurry, however; the metal immediately around their ships would still be red-hot. He used this free few minutes wisely, and grabbed the Amp at his console. At least his nose had stopped bleeding, as Arcturian blood always clotted quickly.

'Every other Enforcer that can hear me come in. Gimme an update here, will you?' Before long, over a hundred different voices of synthetic Draconian and human responded to Murphy's role call. And still kept coming. 'Enough! I.......we don't have all day. I will have to assume most of us survived then. Everybody out, and storm this 'Liner! Kill anyone who has the audacity to resist. We will take this ship in twenty standard minutes, before the damn Marines get here. Or we will rot in a cell.

I'm not going to let that happen, and neither are any of you. Now let's make the poor Gaadyu a very rich Ciakar!'

At that conclusion, Murphy replaced the Amp and banged the control to open the door, almost in one motion. Presently he marched out in a ruthless cadence, Anti-rifle cradled in his arm, two dozen Enforcers following close behind. The smoke caused from the trauma to the 'Liner was finally beginning to dissipate. Murphy did not know where he was. It did not matter. Raids like this worked better when improvised and unpredictable anyway.

'Now all of you!' Murphy barked deafly over his shoulder with telepathy, ears still ringing, and powered by rage and fury. 'Get to the front of the 'Liner. We have some dashing pilots that need killing.'

17.

When Sorjana regained consciousness for the second time in a still-yet-to-be-determined amount of time, she was indeed bound and tied this time. A sack made of primitive fabric was swiftly, if roughly, removed from over her head. The world spun, but eventually she realised her arms were fastened behind her back, and her body was fixed to a cold, primitive chair. It was the type of chair the poorer Oil-Age schools and academies favoured. Steel and wood, with no padding whatsoever. An equally primitive lightbulb was faintly orbiting low above her, casting dynamic shadows about the room. It was the same type of room as her previous cell she had shared with Mishta the Grey. Indeed, it probably was the exact same one.

'Yes, you're finally awake, you Nordic little bitch. You're not gonna cause any more problems now, are ya? Good girl.' It was a spoken voice that entered her mind via her ears, so much unlike the telepathy she was accustomed to. Not surprisingly, it was in one of the main dialects of Oil-Age Terra; English, of which Sorjana spoke fluently.

Or she would, had her vocal cords, voice box and other organic apparatus for speaking had not become as vestigial as a tailbone. She realised after all this time she had forgot about her Holotab. She had to assume it was confiscated by the *Homo sapiens* when she was first captured at the underground subway at some distant city, when she had walked its streets like her primitive ancestors had, among her ancestors. They would undoubtedly be dissecting her holotab, and see if they could not learn from the technology from a military perspective. She would have to communicate with good old-fashioned pen and paper, despite her bound hands, if not to write these *Homo sapiens* a message of obscene defiance.

'You're a pretty little thing. It's a good thing you are,' The ape-like human continued. 'Had all my men working for their pay, you did. Can't let you get away. You're the first Nordic we caught in a while.' The voice, Sorjana slowly realised as she regained full consciousness, was coming from behind her. Sorjana assumed it was a male, as the males of the species tended to make deeper, low-pitched grunts.

Where am I? Sorjana thought. Her head seemed to throb at the effort. She realised she was dehydrated. She hoped the apes would permit her a drink. That previous workout she had running from these animals would have depleted her fluids significantly. She moved her lips; they seemed to have lost all elasticity. Her mouth was desert-dry. *I am probably underneath a desert.* Sorjana realised; the voice of the *Homo sapien* that had recently spoken to her had either an American or Canadian accent. It was Sorjana's job to know the accents of ancient Terra. She knew her ancient Terran geography. That was also her job to know; that in this part of Terra, the only place that could be clandestine was away from civilisation. That meant either the deserts of ancient Nevada or the tundra of Alaska. It was unlikely they would take her to an isolated island in the pacific; that would be logistically impractical.

'Got something to say, Nordic?' The male's voice ventured. 'Oh I'm sorry. You freaks can't talk without you gizmo thingies.' A modern-by-Sorjana's-standards device was waved in front of her. Her ultraviolet eyes now discerned the device was familiar. *My Holotab! At least I can get it back. If only I can't rehydrate, I can use psionic powers.* Sorjana knew, that with a headache, that would soon fester into a migraine as her evolved brain indeed was drying out, that the attempt to use telekinesis would be met with overwhelming protest. It was only a matter of time before even these stupid ancient Terrans would realise she needed water and permit her a refreshing skull of even-brackish tasting water. Her tongue ran over her parched lips habitually, but even that was nearly completely dry. She realised her joints were now beginning to ache as a symptom. Her muscles ached. She gathered saliva, as if her body could squeeze blood out of a stone and quench her thirst with her own body fluids.

Slowly, the source of the spoken voice moved around the chair to face her. Sorjana's ultraviolet eyes focused on a middle-aged male, at least by *Homo sapien* standards, who wore a sharp suit, typical of contemporary professionals of ancient Terra; not a military uniform that Sorjana had expected. The primitive human bent down to look Sorjana in the eye. Its eyes were small, compared to modern humans, and did not see in either the ultraviolet or infra-red spectrum. Unlike the myriad of different species of human that would exist some two hundred thousand Standard Years from now (with the exception of the Tau Cetans of planet Tsorra). The face, presently, began to sneer at her. It was a facial expression not seen for thousands of years. Sorjana doubted her facial muscles would even let her comply to match it.

'Well now.' The primitive pulled up a chair, a companion to the one Sorjana was bound to, scraping it audibly on the ground, deliberately, in the process. It sat down, with its stomach and crotch against the backrest, and glowered at her. *Primitive psychological interrogation techniques?* She thought. 'Where were we?' The *Homo sapien* asked platitudinously. Sorjana simply eyeballed the Terran. 'Oh, yes. The name's Onslow. But you,' it shot a gesture towards Sorjana, 'Can call me Bob. Can you say "Bob"?' Onslow had the nerve to take a patronising tone with a superior species! Sorjana realised these caste of Terrans were significantly different from the Hopi from which she had got on well with. There mannerisms were almost that of a Draconian. *A disguised Enemy? Surely he would have revealed himself by now. It!* She reminded herself. *Itself.* In the ensuing silence Onslow simply scoffed and rose from his chair. It nodded towards the back of the dark, off-sepia room. Moments later, armed guards in military uniform carried a simple, nondescript table in front of Sorjana.

The two then marched off towards the back of the room, behind Sorjana, their primitive rifles slung behind their shoulders. Sorjana turned her head around, with what little movement permitted her, and watched them. They immediately took up positions either side of the steel door. It was exactly like the one in her cell. It showed no signs of telekinetic molestation. *So, this isn't my cell.* She faced forward to the near-bookish Onslow. *CIA? NSA?* Sorjana's Ultraviolet eyes squinted to the tiny plastic badge pinned to the animal's breast pocket. The room was too dark to discern anything. Not that it mattered. Either the animal would tell her eventually, or she would have to kill it with her mind, and, more regrettably, the armed guards near the door. Those two apes in green fatigues bore her no visible signs of malice after all.

Onslow the *Homo sapien* tossed a stone-age bundle of paper and an ancient pen of ink on the table in front of Sorjana. With a nod from Onslow, the two guards could be heard clomping towards her from behind. She felt her wrists were being freed a moment later. In her peripheral vision, she caught a glimpse of the other guard pointing its weapon fastidiously at her, the black muzzle of the *Armalite* almost boring into her temple, even from a metre away.

'Now, bring your hands were I can see 'em, Nordic. And real slow, at that,' Onslow ordered. Sorjana did as the animal instructed. She moved her hands from behind, and rested them on the table, flexing and rubbing her wrists absently at the relief. Now both the guards had their rifles pointed at her. Onslow gestured towards the pen and paper with his eyebrows. Presently it said, 'Now, you're gonna tell us what we need to hear, if you're a smart girl. Use the pen and paper, since you won't talk. But you will talk in the end. Is that understood?' Onslow spoke to her as if she were a criminal. Sorjana glowered back at the ape defiantly.

'Is that understood?!' Onslow almost barked at her. Sorjana finally nodded with pursed lips, eyeballing the animal all the while. The *Homo sapiens*' mouth twisted into a malicious grin, a step above a sneer. 'Good,' it said. 'Now write us what we wanna know. You can write, I assume? Too bad. If not, learn, bitch!' Onslow clearly came from a dark age in humanity where sociopaths were seen as an asset, and went far in life. Sorjana would have no regrets pile-driving this abominations' skull into a hard object with her mind. The only regret would be the fact that these apes would waste time and resources to give this mistake of a human a proper burial. But first the two guards would have to be telekinetically despatched. That would mean Sorjana should eradicate this creature bare-handed, without powers, seeming Onslow is unarmed, it would be a tad dishonourable. *We will see who is whose bitch when I use your genitalia to pick this lock, Homo sapien!* She thought in an uncharacteristic surge of fury. However, she surprised herself when she did pick up the ink pen, and applied it to paper. It came almost instinctively, like a man castaway on a tropical island would automatically know how to fabricate a bow and arrow or a simple lean-to shelter. She began to scrawl, clumsily at first, in near-perfect English.

FIRST NEED WATER, Sorjana wrote on the pad in crooked, wobbly capitals. Onslow watched her hand intently as she wrote. The guards held their rifles pointed true at her head. They glanced at each other. They occasionally drummed their fingers underneath the forward stock uneasily. Onslow glanced up at the guards in the dim room and shook its head briefly. It nodded towards the guards a moment later, and one left the room. The door could be heard unbolted behind. In the ensuing minute or two before the guard returned Onslow said nothing. Sorjana, who had her overlarge Plieadian eyes cast downward at the notepad eventually looked up and met the piercing stare of the bureaucrat, or agent. Onslow had dark brown, almost black eyes, which to the ultraviolet spectrum was drowned out in the luminescent silver that was the whites of the human eye. To an Arcturian, the browns would be merely a shade of grey. The door opened again with a metallic protest. A moment later, and an open flask was plopped in front of her emotionlessly by the guard. Sorjana knew they needed her alive for interrogation; it would not therefore be poisoned. She downed the first half desperately, stopping when she needed to breathe. She was breathing loudly now, still letting the fluid settle, and grasping the flask primally, as if a thief would spirit it away from her. After a few moments, when she regained her breath again, she leisurely began sipping the flask, with Onslow the *Homo sapien* glowering at her as if she had been bathing in her own urine, not saying a thing. It had, however, turned the chair around and sat in it the way in which it was intended. The ape was now lounging in the spartan chair, with one of the male's arms resting on the table, the other dangling behind the chair's back. Onslow's chest rose and fell contemptuously with its breathing. The lightbulb on a wire had finally ceased its swinging, and was no longer a source of distraction or irritation. Sorjana picked up the ink pen, and resumed her clumsy writing.

WHERE AM I? Sorjana finally wrote while the three early-humans watched intently. Onslow, the instant Sorjana put down the pen screeched, 'I'm asking the damn questions here!' The ape sat down again, less wild now, and venomously spoke. 'Now I have a question for you now.' The *Homo sapien* alpha paused, glanced up at both guards who still had both rifles pointed at Sorjana, as if for reassurance. 'What the hell are you doing here, in our country?' Sorjana knew enough about Terran politics to know what a country was. In The Commonwealth, and even the Empire and Sirian and Zeta-Reticulan Republics, there were no nations; just towns, cities, continents and then planets. She supposed that for a species bound to one planet, nations were a must. But she simply scrawled, on the paper with the ink pen, as if she were right handed and wrote with the left, a response. Simply;

I AM HERE HELP YOU. ALTHOUGH CANNOT TELL WHY. This merited a puzzled look from Bob Onslow, whose brown eyes darted around the room thoughtfully. The ape steepled its hands and formed a bipod with its arms. It leaned forward and asked, 'Help us? You say?' It leaned back and lounged on the chair again. 'With what, the Rooskies? Don't you dare think we don't know you come from another planet. We're the government, and we know you come from the Plieades system, about five hundred light years from here.' Sorjana took another long sip from the canteen. *Will have to wait for this stuff to kick in, but feel better already. Why not see what I can learn from this primitive human first?* She picked up the pen and wrote painfully, *NOT TRUST REPTILE FROM EMPIRE.*

To which Onslow got up from its chair and exclaimed, 'The Reptilians? The Reptilians? They're the reason we have nukes, although the Rooskies got them a few years later. We assume through espionage, and not through the Reptilians. The Reptilians have done a lot for our great Nation. And they don't ask anything in return, except the odd worthless bum, which to eat, or experiment on, that we don't care. The point is, what have you Nordics done for us? You haven't done squat, although you look so much like us. Why is that? You look like us so much? I have always been creeped out by that, don't you know? The fact an alien looks so human, even though it came from a different planet. If you, however, were li'l green men with antennae or something......' that merited a smirk as Onslow looked up and caught a glimpse of the guards, evidently grinning. '........It wouldn't be so bad, because that would make sense. But you look so human, so human in fact, no one would even notice you lot from a decent distance, wouldn't even look twice at you's.....' The dominant ape's voice trailed off. Sorjana knew, reading between the lines, that this early human wanted to know why they looked so alike, Pleiadians and Ancient Terrans.

Well that was simple, if you knew your paleoanthropology. But Sorjana could never tell the Terrans that. They would unlikely believe her anyway. Most Terrans, particularly the scholarly ones, believed time travel was impossible, was only the stuff of primitive science fiction and other pagan myths and legends. Sorjana had once read a science fiction novel of Oil Age Terra. It was so scientifically inaccurate, well impossible, that it barely merited to be called fantasy. The Idea that people could travel to distant galaxies! And travel thousands of times faster than the speed of light! (without compressing the fabric of space). Sorjana picked up the ink pen once more, and scrawled, simply replying to the unasked question;

CONVERGENT EVOLUTION? IT'S WHY US LOOK SO ALIKE??

Onslows' eyes met hers. The luminescent silver in ultraviolet wobbled to Sorjana as the Terran's eyes flared. It got up suddenly, kicking the chair behind it, and toppling the chair. It leaned forward to tower over Sorjana, as if to intimidate her, placing its arms on the table, hands first, forming a bipod again. 'You are alone here. You're little blonde friends don't know you're here. You're little Grey friends don't know you're here. And the Reptilians *want* you here. Now you're gonna play ball. Either hard ball or soft, we don't care. But you will play our game. Mark my words Nordic! Convergent Evolution? What do you take me for? Do you really expect me believe that two planets lightyears apart, with different gravity, atmosphere, and what have you, can have two different species evolve to look almost exactly identical, by sheer coincidence alone?! And your DNA; we've recovered your DNA, my pretty. It's a cutting edge technology for us Earthlings, but so far we have determined that you, Nordic, are part of every race on this planet. Your DNA matches European, African, Eskimo..........hell even Mexican all the way to Mexican't!' The joke was lost to Sorjana, but one of the guards snickered behind her. Bob Onslow concluded with, a deadly serious face and venomously quiet tone, however, 'You have a lot of explaining to do, sweetheart.'

Sorjana took another sip of the flask, shook it, and realised it was nearly empty. She downed the last of the brackish tap water and belched rudely in sheer defiance. The dominant ape, in response, simply turned around, with its back to her, and replaced the chair. It then remained there a few moments with its back turned, as if to show disappointment patronisingly. Abruptly, the Terran strode towards the door. To Sorjana's surprise however, it wrenched the primitive assault rifle from the nearest guard, and fired a few rounds into the air.

The alpha *Homo sapien* had deliberately placed the rifle near Sorjana's ear, but the guard had recovered, and, restraining the dominant, had in the process, pulled the deafening firearm away. Even so, chips of concrete rained down from the ceiling and stung Sorjana like so much half-hearted shrapnel. The echo of the shots was deafening in its own right, in the confined, soundproof room. It was a moment before the raging ringing in her ears of protest regained their purpose. She reacquired her hearing, and heard the last of Onslow's demands, just in time, as it was assertively spirited from the room by one of the guards. The other guard had recovered, and had pointed its rifle at Sorjana again. Not that she had even thought of capitalizing on the situation; she was bound to the chair and momentarily incapacitated too. Onslow was screeching from near the exit, '.........ARE YOU, NORDIC? WHAT ARE YOU?'

18.

It was not long before Rion Murphy had commandeered the 'Liner. By the time the Arcturian Navy had finally arrived, well over two Standard Hours later, thousands had already perished. Three warships armed to the teeth with long-range ballistic missiles with Arcturium Anti-warheads were stalking the crippled Timeliner from a safe, if not diplomatic, distance. A dozen or so smaller picket ships were scattered about for good measure. The small, saucer-shaped craft were still in their proverbial motherships. In the initial raid of his never-before-seen kamikaze tactic, Murphy had lost over five percent of his Enforcers. The Timeliner passengers were not all pushovers either. Some fought back with their psionc powers, accounting for a further tenth of his force depleted. Another five percent of the Annunaki Enforcers were still too injured from the initial crash to fight, and were topside tending their wounds. After the 'Liner had been taken, Murphy ordered some Enforcers to administer the Annunaki's wounded, not as a gesture of humanity, but so the Gaadyu would not be too displeased with the losses. Murphy would have to demand over two hundred Sentinels in ransom just to break even. Every Enforcer in the Annunaki had monetary value, and not sentimental. *Just like livestock*, Rion Murphy had once mused.

That had left some fifteen thousand of his forces, armed, against sixty thousand unarmed hostages. On ancient Terra, armed bank robbers and other thugs would have no trouble with subduing about four hostages each. But this was the Modern Age. "Unarmed" civilians had mental powers that could kill with a glance. His Enforcers would have their hands full in guarding the mustered hostages. Strictly speaking, the raid was not going very well, let alone according to plan.

Murphy was on the bridge of the 'Liner, glowering at the captain. The captain, in turn, did his best to glower back. A middle-aged Lyran with a very forgettable face, had faux defiance betrayed by fear clearly in his eyes. Murphy sneered as he could no longer keep a straight face. The Lyran captain swallowed. The Arcturian with a small, pocket-sized anti-pistol, single shot, but with more firepower than an ancient rocket launcher of Oil Age Terra. The rod-shaped weapon (not a true pistol) would obliterate both the Lyran and most of the 'Liner's bridge with it, vaporising anyone in its path in the process.

'Now,' said Murphy simply with his telepathy to the captain. 'You're gonna get on the Amp and tell the Navy to clear off, and don't come back unless its with three hundred Sentinels for the beloved Annunaki. I shouldn't even have to tell you this.' Presently, after a momentary pause, he raised his telepathic voice and continued, 'What are you staring at!? Hurry up!' The Lyran scrambled to the Amp apologetically. Murphy bought the rod-of-death closer whilst the captain used his telepathy, as if to dare him to turn telepathy into telekinesis without warning, letting him know Murphy and his Annunaki was expecting it. But the captain, wisely, complied, and relayed Murphy's command in more formal words. A hostage negotiator replied in Draconian Bird-Song language, assuming the mastermind behind this piratical episode was green and snake-like. Murphy took immediate offence to this and snatched the Amp from the captain's hand.

'I'm Arcturian, idiot. I speak Common. Now when do we get our three hundred Sentinels?' Murphy could have asked for more, but knew most planets seldom carried more than five hundred. Three hundred was a realistic number. 'If you don't have three hundred, we, the Annunaki take Draconium and Arcturium Bonds,' He tittered over the Amp. 'We also take flyer miles with Shrinktime Spacelines!' No one in the Arcturian Navy, however, shared Murphy's amusement. Rion Murphy was accustomed to every sycophant laughing at his jokes accordingly. Whether they were funny or not. And usually with audible effort and fear in the laughter. Rion Murphy had obviously chosen the wrong time to crack a joke, and with no one laughing, he childishly pelted the Amp into the console with an audible *clank*. His face and demeanor immediately took on a sulking fashion for a moment or two. The Naval negotiator, however, took the silence to confer with his superiors. The amp click on and the negotiator began in Common. 'I'm afraid it is just not that simple, my Arcturian Brother. But we will see what we can do. Three hundred is quite almost every Sentinel this star system has. We would be essentially marooned without access to Shrinkspace for months, possibly Standard Years, when an outside vessel finally comes in and goes away for help. As for the Bonds, we simply don't have that kind of wealth here, and if you take all the Sentinels, how can we go away and get more?'

That had never occurred to Murphy. He bit his lower lip ponderously.The captain of the Timeliner replaced the Amp, slowly on its hook. The Lyran looked up at Murphy contemptuously but questioningly. 'Well,' The Lyran asked, 'What do we do now, Annunaki? We have people that want to get out of here, both passenger and crew alike. People of The Commonwealth work hard, you know, and pay good money for time-travel after all.'

'Shut up.' Murphy pointed at the Lyran and replied evenly. He turned to a Reptilian, with his holotab ready to translate dutifully. But the Amp, however, interrupted him before he could give orders. 'Now if we could only see the hostages. Proof that we have human lives to bargain with. I am sure we can come to some agreement. No one else gets hurt or killed. We get our people and our 'Liner back. The Annunaki go home rich men, or reptiles, or whatever. It can be that simple.'

It was not that simple, Rion Murphy knew that. It never has been, and probably never will be. Authorities had never, had always refused to, negotiate with thugs, thieves or terrorists since ancient times. That has always been a policy since ancient times. The Arcturian Navy and Marines was simply searching for an opportunity, a chink, an opening. It won't hesitate to seize that opening, to barge into the Annunaki's fairly and squarely captured Timeliner, kill the Enforcers and or free the hostages without giving a shred of Bonds or other assets. Effectively saving money, face, and the proverbial day. That has always been the plan. Since ancient times. Murphy chose to ignore the negotiator, and return to the reptilian Lieutenant. 'Bring a few hostages to where spying automata can see them; to where the Navy can see them. It's time to play hardball. Every Standard hour they delay, we kill hostages.'

'How many?' The Reptilian lieutenant asked in his bird-song language, translated into Common presently. Murphy, in response, shrugged dramatically, and took on an exasperated tone, rolling his eyes for effect. 'Oh, I dunno. Surprise me!' *Just like ancient times also*. Murphy mused to himself on a private channel of his mind.

The Arcturian Navy knew Murphy and the Annunaki were not playing games when the spying camera eyes showed images of innocent Commonwealth citizens of various human species, with weapons, anything from Anti-Rifles to knives and a taloned claw of a Draconians' hand, pointed at their heads or throats. The Captain of one of the three huge cigar-shaped warships, a Vegan woman who attained the rank of Commodore at the age of forty-five Standards (about a decade younger in *Homo sapien* years), was to be honest, expecting no less. She knew the Annunaki were not ones to demand without actually taking live hostages. Still, it wouldn't do to give a fortune in Sentinels and Bonds in exchange for a Timeliner full of corpses that would cost a third of what it would take to build it to get it spaceworthy again.

Her ultraviolet eyes, blue and large, like those of a Plieadians' darted about the screen as the automata fidgeted the cameras, making them zoom in and out, pan left or right, at the mercy of artificial intelligence. Sometimes the automata zoomed in at the right time, to see the terror on a middle aged Lyran woman's face. Other times it zoomed out, panned left or right, then zoomed in to show a Draconian holding a machete to a humans' throat, or, more disturbingly, a human with an Anti-Rifle pointed at another human's head. But these were few and far between, fortunately. What did matter is the ultra-violet spectrum that she saw masked some of the more terrifying details, and sugar-coated them with vibrant, pleasing and psychedelic colours. She could not see the terror, the anguish, in the hostages' eyes, for example. They were lost in a luminescent off-silver colour that no *Homo sapien* or Tau Cetan had ever seen, and never will.

Her braided, long, dark hair, despite being tied back into a ponytail, whipped about as she turned her head here and there, to bark commands at an Arcturian negotiator, other officers, or just frantically adjust the console of the bridge. With a sigh, Commodore of the Arcturian Navy, Claudia vam Rees closed her deep-sea blue eyes and held them for a moment. She turned to the negotiator, an ugly Arcturian Lieutenant, and ordered;

'We have no choice. We must do as they say. I know the Annunaki. They are either not human, or the ones that are, subhuman. They will not hesitate to carry out their threat. If we do leave, I know they won't kill anyone; the hostages are the only guarantee we will come back with the ransom. The Draconians, or Annunaki, know this, and won't carry out the threat every hour, in case we take too long and run out of hostages.'

'But what if they take the ship away, with all its hostages, to a place we will never find them?' Piped the Arcturian in reply.

'How will they get their precious ransom then? The 'Liner itself is now practically worthless, especially to them. Remember, they are made out of titanium and even more worthless steel. And besides, they, or the crew, have crippled the engines. It's just not going anywhere.'

The Arcturian nodded solemnly in resignation. 'But how can we get the rest of the fleet to follow us? In the end, after all, it is the Admiral that makes the final decision.'

'The Admiral has already considered this. Trust me. If he hasn't, he will when the Annunaki execute the first wave of hostages. But, if he really did care about sparing their lives, he will give the order I just suggested any minute now.'

The Vegan and the Arcturian returned to the spectacle on the screen ahead of them. This time, it had returned to the bridge of the Timeliner, where a large, slightly corpulent, bald and bearded Arcturian in a long black leather coat held a metallic rod to a nervous, unsure Lyran man of middle age. The Lyran wore a uniform signifying he was one of the people that piloted the graceful Timeliner. *Dissidents!* Claudia vam Rees thought angrily. *If only they had joined the human cause against the Empire.* No matter how much you engineer genes and raise a human in a benevolent, almost utopian society, there was always the one bad apple that slipped through the cracks, rebel, resist, and eventually joining the Annunaki. The only place that understands these people. That would accept them. For once, society was not to blame, no matter how much of a left-wing perspective you approached it.

Seconds passed. And the seconds turned into minutes. Still the Admiral held his cause, did not deviate, did not give the order to withdraw. The Vegan and the Arcturian were entranced by what was happening on the screen in front of them. Cameras changed randomly according to what artificial intelligence of the local automata decided what was a priority. It was halfway through zoning on a Tall Grey when it abruptly switched to a Draconian discharging an Anti-Rifle. Instantly, a scorched human body, barely recognisable as one, slumped forward, and out of camera shot. Gasps and moans could be heard both from on-screen, and behind Claudia. Her dark skin shone beautifully from the clinical lighting of the bridge of the warship, her dark green officer's fatigues contrasting with the pearl-white interior, as she spun around to chide the other officers on the bridge.

'Come on now.' She said gently and evenly at her crew, a myriad of different human species. 'You're not being paid good wages to be squeamish and sensitive. Obviously you lot have had too much time away from the battlefield and on a comfortable Navy warship, away from the action. Hold true, harden your nerves. We have a job to do.'

The first wave of hostages were indeed being executed. Claudia lost count quickly, but it was certainly in the hundreds. Coldly and calmly, she efficiently clutched the Amp and asked, 'Admiral, with respect, now would be a good time to withdraw, and fast. We already have the blood of five hundred or so on our hands. Do we need to make it more? However, I await your directives as always.' She added latently, 'This is Commodore vam Rees.'

'Stand down, Commodore.' Came the telepathic reply. 'You will not give in to their demands unless I give the order. Is that understood?' There was a brief hesitation when Claudia replied with her telepathy. 'Yes, sir.' Her telepathy, however, betrayed her shame and disappointment.

'The Admiral is calling their bluff,' the Arcturian negotiator suggested helpfully. 'His strategy is to make them think the Navy does not care about the hostages, that we only want the 'Liner in one piece. The hostages are expendable. When we let them kill a thousand or two, without flinching, The Annunaki will panic. They know that once they run out of hostages, they're dead. They will melt like ice in a volcano against the might of the Arcturian Marines. It is a dangerous gamble, especially when citizens of the Commonwealth are at stake.'

'And if we do falter, they will simply keep the Sentinels and Bonds, and only release half the hostages. Then demand more for the other half. I wouldn't put it past them, and there's no confirming how many hostages are actually *alive*.' The telepathy came from behind Claudia.

Her second-in-command, a Tau-Cetan with the rank of Captain, spoke for the first time since the stand off. Claudia could only solemnly nod in agreement.

'That's just it then.' She concluded. 'The Annunaki can effectively bankrupt this Commonwealth if they're smart. If they clean out every Sentinel we have, not only are we marooned, but this Star system could be significantly vulnerable if the Draconians decided to capitalise on us with a full-scale attack. After we have been weakened by the Annunaki, that is. The Admiral is in command. I trust him that he knows what he is doing, and so should you all. He will be the one responsible if the Commonwealth throws the proverbial book at us for letting hostages die. Just all of you remember that.'

The rest of the bridge went quiet at the suggestion of being finished off by the Draconians. It was, ever since the start of this Cold War against the Empire, something everyone knew could quite possibly happen, but avoided the subject. Just like planning the funeral and will for one's inevitable, distant or tomorrow, death.

Claudia, presently muttered, more to herself than the rest of her crew on the bridge, over a sloppy wave of projected telepathy. 'There is an expression that goes back as far as Ancient Terra. *To the victor, go the spoils,*' Claudia mused sadly.

19.

Darius awoke in the dark shed that served as both a wine distillery and storage silo the most dehydrated he had ever been in years. His mouth tasted like sand. A headache was slowly creeping up inside his head. It was so dark in there, he could not tell if he had even opened his eyes at first. There was no light coming from beneath the door. It was evidently night time. He had obviously been missing from his estranged parents for hours. They would have gone to bed by now, and be fast asleep. His heart sank. Or maybe they were out looking for him? Well his mother would be, at least.

Darius sat there for a few minutes, willing himself to get up, knowing he needed to rehydrate urgently. Again, when he did sit up, Darius crashed and stumbled. He forgot about his missing leg once again. He fumbled to his left for his crutches. He had to go solely by feel. By now, his Tau Cetan eyes, at the same spectrum as *Homo sapiens*, now adjusted and discerned a faint light from under the door. It must be a starry night with a full moon. Darius hobbled to it pathetically. When Darius got to the door he fumbled, feeling the solid mass looming in front of him. His hand moved to the side, and felt only dust and cobwebs. The light switch was found eventually a standard minute later. The room was illuminated with a flicker and a protest. Darius flinched and closed them reflexively. His eyelids were the colour of red. For some strange reason, he only noticed it was cold now. His body tensed as if enduring a freezing cold shower.

He came to the tap, and ran it for a few seconds, before stooping over to take over twenty gulps. He straightened to catch his breath, and still his mouth felt dry. He stooped over once again under the tap. It was a long journey back to the homestead. Perhaps he should make a makeshift bed and spend the night here instead? His eyes presently scanned the inside of the dusty, neglected distillery. He could find no such thing. Only dusty crates, jugs and other winemaking tools, all stacked half-heartedly neat in a corner in front of him. Well, it was a distillery after all. It was not intended for sheltering people. Shivering, by now, Darius went to the door on his crutches and awkwardly opened it, while trying to balance. He turned off the light and slid the door closed behind him. He decided to push on towards the homestead.

The full moon was out, and indeed it was a spectacular night. Darius looked up and gazed at a star above him, lightyears away. Throughout the Commonwealth, everyone was taught to look for the star that nurtured humanity; Terra's Star. Although Darius had seen it "up close" at only one hundred and fifty thousand kilometres, it looked like every other star in the Tsorran night sky.

Darius looked forward and pushed on, with the now-familiar tempo of his crutches.

The pastoral Tsorran landscape was presently illuminated in many shades of blue-grey by one of its moons. The one that was currently out was similar to size and distance to that of Terra's. The second moon of Tsorra, larger, but further away, was generally only seen during the day. Tsorra experienced solar eclipses almost fortnightly. To the people, they were mundane rather than a novelty, naturally. As Darius tri-podded along the dirt road, at a quick pace to build a sweat and keep warm, he became mesmerised by his frosty breath that puffed out visibly with each breath. Soon, he was breathing so fast, the frost before him became a continuous puff of smoke. Dew was glistening in the moonlight on the vegetation everywhere, which, along with the position of the moon in the sky, told Darius that it was roughly midnight. The Tsorran days lasted only twenty-three Standard Hours. Every planet known to Sapients all had their different measurement of time. Most attempted to synchronise their days in multiples of ten minutes and ten hours. It did not work on many planets. So humanity decided to revert back to the incredibly ancient twenty-four hour format.

Presently, Darius came to a shell of a biodiesel powered tractor, and thought, *I have never noticed this before. Why?* Indeed, the farming implement looked ancient, entropied. It would have been here untouched, for a Standard Century, or close to it. He would have noticed it as he was growing up. *Have I taken a wrong turn? Am I still on the family biodiesel farm?* He knew other farms on Tsorra had abandoned tractors too. His frost breath stopped as he had an epiphany. *Did I not pass out, drunk on red wine, with the light on? Then why was the light off? Someone must have been there, in the distillery shed, whilst I was asleep to turn out the light. Or the light was on a timer.* He ruled out the latter. Utterly unfeasible on a rustic, technophobic farm. Technology was forsaken here, used only when necessary. There was no television network out here; Darius or his brother had never watched television, or films, or played video games in their childhood. Their childhood in a way, was more ancient than that of Oil Age children, to a time even more ancient, practically medieval.

So someone was at the distillery while he slept. A shiver ran down his spine, even though he was now sweaty, puffed and warm by now. Hobbling along faster involuntarily, he checked behind him. Just a dirt track and vegetation, faintly illuminated by the moon. But it would have been easy to follow him at night here, at a safe distance. Besides, no one was out her besides other farmers and their families; no would-be conspirators had a reason to be out here. Maybe his father came by, and left him there, with utter contempt? If it were a Draconian agent, Darius would simply not be breathing now in the frosty air. A sleeping enemy agent, who was also crippled, was simply too good of an opportunity to pass up upon. No, it must have been his father. Darius hobbled on at a more relaxed pace. He must be halfway home by now, surely. But the carcass of that tractor still bothered him. *Why do I not remember that thing being here?* He wondered. *Perhaps I have just forgot about it*, he mused.

It was around one in the morning when Darius came to the homestead. Being isolated and down a country road that ran adjacent to the main iron road where levitating Biobrids passed through only every minute or so, his parents had the luxury of not bothering to lock their door. Being on crutches, Darius could not by any means move with stealth. His parents, fortunately however, were heavy sleepers. Living a lifestyle where there was minimal modern conveniences was taxing, and there was nothing to do in the homestead besides reading, (not by candlelight, surprisingly). In the dim light, Darius came to the kitchen and grabbed a primitive ceramic mug from the cupboard. The kitchen tap was just below. He ran the tap for a few seconds and filled the mug, downing it instantly, then filling his cup again. Oh how he was thirsty! He drank it down greedily without even thinking, filling his mug again a third time. This time, however, he took it to the nearby guest room clumsily. His parents surely would have woken up to the sound he made by now. It could be another Standard Year before he could creep and move stealthily again, when he got a replacement for the missing leg. For now he had to endure this life as a wretched cripple, and he did not think he could ever get used to it, as he lay on the rustic cot with his faithful crutches at his side. It would be a while before he could fall asleep, all active and sweaty like he was, but it was better than the cold distillery. He would have to reconcile with his folks in the morning. Especially the father.

20.

Sorjana remained bound to her spartan chair under the constant surveillance of two *Homo sapiens* armed with their primitive, practically stone-age, rifles. She could feel their piercing glare on the back of her head, even after hours of facing the table and staring ahead. *How many more hours are these monkeys going to keep me here?* She complained to herself. Even the two guards behind her were getting weary, she noted. Sorjana was still thirsty, and now she was hungry, too, but the *Homo sapiens* denied her any food or drink for the time being. Her powerful, evolved mind was screaming out for fuel. Pleiadians, like all modern humans, do not fare well with food deprivation. Not only do their brains have higher energy needs than their *Homo sapien* predecessors, but their body chemistry had also evolved. Excess carbohydrates are now excreted instead of being stored as fat, thanks to designer genes, and hundreds of millennia with an abundance of food. Their stomachs have also shrunk, unable to digest foods such as raw carrot. A stomach that was powerful enough to digest foods would have to sacrifice brainpower. That will never do.

As with food deprivation, *Homo sapiens*, who initially felt weak for an hour or so, but soon their non-vital organs shut down, stomach shrinks, and body chemistry changes to burn any stored fat and generally conserve energy wherever it can. However, their descendents some two hundred thousand years later, for reasons mentioned above, no longer had that luxury aroused through lack of luxuries. Sorjana's stomach simply churned and laboured. Her small stomach could not possibly shrink any smaller. She had no excess fat reserves, only fat in essential parts of her anatomy, such as subcutaneous fat under skin for insulation. Her body had forgotten how to shut down organs not essential for breathing and thinking. So she just sat there and got weaker by the hour. She had learned it had been nearly forty-eight standard hours since she left that tram, was captured and bought to an undisclosed location, fraternised, only briefly, with Mishta the Grey, and made her failed escape. And now she had been sitting here for eight hours after Onslow had left. Forty eight hours without food! It was a hunger strike by Plieadian standards. Not that they have ever had a reason to stage a hunger strike in protest. Not with their perfect, utopian sub-commonwealth.

Her thoughts drifted to Mishta the Grey. Maybe his, -*it's*- she corrected herself, kind knew he was missing, and come by to break him out of this abominable place with ugly hairy ape men. She did not know much about the

Greys, their customs, their culture. They were, to most of the citizens of the Commonwealth, an esoteric, if not repulsive, society. She remembered they have no real digestive system, that they obtain nutrients by absorbing an insular protein solution through their skin. But what mattered was if the Greys knew the Terrans held their subject, like Mishta, here. And If they did, would they do anything about it? Such as attempt a rescue or jailbreak? One thing was certain; The *Athena* did not know she was here. If she never knew the Terrans had a facility like this, and its location, then no modern human would. As the Director of Chronophysical Intelligence, the only one for a hundred light years and a hundred thousand years, if she did not know, then no one would.

Right now however, she was in no condition to fight. She was too weak both physically and mentally to attempt another escape. And she was under the unrelenting vigil of two *Homo sapien* armed guards. Their rifles, however primitive, were still deadly. She could only wait until she could eat again and gain strength. Sorjana was beginning to come to terms that that was an *if*.

How hard could it be, to escape these semi-sentient animals?

It was at that moment footsteps could be heard from outside the cell. They were approaching at an angry, or frustrated pace. Sorjana knew by the sound that it was those of a male. The iron door could be heard unlatching and unbolting now, operated deftly, with well-practised movements. The door creaked open on half-heartedly lubricated hinges. The same footsteps could be heard approaching behind, and then the door could be heard closing and being locked again, with an almost perfectly reverse musical sound of metal on metal, drowning out the simultaneous footsteps. Sorjana did not bother to look behind her to see what was coming in. The ugly, monkey-like face of a lower primate appeared in front of her anyway. The *Homo sapien* that called itself Bob Onslow leaned over to both leer and sneer at Sorjana.

'Well now. I see that you are quite comfortable eh? Are us Earthlings treating you well?' Onslow grunted in a voice that was both sarcastic and patronising. Sorjana just stared back at the animal in defiance. 'Now is that any way to treat your hosts?' It turned its back on her and mused. At a signal from the early man, the table and writing pad was bought in front of Sorjana by the two guards. The dominant *Homo sapien* must have known Sorjana was too weak to struggle out of her bonds and escape. The guards quickly pointed their rifles at her afterward, regardless. One unbound her hands again, more nervously than before, as if it sensed Sorjana would make one last desperate attempt to attack and then flee. If she had enough strength, she could wrench the rifles out of their hands with her mind. Not now. She barely had the strength to think a way out of here. Just reaching forward to write with the ink pen was becoming taxing.

FEED ME PLEASE, Sorjana wrote with an even messier hand than before. When Onslow the *Homo sapien* finally read it, watching expectantly, he sneered with even more conviction.

'So blondie here is hungry,' it said in a musing, if

theatrical tone. 'Well, how is she going to pay for her meal eh? And how is she gonna pay her rent? She owes us two days so far,' the *Homo sapien* chucked sarcastically. The guards just stood there, rifles drawn, and unamused.

Presently, as if oblivious to Onslow and its cruelty, Sorjana began to scrawl, FOOD FIRST. THEN TALK I.

Again, Onslow watched her write like the stupid animal that it was, stalking its prey. 'Well now,' it said as Sorjana put down the ink pen, 'it seems we are getting somewhere. Finally!' The dominant *Homo sapien* male said in a childish tone. It nodded and puckered its lips to one of the guards. Sorjana felt a blow to the side of her neck. As she buckled and flinched, she caught a glimpse of a guard withdrawing its rifle, butt-first.

'That's for making me wait,' Onslow barked. 'Now, you will answer my first question. Who are you, and what are you doing here in the good old You-ess-of aye?' Sorjana's ultraviolet, Nordic eyes widened at the revelation. So she was still in the same country as she was in when she fought those three *Homo sapien* degenerates. That was something, at least. It ruled out an island somewhere in the Terran oceans. She thought it no harm, however in telling the primitive humans some useful information, even though they have greatly mistreated her. She picked up the ink pen and scrawled, HERE HELP YOU FIGHT REPTILES. REPTILES WILL KILL ALL US. REPTILES NOT TRUSTED. REPTILES IS EVIL.

Sorjana could never tell the dominant *Homo sapien* about The *Athena*, The Commonwealth, her home Planet of Erra in the Plieades cluster, orbiting the star Taygeta.

Especially not about the part where she is from a future well over two hundred thousand Standard Years from now. She however, added latently, writing ever more feebly as she got weaker, I AM SORJANA. I FROM ERRA PLANET IN PLEIADES. AM PLEIADIAN. PLEIADIAN FRIENDS. DRACONIANS NO FRIEND OF HUMAN. NOW FEED I. I TALK. NOW HOMO SAPIENS FEED SORJANA.

That, at least, was true. Sorjana regretted instantly referring to these Terran as *Homo sapiens*, but realised to her relief instantly, they lacked the brain capacity to draw the fatal conclusion from it. There was no way in all The Great Commonwealth they would put (x+2=4, *therefore* x=2) together, and how peculiar and queer it should be that Plieadians use the same taxonomy as "Earth-lings," and therefore must be related or interconnected somehow. But if Onslow had indeed made contact with Draconian agents like it had claimed, then surely Onslow should know that Plieadians are in fact *Homo sapiens* of the future?

Onslow, however, simply shook its head and said, 'I told you before. Now listen to me carefully. The Draco-nians have been an asset. They have done for us more than you Nordics have. You're refering to an alien invasion? Don't you think they would invade us by now, if they were? No. What is on the Reptilians" agenda, the reason why they have provided us with nuclear weapons technology, decades ago, and have asked for practically nothing but a few worthless lives in return, that we don't know, don't care.' Sorjana wondered why the Terrans were not sceptical about a Draconian offer that sounded too-good-to-be-true, only perhaps their new toys blinded them. Onslow continued, 'But it's good you have finally decided to cooperate. What you have told us, most of it we already know............Sor.....jana is it? Well, Sorjana, all you have to do, now is tell us what you are doing here, on "Earth." After that, you may eat and drink. You will never leave here, of course, unless the Draconians make us an offer we can't refuse for you. But you may live another day if you tell us what we want to know. Now what is the *real* reason you are here? And none of this crap you're here to help us. Second, why do you look so much like us? And don't you dare bring up this "Convergent Evolution" bullshit. I wanna know, is this your true form? Or are you simply disguised as a human, huh?' Onslow the *Homo sapien* raised its eyebrows at her.

Sorjana shrugged her shoulders, and wrote, THAT ALL SORJANA KNOW. SORJANA IS HUMAN. SORJANA IS SORJANA. PLEIADIANS AND TERRANS BOTH HUMAN. SORJANA HERE HELP TERRANS. THERE MANY PLEIADIANS HERE HELP TERRANS. And that too, was true. NOW SORJANA EAT. SORJANA DRINK. SORJANA DID TERRANS WANT. SORJ-

Sorjana's hand went limp. Both her hands were now shaking. There was no way she could continue to write; writing was taxing to a species that communicated with telepathy for countless generations. Her wrists ached. Her hands throbbed. She had never actually written before, until today, although she had read the Terrans' language until she knew it fluently.

'Aww for Chrissakes! Give the blonde bitch some food already!' At that, the Dominant *Homo sapiens* walked away from Sorjana contemptuously. Before long, it rapped on the iron door to her cell. A guard beyond unlatched, unbolted, and opened it. The reverse was repeated seconds later.

It was not the best meal Sorjana had eaten. Far from it. It was meat of such poor quality, it was beneath feeding even to a Neo-Terrier. It was slopped onto a steel tray, that was dumped in front of her as if she were, herself, a Neo-Terrier. Hard-to-digest Terran vegetables were mixed in and cooked together. But Sorjana hungrily ate it regardless. A jug of water and a steel cup full of water flanked the plate, like a medieval convict's last meal before his execution. It did not taste so bad. To Sorjana, it was more than food. It was a ticket to *freedom.*

'Good. Now eat your stew.' Onslow said in a voice that was almost serpentine. 'And eat it slowly. It's the only meal you're gonna get until you tell us everything. You're probably used to eating green blobs or rocks or whatever it is Martians eat. Down here on Earth, we have something here called Mama's Home Cooking. Mmm-imm.' The *Homo sapien* rubbed its belly and licked its lips theatrically.

And Sorjana did exactly that. Of course, she had to eat it slowly. Her digestive system was in tatters. It took her nearly half an hour to finish off the dish, even though it was a small portion. Not being foolish to fill up on water, Sorjana washed down the last of the Terran dish with the cup of water. She poured herself another unhesitatingly, and began sipping it. Presently, Onslow sat down in front of her, and glowered at her. It stared at her for a few minutes. Sorjana simply sat there now, waiting for the food to digest. She felt bloated. She could only sit there and wait for the nutrients and fluids to kick in. For her body to regain its integrity.

Onslow ventured after a few minutes passed, 'So, now you have no excuses.' The plate was taken away, and replaced with the notepad and ink pen. 'Tell us what we should know,' the *Homo sapien* gestured at the notepad pointedly. There was a brief hesitation as Sorjana looked around, down at the notepad, and up again at Onslow. Her deep blue Pleiadian eyes un-nerved the creature. It swallowed despite itself. Sorjana wrote with refreshed vigour;

TERRANS FOOLISH. HAVE TOLD ONSLOW EVERYTHING. NOT TRUST REPTILES. PLEIADIANS HELP TERRANS. I PLEIADIAN. AM SORJANA. PLEIADIANS FIGHT REPTILES. SORJANA FIGHT REPTILES. THANK YOU EAT AND DRINK.

At that Onslow the Ancient Terran got up from its chair, and turned its back in its trademark show of disappointment. It turned its head and addressed the two, guards in green fatigues.

'We're wasting our time with her. We don't know enough about Nordic Alien anatomy to inflict pain for physical interrogation. We don't even know if they actually *feel* pain. But she does have value on the open market however.' The Terran's voice increased with excitement as if it had an epiphany. 'Secure her again. Tie her to the chair, and keep an eye on her,' Onslow called to the guards it knocked on the cell door. The door instantly unbolted and opened, and Onslow added maliciously as it exited the cell, 'I will talk to my contact. I'm sure The Reptilians would give us a nice juicy reward for a captive Nordic. We don't know much about her, but she could be the Goddamn President of Mars or Saturn or something. She could be a nobody. Either way, she's gotta be worth something,' the Dominant *Homo sapien* concluded as the door was slammed shut and it marched off down the hall beyond.

Sorjana felt her heart rate increasing as the two soldier class early humans grabbed her wrists and began to bind her again. She felt her mind twitch in desperation, almost instinctive. Her mind throbbed again. Behind her, a guard gawked, lowering its rifle, as the ink pen was now floating in the air, levitating as if by the hand of a polter-geist. Sorjana felt her bonds no longer being fastened. The other Terran guard had noticed it, too.

Sorjana knew she no longer had the luxury of hesi-tation, the luxury of not seizing this opportunity. Her wrists found themselves wriggling free of the half hearted bonds. With genetically engineered speed, and with rope still tangled around one wrist, she rose from her robust, spartan seat. Her legs and buttocks felt numb, but already adrenaline had blocked it, and Sorjana found that she had effortlessly despatched one of the surprised guards, and taken the Terran's rifle. Sorjana instantly dove under the steel table as the other *Homo sapien* guard removed the safety on its rifle and opened fire. Bullets sprayed about the room as it followed Sorjana. She rolled and got to her guard. A cursory look at the primitive weapon, and Sorjana remembered how to operate these things as she had learned as a novice many Standard Years ago. When the echoes from the shots had dissipated, the guard made its ape-like grunts and hoots of distress, calling others within earshot. The shots would bring them regardless. That would mean the cell door would have to open to permit them in. Sorjana would have to seize that opportunity, as well as fight her way out here. She had primitive weapons now too. If she could gather enough, she could perform a makeshift jail-break, and use the aid of other Sapients in her escape.

There was silence for an agonising few seconds. The guard was stalking Sorjana, moving slowly around the table like a Neanderthal stalking a superior Cro-Magnon for the first time in history. But Sorjana was smarter. The intellectually inferior guard had forgotten that Sorjana had a clear view of its legs from under the table. She leaned around and opened fire between the table legs. The *Homo sapien* shrieked in pain and fell to the floor, dropping its rifle and holding its shins instinctively. Sorjana rose from behind the table and casually strode past it, and past the wounded primate. She took its rifle, and slung it behind and over her shoulder, mothballing it for later use. She took up her position behind the cell door, and ignored the whimpering animal. It should survive, and sire future generations, maybe even someone Sorjana knew. It had no sidearm. She had, however, had to kill the other guard.

That was a necessary evil. Sorjana surveyed the room. It was the same hellish sepia as her cell.

Sorjana could do nothing but wait for the guard beyond to open the door. He would not do that until other *Homo sapien* reinforcement arrived. When they did, Sorjana knew it could be a stalemate. But it was better than being sold to The Draconians as a prisoner of a cold war. The Draconians knew enough about Plieadian and other modern human anatomy to inflict physical pain. That much, at least, was certain.

21.

Skyler Tjeons lounged in the clinical training room. Magne Mimee sat upright, paying full attention. Master Pteru Hoolde of Shrinktime Enterprises was busy scrawling notes on a primitive whiteboard. Holotabs are capable of projecting a lecturer's writing, but Pteru thought that a whiteboard would suffice. Skyler did not have any opinion on that. He just wanted to get this over with. Magne thought it odd, at first. She had never seen or even heard of the archaic writing apparatus until recently. Pteru was summarising the last of the upcoming exam concerning cargo manifests and other mundane logistics. Then, he said, would come the final practical assessment. Still on a simulator of course. The Commonwealth would not spare an expensive and useful Timeliner just to train a couple of interns. That will never do.

Presently Pteru, in a grey tight-fitting robe and orange boots, turned around, his long Plieadian hair tied behind him as usual. Immediately, he grinned, and said, 'What are you two still doing here? Class is dismissed for the week.' It was nearly a standard hour before they typically ended class for the day.

The two adolescents thanked Pteru in unison, got out of the chairs, and left. Pteru wished them well over the weekend as they left the training room, down a clinical corridor and out of the dome-shaped building that served as an administration block at the continent's only spaceport. Magne and Skyler walked together as they both exited the building. They squinted their ultraviolet eyes as the clear blue sky and the star Electra, three quarters towards the horizon, dazzled them. For a few Standard Minutes, neither of them said nothing as they followed the allocated walkway, at a safe distance from a myriad of saucer, bell, and dish shaped civil spacecraft. Some were privately owned by commercial tourism pilots and the occasional entrepreneur. Most, however, were state owned shuttles that ferried passengers up beyond the planet's stratosphere, and onto an awaiting Timeliner. These were considerably larger than the civil craft.

It was a warm, mid-spring day, especially by Plieadian standards. It was the type of weather and time of day that made humans feel sleepy. Even modern humans were afflicted from the time when early man, even more ancient than *Homo sapiens*, slept under a tree in ancient, prehistoric in fact, Africa, on a warm day after eating a kill. Magne began to yawn as they reached the halfway point between the administration building and the spaceport's Biobrid parking lot. Skyler did the same, as if it were a flu. He decided to be the one to spark up telepathy.

'I can tell you won't have any problems with the exam, both written and practical. I never did that well at the academy. I think I'm doing better at the internship, because I can see the point of it. I hate algebra, and calculus, and writing exams on my Holotab. I never saw the point of them, so I didn't really try with them. To me, it's like learning ancient Latin or English. They're hard to learn, and nobody really speaks anymore, so why even bother learning them?'

'True,' Magne replied with her telepathy. 'I did okay at ancient mathematics, although I also, did not see how I could use them when I was an adult. Geometry, for example. I have never known my parents to use it. Or trigonometry. My father runs his own business selling travel passages, tours and accommodation to people on Erra. What the ancients referred to as a "travel agent." My mother is a psychiatrist specialising in treating war veterans with post-traumatic stress. I followed in my father's footsteps and decided to pursue a life in the Timefaring Industry.' In the socialist Commonwealth, a travel agent and psychiatrist earned around the same wages. 'But to me, most of the subjects at the academy were pointless, but it was a proverbial hoop I had to jump through to be where I am, today. I did what was asked of me at the academy, and I did my best.' She shrugged and grinned, which made Skylers heart melt spontaneously. Magne had looked so coy, yet mischievous just then. 'But you're right, and in the end, a pass is a pass. In the end, so what if you don't know a skill that you will ever use?' She strolled with Skyler with a feline, ladylike grace as she faced forward and mused. Skyler tensed and tried to act cool as they neared the Biobrid parking lot. He just nodded and smiled, and began, 'How are you getting back? To where you are staying I mean?' He asked in telepathy that betrayed a nervous shaking.

'I'm being billeted by a local family about ten kilometres from here, until my, well, our, internship, is over. I wait for a Hycoach, that picks me up near that parking lot, that won't leave for another half an hour or so.' Magne's raven hair bobbed and swayed as she swaggered down the walkway. They both were about three-quarters of the way to the lot. As they continued on in silence, Skyler knew that his time was running out. He had a minute and a half to pluck up his courage. What was a small burning in his stomach that was his nerves, rose hotter and hotter as the two adolescents as they got closer and closer to the lot. Skyler felt his heart race and his body language betrayed hesitation. They were almost at the point of departing when Skyler, in a shaky telepathic voice ventured,

'Magne?.......Can I. Can I..........offer you a ride home? To where you are billeted I mean?' Magne thought Skyler was, for the first time in the two weeks since they had met, being uncharacteristically kind, almost gentleman-like. *Well*, she thought. *I have nothing better to do, and he doesn't seem the type to try and frisk me. Its' kind of cute the way he is acting; all shy and innocent.*

They were both at Skyler's Rugged Biobrid, A black lump of a thing, with the back part open to the sky, like an ancient pick-up. Skyler coyly, on trembling legs, and furtive, frantic movements, opened the passenger door for Magne. It was a truly ancient custom of chivalry. Or it could be the door did not open properly on that beater of a Biobrid, and Skyler was trying to hide it, but

Magne, climbed on to the high bucket seat and threw her legs together inside with a delicate grace. She reached up and shut her door, that was suspended on a pair of gas struts, as Skyler trotted over to the driver's compartment. Whether it was an uncomfortable, bumpy ride and slow for a Biobrid, Magne could not know. She had, after all, never been in one before.

As Magne and Skyler neared the residence where she was being billeted, Magne had a change of heart. She quipped; 'You know, I have been on Ptaah for a little while, and I have not even got around to seeing the sites.' She raised her eyebrows at Skyler intently. Skyler felt a new, stronger surge of nerves shoot through his body. He faced forward and kept his eyes on the road and replied, 'That's okay. I have been here all my life and have only seen like half of what there is here. Umm, where can I, I mean, where would you like to go?'

'Surprise me,' she giggled telepathically. 'You're the local after all.'

'Uhh, how long have you got? Before your hosts are expecting you?

'Don't you worry about them. They have suggested I go out and see the sights anyway, and that was a while ago.'

Ptahh was a comfortably warm planet in the Commonwealth, with a semi-temperate climate similar to ancient France or Spain. The planet had its decent share of scenic natural landscapes. The dome-patterned Capital Commoncity of the continent was surrounded by mountain ranges and autumn coloured, peaceful farms. The land was fertile, and the Pleiades economy relied on agriculture, tourism, and other renewable resources. Ptahians, like all Nordics, preferred a clean, unpolluted planet, even at the expense of a wealthier economy that spoiled their planet. Most of the fuel to power their machinery, trucks and Biobrids was grown locally; the local population was kept to roughly one billion. There was plenty of arable land to grow edible crops and biofuels. Like the only other inhabitable and Terraformed planet in the Plieades System, Erra, Ptah followed the human tradition of naming planets after ancient, long forgotten gods. Calling a planet "Earth" in the days of interstellar travel was obsolete. Most modern humans now have no kinship with the ancient Mother planet, and what the ancients called home, was just another planet in the galaxy, now uninhabitable. Except for those who would ride a Timeliner to time when the planet was precious.

'There is really not that much do on Planet Ptah, Well not on this continent anyway.' Skyler replied after a moment of silence. 'We have a few local novelties, like some ugly sculptures here and there.' Magne looked out of the Biobrid window, but could only see dome shaped buildings of varying sizes. 'What I like to do for fun involves tinkering with Biobrids and listening to ancient rock music. The ocean is over a hundred kilometres out of the Commoncity. There is only rural landscaping between here and the ocean-' Skyler abruptly pointed to a statue ten metres tall and yelped, 'Oh look it the stupid deity our planet is named after.' To Magne, it was just like every other god of Prehistoric Egypt she had learned about briefly at her Academy on Erra. It looked more androgynous that god-like. She looked away, only half impressed. Dome building after dome building followed as they cruised down the congested Iron Road, stopping occasionally to give way to perpendicular-bound, hovering traffic.

'Okay,' Magne said after another moment of silence. 'Take us to a theatre or something.'

'There is a drive in film theatre just outside the city in the country,' Skyler suggested. 'It's a nostalgic one, similar to how the ancients did it. We are going to the Oil Age one day, after all. So why not get some knowledge of their culture?' He grinned and telepathically added, 'Think of it as homework.' Magne shrugged in agreement.

It was another half an hour before they emerged into the outskirts, and the traffic moved faster as the area got less built up. Presently, Magne asked, 'How much further is this theatre? I'm starting to get hungry. How are you coping?'

'I could eat.' Skyler replied diplomatically. His nerves had killed any hint of hunger an hour ago. The star Electra was approaching the horizon, blinding them. Skyler put down a visor, practically unchanged from that of Oil Age automobiles. Magne did the same a moment later in conformity. Skyler continued, 'Not too much, about twenty kilometres or so. They have an Oil Age style diner there too, in keeping with tradition and all that. Have you ever eaten a hamburger? You're probably used to eating tofu, chia seeds and wheatgrass, being Erran?'

'Hey!' Magne giggled in pseudo offence. 'I've eaten

meat before!' Skyler flinched at first, but then read Magne's body language. 'On Erra, I've had fish from Selonabus, Xenotitanosaur from the Empire, as well as local poultry.'

'But have you ever had steak before? From a Terran cow?'

'Can't say I ever have.' Magne replied. 'Our farms are more devoted to growing fruits and vegetables.'

'Well, you're on Ptah now, so why not eat like a Ptahian?' He put his foot harder on the accelerator. The ethanol-hybrid engine responded instantly, sending a more intense electrical surge to the four Draconium pods. They were now travelling so fast, they reached the diner in under ten minutes. Skyler slowed his biobrid a little too post-maturely. Magne rocked forward in her seat with the momentum. The diner was another large dome-shaped building situated at a turnoff adjacent to the Iron Road. They were soon at their same cruising speed as they approached the diner. Magne picked up her holotab, and informed the host of the residence where she was being billeted she will not be home for dinner. Skyler informed,

'This is something the ancients called a drive-through. You can get food without even leaving your seat. Or we could go inside?'

'Why not try this drive-through? How does it work?'

Skyler rolled down the driver's door window with a button on the Biobrids' control wheel. 'It's easy. You just tell that box thing there what you want, and follow the instructions. Just watch.'

There was only one Biobrid in the cue ahead of them, so they did not have to wait more than a few moments. The star Electra had half disappeared over a mountain range by the time Skyler coasted his 'Brid up to the automated ordering box. He asked Magne latently, 'what would you like, Magne? There is a list next to that box on that sign.'

Magne's lavender eyes scouted over the photographs of Oil Age culinary and dishes, with a description accompanying then in Common. After a few moments, a robotic voice over the Amp urged, *Can I take your order, please?'* Magne hesitated another moment, slightly under pressure and said, 'Just get me one of those hamburgers you were telling me about.'

Skyler turned to the amp and commanded Magne's choice to the computer in a neutral, well-practiced tone. His nerves were beginning to ease off. He had heard from his peers that women liked a man with confidence. Whatever that means. *A euphemism for a smooth talking sleaze with ample pheromones*, he once thought. He ordered the same for himself, as well as some other Oil Age foods that he thought Magne would like. He followed the automata's prompts, and drove to the window like an Oil Age Terran would. Magne was surprised to see a *human* serve them food out the window in a large paper bag, followed by two cups with a straw each and a disgusting looking black liquid that boiled despite it being ice cold. Skyler took them, and thanked the young Ptahian woman dressed in Terran clothing. She stamped his debit card, and returned it to him, after charging him only a pittance by Erran standards.

Skyler asked Magne if she could hold on to the food while he drove to the nearby film theatre. He pressed the button on the control wheel, and the 'Brid's automata rolled up the window again. The two young Plieadians of two different races cruised on for a quarter mile to a parking lot half filled with other 'Brids. Ominous pine trees surrounded an iron pad roughly a hundred metres square that was the parking lot. As Skyler chose the first convenient place halfway down the lot and to the left, Magne noticed that all the other vehicles were facing the same way, parked with their occupants facing forward. Magne followed their direction, and saw an enormous blank screen mounted to primitive scaffolding. A moment later and images appeared on the screen accompanied by a long musical jingle. Humans with primitive, ugly, and apelike facial features came on the screen and made loud hooting and chittering noises. Texts in Common appeared at the bottom of the screen at the same time, promoting a liquid to wash a person's hair with.

'What in the Commonwealth are *they*?' Magne asked, slightly startled.

'It's an Oil Age themed place. They roll advertisements from ancient Terra, Contemporary from when this film was made.'

'When was this film made?'

'Oil Age. The people you see on that screen are our ancient ancestors, *Homo sapiens*. Look how little their eyes are and how square their jaw was!' He telepathically chuckled. 'They look like shaved monkeys!' He was trying to cheer poor Magne up, who was now settling in her seat and rummaging through the bag of food. She handed a parcel to Skyler, and ripped open hers like a child with a gift. Skyler gently chided her and said, 'You're supposed to unwrap it, like this.' He gently grabbed at what remained of the wrapping and peeled it off carefully, then handed it to her, along with a small bag of thick-cut fries. 'It's a Terran themed restaurant, serving Terran food. I hope you like it.'

Magne tentatively, of course, took a reluctant small bite after examining the ingredients. It appeared to be well-cooked red meat with vegetables and cheese, piled between two thick slices of bread. She took a bite from the top, before Skyler interjected and said, 'Hold on, you're supposed to eat all the ingredients together. Like this.' He unwrapped his, compressed the dish, and took a *whole* bite out of it, like a Terran would. After he masticated his bite, (although with telepathy, one could talk whilst eating) he grabbed a fry out of his bag, and said, 'You eat these too. It's essentially fried potato. And this black liquid stuff, is cola. It's not the original recepie from Terra, because the ancient makers of this stuff disappeared before the Third Ice Age.' Magne picked up the cup questioningly, and looked at Skyler playfully. 'You put the straw to your mouth and suck.' Magne tried this, and finally managed to suck up a sip after many attempts. She coughed as the bubbly liquid went down into her lungs and into her stomach.

'No, sorry, you suck up a mouthful, and then swallow it as if you are drinking water.' Magne managed to suck a mouthful after three attempts. She swallowed as instructed. The liquid! It burned her mouth and throat! And it was so sweet! She took a moment to recover. Skyler said, 'Of course, this diet isn't that good for you. You're not supposed to eat it with every meal. That is why, I've heard, that when you go to Ancient Terra on a Timeliner, you will see some of the *Homo sapiens* are overweight. I know. I don't get why you can gain weight by eating too many calories, either.' Magne had never heard of such a thing. All the humans in the Commonwealth had muscular and/or slim physiques. Generations of designer genes meant there was no such thing as a "fat kid" at the academy. 'But don't worry. Modern humans aren't affected by this. I was told we get rid of excess calories easily. Take a bite of the hamburger.'

Magne copied the way Skyler ate his, and chewed tentatively. The hamburger was greasy and flavourless, like cardboard. She grabbed a French fry, shook it to cool it, and took a bite of that too. It was even worse. 'Terrans actually *ate* this stuff?'

Presently, another loud commercial, translated into Common, ended. The screen went blank, which dimmed the immediate area in the twilight of Electra. That caught Skyler's attention. He looked away from Magne and forward towards the screen.

'Yes, but only one culture on Terra. There were many cultures on Terra, that was one thing I learned at my academy. Anyway, this is the diet of the dominant culture there. But even they ate other foods. Oh look. The film's about to start.' He took another bite of the burger, and Magne did the same. 'Your stomach might disagree with you, later on. It took me a while to get used to this exotic dish. But I hope you enjoy your meal, nonetheless.'

Magne only ate the meal, both as a gesture of diplomacy, and because she was hungry.

The film went on for over one and a half Standard Hours. A primitive language was blocked out, dubbed over by Common. Adjacent speakers either side of the screen boomed out a robotic voice in a poorly emulated Ptahian accent. Magne was soon mesmerised in it. The ugly, ancient peoples, gathered in a crowd were flashing coloured lights at a spacecraft that resembled a scout-class military vessel in the Arcturian Navy, only more primitive looking. The spacecraft flashed coloured lights in response. Magne said, 'Is that a Terran's impersonation of *us?*'

'Well yes and no.' Skyler replied. 'I have always been fascinated by the Terran Counter-culture, but I know a little about these sorts of films. This is something called Science Fiction. It came at a time before humanity knew about the Zetans, or the Draconians, or the Sirians. They would look at their night sky and wonder if there are other lifeforms out there. They didn't know, so they guessed and speculated and made films like these.' Magne looked at Skyler with her lavender eyes intently as he stared forward and mused with his telepathy, as if reciting a nearly-forgotten lesson. She grinned coyly, nodded, and looked forward, watching the film again.

When the film finally ended, hieroglyphic writing scrolled up the screen. 'What are they?' She asked. It was an esoteric writing she had never seen before. It looked needlessly complicated at first glance. 'Credits.' Skyler telepathically replied. He fired up his Biobrid, and cruised off. It was dark beyond the parking lot by now. The Biobrid's automata turned the headlamps on for him as they left the lot, giving way to a few 'Brids that left slightly earlier. 'They acknowledge what *Homo sapien* made the film. Most people in the Commonwealth regard Prehistoric Terrans as *"it"* by the way.' Skyler added as his rugged black Biobrid left the diner-theatre complex. As he merged onto the main Iron Road that took them there, Skyler Tjeons planted his foot on the accelerator again. The Biobrid roared to life again, exceeding the two hundred and fifty kilometre-an-hour speed limit, in a few seconds with ease.

22.

Planet Selonabus. A marshy, humid world less than a dozen light years from the Mother Planet. It orbited the star that humans called *Sirius B*. Cloud shaped metallic Megapolises floated kilometres above the surface. There were hundreds of them. Each was roughly a hundred kilometres across. The advanced technology, frighteningly advanced even for the Commonwealth, meant that the Sirians could build floating cities as easily as typical, surface- bound ones. They preferred to keep their Terra-formed planet, the first ever, unspoiled, a swampy, humid paradise.

Planet Selonabus, from space, was a brown and blue sphere with the odd patches of green, and silver where the Megapolises were suspended. Terraformed in the likeness of Cretaceous Terra seventy million years before the Oil Age, it was prehistoric enough to sire a totally different species of Reptilians, isolated from their Draconian cousins for millions of years. The first Sapient Dinosaurs migrated and settled here, five million Standard Years before the Cretaceous Nuclear War. The prehistoric

Reptilian survivors on Terra, victims of the Nuclear War, evidently fled to other frontier planets in a mass exodus on their spacecraft, and forgot about their Sirian cousins. Over seventy million Standard Years is the Sirian civilisation. In that time, they were now quite distant from their Draconian relatives, both in genetics and in kinship.

Xankyu, for on his homeworld, rather than the Commonwealth, he was simply known, disembarked the shuttle and stepped his amphibian-like foot on his native world for the first time in months. He glowered at the scenery, taking his home in, and ignored the other conehead passengers. A moment later, he marched forward, with his jasper-coloured gown of office flowing behind him. Here, he was just another Sirian. His fellow specimens walked past and cut in front of him apathetically. Only the occasional offworlder broke the monotony of seven to eight foot tall coneheaded, erect-walking, eel-skinned, Reptilians. Xankyu nodded toward an offworlder he recognised, a nondescript, forgettable Lyran diplomat, slightly past middle age. Someone not even an acquaintance, but merely he had seen around from time to time.

It was midday, a clear blue sky, in a bustling Megapolis. Pedestrians mixed with Sirian style groundcars. Most kept to themselves and avoided eye contact. Xankyu continued to march forward. His destination was a skyscraper ending in a dome roof, just under a kilometre away. He was, however in no hurry to get there. He longed to be on the surface of Selonabus, to relive his juvenilehood. To swim in the lakes and swamps, hunting shellfish to eat. It was what his amphibious body was designed for. He did not like being on Megapolises, where it was frigid cold, high above the surface, where there was no humidity and the air was thin. Offworld, he could tolerate unnatural, man-made environments. It was part of his duties as an ambassador. But on Selonabus, it was different. Xankyu could not explain to himself why.

Despite walking at a brisk pace, Xankyu soon had to hunch over and cross his arms to trap body heat and shield himself from the cold easterly breeze. On this part of the Megapolis, it was open to the elements. A bank of skyscrapers loomed ahead at the centre of the floating city, for balance as well as aesthetics. The metallic, artificial ground felt cold on Xankyu's bare feet. The only reprieve was the proximity of other Sirians and groundcars, occasionally acting as windbreakers. To either side of him, merchants had set up stalls with high-tech, instant and efficient, huts. Xankyu had been to these markets so many times. They had always sold things that were downright superfluous. Others peddled fresh sea and swamp food. A few even sold fruit and vegetables, catering for offworlders only.

With his long strides, credited to him by his height, Xankyu reached the embassy in a little under eight standard minutes, jogging pace for humans. Two pyramid shaped robotic guards armed with built in anti-guns flanked the entrance, a transparent arch two stories high. After identifying himself to the two automatons, Xankyu stepped through the transparent door, feeling the endoplasm mould against his skin as he emerged inside the government building. The lobby was relatively dim, with burgundy draperies and sandy-brown tiles, decorated according to Sirian's tastes. Xankyu's reptilian eyes took a moment to adjust, the catlike, sinister slits opening and contrasting against his inferno irises. He surveyed the lobby with a sweeping motion of his conehead. Afterward, he joined the queue of other cone-headed sapients to confer with the robotic concierge.

When Xankyu strode forward to the desk, after ten Standard Minutes, another pyramid shaped automaton, two metres tall, greeted him with as much sincerity as seventy million years of artificial intelligence could muster. Xankyu told the robot he needed to see the Chancellor, or someone available that was high up as possible. He added afterward, as the robot hesitated and resisted, that it was a matter of "potentially jeopardised diplomatic relations." It was a slight lie. The human Commonwealth was expecting his answer anyway, in fact they would be more surprised if he told them the Sirian Republic would agree to join them. There was no offence taken, and no diplomatic emergency. But the robot did not need to know that.

Xankyu reflected, latently, after the robot ushered him to the appropriate floor, that it was nice to finally see machines that did *not* emulate humans. He could not understand the concept of androids, which by far was the most common form of robot in The Commonwealth.

Xankyu embarked one of the many elevators in the government skyscraper, a transparent bubble of a thing with a base of electrified Draconium. Three others got on with him, fellow Sirians that he did not recognise. He was the last one off, of course, because the Sirian that he needed to see was on one of the top floors. It was not the Chancellor, but it was close enough. It had to be. The Sirians did not think him important, but his human counterparts in the Commonwealth did. He had grown quite fond of his mammalian diplomats and co-workers.

Presently as the lift opened, Xankyu's eyes were exposed to the exact opposite of the lobby. It was bright on the upper floors, its walls transparent, almost window-like and open to the bright light of Sirius B. He squinted reflexively, and approached a final robotic guardian that barred his way to an office beyond. Xankyu could see the very Sirian he wanted to see, seated at a desk; for the office was, in fact, a transparent cuticle. The automaton, in a voice that spoke emotionless Sirian, demanded that Xankyu state his business and identify himself.

'I am Xankyu, Sirian ambassador to the Arcturian Commonwealth. It is imperative that I see the Secretary as soon as possible. It is a matter of diplomatic duress.' Xankyu lied of course, or rather, exaggerated. His time was precious to him, however, and what the automaton did not know, would not hurt. Presently, the pyramid shaped armed drone made an audible beep, its top quarter of the pyramid turned electric blue and swivelled, indicating that it had synchronised itself with the Secretary's console and relayed Xankyu's message. Xankyu waited in silence, eyeing the robot for a moment, when it made another, different beep a moment later. The robot then ushered him through.

The Secretary Of Foreign Affairs was an elderly Sirian female, with over fifty standard years experience in her current role, and wearing a fuchsia-orange flowing silk robe of office, exposed at the arms entire length of both arms. She looked up from her console, doing esoteric work that was beyond even Xankyu's comprehension. Her inferno red reptilian eyes dilated, and her irises widened with the change in light. She regarded Xankyu with business-like irritation, rather than anger or annoyance.

'Ambassador Xankyu, this had better be good news. Have The Commonwealth taken offence to our decision? Speak!'

'They were surprisingly indifferent, as if they expected it, Your Excellency.'

The Secretary looked back at her console and made a Sirian equivalent of sighing. 'The humans brought this on themselves, you know!' She flared up unexpectedly. 'They made us choose loyalties, to choose sides. How could we turn our backs on our genetic cousins that we have had stable, diplomatic relations with for seventy million Standards!?'

'With respect, Your Excellency, The Draconians have increased their belligerence in the last millennia, with the Feekoozh Dynasty of the last five Empresses.'

Ciakars typically live well over two hundred Standard Years. The first Empress Feekoozh had cloned herself to produce a serial reign of tyrantesses. On the Draconian Capital Planet, simply referred to by their Imperial inhabitants as Draconia Prime - as Reptilians do not share the custom of naming planets after ancient gods - no human,

Grey or even Sirian had ever visited. Outsiders were strictly forbidden. Hence, no one but the Draconians knew what sinister plan was being brewed, or monster was being bred, or weapon was being tested. Not even their Sirian Cousins, which troubled much of the masses on Selonabus, especially Ambassador Xankyu.

Unlike their Sirian relatives, who had bothered to name a planet, the Draconians have simply given their many worlds in their Empire a number. One planet among many where *Xenotitanosaurs* were bred and farmed, for example, is simply known as Draconia-VII, or seventh planet to be inducted (or more recently, conquered) into the Empire. Another Planet, which is Terraformed in the likeness of a snapshot of Mesozoic Terra, was known as Draconia-XXI. Similarly, another planet devoted as a prehistorical snapshot, in this case the Cenozoic Period, was called Draconia-XXVI.

Needless to say, these planets, affectionately known as a "Time-Zoo" by the people of The Commonwealth, were quite an epic and ambitious project to complete. The unmanned, or rather "un-reptiled" mission to retrieve these prehistoric reptiles of Terra, took a five hundred Standard Year round-trip through Shrinkspace. The idea of sending ships, probes and robots back even further to the Paleozoic, was ridiculously expensive and too long-termed, even by Reptilian standards. Besides which, The Draconian Empire was, in a rare and unfathomable show of benevolence, good enough to build up these so called "Time-Zoos." Although fabricated long before the Feekoozh Dynasty, Draconians had, quite frankly, nothing more than disdain for non-military science. Thus, it was rumoured by Citizens of The Commonwealth, The Zeta Reticuli and Sirian Republics, and even the Annunaki Syndicate, that these planets were a covert and back-handed way to engineer biological weapons. As if the deadly pathogens, *Titanosuchids*, and indeed, the Ciakars themselves, were not enough to conjure up the proverbial Bogeyman in the hearts of those whom even considered standing in Her Imperial Majesty's way.

The Secretary's inferno eyes narrowed at Xankyu, but she could not bring herself to raise her voice in anger or reprimand the Ambassador. Presently she said in a defeated and tragic tone, 'Yes, Ambassador. The Draconians have become a concern, and between you and I, Planet Selonabus of the Sirian System cannot assume we will be immune to the wrath of The Empire, simply because we share the same common ancestor.'

Both the Sirians and Reptilians came from one species of unknown Dromeosaurid. Unknown for two reasons; because it is impossible to completely reconcile human and reptilian taxonomies, and secondly, the Draconians and Sirians simply did not bother to fastidiously catalogue their family history, and lost track of the common ancestor. The Dromeosaurid concerned, was exposed to similar evolutionary stimuli to that of primates in the late Cenozoic, thus giving rise to an erect, sapient dinosaur, unknown to human science until well after the Oil Age.

'I am not going to lie or dally with euphemisms, Your Excellency. It is only a matter of time before Selonabus will have to choose sides.' Xankyu stood at attention, opposite the Secretary's transparent desk, with his arms crossed in front of him. It was a textbook human gesture of toadieness and/or submission. Xankyu, noted recently, that his mammalian friends and acquaintances' habits were rubbing off on him. *Well.* He thought. *You are on Selonabus now. You are in the Sirian homeworld now. So it is time you started acting like a Sirian again!*

The Secretary, in response, swivelled in her seat, turning her back to the Ambassador, and rose. She musingly strolled over to the transparent wall of her office, and stood there for a while, with her back remaining visible. Xankyu stayed standing behind the desk, and stared at the Secretary's back. He too, remained silent. The Secretary was looking out beyond the transparent wall, and at the structures, traffic, and sapients outside, like an Oil Age executive glowering at the view ancient Manhattan Island from his office.

For the first time in his life, Xankyu was left without a word to say. He knew he should say something gentler, more consoling. Or at least change the subject with idle platitudes. He simply stood there dumbly, with his arms crossed at his side. The Secretary, however, seemed to take the lead. She turned after more than a standard minute and faced her subordinate. Her facial expression formed the Sirian equivalent of a smile, and her body language relaxed and became casual. Presently she said,

'You know, Ambassador, I have only met you a few times, but I can read you like a book, as your human friends like to say. And, I can tell that you are serious and devoted to your career. You are also unmated. You have no offspring, and will never will. Unless of course, you learn to be more carefree and confident, every eligible female will find you unattractive. So this is what you are going to do. You are going, on the earliest convenient Timeliner, to The Ancient Motherplanet, Terra, in the time the humans call the Oil Age. I do not care which governing entity you travel under, be it Sirian, Draconian, human or even Zeta-Reticullan, but off to the Oil Age with you.' Xankyu's body language visibly slumped, but reading between the lines, he knew the Secretary was dismissing him, and as he turned to leave, the Secretary added, 'And Xankyu,' she addressed him to emphasise the informality of his new directive.

'You are to consider that an order.'

23.

Sorjana had made an effort to incapacitate or stun, rather than kill, the *Homo sapiens* who hunted her from just outside the cell where she was recently interrogated. She stepped over the primitive humans almost too casually, shouldering a few more rifles in the process. Over a dozen lay just beyond the cell door, as one had finally unbolted it for her, the others with tear gas canisters at the ready, about to throw it in her cell. It was not an easy task, by any means, to best a dozen *Homo sapiens* single-handedly. Despite using a mix of telekinesis and high-efficiency martial arts, Sorjana had still sustained a few blows. The guards who were not too close to use their Armalites, were dealt with by Sorjana's superior brain to even the score. The other six guards, who were immediately next to the door, and within striking range, caused most of the problem. One had landed a blow at her lower back with the butt of its rifle. The other had unsheathed an even more primitive combat knife and scored a slash on Sorjana's upper right arm, but at only marginally more deep than superficial.

Presently, Sorjana knelt, placing the rifles on the ground, and frantically wrapped a makeshift bandage around her wound with a conveniently-found piece of cloth on a simple, stout bench located a few metres down the hall. It was not a tidy dressing, just looped around and tied up using her left hand and teeth. Her back throbbed, even though she was over ninety kilograms of pure, genetically enhanced Pleiadian muscle. A lesser species of human would be incapacitated with no flesh to absorb the blow; Sorjana was lucky to walk away with a stiff leg caused by a pinched nerve in her lumbar. She hastily leaned back with her hands on her buttocks and stretched, willing her traumatised lumbar to miraculously heal itself. Sorjana silently gritted her teeth and grimaced as she endured the pain. A moment or two later, she tenderly squatted down on one knee and picked up the Armalites by their straps, mothballing all but one over her shoulder once again. The one reserved for her hands and arms was pointed forward at the ready, with the safety off. She hoped she would not have to use it as she began, reluctantly, trotting off, only to increase her wounded jog as haste and adrenaline over-rid the pain.

As she trotted down the metallic hallway built by early man, she became immersed in deep thought for a moment. Abruptly, the claxons alarmed again, startling her out of her reverie. She knew this would be her last chance to escape; the Terrans would surely render her comatose until the Draconians took her away. They would not, under any circumstances, be humiliated for the third time. Sorjana hated the thought of being a trophy to those vile Reptilians. She wondered how her cousin, Pteru, could even stand to be in the same room as one, let alone befriend that Draconian Meerkah.

I can talk, She thought. *I'm about to release a Grey. And collaborate with it.* Sorjana frowned as she tried to remember where her old cell was in this ancient Labyrinth. She involuntarily began to slow, and realised it would do no good to think; she did not know this dungeon's layout in the faintest of degrees. She decided to push on and take a gamble, a guess. She increased her pace again. She had forgotten about her back pain already. As she neared a T-junction, it became surprisingly damp and chilly. When she reached the junction, she found out exactly why.

This is the main corridor, the exit from where I had to turn and go back. But I can't leave yet. I have to go back for Mishta, and whatever other Sapient is captive in here. Her head darted around for something she could use to mark a trail, as the claxons rang in her head, and began to reawaken the familiar melody that her evolved brain had caught onto recently. The cacophony was hindering her from thinking. There was nothing but the odd piece of solid trash and furniture. At an epiphany, she turned back and released the clip on her captured Armalite. She began her trot again as she dissected the magazine, dropping a five point five six millimetre full metal jacket round. Every dozen or so steps, she did the same. After five bullets were discarded, she came to her interrogation cell again. The *Homo sapiens* were still unconscious. She ransacked through them for more magazines and discarded the rifle in her hands; her hands were now too full, and she was in too much of a hurry to stop and reload it anyway. Sorjana stole away five more clips, and was on her way again, dropping a bullet regularly.

She had just emptied the first magazine when she came to a door on her left. Looking both ways to check for Terrans, Sorjana frantically tried to discern the primitive lock and door. It was surprisingly complex. Nevertheless, she had it open in just over ten standard seconds. She kicked open the door, heedless of what was behind it. It was dark inside, and now Sorjana wished she had the foresight to take a flashlight from a Terran. Her right arm darted around the corner of the cell, just beyond the doorway, dropping the now-useless magazine as she fumbled for a primitive light switch. She wasted precious seconds before she realised there was only cold metal. Whatever was inside, if it was living and not bounded to the bed, would have attacked her by now, mistaking her for a *Homo sapien* in the dim light of the corridor. She could not waste anymore time here; it was a miracle that there was not thirty Terran guards opening fire, or trying to capture her again, as it was. Sorjana was most certainly working on borrowed time now. Sorjana spun and left.

What is keeping those ugly, ape-faced men? With their low cheekbones and tiny, beady eyes?

Her head spun around as she tried to block out the insistent droning that was the ancient claxon. As before, she tried to listen for running footsteps or anxious bellows of the primates she was escaping, but everything was drowned out by it. She would have to choose a direction and hope for the best. Sorjana resumed her aching trot with surprising grace despite her back injury. As she discarded another bullet, she came close to another T-Junction, and caught a glimpse of her reflection on a one-way mirror. Her Terran costume was dirty and tattered, as expected. Her body had only a few other cuts and bruises visible, and despite being depraved of nutrition, she was still in her prime; toned and firm muscles, yet still retaining her feminine curves. Sorjana had no more time to assess her physical integrity in the one-way mirror. The prehistoric humans should be on her by now. Sorjana thought it must be too good to be true as she turned to her right and away from the mirror.

The one way mirror! Did my cell not have one, so the Terrans could spy on me? And Mishta? If that is my cell, then the door should be opposite or adjacent to the mirror.

Sorjana leaned in and tried to make out Mishta inside. This room, as well was too dark to see inside. She squinted her eyes for another second, and continued on, looking for the door.

It was almost another minute before she found another door. *Not making good time here. I should have to turn back any minute, and escape without Mishta and any others held captive in here.*

Again, she unbolted the door with new, once-practised efficiency. She had it open in less than five seconds now. With all her might, she violently shoved it open to despatch any *Homo sapien* guard that could indeed, potentially be waiting to ambush her. It was dark inside, but not as dark as the previous room. As sorjana regained her balance, her ultraviolet-spectrum eyes widened to frantically let more light in. Once more, she held the Armalite with one arm and fumbled for a Terran-style light switch. Again, she felt nothing except cold, metal and concrete. This facility that the ancient humans built was unlike typical contemporary dwellings. The lights must have either a primitive form of automation, or are remotely switched on via some distant control room. Sorjana thought it must be the latter as her ultraviolet large Pleiadian eyes slowly adjusted to the dim light.

She saw only movement at first. Then, a second later, her eyes vaguely discerned a humanoid shape. It was getting larger. Whatever it was, it had seen and was definitely stalking her. Sorjana's heart was now racing. She took a step back like a cornered animal. She had never known terror like this before. By the way the shape moved, it was clear that it could see her quite well, with her only barely tracking it. There could be more. Sojana inched herself back another step. She lifted her Armalite at the shadow.

'Pleiadian?' A whiny accented telepathic voice intruded inside her head, now familiar. 'Is that you? I do not recall your name.'

'Mishta! Come! I'm getting you out of this shithole! Hurry up!' That outburst, mixed with Oil Age slang, surprised even Sorjana. It was high time she returned to a more civilised time, two hundred and thirty thousand standard years from now. For some reason, Sorjana's thoughts wandered off, for a fraction of a second, to her sister on Modern Erra, the wedding she had attended with Obron Altemeus and her parents. Her father, leader of the Pleiadian Conservative Party, her mother, a retired executive in Shrinktime Enterprises. Had her family lived two hundred and thirty thousand years before, they would have been a poster-family of the very ancient Republican Party, The Elephant Tribe, the epitome of capitalism. On Modern Erra however, as on most Commonwealth worlds, conservative political parties remained an unpopular minority. Her family was barely more than nobodies. She remembered, in her youth, being in the shadows of the offspring of the dominant socialist parties, at functions, academies and other myriad jubilees. As a child, her classmates at her academy did not even know her father was a politician. Sorjana shook her head slightly, as if to shake herself out of her woolgathering.

Presently, a Tall Grey from Planet Serpo in the Zeta Reticuli system emerged silently from the shadows, and moulded into the light. Its large black eyes stared Sorjana in her eyes. It had merely two nostrils for a nose that did not protrude. Its tiny mouth puckered, giving the hom-inid-cetacean hybrid created long ago an almost cute, innocent, hush-puppy expression. Had the overlarge head of the thing not been amusingly out of proportion to its body, which wore a one-piece black jumpsuit, like every Grey she had ever encountered. This jumpsuit was also soiled and torn. Sorjana, however, could not tell what the creature was thinking by facial expression alone. It remained neutral, implacable.

'Can you operate a Terran's weapon?' She asked hastily, unshouldering a mothballed assault rifle and handing it to Mishta without waiting for an affirmation.

'No.' it said. 'The thing is heavy and clumsy. And my hand muscles are not conditioned to operate the trigger.' Sorjana reached over and disabled the safety mechanism for Mishta. It made a *click*, barely audible over the persistent claxon. Sorjana and Mishta were telepathically shouting in unison at each other, a primal habit deep in their Terranic Genes to talk over loud noises.

'Just do the best you can, maybe pull the trigger with your entire hand. With a bit of luck, you won't have to use it, regardless. I'm Sorjana, if you recall, by the way.'

'Very Well. Let us leave. There are no other Serponians here, in this Terran penitentiary complex. You and I are the only fully sapient species here.'

'Yes. Well. Good,' Sorjana continued to shout over the claxon. 'The Terrans aren't here yet. They have likely staged an ambush. Do not underestimate them. They are surprisingly cunning for a lesser animal.' At that, Sorjana's head darted around, searching for *Homo sapiens*. 'Now let's make like a banana, and leave, as the locals on this planet would say.' Sorjana the Nordic smiled for the first time at Mishta the Grey, both as a show of kindness and newfound friendship, and also because she realised she had got the expression wrong.

24.

'Master Tjeons, have you not been paying attention?' Pteru said in a telepathic tone that was vaguely betraying his frustration, but cool and even nonetheless. 'It is absolutely imperative to enter Shrinkspace with Sentinels, exactly which kind is beside the point. Why? Because when an object of any kind exceeds the speed of light, they also exceed the speed of reality. It exceeds the speed of chemical reaction. It exceeds the rate in which energy is converted to one form to another. It exceeds the speed of science, exceeds the speed of time itself. Therefore, it is a paradox to exceed the speed of light. Virtually every scientific principle is governed by this fundamental principal.' Pteru lectured, his voice calming as he entered a trance of science.

'But hypothetically, *if* we could provide enough energy,' Skyler insisted, 'For a spacecraft of any kind to perform *faster-than-light* travel, without entering Shrinkspace, what would happen to you?'

Pteru sighed with his telepathy, and closed his eyes. After a moment of silence, he opened his eyes and said,

'Theoretically, you would die of thirst in a few standard seconds. You would, at first be frozen in a kind of suspended animation, because time is now exceeding the speed of reality. Body chemistry would effectively cease. Your teeth would decay and fall out in less than a minute, and you would be an old man in less than five. But then again, come to think of it, nothing would happen, because you are exceeding the speed of entropy. Radioactive half-life of matter simply would not happen. You would therefore die instantly, because your cells cannot function, could not produce ATP with their mitochondria. They would effectively be snap frozen in the "breach-of-speed-of-reality" and therefore become a paradox of existence. In other words, you would either disappear completely, or die before your brain had time to process any pain. Either way, it would be a quick death. Your spacecraft would be destroyed also, or would vanish from existence as well.' Pteru presently shook his head. 'This conversation is getting beyond even my comprehension.'

Magne, who had been quiet all morning until now, asked, 'But what about the fact that time-faring starships and beamships travel, through Shrinkspace, about one lightyear per sixty or so standard seconds? That equates to...........' Magne crunched some numbers on her Holotab conveniently located on her desk without Pteru even noticing, 'Roughly five hundred and twenty thousand times the speed of light. Would not that freeze reality to a factor of five hundred thousand or so more than what you have just described, Master Hoolde?' Magne had been thinking about her "date" with Skyler on the previous weekend. Now, roughly the equivalent of a fifteen year old *Homo sapien* that was the ancestors of all species of modern humans, Magne had only been thinking about boy Pleiadians in the last six standard months or so. If it was indeed a date, it would be her first, despite having hair and eyes that made her exotic to the Pleiadian male. Only about one twelfth of Pleiadians did not have blonde hair or blue eyes; evolution had considered that an advantage in the cool planets of Erra and Ptah, Terraformed in the likeness of ancient Scandinavia. Any other eye or hair colour would have been obviously, manifestations of recessive genes.

'True, Magne. But do not forget, the anti-matter produced from Arcturium nullifies only time, and not space. It effectively separates the two, which are, typically, synonymous.' Pteru ran a hand through his long Pleiadian blonde hair, which he wore loose for a change. The Chronophysics guru presently returned to his beloved, signature whiteboard and scrawled some esoteric equations that looked the lovechild of algebra and calculus. It took him well over a standard minute to complete it. It nearly occupied the entire whiteboard, which rocked back and forth on his plastic castors as he wrote. Magne wondered if Pteru had not stolen his precious whiteboard from an Oil Age Terran and carried it with him to the present day on a Timeliner. She had lain awake after her date, not just thinking about Skyler, but what he said about the prehistoric *Homo sapiens* of the Oil Age.

As if reading her mind, Pteru said, 'Now, as you may

know, tomorrow is the day of the final exam on your internship, but please, if you could fill out this anonymous survey first,' Pteru handed the adolescents a sheet of primitive paper each, 'both of you can get more practice in the simulator first, followed by any final questions you have of Chronophysics. But first you have to memorise this formula and know how to solve it as if it were two plus two.'

Skyler, and even Magne's large eyes widened even larger, complimented by a moan from Skyler and a gasp from Magne. It was a cold morning, and had an unusual low amount of humidity. The training room was cold inside as well, with no heating of any kind, and Magne shivered even more with the momentous task. Her chair felt even colder, as did Skyler's. After a few moments silence, however, Pteru's expression lightened. He grinned mischievously, as if no longer able to suppress a smile, and said, 'I am only joking. The day after the test, I am leaving for Selonabus for a standard week or two, and then off to Oil Age Terra. You two do not have to return to the academy for over two standard weeks, so both of you are welcome to come along if you wish.' Skyler stirred and said, 'Does that mean we *don't* have to learn that formula on the whiteboard after all?'

'Not at all. I don't even think it has anything to do with Chronophysics. I just made it up. It is probably not even solvable. In any case, all the complicated mathematics and calculations, and everything else Prehistoric Terrans colloquially called *"rocket science"*, is performed using computers and other automata. Your job is to do the thing AI is not capable of, and hopefully never will be, lest I will be out of a job. Like knowing when to launch the Sentinels, and guiding it into the indigo triangle and into Shrinkspace, as well as other things like watching out for those damnable Anunaki.'

What are the Annunaki?' Asked Magne presently.

'Space-time pirates essentially. At least that is all a Timeliner pilot needs to know. They steal Sentinels so they can go back to prehistoric Terra, thousands of years earlier than even the Oil Age.'

'Why do they go back to that time?' Magne pressed.

'No one in the Commonwealth knows for sure, but think it has something to do with the previously-valuable metal of gold, now scarce but not entirely valuable on Terraformed planets. They have been thought to have enslaved early man, convincing them they were vengeful deities and had them mine gold and build them monuments. But I am digressing now.'

Magne said, 'Well I will have to pack and terminate my billeting a day early, but I can manage. I'm in, Master Pteru!'

'Well as long as I don't have to learn that damnable equation for the exam, I can get time off from my father at the family workshop. I'm over Biobrids at the moment anyway, and haven't had a vacation like father promised anyway. It will be good to get offworld. I am also in, Master Hoolde.'

Pteru nodded and smiled in affirmation, and resumed the class with a renewed haste, knowing that his two young interns had an insatiable passion for time travel indeed.

* * *

Magne passed the final exam the following day with flying colours, as can be expected. Skyler, however, passed with an above average score, which surprised all three Pleiadians. Magne only needed a cursory swatting of her internship; Skyler was up half the night in his room that was the basement of the Tjeon family residence, adjacent to the family workshop, and practically attached. The Tjeon patriarch was, unsurprisingly, disappointed and surprised by Skyler's decision to work in the Timeliner industry, rather than follow in his father's footsteps like his elder brother, Dannery, had. Not that Skyler would have spent the rest of his life being Dannery's subordinate. Is it any wonder that Skyler had gotten into the counter-culture of prehistoric Terra? And had wanted to travel through time and be with that counter-culture, when his elder brother had dominated and occasionally, bullied him? Of course Skyler would become a Timeliner pilot! He would do whatever it took, no matter how irrelevant or hard it was. He had learned that indomitable, unbreakable spirit from ancient punk rock, which Magne now found so appealing in him. She had never known a Pleiadian boy quite like him. Most on Erra were far-left conformists overly devoted to benevolence, altruism and empathy. These were the Holy Trinity of Pleiadian philosophy.

That god (no capitalisation because there is no deification of pronouns in modern times) is an abstract thing, manifesting itself in kindness, love and unselfishness. Unlike the ancient Terrans who believed God was a giant man with a beard who lived in the sky and created man, Pleiadians, and many other species of human, believed the direct opposite. That an instinct, a force, that compelled humans to act with kindness, whilst their body produced endorphins when they bestowed or witnessed said kindness. This instinct can be strictly and semantically labelled "god." God did not create man, man created god the instant an ape-like ancestor even more prehistoric than *Homo sapiens*, felt compelled to help an injured or sick specimen, or nurse it back to life and feed it while it recovered. It was long thought by anthropologists that *Homo erectus* was the first hominid capable of benevolence and altruism, and god, therefore, was the abstract manifestation created sometime back then.

But Skyler was different, Magne had realised. Though still kind and capable of considering others, he was also a free thinker, a free spirit. Magne felt in her heart a growing fondness for the Ptahian boy. He was a rebel and a gentleman at the same time. Though not the best looking boy she had laid her purple eyes on, he nevertheless had good genes like every designer human of the Commonwealth. What set him apart from the rest of the mass produced supermen was his free spirit, which Magne was finding more and more irresistible about him.

'Congratulations,' Pteru finally said after many painful minutes of silence as the interns waited patiently for him to mark their exams. 'Both of you have passed, with pleasing results. If you both wish it, Shrinktime enterprises will be more than happy to accept both of you as potential Timeliner pilots when you graduate from your academies. But do not, by any means, feel obligated to accept Shrinktime's offer. You both still have two Standard Years before you graduate. Now, on another note, my offer still stands; I will be leaving Ptah for Selonabus tomorrow, and both of you are welcome to come along. My personal Beamship,' Pteru nodded outside where all the myriad starships were being docked, 'will be leaving here first thing tomorrow. Be here at dawn, and pack light. Planet Selonabus is borderline-bearable for humans in its humidity.'

Pteru looked across the room, where his two interns were clearly close to each other now, manifested in the way they sat close to each other, and coyly, awkwardly, tried to mask it with huddling for body heat on another cold morning on Ptah. A moment later, they both called out in unison, with their telepathy, 'We are both still coming, Master Hoolde.'

The rest of the day passed without any significant events. Pteru answered any final questions they had on Chronophysics, Timeliners and time travel, and unwound the day by throwing a jubilant luncheon for his two interns about one standard hour past midday. Magne offered to help clean up the two platters of sandwiches, sushi and other processed, easy to digest food. Pteru, however replied, 'You two have to be up early tomorrow. I advise you go start packing, and then unwind. Make sure you get your full four standard hours sleep that your body needs. You two are dismissed. I will see the both of you outside this training room at dawn, with your bags all packed. From there I will take you up to tomorrow's Timeliner on my Beamship. But today, I must go too. I also have a lot of packing and loose ends that need tying up.

Skyler and his new found female companion, Magne, were waiting outside the training room, as promised, over a quarter of a standard hour before the star Electra was even considering rising up over the eastern horizon. The two adolescents took advantage of the freezing, early winter morning by huddling close together. They had both dropped their primitive duffle bags and had embraced to conserve body heat. As Pteru arrived at his training room just as Electra was rising, he saw his two former-interns' icy breaths, with steam shooting out alternately and in synchronisation, before he saw their faces.

'Good Morning, you two.' Pteru said in a cheerful tone of telepathy that would otherwise irritate most people on this frigid morning. The two youngsters telepathically grunted in reply, as if disagreeing. 'Now,' Pteru scolded. 'I understand you two may be practising your languages of the Oil Age, in preparation of one day travelling there, but I do not understand the grunts of early man. Now let us have a "good morning" in response, if you will.'

''Good morning, Master Hoolde,' the two adolescents said in unison. The enthusiasm was clearly laboured in their telepathies.

'Oh no. You are no longer my interns, officially anyway. You two can call me Pteru from now on. You are, after all, fellow Chronophysicists now.'

Skyler and Magne picked up their duffle bags and followed their former tutor. Pteru had immediately begun a beeline for his personal Beamship as soon as he had affirmed that Magne and Skyler were following him. It was roughly a kilometre to where all the starships were resting, on a concrete pad waiting across a neatly-manicured meadow. At this distance, they were tiny, just silver specs reflecting of the half circle of Electra. As Pteru, Magne and Skyler crossed the meadow, they made snow prints with their boots in the genetically modified Kikuyu grass covered in frozen dew. Pteru could have chosen the long way, via the designated concrete walkways, the two adolescents realised as their former master lead the way across the meadow with his leather duffle bag slung over his shoulder, bouncing from side to side as he walked. Electra was now blinding them as they walked directly towards the star. Only their frosty breaths could be discerned now.

The etymology of Beamship is widely unknown, but most experts have agreed on two theories; firstly they are named after their primary role of "beaming" personnel up beyond the stratosphere of a planet, ferrying passengers onto an awaiting 'Liner beyond the planet's gravitational pull. The second theory was more esoteric; that the original Draconian design emitted beams of light for propulsion, and the name hence, had stuck. Pteru knew the latter made no sense; light itself was very weak, and rays of light could never provide enough energy or power to propel a starship to incredible speeds. That could only be achieved through anti-matter propulsion.

At last, the three Nordics came to where the saucer shaped starships were being stored. To a prehistoric *Homo sapien*, the design was synonymous with what they called UFO's and alien spacecraft responsible for Grey abductions. To a modern human, however, they were merely mundane spacecraft, their saucer shape being more practicable in space than the prehistoric, bird-like design. Pteru's Beamship was nearly the furthest away. After about seven standard minutes marching across the meadow, and on hard, cold asphalt that stung their cold, frozen soles of their feet, they strode past many Beamships and scouts, all cradled upon their tripods. Pteru's Beamship was nondescript, indistinguishable. Magne wondered how he even knew this was his. All were essentially the same; Draconium-titanium alloy, wet with now thawing-out-frozen-dew. They all glinted and glistened in Electra's sunlight, blinding them as they carried their now-heavy duffle packs. At last Pteru came to a halt, then made a beeline to his right, to the nearest Beamship.

Pteru opened the semi-automated hatch, and climbed on board, up the fallen door that doubled as a flight of stairs. 'Place your luggage in here,' Pteru gestured to a compartment at one end of the starship as Magne and Skyler squinted in the dim light of the dormant space-craft. It was perhaps six or seven metres across in a round interior, and two metres of it was the anti-matter drive that obstructed the centre. Presently Pteru activated the lighting, and luminescent blue-purple ultraviolet lights awoke at his command by the Beamship's automata. There were two rows of ivory-coloured chairs among an ivory interior. The chairs had jet-black harnesses, which looked out of place compared to the ivory and ultraviolet blue-purple decor. The chairs were arranged in a double semi-circle around the propulsion system. The other half of the semi-circle was devoted to pilots' quarters and cupboards for luggage. That was where Pteru, Magne and Skyler were now, unburdening themselves of their packs. Pteru closed the lifting door suspended on pneumatic struts when all the duffle bags were packed in.

'Beamships are typically designed to ferry passengers into outer space, and to rendezvous with an awaiting Timeliner. That is why there are so many empty chairs here. But please, go ahead and choose one, and strap yourselves in. I will be at the pilots console.' Pteru presently placed himself on the pilot's throne and fastened his harness. The others chose their seats (side by side, of course) and did the same. Pteru listened behind him to ascertain his passengers were indeed buckling up, whilst simultaneously firing up the Arcturium engines. They were whisper-quiet, and only needed a few moments to be ready to get the Beamship airborne. After an audible sound from the console, and after double-checking instruments, Pteru pulled back on the control wheel, slow at first then hard. The "flying saucer" was only barely making any noise as it lifted off vertically. It climbed at a mundane rate for a few hundred metres, and Pteru looked around, as if double-checking the world outside. He then jerked the control wheel backwards, at full throttle.

The Beamship accelerated dramatically, and they all found themselves thrust into their seats with the rapid increase of gravitational force. On cue, the ship's automata oscillated their seats backwards, so that a human would not black out and eventually die. All the while, the Arcturium anti-matter propulsion system only faintly laboured, and grew louder. Magne did not know how fast they were travelling, but it was at *least* one hundred kilometres a second, and doubling every moment. She caught glimpses of the sky, and it turned from blue with the occasional tuft of white cloud, to a darker blue, a purple-blue, and finally a deep purple, all in a matter of half a standard minute.

Finally, the chairs pivoted upright once again, and Magne saw only night sky out the window, as the Beamship slowed in its acceleration and the gravitational force was reversed. The anti-matter engine barely became quieter, as all chairs were now upright, and Pteru had annexed the Beamship's controls once again. They were still rising now, but at a more civilised rate of climb. Magne looked out the window at the beautific night sky that was space, the Milky Way galaxy. She had done this before, recently, when she commuted to Ptah for her internship. Skyler however, did not fare so well. This was his first time off world, and it was far from mundane. He clenched the armrests of his seat, his hands becoming eagle's talons.

'Keep your harnesses fastened until I say you can get out of you seats,' Pteru ordered with his telepathy cast over his shoulder, whilst simultaneously and deftly operating the Beamships' controls.

'Where are we going?' Skyler asked, whilst scraping himself off his chair, his nerves calming, his heart rate returning to normal. Pteru pointed out a viewing port to their right. Magne and Skyler had to stoop and crane their necks to look upwards and out of the viewing port, but when they finally saw it, an elegant, cigar-shaped starship, the same ivory colour as the Beamship's interior, could be seen. It was evidently far away, but Magne and Skyler could tell it was incredibly large, the size of an average Commoncity.

'Get a good look Magne and Skyler. You too, could be piloting one of those in a few years.' Magne and Skyler stared at the 'Liner, so luminescent white, it nearly blinded them, and drowned out the light from the surrounding stars.

'Why is it so big?' Skyler ventured feebly.

'Time travel is incredibly costly, as you can imagine. A starship large enough to carry a few hundred thousand passengers and thousands of standard tonnes of cargo, is the only way to make it economically viable.' By now the Timeliner loomed ahead, and could be seen clearly out of the port, without ducking one's head. They were close enough that it monopolised the entire viewing port, and was growing larger by the second. Pteru, Magne and Skyler all travelled in silence, as the Timeliner grew in size. Within five standard minutes, they were within the cavernous hold of the 'Liner. Pteru was expertly operating the controls, and managed to dock his Beamship among many others in the Commonwealth, their Draconium hulls dormant, like resting horses in a prehistoric Terran stable.

25.

The Annunaki raid on the Timeliner had gone from bad to worse. Two more waves of hostages were executed before the Arcturian Navy and Marines had finally caved in. The Hyadean Commonwealth were in the process of mustering up the demanded ransom. Solemn-silence ensued on both sides. The Annunaki were silent, because they were growing increasingly nervous and impatient. The Commonwealth were twice as solemn merely because of all the human lives that were terminated, and the prospect of even more.

Claudia vam Rees was taken aboard in exchange for fifty civilians. She now saw this ugly Arcturian traitor in the flesh, and up close. The beast's body odour was borderline on the bearable. Even though he also communicated primarily with telepathy, the Annunaki Lieutenant's breath was no more pleasant.

'What is taking so damn long, Vegan?' The sociopath demanded inside her head.

'Patience, now. It has only been six standard hours. The Commonwealth cruiser that is gathering your precious ransom is not travelling through Shrinkspace, as it is not practical with only having to travel about two dozen or so astronomical units. That alone will take a standard day. The Sentinels are on their way as we speak, along with the freighter carrying them.'

'They should have gone through Shrinkspace! They would be here by now!'

'What, and have three less for the Annunaki's treasury?' vam Rees sneered at the Arcturian defiantly. 'You and your band have cleaned the Hyadean system out, remember?'

'Shut up! Just make sure they get here as soon as possible. I want my three hundred sentinels, and I want it without any screw ups, for once! Think you and your snooty Commonwealth can handle that?!'

Of course,' vam Rees countered. 'Just make sure you and your pieces of cockroach-shit band of pirates keeps up their end of the bargain.'

'Here now! You mind your proverbial telepathic tongue if you knew what helps ya!'

'Or what, Sociopath? What are you planning on doing with those Sentinels anyway? Go back through time and kill my ancient ancestors? You can just forget it, *sub-human*, The Draconian Empire has beat you and your sorry mistake of an army to it, I will have you know.'

'Humph.' Murphy telepathically sneered. 'If it is *really* that important that you know what business we Annunaki have with your Sentinels, it is this; we are off to prehistoric Terra. And not the Oil Age where all the action is. No. We are going further back. Think big. Bigger than your pitiful

Cold War with the Empire. Think of a time where *even* the prehistoric Terrans who drove dirty groundcars and flew rudimentary aircraft, would have called ancient. I'm thinking the Bronze Age, or maybe late Stone Age. There, we will change history. We will make slaves of the *Homo sapiens*. We will make them build massive monuments in out honour. We will make them mine gold for us. We will be worshiped as gods.' Murphy spread his arms out at conclusion of the Annunaki's grand master plan.

At that, vam Rees cocked a skeptic eyebrow at her Arcturian adversary. 'Gold, you say? It's borderline more valuable than titanium in these modern times. Rare, yes. Hard to find, absolutely. But valuable? Only to those who make jewellery on behalf of those who still celebrate pagan rituals like Christian marriages. That counts out practically every Modern Human. You might get lucky with a few lovestruck *Pan sapiens*, better known as Terran Simians, or Bonozees. And I don't think you would see any Neo-Terriers dressed in bridegroom garb, either. They are semi-sentient pack animals, and certainly not monogamous sapiens. Face it, Annunaki. Your plan is worse than futile. You took a wager and you lost. Can you do that, sociopath, without sulking like a child?'

Canis erectus, or Neo Terriers, are the descendants of domesticated dogs of prehistoric Terra. Resembling a lovechild of a dingo and kangaroo with a swollen cranial capacity, they have grown intelligent over the past two hundred and thirty millennia, through a diet of processed meats. Processed meats that ancient peoples have fed their dogs, consequently, are high in protein and easy to digest.

The perfect recipe of evolutionary brain and intelligence growth. Though not fully upright, they are nevertheless bipedal, with powerful hind legs that carried them like an ostrich. Their forearms have shortened and have became more flexible, with their front paws developed into two toes that can grasp objects in a pincer-like manner.

Pan Sapien, is an example of semi convergent artificial evolution; their ancestors were a crossbreed of a bonobo and a chimpanzee, hence their common name. Early man had adopted them under their wing after deforestation had compelled them to walk upright. They were taught to make and control fire, rudimentary technology such as the bow and arrow and spear, make stone tools and shelter. Prehistoric *Homo sapiens* had given these simians an evolutionary hand-up, for reasons known only to them. Perhaps it was guilt. Perhaps they merely wanted to find out if ape could evolve into a man-like creature, given time and evolutionary pressures. Or perhaps it was just because *Homo sapiens* needed to civilise them. Regardless, they got their wish. *Pan sapiens* was now an almost upright, bipedal creature, like that of *Homo erectus*. Today, in modern times, they were regarded as citizens of the Commonwealth, having the same rights and responsibilities, and treated with love and respect by their *Homo crononaughtilus/Homo cras* cousins, as they both dwell and coexist on all Commonwealth worlds.

Rion Murphy merely turned his back on vam Rees and said in a venomously quiet telepathic tone, 'You know, in prehistoric times, the ancient Mafioso would have had you tongue cut out for your cheek and backchat.

Nowadays, not only is the tongue a redundant organ for communication, but we are far more civilised than that. But that doesn't mean I will tolerate you insolence, Vegan.' He turned his head to the right and nodded toward a Repillian Enforcer. A moment later, and the body of a Lyran civilian could be heard or seen slumping and hitting the ground with a sickening *thud*. It reminded vam Rees of a raw steak being carelessly dropped on the ground in an ancient kitchen.

'Like I said,' Murphy continued. 'More civilised.' He gestured to the executed hostage and casually strolled off, as if he merely needed to use the bathroom. Claudia vam Rees could only glower at the hapless Lyran, whose spinal chord at the base of her skull was pierced by a Draconians' talon. Murphy had been right. It was a clean, quick death, with very little blood. About as civilised as the Annunaki got.

26.

Sorjana The Nordic and Mishta the Grey squinted in the daylight of Terra for the first time in days. For Mishta, it was months. It burned as delicate, grey, cetan skin instantaneously.

'The star of Terra is excruciating,' Mishta informed Sorjana. ' We need to commandeer a groundcar. I can last about ten Standard Minutes out here, no more.'

'Just a moment,' Sorjana took her time in adjusting to the mid afternoon sun with her ultraviolet eyes. She frantically scanned the immediate area, knowing the Terrans were not too far behind. It was fifteen standard seconds before Sorjana made an assessment of the alien compound and compiled a calculation where a groundcar was likely to be. She had been right in her assumption; she and Mishta were indeed somewhere in the desert. Mesas could be discerned in the background some five kilometres away and surrounding the entire area, evidently aiding the secrecy of the prison. At an epiphany, she slid the manhole cover that she and Mishta emerged from shut. 'Wait here,' she ordered, and sprinted off toward the nearest Terran Groundcar. She recognised the design; a Chevrolet Impala about two decades old in the current time of Oil Age Terra. It was an ugly beast made elegant, with fins, and used to have, once upon a time a red coat of paint, now faded into brown. Sorjana, however lacked the time or enthusiasm to behold the Stone Age automobile. Sorjana was at the door and opening it in ten seconds. The door did not open, and Sorjana knew that the *Homo sapien* that owned this thing had wisely locked the door. She unhesitatingly skipped back and booted a foot through the window. As she had been trained, and her back now almost much better, she reached in and unlocked and opened the primitive door from the inside. Sorjana ignored the cubic shards of glass as she dived into the driver's seat, and tossed her gathered assault rifles on the passenger's seat.

She knew how to operate these things, and that they required a metallic key to start. Of course there was none, so she had to resort to breaking open the trim with the butt of her *Armalite*. It was well built and sturdy; Sorjana had only just managed to crack it open and expose the wiring, when she heard shouting and gunfire from behind. The rear window shattered, losing cube-shaped glass all over the back seat. Sorjana turned around and saw a greasy, corpulent *Homo sapien* male armed with an unsophisticated shotgun. It had emerged from behind an old caravan some twenty metres away, and obviously its dwelling. It took another swill of a potent alcoholic beverage and staggered closer, shouting incoherently in drunken English. Sorjana did not recognise what it was saying. She grabbed the comparatively efficient assault rifle and ducked, just as the *Homo sapien* fired again. It missed completely, about a metre and a half to the side of the driver's door, but spraying gravel and shrapnel unpredictably in every direction, nonetheless. Sorjana did not hesitate to return fire as the Terran staggered closer. Her rifle bullets missed it too, as if in warning, but it staggered closer and prepared to fire again. Sorjana aimed this time at the Early Man's torso and fired a few automatic rounds; it would not sire beneficial offspring, and she had wasted enough time regardless. The *Homo sapien* soldiers were on their way. She heard Mishta shout out to her in its telepathy, saying that it can hear shouting from underground. The Terran soldiers were climbing up a runged ladder toward the manhole. She did not even bother to check whether the drunken peasant was alive or dead, she only cared that it will not bother her again.

Sorjana expertly ripped the wires and hotwired the thing with her evolved brute-strength, hoping it was not too late. The ancient groundcar roared to life as she twisted the wires together, and took a cursory observation of its controls and its operation. That would be the only time that the rudimentary combustion engine would be permitted to warm up. She slammed the column shift into first gear – Sorjana now knew it was a four-speed manual and exaggerated the engine revolutions as she tenderly took her foot off the clutch, careful not to stall the Impala. It lurched forward at her command and she had it revving high at thirty kilometres per hour in seconds. It was surprisingly punchy, but nothing compared to even the cheapest, most underpowered Biobrid.

Sorjana did not bother to change gear as she neared the manhole and planted her foot on the middle pedal, Mishta the Grey was still there, standing on it whilst rocking up and down and to the side, trying to weigh it down. It bent its knees as it tried to balance. The manhole was now roughly ten metres away, and the *Homo sapiens* were now clearly just beneath it, trying to get it open. Mishta could not hold them off for long; its body mass would be pushing forty Standard Kilograms, and the steel manhole lid only weighed about ten. It would be only a moment or two until the Terran Soldiers overpowered the puny, unarmed, Grey. Mishta looked up in time to see the rugged old Impala skidding to a halt only metres away. The Grey dived to the side, aided by the lift of the *Homo sapiens*' arms. Immediately, the lid was tossed open, and a monkey-like arm emerged and tossed an *Armalite* from up underground, which was the last thing Sorjana could see as the Impala came to a halt over the manhole. A sickening thud could be heard as she realised, regrettably, that the Terran was now hit in the head with a fifteen-hundred-Standard-Kilogram groundcar at ten kilometres per hour.

'Get in the back seat, Mishta!' Sorjana barked telepathically out the Impala's passenger window. She knew there was no time to move the half dozen Armalites, and besides, Mishta could more easily provide covering fire from there. She reloaded a clip in her assault rifle as Mishta trotted over to the nearest rear door. The Grey stood there dumbly for a second or two, and Sorjana realised he did not know how to open a Terran ground-car's door. Ignoring the remnant pain in her back, she leaned over and opened it for the Grey.

'Get in, quicksmart!' She ordered with her telepathy. 'Doesn't matter how, sit, dive, I don't care. Just get in!' Sorjana barked as Mishta hesitated. It would only be a matter of time before it occurred to the wily *Homo sapiens* to shove the unconscious or dead soldier aside and open fire. That would be the last thing she needed; Terran groundcars are vulnerable from underneath, and she would have to abandon this one and find another if even only a few rifle rounds were discharged by the primitives underneath. Mishta, however, elected to haphazardly dive in and ignore the glass a moment later. Sorjana, unhesitatingly, exaggerated the throttle and released the clutch pedal with upmost care; stalling now would be disastrous. At her unorthodox command, the Impala's rear wheels spun for a second on the desert's surface, but miraculously found purchase and darted forward like the startled animal of prehistoric Terra from which it was named after.

As was expected, the Terran soldiers opened fire from below, but just as the groundcar was clear of the manhole, the bullets discharging uselessly into the sky. Sorjana grabbed an Armalite and handed it to the Grey, who ignored the rear door flapping uselessly open.

'Use this to return fire.'

'But no one is firing at us,' retorted the grey. Sorjana pumped the clutch pedal and selected second gear. It was a foreign procedure; Biobrids did not have transmissions, as expected. Sorjana found it easier to change gear now, even though it was over five standard years since the last time she actually drove *anything*, it was nevertheless coming back to her quickly. She felt the prehistoric groundcar pull back as she released the clutch clumsily, its revolutions dropping. At that moment, a flotilla of full metal jacket bullets hit the rear of the Impala, and both the Nordic and the Grey ducked reflexively.

'They are now!' She screeched with her telepathy. Inside the Impala's side mirrors, a *Homo sapien* could be discerned half out of the manhole, about fifty metres away, aiming an assault rifle. It reminded Sorjana of an ancient cartoon gopher with a bazooka she had once seen on Terra. It unleashed another flurry of bullets, and one even pierced the passenger's seat. Both Sorjana and Mishta were hunched over, taking cover, and hoping for the best. They were fortunate these early Oil Age groundcars were covered in a thick shell of steel, which halted the fury of the bullets (unlike groundcars of the mid-to-late Oil Age, which were primarily plastic and fibreglass).

'Now would be a good time, Mishta!' Sorjana advised. The Terran had stopped firing and was now climbing out of the manhole, obviously to permit more soldiers through. No sign of the soldier that was hit; Sorjana assumed he was just below and would be dragged out eventually. That hindered the *Homo sapiens* enough to for her and Mishta get away. The Grey did return fire, clumsily, but it was enough too stall the Terrans another ten seconds or so as they remained in the manhole, taking cover. The first

Terran took cover as it reloaded its *Armalite*. Sorjana looked in the groundcars' mirror once more as she changed up to third gear. By this time they were over two hundred metres away, and the manhole was now a speck in the distance. Humanoid figures were tiny as they heaved out of the manhole frantically, one at a time, and took aim in succession. This time however, the majority of them missed completely, as Sorjana the Nordic and Mishta the grey were leaving the effective range of the Terrans' weapons. They were well over four hundred metres away by the time a few soldiers got themselves organised and took aim. The groundcar would have looked the size of a child's toy groundcar by now.

'Don't bother returning fire, Mishta,' Sorjana cheered. 'We are free. There's no way they can catch us now.' The Impala was now travelling eighty kilometres an hour when she checked the speedometer (it actually read fifty miles an hour, and not many Modern Humans could fathom the Imperial measurement system), which was the most that Sorjana dared to travel offroad in this primitive groundcar. It was surprisingly smooth on this gravel road, and Sorjana shifted into fourth. Neither of them had any money on them, and the Impala had barely half a tank of fuel. She remembered that these things used less fuel if the revolutions per minute were kept low. The groundcar cruised at the most efficient speed it could now. Sorjana gunned the middle pedal tentatively, slowing the beast as they were approaching a corner. Sorjana dropped to third and released the clutch only just in time. She had no idea how this thing would handle, so she took the corner at thirty miles per hour. Mishta finally chose this time to slam the door shut. The Impala handled surprisingly well.

Sorjana took the time to survey the landscape as she accelerated and shifted up to fourth. The Mesas were growing, encroaching, but she assumed if she followed this road, they would be out of this desert basin. Hardy shrubs and the occasional cacti were the only vegetation here. There was no sign of civilization except the caravan and manhole about a kilometre behind them, and another approaching groundcar and its plume of dust about a kilometre ahead.

'Keep your head down, Mishta,' Sorjana warned. 'I have the exclusive fortune of blending-in on this planet, as you can imagine.'

27.

Darius lay in the rustic cot of the Ferrari residence. *Lieutenant Ferrari*, Darius reminded himself. *Or, rather, former Lieutenant of the Commonwealth's military*, he thought sadly. *Still, I have only myself to blame. I shouldn't have taken on that Ciakar. I should have waited for help. If only I had. I would still be with my 'Real' family. With my 'Real' species. I don't belong here. On this Planet. With these people. How can one pledge allegiance to an entity that does not accept them as one of their own? To do otherwise is simply, a paradox.*

Darius knew he could not indulge in self-pity much longer. It had been two standard hours since he woke, and now he needed to urinate. Tau Cetans had, for reasons still unknown to Modern Science, weak bladders. And he could not hold on for much longer. The wine and water had been processed long ago. Darius moved his head to the side and looked at his crutches. They seemed to weigh a standard tonne each, in his current state.

Nevertheless, he rolled over and heaven himself upright, remembering his missing leg for once. Well, he had two hours to remember it. Darius Ferrari reached forward and gathered his crutches that leaned against a matching, rustic, bedside cabinet. Hoisting them, one under each armpit at a time, he was on his one foot in seconds. He was getting good at this. Darius took a deep breath and began his quest for the one bathroom at the other end of the Ferrari dwelling. Two bathrooms were decadent, especially according to his father.

Clip hop. Clip hop was all that was heard in the dim, dingy and stuffy dwelling. Not even an ancient clock could be heard ticking, which would have gone well in this spartan place. But clockwork timepieces were phased out and forgotten long ago, around the time Terra's nearest neighbour, Mars, was terraformed, and no one was re-apprenticed to build or repair them, not even for sentimental purposes. There was not even any time keeping device here, and there never had been. Darius knew his parents always ran on their own bodyclock, and got up when the star Tau Ceta was rising. That, his father once told him, ironically made their family better at managing time, by neglecting to keep a mind on it, an unnecessary distraction.

The only bathroom was adjacent to the kitchen and laundry. He passed through the unoccupied kitchen. Both his parents were out managing the winery. Darius noted a piece of paper on the table. But it would have to wait until he relieved his bladder.

Paper! In the age of interstellar space and time travel! He thought. *Well, it does the job.*

Darius hobbled to the note a minute or so later, he did not bother to wash his hands. *My own germs, anyway.* He thought. Darius leaned one crutch against the table, balanced on the other, and reached for the note. What was written on there was in his mother's handwriting:

To our Beloved son,

Your father and I have talked and talked. Your father is disappointed in the fact that neither of his sons are following in his footsteps, but he still loves both of you. Do not take his demeanor personally. He is not angry at you, but angry at your recklessness. Angry at the fact that we nearly lost an heir, all for fighting a war against giant lizards.

But I have talked him into a compromise. We have agreed to let you go back to where you are happy. Where you can fight side by side with your comrades of other human species. We have been in touch with a cybernetic specialist while you were sleeping. The best on Tsorra, so we are told. And he will do it for a good price. He said he had a deep respect for war veterans. There is an envelope on the table. Darius lowered the letter and found a white rectangular piece of paper sitting partially under a clean, ceramic dinner plate. Probably placed there, simply as ballast, a paperweight. He pulled it out with a swift careful jerk, barely moving the plate. It was an unsealed envelope, just like the letter said.

Darius looked inside. A familiar, sepia coloured set of contents filled his senses. He pulled the contents out. Draconium bonds! A small fortune of them. Darius thought it would be rude to count them, at this time, for some reason. He continued reading:

Inside, you will find thirty standard tonnes worth of Draconium. Don't worry. I am sure your veteran's pension will more than cover it, when the Artcurians finally pay you out. Pay me out?! There is three standard years of wages here, easily. Nearly enough to buy a Beamship. How generous do you think the Arcturians are? But he continued reading. *There is a coach scheduled to pass by here, late afternoon today. Take it to the spaceport. There is also five standard tonnes of titanium bonds. That should more than pay your coach fare and passage to the other end of Tsorra, to the Southern Continent's capital. When you get there, go to the workshop of a Mr. Nero Suzuki. The locals there should know where that is.* Yeah, right. The average Commoncity has a population of about twenty million, all crammed in rows upon rows of skyscrapers over two thousand metres high. And each skyscraper could contain as much as five thousand apartments. Hopefully this Nero fellow is a local celebrity or legend, and not a nobody. He continued reading.

When you get there, give him the Bonds, and he will measure you up and fabricate a cybernetic leg. I know you must be in hell right now, waiting years for another leg to grow in the Commonwealth stem cell laboratory, or wherever new arms and legs come from, so you father and I have dipped into a hefty part of our retirement fund, our nest egg.

Don't wait for us to get back to the dwelling to see us off. It would only make things harder for you and your father. Just make sure you are outside our estate when that coach arrives. There won't be another one for four days. Just take these Bonds and letter with you, and keep them safe with you. On Tsorra, people will not hesitate to rob a, how can I put this, Disliked? War veteran. Go, as soon as you are ready and packed.

We will always be thinking of you, son.
Love, your Mother and Father.

Darius folded the letter and placed it in his pocket, the same trousers he wore the day before. He would have to bathe and put on clean clothes, he knew. What he did question, however, was if he should take his father's charity. He would be indebted to him. If Darius decided yes, then he would pay his father back as swiftly as possible. The sooner, the better. He picked up his crutch and hobbled to the bathroom again. He would decide while he bathed, make a decision over a long, refreshing bath. When he got there, however, he checked his Holotab in his pocket for the time. Late afternoon was a bit vague for Darius's liking, but he guessed if he was waiting out the gate three hours from now, that would certainly cover it, guarantee he would be there in time for the coach. But late afternoon of what season? No, far too vague and sketchy. He decided to check his Intradata on his Holotab instead, after inserting the plug in the stainless steel tub and running the water, with taps and valves marginally more advanced than the ones he had opened back in the Oil Age.

On CoachTracker.data.info, a Tsorran atlas appeared, projected about the bathroom, a hologram in three dimensions. Darius selected the continent he was on, and entered the parameters about the coach he needed to catch. A few seconds later, and his Holotab informed him today's coach would pass here approximately four hours, fifteen minutes, standard, from now, not three. Darius rolled his dark eyes and placed his Holotab on the porcelain counter, after deactivating the hologram. He turned the water valves off and undressed awkwardly, propped his faithful crutches against the nearby bathroom counter and slid in the tub like a gastropod. The tub, and entire bathroom, was old with deteriorating tiles, but nonetheless clean. Not that Darius cared. He had a decision to make, and only half an hour to make it, before the water was unbearably cold. He had to make it warm, as he could not get in one-foot-at a-time. He rolled over on his back and scrubbed absently, weighing up the pros and cons. His mind raced and eddied. He lay back down, submerged in the water, and contemplated. Before long, it seemed only a few minutes, the water was cold.

Darius Ferrari hoisted himself up on the side of the tub. He got to his feet. He had made his decision. He would take up his parents offer. Regardless of the crippling price of a cybernetic leg, he could not psychologically last five or so standard years as a hapless amputee. Besides, The Arcturian Department of Veteran's Affairs might reimburse him. *We are a socialist galactic commonwealth, after all.* Darius had three and a half standard hours to get dressed, pack, and trundle to the main road, where that first coach had dropped him off, nearly one week ago. He was in no hurry now. Darius felt his face, and was aware of a six-day stubble, which began to itch. He had time to shave it, and he would, of course.

While he shaved with a primitive razor, brand new and found in the bathroom cabinet, Darius pondered why men of all species of human still had facial hair. Why evolution would allow it, when men endeavour to shave it off regularly. Women did not find it attractive, either. *Or did they?* He wondered. *I have heard that beards come and go, in and out of fashion, every five hundred standard years or so. Perhaps sexual selection will allow men to have beards in the future. And we probably always will,* Darius mused as his razor scraped harshly over his forty standard year old chin.

Having the foresight to get there very early, and take drinking water with him, Darius hopped on the coach with his crutches. It was a warm day, not scorching, even so, he had consumed nearly half the contents of his flask, despite waiting out in the heat of Tau Ceta barely half a standard hour. He tweaked and fiddled with his Holotab while he waited.

Darius offered a generous half a standard tonne of titanium in Bonds in lieu of a coach ticket, or the equivalent of about two days of wages. The coach driver, the same that had taken him here, could not refuse. It was worth nearly twice the fare. Taking his mothers advice, he found a seat at the back, where no one could rob him easily. The coach was sparsely occupied, about one quarter full, and he would stay awake, alert. For the whole coach ride, he promised himself. He kept himself entertained by looking out the window, at the passing Tsorran landscape, always occasionally watching out for the other passengers.

It was night time when he reached the continent's spaceport. It was a warm night, and the coach driver did not offer him any help disembarking, despite his benevolent tip. 'I will buy a ticket on your behalf, and keep the change.' The driver told him stoically with telepathy. Darius's issue duffle bag was dumped in the usual place. Darius told himself not to advertise the fact he was a veteran, in future. Especially on Tsorra.

When he made the trek across the Biobrid parking area to the spaceport's terminal, sweat secreted from his forehead as soon as he entered the sanctuary of the airconditioned dome-shaped building, twenty metres high, with the interior decor of spartan steel and titanium rafters and crossbeams. A few screens devoted to advertising changed every standard minute littered the walls and ceilings. There was token potted tall palm trees here and there, nearly reaching the framework at the top of the dome. Some even had branches that partially covered the screens at some angles.

Darius wiped his forehead whilst queing up at one of the booths to purchase a ticket. Someone let him go to the front of the que, when they took in Darius's crutches and missing leg. The man and his family were offworlders, Arcturians, by the look of them. Either they did not peg Darius as a veteran, did not care, or looked favourably upon him. Either way, Darius thanked the Arcturian tourists sincerely with his telepathy. The Tau Cetans behind them looked irritated and annoyed as Darius hobbled up the place in the que. They disagreed passionately that he deserved or merited it.

'Need the next available passage to the Southern Continent's capital, please. I need a return ticket back to this spaceport, at a various, to be announced return passage, if possible.'

He leaned foward into the booth at the android, placing his elbows on the sill. 'I have titanium Bonds. Do you still take them as currency?' Darius almost pleaded with the artificial human.

'We do, sir.' The synthesised voice was an almost perfect natural Tau Cetan accent. The android had a device on itself for communicating with telepathy, and audibly responding. 'Three point seven standard tonnes. It is the peak season, I am afraid. If you would like to wait three weeks, it drops to three point one standard tonnes.'

'No thank you. I must board the next available Beamship. I have no accommodation here.'

'Very well, sir. Do you have photographic identification?' Darius fished his Biobrid license out of his veteran's fatigue jacket, the same sky blue as his one-piece uniform he wore on Oil Age Terra, with the Tau Cetan constellation sewn on the upper sleeve in the shape of a circular badge.

He passed it to the android under the bulletproof-looking screen. *Why do they need a reinforced screen here? It's not a bank!* Darius riddled himself. As the android handed him back his card, it dawned on him why. *Tsorrans are militant about machines replacing humans, especially taking their jobs. It is to protect...her? Protect her from the riff raff I call my species.* Darius met the androids' eyes and almost read the abuse and antagonism the Artificial had to endure daily in its career. *I thought we knew better, Modern Humans. I thought androids were seen as equals everywhere.* Darius not only appreciated his old job in the Navy, but could not wait to get offworld also.

'The next Beamship to the Southern spaceport does not depart for another ten standard hours, sir.

'That's okay. I don't mind waiting. Could I have that passage, please.' The android turned and processed the human's directive, then printed off a pass in the form of a thin, waterproof tablet. 'And its definately an open return passage? I don't know what day or time I will need to catch the Beamship back here, is all,' Darius confirmed politely the parameters of his passage with the Artificial.

'It is a return passage, sir. I have issued you a standby passage. All passages are flexible, sir. We have come a long way since Oil Age airline travel, after all.'

He thanked the Artificial as he handed over four tonnes of titanium's worth, and refused the change. The android looked oddly perplexed at the gesture of kindness, but handed him his pass. Darius pocketed the pass and resumed his familiar tripod gait, to the terminals' only kiosk. He still had enough credits in his left iris to buy refreshments. He was hungry, and would eat slowly to pass the ten standard hours by.

28.

Ambassador Xankyu boarded the Commonwealth's next available Timeliner, drifting hundreds of kilometres above Planet Selonabus, two standard days after his appointment with the Secretary, via an efficient, if spartan, Sirian beamship. It was another warm, humid day on Selonabus, and Xankyu was only just getting re-acclimatised with his native planet.

He was ushered on with a nondescript android, who directed him to his appropriate seat. Xankyu let his thoughts wander for ten minutes as he finally arrived at his appropriate wing. Before long, and after he sat down, he turned his attention to a screen with a massive database of films and entertainment. Xankyu scrolled through the various programmes with a near amphibian finger. The time passed, and by the time Xankyu browsed through all the pictogrammes representing entertainment programmes, nearly one and a half standard hours had passed. His mind was on other things. He had elected to choose nothing.

It was at that moment that the lazy Timeliner had finally decided to cast off. Xankyu barely noticed the

'Liner's movements, it was so incredibly large, with he so insignificant. Upon the VIP wing, the 'Liners anti matter propulsion engines could not be heard. He only knew they were moving because the loud and proud Vegan diplomat next to him said, 'Well its about time they moved off, don't you think?' Xankyu turned from the screen to face the human who initiated telepathy. The dark skinned human was half bald, as if he had no interest in curing his male pattern baldness (found millennia ago, and is now relatively inexpensive), and facial hair underneath its nose. Xankyu never understood why humans had hair, or why they found it either attractive or unattractive. He wore a two piece suit of office, a black vest and trousers, with a puffy white undershirt, covering the diplomat's arms, masking his genetically engineered, powerful, muscular arms (the same arms of practically every Modern Human). Around his neck, a medallion of office, identifying him as the Chancellor of Commerce.

'Marlon vam Rees.' The Vegan offered his right hand in greeting. Xankyu took it and shook with well-practised diplomacy, performing the ancient human custom still alive today.

'Ambassador of the Sirian Republic to The Commonwealth, Xankyu.'

'Formalities, huh?' The Vegan released the handshake and telepathically mused. 'Xankyu. Xankyu? Do you have a last name?'

'No last name. Sirians are not as feudal or ancestral as you humans of any species are. We have never had a need for them.'

Marlon nestled back in his seat and tilted his head back in thought. 'You look familiar, Sirian. Have we met before?'

'I do not think so. Although the thought is mutual. You, too I know I have seen before.' They both faced forward and stared at the ancient cartoons of the Oil Age being run on the screen, the Timeliner's default entertainment programme, if nothing is selected. Xankyu turned his personal screen off. He could never understand the appeal of bright colours to humans, especially the youngsters.

'The convention!' They both exclaimed telepathically, simultaneously. Marlon looked down and then up, recalling that conference a few standard weeks ago. 'The one where the Draconian Ambassador made a hell of a scene. What's with those lizards, anyway?'

'Why look at me like, that, Marlon. Sirians and Draconians are distantly related now. Our personalities and psychology are twice as removed. I do not know why she suggested that The Commonwealth allow the Empire to farm your ancestors for their meat, and why she thought it would not offend anyone. I can however, confirm she suggested that not merely to antagonise Modern Humans. They really do see *Homo sapiens* as a delicacy. They may one day feed upon Modern Humans, and for all we know, probably do. But *Homo sapiens* are much easier to control and breed. Modern Humans would put up more of a fight.'

'The nerve of The Empire! Suggesting they farm and consume humans! But that would mean time travel to farm and consume them. How costly! It just doesn't make sense.'

'Not if they mustered up just a handful or two of your ancestors. One thousand would be plenty to bring back to Modern Times, to establish a breeding population. Just one Freighter Beamship full, and we would have a living fossil being bred for their meat, on one of the many Ranch planets of The Empire. Think about it, Marlon. Can The Commonwealth account for every world in the Empire? Maybe The Draconian Ambassador suggested what she did, merely for psychological reasons. That the Draconians *can and want to* consume humans. But I repeat, Marlon. Can The Commonwealth account for every Planet in The Empire?'

Marlon processed what the Sirian Ambassador just said to him, almost daring him to read between the lines. His large, dark eyes of the ultraviolet spectrum widened as the hidden message occurred to him, not directly said, because Xankyu was a trained diplomat.

'You mean they *are* consuming Modern Humans already? Or prehistoric hominids, at least?'

Marlon's telepathy was a whisper. It was just as well. A refreshment-serving attendant appeared from out of nowhere, and in telepathyshot. The android asked the two diplomats if they would like something to eat or drink, and if so what.

'I will just have water and a platter of Terran-pedigree scallops, please.' Replied Xankyu.

'And for the Vegan gentleman?'

'Make it a scotch and cola, with ice. And some tuna mornay. I have a craving for that.' Ordered vam Rees contemptibly.

When the android left out of telepathyshot, Xankyu simply said prudently, 'I mean whatever you want me to believe, Marlon.'

Their meals came within twenty standard minutes, and Marlon ordered another scotch when his mornay was served before him on a folding, perspex tray, built-in the seat in front of him. He ate the dish silently, not stopping to make idle conversation. He polished the dish just in time for his next scotch, which was served by a different android this time. Xankyu was only half finished. He stopped eating, and requested a seaweed-laced glass of mineral water, just the way the Sirians liked their beverages. The android confirmed his order, and served the next lot of passengers nearby, but still far enough not to "hear" the Vegan and Sirian's conversation. Xankyu resumed consuming his plate of scallops. Sirians never ate with utensils, but this dish, served with borderline-digestible (to a Sirian) cheese, required a fork to eat. It was just as well. Marlon would have found eating with one's hands, or talons, uncivilised. Marlon downed the dregs of his scotch impatiently.

'You know, the food on Shrinktime Enterprises, may be mediocre at best, but the drinks are free. I'm not complaining.'

'Remember, that is taxpayer's dues you are drinking, Marlon.' Xankyu replied coolly. 'Only non-alcoholic beverages are complimentary.' The Sirian finished off his cheesy scallop dish, and had to wash it down with all the water available, and only barely being able to pass it down to his gizzards. Xankyu practically choked, as his digestive system, his gizzards, were not adapted to processing melted cheese.

'You know, Xankyu,' Marlon retorted. 'Your problem is, you don't know what to take what you have earned. What you deserve, what you are entitled to. I-'

Marlon's telepathic rantings was cut off by audible, emergency klaxons. The klaxons only stopped half a minute later, to be complimented by a voice over a nearby Amp. The voice had a thick annoying Arcturian drawl.

'Ladies and gentlemen. Citizens of the Commonwealth, and esteemed Sapient patrons. Do not panic. Please await instructions from a 'Liner attendant, and return to your allocated seats. We will inform you of further instructions shortly.'

The klaxon resumed its annoying, inconvenient wailing. 'What is going on here?' Marlon demanded rhetorically. He was telepathically shouting, to be heard over the klaxon. The klaxon sounded for a further five standard minutes or so, but still no instructions came over the Amp. Finally the klaxon terminated, and the drawl took over.

'Attention all passengers aboard Shrinktime flight seven-zero-eight. We are under attack-by-as-yet-unconfirmed, military force. A distress call has been transmitted to the Commonwealth Navy, at the last stopover. Again, please stay in your allocated seats and await further instructions.'

The klaxons resumed. They became irritating again before long. Marlon began to protest with his telepathy again, as if Xankyu can fix the situation, when a deafening *boom* shook the Timeliner. And then another. And another. Now, other passengers were certainly panicking. They began to stir and scream. The interior lights went out after the fourth *boom*. Now, the only illumination inside the entire beamship was the rotating, red beacons that complimented the siren. And the occasional emergency lights that illuminated exits signs and the like.

'The main Arcturium power plant has been hit, I think.' Xankyu telepathically shouted. 'The Timeliner is running off secondary, standby power.'

A moment later, however, and the main power hummed to life again, but was drowned out by the persistent klaxon. Interior lighting resumed its integrity, and the luxurious decor of the VIP wing of the Timeliner could be seen. The other passengers seemed more pacified, as if seeing their opulence and status and luxury, alone, would guarantee their safety. Their screaming and shouting died down significantly. A final *boom* however, shook the Timeliner again, and the other passengers resumed the volume of their panicking.

'I want my scotch!' vam Rees shouted, to be heard over the others. He was more inconvenienced than scared. 'Does this mean I won't get my free booze, Xankyu?'

29.

Sorjana had never expected the approaching utility groundcar to turn around and follow them. But that was exactly what it did. Sorjana could not help but watch in the side vision mirror (the rear vision mirror was destroyed when the *Homo sapiens* fired at the Impala) as the Ford F-truck not only turned around but matched their speed in ten or so standard seconds. Such incredible performance for an Oil Age groundcar. Sorjana realised it was because it was a late model pick-up, and easily outclassed the decades-old sports-sedan. She returned her ultraviolet Pleiadian eyes to the road ahead as the now-belligerent utility groundcar no longer diminished in size.

Taking a deep breath, she passed a couple of assault rifles to Mishta, and said, 'We're being followed. You may need to use these again. I am going to have to hazard going faster. Hold on, Mishta.' Sorjana stomped her foot harder on the accelerator pedal, slowly at first so as not to lose control. The Stone Age groundcar protested at being told to abruptly increase revolutions and speed at under two thousand revolutions per minute. It was sluggish in climbing to seventy miles an hour, and Sorjana no longer cared what that was, in Commonwealth (metric) units of measurement. She had bigger worries now. In the side vision mirror, the dark blue F-truck was increasing in size, gaining on the Impala.

'This is as fast as I would dare to go on this road. Do you remember how to release the safety mechanisms of a Terran's weapon?'

'Yes a primitive, unsophisticated design. With ease, Sorjana.' The Grey, unaccustomed to manual labour, grabbed the knob with its rubbery fingers and released the safety of the *Armalite* with some considerable effort. Mishta repeated the action on the second assault rifle, and Sorjana eased off the accelerator, her heart racing, uncomfortable with these break-neck speeds on an unsealed road. The F-truck increased in size even more rapidly now. Sorjana realised her new-found adversaries' advantage; heavy-duty, wide and grippy, pneumatic tyres specialised for off-road travel. She estimated the enemy Oil-Age groundcar was doing eighty miles per hour, and it was evidently doing it with ease. There was no way she could outpace it; the Impala was already losing grip on the loose surface as it was.

'You might just have to use those after all, Mishta. Don't open fire on him just yet. Wait until I know for sure he means to harm us, to run us off the road.'

'Oh? Why is that?'

'That groundcar behind us could be just a punk teenage *Homo sapien* merely wanting a race. It certainly does not seem the type of vehicle the CIA would use. To open fire on him could bring the wrath of every authority in the area, and not just the military. Also, he could return fire.'

'As you wish, Sorjana. I just hope you know what you are doing.' The pick-up groundcar had now doubled in size in her mirror. The Grey prudently ducked his head again, attempting to minimise attention.

'Oh, I hope I do too. I am trained to indentify and perhaps combat Draconian agents, among other things. I have only had elementary training in driving Terran groundcars. High speed defensive and offensive driving is not my speciality.'

The Mesa ahead loomed in front of them, casting shadows about the landscape in the mid afternoon Terran sky. As the Impala entered the vast shadow cast by the mesa, Sorjana found it difficult to see the more than a hundred or so metres ahead. She turned the groundcar's headlights on, which only marginally helped. Presently, a dusty, decaying sign could be discerned ahead. Sorjana glanced in the side mirror once again. The utility was almost close enough now to read the license plate, thirty metres at most. It would close the gap in seconds. Sorjana could only read the sign ahead. Her English took a moment for her mind to translate into Common.

'State Highway, route sixty-six. Three miles ahead, Mishta. That means we will be on a sealed surface where we can travel faster in about three standard minutes.'

The Impala was just entering the road that cut in between two mesas, when the enemy groundcar was immediately behind them, so close, the drivers face could be seen, if Sorjana had cared to look behind her.

'I don't know as much about Terran geography as you,' Mishta intruded. 'But don't you think it is wise to avoid the main highway, where there is bound to be many law-enforcement Terrans? This damaged groundcar and me inside of it will be noticed within minutes.'

'Brace for impact!' Sorjana simply barked in response. She gripped the steering wheel with both hands, preparing to be shunted out of control. The Ford F-truck was now only three metres behind. She had just enough time to glance in her mirror and look ahead when the Impala was indeed struck at about ten miles an hour from behind. Sorjana wrestled with the Impala as it swerved and drifted. She took her foot off the accelerator and gunned it, barely retaining a sense of rationality. Her heart was racing. Adrenaline was being shot into her. Sorjana practically closed her eyes and hoped for the best, hoping the prehistoric groundcar would not spin out of control. At least she was not foolish enough to slam her foot on the brake pedal, she could grant herself.

Seconds later, and the Impala had indeed returned itself true and in a stable, forward direction, but only after losing nearly a third of its speed. She decided to stay at this low speed; she could never outrun it. She glanced at her side mirror; the F-truck was now about to ram her again, so close the headlights could not be seen.

'Brace for another impact!' This time, however, Sorjana had no problems in controlling the bullied groundcar at these lower speeds. 'Mishta. You may fire at will!' The Grey sat up whilst cradling the assault rifle like a child-soldier would; the weapon was evidently too big for it.

'Aim at the driver! Right hand side!' The windows were darkly tinted; Sorjana could only make out a human silhouette. She did not know what a Grey could see. 'About half a metre from the edge of the right side, in the centre, is where driver's torso should be.'

Mischta heaved the *Armalite* up and over the back seat, and took aim where its new-found *Homo chrononaughtilus* ally had instructed. The F-Truck braked and swerved when the driver saw that Mischta was about to open fire on him (or her). It was at that moment that Mischta chose to open fire.

The Grey naturally had trouble with the recoil of the relatively heavy weapon, and its aim was equally shaky. Only two thirds of the bullets actually hit the belligerent groundcar, and a couple even penetrated the windscreen. The assault rifle made an audible *click* to indicate its magazine was exhausted. The Grey ducked down to grab the second rifle as the F-Truck recovered.

'Stay down!' Sorjana ordered. There could be two in that vehicle, and now would be the time that they would return fire, if they are armed. But the pick-up groundcar merely increased speed. Either they were unarmed, or there was only one occupant.

'Okay Mishta. Let them have the second barrage! We have plenty of ammunition. Don't worry if you don't get them this time. Maybe they will take a hint now!'

Again, the Grey nodded and lifted the heavy Terran weapon over the seat. As Mishta jerked on the trigger painfully, a flash emitted from the enemy groundcar, followed by a nearby explosion. This time, the ancient sports-sedan lost control, and the Nordic and Grey were tumbling inside the prehistoric deathtrap a second later.

That was an Anti-pistol! Sorjana thought as the adrenaline from the crash dissipated inside her body. The prehistoric Chevrolet was a battered mess. She was reminded of a crashed and totalled groundcar from a contemporary Oil-Age action movie made recently; she had seen it while blending in with her ancestors. *Whoever was in that pick-up, was no* Homo sapien. *It could be a defector.* Sorjana's Pleiadien eyes widened at an epiphany. *It could be a Draconian!* She gasped.

It was fortunate that the groundcar came to a halt the right way up. The bad news was that Mishta was not wearing its harness. Sorjana looked over at Mishta. The Serponian was alive, but unconscious. Its soft, rubbery and flimsy body lent it much purchase and flexibility. Its black jumpsuit was torn. It was haemorrhaging a respectable amount of blood, but nowhere near enough that it would bleed to death. Sorjana checked herself. Human blood. She was bleeding.

Her heart was racing and her ears were ringing. More drops of blood seemed to fall from the heavens. Sorjana touched her forehead and felt a mix of wetness and stinging. A deep cut on her forehead. Oil-Age medical science would dictate stitches. Sorjana did not have that luxury.

No time to ponder. The driver of the pick-up slammed

its door and began to stalk forward, as if the Impala was a kill. Sorjana had to get out and fight the driver. She was vulnerable here.

Sharp pain in her left side of her torso. A rib or two was broken, or at least bruised. Her legs! Sorjana checked them, quickly but tentatively patting them down. They were not broken, she thanked her own good fortune. At least she could move.

Instinct compelled her to nurse and favour her broken rib with her right hand and crawl with her left, after she released the seat's harness. She opened the groundcar's door. It was stiff and would only open a quarter of the way. The dented panels effectively jammed the door. It would have to do. Sorjana awkwardly slipped out of the narrow gap and limply confronted their mutual nemesis. A humanoid figure was now only a few metres from the groundcar when it saw Sorjana and fired. She ducked reflexively, and heard the trademark sound of a prehistoric bullet hitting a groundcar's panel. Whatever was shooting at her, was using contemporary firearms. It was then Sorjana peeked over and saw the Terran's face. Terra's sun was at the right angle, at the right time of day, for the light to catch its skin. Subcutaneous scales could be discerned to the trained eye, like watermarks on prehistoric dollar notes.

No doubt! A Draconian indeed! Sorjana dived inside the groundcar again, ignoring the pain, and laid on top of both seats. Then she took a deep breath and reached for the last *Armalite.*

* * *

Unkaalah, a senior field agent in the Draconian Empire's Chronophysical Intelligence corps, raised his *Homo sapien* Browning pistol at the groundcar again. He crouched, knowing the enemy *Homo chrononaughtilus* was seeking refuge behind the drivers seat. He sadistically sneered and discharged a few rounds into it.

Unkaalah crouched forward in his human form, scanning and stalking. He reflexively dived and rolled when he saw the glint of a Terran rifle reflecting off of Terra's star. Presently, rifle rounds unhesitatingly shot overhead as he rolled sideways. He stopped on his stomach at a forty-five degree angle to the groundcar, where the Modern Human could not fire at him. His peripheral vision caught a ditch on the side of a gravel road. He decided to risk it. He got to his feet and scurried into the ancient aquaduct. Rifle rounds wizzed over his head harmlessly as Unkaalah dove into the ditch and lay flat.

Stalemate. Unkaalah scolded himself. Although the ancient game of chess was not popular in the empire, Unkaalah was a keen and seasoned player. Often, to build rapport with *Homo sapiens* that he hoodwinked as one of their own, he would play in Oil-Age tournaments. This, which The Empire encouraged, also aided in his anomynity. He often heard rumours, more often than not, which to a seasoned Agent like himself, would lead to clues about his archenemy, *Homo Chrononaughtilus*. Even if it was merely these animals bragging about their love-making prowess to a tall, Scandanavian looking woman they had met in a Terran den of vice, in their free time.

Now, as he lay here in a ditch, he considered playing guerilla tactics and exhaust the human's ammunition. He had plenty; another three clips, plus half in his *Browning*. If he played *weasel* at different ends of the ditch, the dumb human would take the bait. *Except the fact they have telekinesis*, Unkaalah thought bitterly. *She would use that if she ran out of bullets.*

Unkaalah tried to remember his adversaries' name; Onslow the *Homo sapien* informed him of her recently, and he had rushed here, in this desolate place on Oil Age Terra, unhesitantly. A live Agent of The Commonwealth would merit him his long-deserved promotion. Or so he hoped.

But now this happens! The idiotic Terrans' let her and a Grey escape! Sorjana! That was the Plieadian females' name!

And so, thus, Unkaalah tried it. At first, he crawled towards the front of the crippled groundcar, where this Sorjana could aim at him with ease. Unkaalah raised his hand and discharged two pistol rounds, and strictly no more. He too, had to conserve ammunition. With the reflexes a higher bird-dinosaur could muster, Unkaalah flinched his arm downwards, towards the sancturary of the ditch.

As expected, the mammal fell for it. The female exhausted her ammunition even more. Five point five-six millimetre rounds wizzed over Unkaalah harmlessly. He crawled along the ditch a few metres, and repeated the process. Again, the inferior mammal with the affliction of empathy returned fire. The third time, however, was met with an audible, *click*, a characteristic of an empty magazine. Presently, a howl of despair from the wrecked primitive groundcar denied all doubt in Unkaalah's mind. The contemptible *Homo chrononaughtilus* female was out-witted by the superior mind of the predatory *Sauro-sapien draconii*.

Yes, in nature and evolution, the predator is always smarter than the prey. Empirically, they have to be.

At that thought, and with typical Draconian glee, Unkaalah got to his feet with only the faintest trace of hesitance. Simultaneously, he prudently ejected the clip and replaced it with a fresh magazine. He emerged from the ditch like a contemporary helicopter gunship, (now primitive as a hand axe by both Empire and Common-wealth standards), rising over from behind a hill and making a kill on a herbivorous tank. He never let down his guard, pistol perpetually aimed at the groundcar, as he pounced on his mammalian quarry. He could see her now; hapless and out of ammunition. The Grey, there was no way it could have survived with its flimsy, weak body. All Unkaalah had to worry about now was telekinetic backlash from Sorjana.

'You have mental powers,' Unkaalah flatly said in his mimicked American accent, knowing the Nordic would understand him. 'Do not pretend I don't know.' As Unkaalah sneered with his pistol pointed forward at near point-blank range, the local star emerged from behind a cloud. His reptilian subcutaneous coating would have glistened in the light to a trained eye. He crept forward even closer, not daring to let his guard down. The human was now clearly trembling with fear. *Like an ancient primitive shrew-like mammal cornered by a superior dinosaur in the Cretaceous Period.*

That split-second philosophical thought was the last poetic impulse Unkaalah indulged in before he took four rifle rounds in his torso and heart. Unkaalah was barely alive and dying by the time he hit the Early Man's gravel road.

30.

One of the many *Pan sapiens* aboard the *Athena*, Kokodo, a highly evolved simian, lounged in her quarters after a hard twelve standard hour shift. Essentially, Kokodo's ancestors; hundreds of millennia ago, were chimpanzee-bonobo hybrids, or rather, naturally interbred to overcome evolutionary pressures, both with and without the aid of seemingly benevolent *Homo sapiens*.

In the background, her mate, Ginki, played the ancient game of checkers with another male whom she had only been partially introduced to and did not associate with. Her mate's intellectual sparring partner was a cretin, in her opinion, and their personalities had evidently clashed. Although every *Pan sapien* on board wore the jumpsuits that served as the respective careers, they had all retained full body hair and a semi-erect gait and posture; these animals did not need to sweat to hunt, and sexual selection did not entail a hairless mate.

In The Commonwealth, however, every being that could recognise themselves in the mirror was treated equally, with the same rights and responsibilities as

Homo crononaughtilus, (the taxonomical prefix of all Modern Humans, sometimes shortened to *Homo cras*, or "Tomorrow Man"). Even androids were not excluded; the idea of creating a machine with sapient behaviour and feelings and not treating it as such, seemed *inhumane*. It seemed evil and sadistic. It disgusted most Modern Humans, such as the Nordics.

Though they had superlative intelligence compared to their ancestors, they still lacked the capacity for strategic thinking. Their intelligence is estimated to be somewhere between that of *Homo erectus* and *Homo neanderthalis*. They were incapable of playing games such as chess, which required high cognitive and strategic thought. Still, with all that said, they had achieved a degree of evolution in a little over two hundred thousand standard years, that took humans roughly three million.

Now, the Bonozee female passed the time by playing an ancient digital game, itself a modified clone from the Oil Age (Bonozeed both hated and could not comprehend, video games requiring more than three buttons and a directional pad) on her inset, built-in console in front of her cot. The *Athena's* automata had near-infinite films and games in its system, though physical exercise and other proactive pastimes were still strongly encouraged. As far as Kokodo was concerned, anything was better than golf or cricket.

'King me,' her mate's chauvinistic friend said evenly. That's the second king I have on the board. Are you going to yield, or fight to the bitter end, Ginki?'

Ginki merely leaned back, steepled his fingers, rotated

his wrists, and stretched upwards in his chair. He then put his hands on the back of his head, leaned back on his chair, and smirked defiantly.

'I will take that as a "no" then, Brother Bonozee.'

Of course, it was not telepathy that Kokodo was hearing, but actual sign language she was seeing. Once their ancestors were taught sign language by humans, verbal communication was evolutionary taxing, and evolving vocal chords and other organic speaking appa-ratuses was, simply, *redundant*. Kokodo un-paused her game and returned her troglodite eyes back to the screen. It was a simple, though nearly addictive game where a paddle bounces a ball at the other side of the screen and breaks bricks, which in turn, merits points and occasion-ally drops a *power up*.

Her mate and his *douchebag* of a friend resumed their boardgame and drank their cheap Tsorran wine. Kokodo thought the stuff tasted like vinegar with a hint of grape juice. Ginki only laughed at her and gently signed her to "lighten up."

It was only minutes later when the visitor exclaimed, 'You can't do that!' with his sign language.

'You are allowed to do that,' came the signed reply. '*You're* the one foolish enough to leave a square behind a piece, then another piece, and then another empty square.'

At that moment, Kokodo was started by the sound of checker pieces hitting the ground, and a high-pitched growl, a cry of frustration that sounded like a mix of a *Homo sapiens'* growl, and a wild *Pan troglodytes'* excited shriek of aggression.

Kokodo, in a show of contempt and maturity, paused her game once more, got up off her cot and signed, 'I think both of you have had too much of that stuff. And Ginki, tell *your* friend that its time to leave and get a good night's rest.'

Her mate shrugged in agreement. Even though they both had deep and beautiful grey-green eyes, Kokodo was raised on a different planet to Ginki in the Commonwealth; he, on New Terra, and she on Erra. Kokodo was therefore cultured differently.

As her mate assertively showed his friend to the door in their small but efficient quarters (only taking up nineteen square metres but had a kitchen, lavatory, double bed and family room) she recalled her species evolution. First at around fifty thousand standard years after the Oil Age, *Propan erectus* was semi-upright with a shrunken digestive system and an enlarged brain. Next at around one hundred and thirty thousand years A.D. came *Pan erectus*, with an ever more compact digestive system and a larger brain, and finally her species came only about twenty thousand standard years ago. They earned their taxonomical *suffix* when they had a self aware concept of commerce and trade, and an understanding of complex machines and tools such as being able to readily engineer a bow and arrow and instinctively move heavy loads with the aid of a self-engineered, though crude, wheel. It has been widely accepted that a *Pan sapiens* intelligence is equal to that of a thirteen standard year old *Homo sapien*.

Their culture is now incredibly complex, in having a

three-tier hierarchical system, (humans took over three million standard years to evolve this) which is firstly;

One: The alpha or "general"

Two: The betas or the alpha's Lieutenants

Three: The gammas or "troopers"

The alpha would delegate to his or her betas and despatch multiple hunter or gatherer parties, comprised of one beta and several gammas. Gammas would report their concerns to the alpha via the beta males or females. In turn, the alpha male and female would, whilst looking out for predatory packs of *Canis erectus*, educate and protect and entertain the beta and gamma's young offspring in a kind of school where the *Pan sapien* troop was based. Here the young learned Commonslan, shared by Bonozee's and mute or deaf Modern humans alike. As well as language, the young bonozee's would be educated in simple mathematics, toolmaking, firemaking and control, rudimentary science and technology, Bonozee evolution and prehistory, and elementary Common-wealth politics and culture.

They lived in harmony with their Modern Human genetic cousins and did not compete for resources; Kokodo's parents would regularly take her from the troops' simple but peaceful hunter-gatherer settlement comprised of the same environmentally friendly dome shaped dwellings that their human cousins lived in, and to the nearby human Commontown to trade their wares. Her father and mother made flint sculptures which they traded for medical supplies, (A human doctor was more than happy to come out if first aid would not do) education supplies and stationary. Even simple toys for the youngsters were traded to Bonozee's in exchange for gathered fruit.

Later, as she was an adolescent, she heard about the Draconian threat on her chimpanzee and bonobo ancestors, how they were indirectly responsible for their poaching, and wanted to help. Her human cousins welcomed Kokodo to their cause; said both *Pan sapien* and *Homo cras* was equally under threat on Oil Age Terra.

Now, however, Kokodo realised she was still in her shopkeeper clerk's burgundy leotard uniform, where she worked in the *Athena's* shopping district. She and Genki had been working extra hours recently, to fund their impending wedding. She thought that working over seventy standard hours a week for eight weeks straight was making her short tempered. The two engaged Bonozee's only took one day off for sermon and rest. The only Organised Religion permitted in the Commonwealth was a watered-down hybrid of prehistoric Terran religions. And this spiritual orientation dictated they had to get married before having offspring (though contraceptual mating was permitted).

'I am going to bathe and retire, Genki.' The female Bonozee signed after her mate closed and locked the quarter's door. She undid the belt and let the burgundy robe fall to the floor, then stood there unclothed while she waited a response from Genki. The male was not aroused by any means. Not because he found her unattractive, but because nudity was neither erotic nor indecent in Bonozee society. They naturally wore no clothing and were apathetic to the sight of another naked Bonozee. She stood there, looking like a hybrid between a human and a chimp, covered in moderate body hair. Her white skin, evolved pale to absorb vitamin D on temperate Erra, could be discerned underneath her light black down that covered her body.

Her deep grey-green eyes, also evolved to absorb Vitamin D, read his signed response.

'I am sorry about him, my Love.'

'That's ok, Genki. Just go easy on that Tau Cetan wine from now on.' At that, Kokodo turned and strode to the bathing room, her strides and gait eerily similar to that of *Homo sapien*, because convergent evolution dictated that a long-distance hunter-gatherer hominid had to walk like that, lest they would not have existed in the first place.

31.

'*Homo tyrannis*', vam Rees mused to herself aboard an emergency Beamship. She could only seethe as Murphy fastidiously kept the Anti-pistol pointed at her head. '*I thought our Homo sapien ancestors wiped them out for good during the Great Cull.*'

The Great Cull was a colloquial term for when the good of humanity revolted against the psychopaths who controlled the governments (both Left and Right) and corporations up until the late Oil Age. It was a shameful history in *Homo chrononaughtilus*' ancestry, but an absolute necessary evil that saved humanity, and most of life on Terra, from extinction. Claudia remembered watching remastered footage from those hundreds of millennia ago, stored on DNA, as well as reading written accounts of this mass, global *pathocide* on ancient Terra. Politicians were dethroned. Greedy corporations were overrun and disbanded. Surprisingly, there was minimal anarchy; early man had an inbuilt instinct to govern itself and follow instinctive laws.

One film she remembered most well, that haunted

her the most, was a scene where thousands of prehistoric humans were mustered and lined up before this massive row of machinery. The machinery, she was told by her history tutor, was many woodchipper-like refinery plants engineered to turn human corpses into fertilizer. She remembered a scene where soldiers would, with a spiked object, pierce an unarmed man's cerebral cortex with the upmost contempt, and toss the now-dead *Homo sapien* into the refinery.

"'Why don't we just shoot them?'" A soldier being interviewed responds rhetorically (translated into Common subtitles, of course). 'Because they are the shit of humanity. Psychopaths, paedophiles, rapists, murderers. The Revolution views them all as cockroaches in a human body. Would you waste a valuable bullet on a cockroach?!'

Another scene, where a man who pleads not to be turned into fertilizer, to at least be given a dignified, proper burial, (again in Common subtitles) only earned him an equally contemptible response from another soldier. "Only humans get a proper burial. We don't see you as human. We see you as rats. And who, in their right mind, would bother to give a rat a funeral? Huh?!' At that moment, another spike shoved into a sociopath's (possibly a former politician) cerebral cortex, with the *Homo sapien* soldiers tossing another body into the human flesh refinery.

Because the prehistoric psychopath caste of Early Man lacked empathy, among other traits that made one truly human, they consequently failed to see the actions of their domination over their perceived "weaker" caste.

Ancient Oil Companies, obsessed with their monopoly on powered transportation, saw biofuels as a threat to their power, as a good psychopath should.

Oil Age overpopulation was caused by this psychopath caste of *"Archo-Hominids"* suppressing population management controls such as family planning and education in the poorer Terran tribes, supporting anti-abortion idealists and installing religious ideals that encouraged having as many offspring as possible. In turn, overpopulation simultaneously obstructed arable land with food crops and farmed animals, and there was hence, simply not enough land to grow enough biofuels. Early man was bonded to fossil fuels and coal this way.

Of course, other species on Terra faced extinction because of *"Archo-Hominids"* or *Homo tyrannis* manipulation over contemporary *Homo sapien* due to this behaviour. The Early Humans that cared had no power to change this. The ones who had the power simply did not care because they lacked or had no empathy. Claudia vam Rees was reminded in her schooling about bigotry such as racism, sexism and homophobia (which in her youthful innocence confused the latter with misanthropy due to the confusing scientific prefix, "homo") and thought it was all as trivial as hating another human because of their eye colour or how long their fingernails were. Then she remembered her history lessons; *"Bigotry among Early Man was the result of the propaganda emitted from Homo tyrannis in order to divide and conquer Homo sapiens and thus keep them under control. The Sapient caste outnumbered the Predatory caste twenty-five to one, after all."*

Of course, some *Homo sapiens* knew this. They were dubbed "Anarchists" by the psychopaths. They had many myths and legends to explain this phenomenon, such as the Tale Of The New World Order, where a pyra-mid-shaped deity with an eye controlled humanity. One Prehistoric legend even told of "Lizard People" disguised as humans manipulating Oilman's Social Hierarchies. *'Close, but no cigar,'* vam Rees thought in the ancient ex-pression that had lost all meaning. Tobacco was abolished and forgotten about over two hundred Standard Years ago. She could not help but look pointedly at her reptilian Annunaki abductors as she was thinking this.

Both her and Murphy were travelling space and time aboard a respectable-sized spacecraft along with over one hundred Sentinels as plunder, with two dozen or so Annunaki Enforcers for good measure. Claudia did not know why Murphy had taken her captive. It would not be for unconsentual mating, as she and the Arcturian were different species of space and time faring hominids. And there was no other *Homo cras vegas* on board. In-terbreeding among different species of Modern Humans was considered a form of beastiality, and both reviled and forbidden.

'Don't you worry,' Murphy said in a psedo-soothing tone. 'I'm not going to kill you. At least not until we enter Shrinkspace.' He bonded her to the structured support railings of the three-hundred metre Beamship with a pair of Anti-Cuffs, designed to resist telekinesis. 'Then again, we may keep you alive after that. If one is resourceful, one can always find a use for a hostage. We may be able to trade you for a Sentinel or two with the Oil Age-based Draconians, for instance.'

Claudia's deep green-grey eyes, irresistible to the male of her species, could only show defiance rather than seduction at the sinister looking and ugly Arcturian male. 'Need I remind you, Commonwealther, that I, too have Powers.' Murphy pressed the Anti-Pistol against Claudia's cheek painfully, distorting her face. 'Don't try anything I wouldn't do.' The sociopath telepathically whispered gently, as if into her ear.

The crippled Timeliner and two Commonwealth warships were now far behind, and the familiar sound of a Sentinels ready to serve could be heard on a nearby console.

'What are you waiting for? Can't you hear the fact we are ready for Shrinkspace? Hurry up!' Murphy's fury was evident over his translating console, but to Draconian society, "vinegar was a virtue." A Reptilian Enforcer nearby toadily confirmed the directive to the Beamship's automata. Although Claudia could not see out of the bridge's viewing port, the unmistakable sound of Sentinels being launched meant only one thing; The Commonwealth and its Navy will not help her here. Commodore Claudia vam Rees, of The Commonwealth's Navy, a strong and beautiful woman in her own right, was at the mercy of wherever in space, or whenever in time The Annunaki would take her.

32.

Sorjana helped Mishta out of the battered, half dead Chevrolet. The Grey, as she had previously thought, had only superficial wounds. Of course, she had made sure the enemy reptilian was indeed dead first.

Terra's star was setting, and it was not as hot as it was when Sorjana and Mishta escaped the compound. However, they had wasted nearly eight standard minutes already, and Sorjana had to urge the Grey with haste. The Terran soldiers were likely not far away. It was foolish to assume they had not been commandeering primitive groundcars and despatching rudimentary rotary-winged aircraft in their animalistic effort to track her and the Grey down. The Grey reluctantly slipped out of the Impala and got to its feet.

'We will be taking the Draconian's groundcar, of course. The key to operate the thing should still be inside it.'

Mishta grabbed the last *Armalite* and walked after its Nordic guardian. Sorjana nursed her injured rib as she led the way. It was less than forty metres away, but to the injured extraterrestrials, that may as well have been a marathon. Sorjana assumed the driver, of course, when they finally got there an agonising minute later. Mishta took its own initiative and figured out how to open the door in a few seconds. As it climbed in, Sorjana was only just figuring out how to operate the newly captured, prehistoric groundcar, when The Grey pointed toward the Terran sky and said, 'I can hear a Terran aircraft. It is probably their military.'

Sorjana, who only just turned the key and fired the clanging, primitive ancestor of Biobrids, looked out the driver's window and behind. Sure enough, Mishta had been *partially* right. There was not one rotary-winged aircraft, but *four*. They were roughly four kilometres away, and they were tiny, but large enough for her to count four *helicopters*. The purr of the F-Truck had now drowned out the still-distant Terran military craft.

Unhesitatingly, she wrenched the groundcar into first gear and released the clutch a little too quickly. Sorjana gasped as she realised it would stall and lose precious seconds, but the F-truck had so much torque it merely bunny-hopped and regained revolutions again. Sorjana planted her foot on the accelerator. It roared to life and quickly redlined at twenty-five miles per hour. Sorjana realised this thing had close gearing and would need more attention. But it had *five* gears rather than the poor old Impala's four, and it was turbocharged. Not that she really cared about the oil man groundcar's *"bells and whistles"*, she only cared that this thing would be incredibly thirsty. She would have to either make more frequent stops or steal another groundcar. *First*, she thought, *I have only to worry about escaping the Terran war flyers. If I can escape.*

Still, the decadent and masculine utility groundcar was better than walking.

The Oil Age flyers were now three kilometres away when she reached seventy miles an hour, and changed the thing into fifth gear. The revolutions dropped to two thousand three hundred at this speed, compared to the Impala's three thousand one hundred. Sorjana, indeed, found the F-Truck handled better on this road, as she had thought. The heavy-duty off road tyres gripped the road like tank tracks. She hazarded a look behind her on a straight; the prehistoric flyers were slowly gaining, but Sorjana decided not to increase speed. This was fast enough, and they were now about two kilometres (or one and a half miles, according to another decrepit, faded green, sign to her left) to the main highway. Sorjana gripped the steering wheel and kept her Ultraviolet, Pleiadian eyes on the dirt track made by prehistoric *Homo sapiens.*

It was another half minute or so before she had decided to check her *six* once more. This time, the helicopters were hovering, and two were descending, where the Impala had rolled and crashed. The *Homo sapiens* had assumed her and the Grey was still inside the wreck!

'They are not going to bother us anymore, Mishta.' Sorjana called over her shoulder at the Grey. 'They don't know that we are in another groundcar. All we have to do is find another groundcar, and we will be fine. Until they start setting up roadblocks.'

Sorjana and Mishta could now see more prehistoric

groundcars crossing perpendicular on a long grey oasis of a strip of asphalt, all different colours and shapes, heading both east and west-bound. At this distance, they all looked like a child's' toy groundcar only two inches long each, at a lower altitude. The Nordic and the Grey realised latently, that the track was descending downhill. Sorjana looked in her rear vision mirrors once more, and could not help but cry out in disappointment. Two out of four helicopters were now following the track behind them, heading towards them, and gaining speed. The prehistoric highway was now less than half a kilometre, with the two pursuing helicopters, Sorjana estimated, just over two.

'They are following us once again, Mishta. But don't worry. They wont know what this groundcar will look like from this distance; we would, to them, look like a puff of dust and smoke. If we can get on this so-called *Route sixty six* before they get a clear visual on this groundcar, and if we can slip in on this road up ahead without having to give way, we can blend in with the other groundcars. Do you follow my plan? Yes? Then hang on, Mishta. We have some traffic merging to do in a few standard seconds.'

Sorjana was slowing the beastly groundcar down as they neared two hundred metres away. At this distance, she realised the highway had *four* lanes in total, and there were frequent intervals of groundcars and groundtrucks, not more than eighty metres spaced from one another. It was going to be a tight squeeze, she realised, but fate was on her side as she was only fifty metres away and a massive semi-trailer groundtruck was approaching, using the side of the road closest to her, on the far-right hand lane. She glanced at her speed, thirty-five miles an hour, and in her rear vision one last time. The two helicopters were less than a kilometre and a half away, closer to a kilometre flat.

The long groundtruck passed across her at twenty metres to the intersection. 'Hang on,' she telepathised to the Grey as she turned the steering wheel at the last second, shooting off the dirt track and instantly parallel with the highway. She was in second gear now, and floored the accelerator and into third, desperately trying to catch the semi-trailer and slip in on its left-lane. She merged onto the highway and changed into fourth about five seconds later, and now gaining on the groundtruck. The two helicopters were now just under a kilometre away, close enough for the Early Humans to identify each individual groundcar. Sorjana did not bother to change up as she caught up to the prehistoric groundtruck and slowed down to stay side-by-side with it. She was now matching its fifty-five miles per hour, and practically held her breath for the twenty or so seconds for the two helicopters to reach the highway. Sorjana checked her rear vision mirror as they did. They were flying low and were noisy. They were now splitting up and banking either way, circling the few hundred or so groundcars and groundtrucks in the immediate area, in an almost vulture-like gesture. They had not spotted her and Mishta. Thank the good in Modern Humans.

'Stay down, Mishta.' Sorjana warned.

Still, the vulture-like prehistoric aircraft circled, as if to look for any evidence of a groundcar having recently been off-road, and searching desperately. Sorjana did her best to remain incognito next to the semi. The helicopters did one more loop, then seemed to give up the chase. Sorjana knew that their *Homo sapien* commanding officer would have given the order to abort, lest it create a public and media spectacle that the military would have to cover up. Sorjana glanced around her, and sure enough, the only aircraft she could see had its back to her, and was increasing the distance.

'Looks like they are gone, for now. We did it, Mishta. But stay down every time we approach another groundcar. And it is only a matter of time before we will come to an Early Man's roadblock. We will have to deal with it when it comes, I suppose.'

'Where are we going, Sorjana?' The Grey ventured. 'We need to get offworld.'

'Indeed, we both do. There is a large Modern warship based near the largest planet in the Terran system. A Commonwealth *Persephone* class called *The Athena*. That is where I am stationed. I am sure we could spare a Beamship to take you to the next awaiting Timeliner.........' Sorjana paused to do a cursory tally of the date (in the Commonwealth calendar, of course). 'In approximately two Standard months. Did you Time Travel from the distant future from Planet Serpo? Or is this your time? Sorry, Chronophysics astounds even me sometimes.' Sorjana had to subconsciously shout with her Telepathy at the Grey, as if to be heard over the torquey diesel engine. She kept her eyes forward, at the Prehistoric road, as she shouted.

'My Beamship crashed on this planet a decade or so ago. I am from your time, about two hundred and thirty years from now, on your calendar. But these details are trivial. I just want to get off this planet and into Modern Civilisation once again. But first, we need to get your Beamship.'

33.

These early hominids have arrogantly declared themselves *Homo sapiens*. As if they were the pinnacle of evolution. Meerkah was inclined to use their more conservative taxonomy of *Miapiapithecus*, or "Good Mother/Father Monkey."

This was the actual *Draconian* taxonomical classification, translated into Latin, which denotes an avian dinosaur pedigree and perspective of evolution. Although his good *Homo chrononaughtilus pleiades* friend and fellow scientist was slightly offended. Meerkah was calling his direct ancestors apes, and the effort for Pteru to hide his offence was clear to Meerkah.

Pteru, Magne and Skyler had managed to escape the galactic-wandering Timeliner, now ill-fated by an Annunaki raid in the outskirts of the Hyadean stop-off. Meerkah had opted to go with Pteru, as he needed time away from his own species. Scientists were underappreciated in the Empire, and Pteru had to agree with his friend. Only a handful of Beamships escaped, with three Sentinels, and all followed the same path into

Shrinkspace. They had simply time-travelled first, asked questions later.

Pteru's Beamship had now landed on prehistoric Terra, with other refugee Beamships following suit, with the exception of one heading of to Planet Serpo. Obviously a family or group of Tall Greys.

At first, about sixteen hours before the Annunaki piratical attack on a peaceful 'Liner, Magne and Skyler were sceptical about having the company of a feared and often-vilified reptilian. They were introduced to each other sometime during the Arcturian stopover. Soon, however, they took a shine to the avian-dinosaur sapient. Meerkah's personality was very human-like. Skyler was secretly amused by the irony of a dinosaur being a paleontologist, and was thankful that Draconians lacked the ability to read minds. *Not the same as Telepathy*, he reminded himself.

Presently, the off-duty Imperial Parapaleontologist and the Commonwealth Chronophysicist puzzled over where in time they indeed were. They were beginning to argue with a dark-skinned male Vegan diplomat who indeed should be in charge. Meanwhile, a Sirian diplomat in resplendant jade livery, endeavoured to calm his beauracratic friend.

After much heated debate, with about fifty or so others in the background, and staying, sheepishly in the background, fifteen standard minutes had passed with no result. A few refugees of various Modern Human species, lounged about against the eight landed, docked Beamships.

'I think we all need a respite,' Xankyu offered as his translating console performed his duty for him. His Vegan friend, the same he had met at the Conference about one Terran month ago with that unruly Draconian female stirring up a hiatus, cocked a sceptical and sarcastic eyebrow at the Sirian. 'We will be able to function again as a group once we have all eaten and drank, and got to know each other, as you humans would say, *break the ice.*'

'Just *whose* side are you on, Xankyu?' The Vegan man with a bald head and a mustache accused, via his Holopad translator.

'Let's be clear,' Pteru's Holopad this time audibly communicating. 'We have no more Sentinels. Unless we can find Modern Civilisation, we are stuck here, on Prehistoric Terra. As a seasoned Chronophysicist, and judging by the fact we were travelling through Shrinkspace for *nine* Standard hours, rather than eight, which would take us to *The Athena*, I have the most reason to get us out of this mess.'

'*Where* are we?' A feminine-voiced Holotab with a thick Lyran accent from the back echoed from a sleeping Beamship.

'I estimate twenty thousand Terran years before the Oil Age of humanity. Perhaps thirty thousand.' Pteru's response was coldly calculating and scientific, even when spoken with a Holotab.

'Twenty to thirty thousand B.C.E.?!' The Vegan diplomat screeched, clearly schooled in his history. He had intimate knowledge of the Gregorian calendar. 'I have a daughter that is an officer in the Commonwealth Navy,

I will have you all know. She knows where myself and Xankyu were heading before we entered Shrinkspace.'

Xankyu said, 'I would not be so sure of that, Marlon. True, Commodore Claudia vam Rees was in the rescue fleet for that disabled Timeliner, but you and I were long gone before the Navy arrived, remember? In any case, the one most likely to get us back would be a Chrono-physicist. Conversely, the one who will help us survive on Terra, two hundred and fifty thousand Standard Years ago, in the *meantime*, would be a Parapaleontologist.'

'So it comes down to this, my dear Ambassador? Mutiny? Anarchy?!'

'What was that?!' Intruded a telepathic voice from the back. A completely new one this time. 'I saw another person, behind the Sirian ambassador over there.' Pteru, Meerkah, Xankyu and Marlon all turned around and looked at the row of trees behind them, not fifty metres away.

'*I* don't see anything.' Marlon boasted after some time of staring. 'Maybe it was just your imagination, or that thing, who or what, is gone.'

'In any case,' Pteru cautioned. 'We must not split up until we ascertain our plans and goals, and delegate accordingly-'

'*I'm* the one who delegates around here!' Marlon tele-pathically intruded.

'I am just getting to that. If anyone is the most qualified to delegate, it's the Imperial Parapaleontologist. He knows more about the Paleolithic period of Early Man than most Modern Humans do.'

'But first, I suggest we have a long refresher break, a Standard hour or so, and get to know one another. We should get out one ration pack each.' Xankyu this time, 'Marlon and I had the initiative to grab six months of food for ten Sapients before we fled that Timeliner as the Annunaki attacked. First, I suggest we do a tally of how many Sapients *are* here, so we can delegate and ration resources accordingly.'

Meerkah said, as he looked his distant genetic cousin in the eye while his Holotab translated, 'Finally,' Meerkah cried. 'Someone who thinks as pragmatically as I do. You Sirians may look down to us Draconians, just because your water is safe to drink and you have far better public healthcare, but our Species are not so different after all.' And Meerkah give the Sirian ambassador the *Saurosapienia* equivalent of a jovial smile as he said this, as if to both reinforce his words, and as a gesture of fraternity.

After every refugee was given a substantial meal (ten to twelve standard hours without food made most Modern Humans irritable with hunger as their bodies re-metabollised on starvation-mode, feebly with a many hundred millennia neglected adaptation) it was tallied that *ninety-three* Sapients in total were in the group. Meerkah, the Parapaleontologist, suggested that was ample to set up a three-tier hierarchal system. Marlon vam Rees, of course, suggested assertively that he and Xankyu should be the *generals*, with Meerkah, Pteru, a Hyadean Physician and a well-off Arcturian woman should be the *Lieutenants*. Whoever was left, of course, would be the *"troopers"*, and a so-called *"buddy-system"* should be in place. Everyone agreed that the ninety-three Sapients could be chrono-logically marooned here for a long time, and possibly forever. Eventually, parties would have to be despatched to find food and water, perhaps on foot, as most of the Beamships had less than half their Arcturium crystals left.

'Why didn't we take more Sentinels, You ask!?' Marlon raged back with his telepathy at the Arcturian entrepre-neur, who was halfway between middle aged and elderly. 'Xankyu and I did not release or control the Sentinels, the 'Liner pilot did! We had no control where in Shrinkspace they would lead us, the main goal was to get us to safety! Furthermore, we did not ask for the other...nine Beamships to follow us into Shrinkspace. *You* lot must take some, if not all, responsibility for our current predicament. We initially thought we had enough supplies to last us three to five Sy's, and then we find out that *all* of you followed us here! Think of how...........upset Xankyu and I are now that we have an extra eighty-seven mouths to feed!'

There were six Sapients in total on Marlon's Beamship. Xankyu's personal bodyguard was an Arcturian Marine that was easily a match for Gunnery Sergeant Klaan O'Brien. Marlon's bodyguard was another Vegan; a bat-tle-damaged former Marine hard muscled on the outside, and twice as hard on the inside. The others, a Beamship engineer, was infinitely indispensible, (and Pteru said arguably *the* most important), and Marlon's personal physician. Two doctors in total. At least that was good.

'Let us make the best of this situation,' Pteru countered with his telepathy. 'If we hadn't followed you through

Shrinkspace, you and the Sirian ambassador will be stuck here, hoping help from the distant future will arrive. Yes, without any Sentinels it would take decades to travel to Selonabus, which is the nearest non-belligerent civilisation. You need a Chronophysicist to get there.' Pteru let his conclusion hang in the air and let the hidden message take effect.

'Right now,' Meekah added, I think we should fraternise with a *Miapiapithecus* tribe. If we are stuck here until help from Selonabus arrives, a troop of prehistoric humans can help us gather food and drinkable water. Our Beamships would provide adequate shelter. We need to find a safe river to swim in for ablutions. I am sure there are those here already that are thinking that they would appreciate a bath already.'

Later that afternoon, a Beamship was despatched by the newly-established hierarchy, and came back less than an hour later. The ubiquitous saucer shaped craft came to a hover at the hands of a competent pilot that the *Generals* of the hierarchy forgot about, as they had more strategic decisions to make. Like all Beamships, it was whisper quiet. Only those that were looking in its general direction even noticed it. The rest of the bored Sapients either lounged around or set up their beds. Most were happy, despite themselves. They saw it as another camping excursion. They only noticed the scout Beamship had returned when it landed with a *whump*.

Presently, a young Lyran male came trotting up to the *Generals*, this time bypassing the *Lieutenants*.

'There is a tribe of stone age humans, about eighteen kilometres that way.' He pointed to the south east. 'I did not land, of course, without knowing the Chronophysical ramifications of it. There are approximately seventy-five members of this tribe, maybe one hundred at most. About the same amount as our little group.' The Lyran pilot's Holotab was turned off, and used raw telepathy to communicate.

'And a river?' Asked Marlon.

'I haven't seen one as of yet, but it has to be close to the tribe's little village, wouldn't it?'

'Leave that sort of deducing up to the Parapaleontologist!' Ordered Marlon curtly.

The pilot nodded sheepishly, as if instinctively learning his place in this makeshift hierarchy.

'That was unnecessarily and excessively assertive, Marlon.' Xankyu chided. 'He meant no insubordination. Perhaps you have gotten out of touch with the ordinary folk and become a robotic autocrat who cannot be reasoned with, as you humans used to say, "A slave to the system."'

Marlon dismissed the young Lyran man with a contemptuous wave, and said, out of telepathyshot to Xankyu, 'Do not ever humiliate me again, Xankyu, especially in front of a low ranking subordinate.' Marlon's tone was silent but infinitely venomous.

Xankyu was about to retort, raising a pointed finger as he was about to "open his mouth" and use his telepathy, when a cacophony from the heavens, and two large Beamships could be seen descending to where the young

Lyran had pointed. A loud boom could be heard as the Beamships entered Terra's atmosphere.

'That was where the Lyran said the primitive human tribe was. We need to get there before those two large Beamships do. It is our last chance at an early escape. It is impossible to know how many there are, or if they are friendly. But even in a worse case scenario, we may be able to, with careful planning, spirit away enough Sentinels to escape this Time, at least. Let's go.'

34.

The roadblock came after about two hours of driving, at the State border. It was getting dark, and the star of Terra was halfway through disappearing underneath the horizon. Sorjana and Mishta were bored, as the traffic came to a crawl along the highway. It was another hour before Sorjana could discern a law enforcement *Homo sapien* ahead, evidently checking identification and the groundcar four places in the cue ahead. Mishta saw it too, and shrieked,

'Turn around, Sorjana! Before it is too late!'

'It's no use, Mishta.' Sorjana was coolly pragmatic in her telepathy. 'I would only draw attention and make matters worse. I know these animals, after all.'

'But they will see me! And they know we have Powers!' Mishta was very careful in not being seen, it hunched desperately on the floor on the passenger's side of the F-Truck.

'Not these Terrans. The military of this planet will tell them a need-to-know only basis. They still cover up the existence of extraterrestrials here, remember? They will be only looking for a Caucasian female with blonde hair and blue eyes in....' Sorjana paused to calculate how old she would look to a Terran. She kept her Pleiadian eyes forward all the time, not looking around and guilty, but apathetic and inconvenienced. '...her mid thirties. I am all they will be looking for. Not you.'

Another pace up the queue. Sorjana could see there were about a half dozen Terran soldiers of the National Guard class and a military groundtruck, and one police groundcar. Sorjana was surprised that the Terrans would risk this much. Surely the animals in front would be asking inconvenient questions, in their primitive language that Sorjana understood. Already that was bad public relations. The *Arco-Hominids* in the Whitehouse would be frantically trying to cook up lies and propaganda to explain these blockades with a military presence. *Military exercise!* Sorjana thought with almost a sneer. *How convenient.*

'How are you holding up anyway, Mishta?' The Grey looked at her perplexingly. Sorjana thought she had to be more specific in future, with Mishta. 'You were bleeding before. How are you doing now? Have you managed to stop the bleeding?' She and the Grey pulled over to tend to their wounds, long after the two helicopters were gone, when she was certain they were tactically safe.

Sorjana had found a first aid kit under the passenger's seat. Her forehead was bandaged, and Mishta had informed her that her rib was indeed fractured. She would be okay for the short term, but was in no shape to fight a Draconian Agent in hand-to-hand combat, or even a

Homo sapien with respectable martial arts skills. In turn, Sorjana had sterilized and dressed the Grey's wounds, which were largely only superficial.

'Of course. I can survive until Modern medical science is found, with ease. How much longer until we get to your Beamship?'

'About another day, assuming this is the only trouble we will run into.' Sorjana still faced forward, as if to reaffirm she was alone in the groundcar to anyone who might be watching her. 'There is a farm in a landmass that the Terrans refer to as the "Midwest," where my Beamship is stored in a building. Don't worry. It is safe there. The owners of the farm are fellow Pleiadians and personal acquaintances of mine. I trust them.'

The Grey and the Nordic sat in silence as the hairy utility groundcar sat idle. Mishta thought that the bullet nicks on the windscreen would draw attention. Sorjana replied simply that they look like stonechips on a normal windscreen (as the windscreen on the F-Truck is actually bulletproof.)

Another pace forward. It seemed like an eternity before the Grey and the Nordic were next in the cue. Only three standard minutes had passed, but as the groundcar in front pulled off as the *Homo sapien* officer waved it away with a cheerful smile, Sorjana said to Mishta in an almost soothing tone, 'Places, people. It's showtime.'

Sorjana leaned over and grabbed the one Anti-Pistol that was in the utility's glovebox. The Grey flinched reflexively as the lid to the glovebox flipped open. Sorjana closed the glovebox and coasted forward. She timed it perfectly; The *Homo sapien* officer and soldiers would not have noticed her grab the Anti-Pistol, because they were distracted with waving off the Terran civilians in their yellow *Datsun* groundcar, that they had just scrutinised. The yellow groundcar was diminishing in size as Sorjana concealed the Rod-shaped weapon underneath her Terran denim jacket.

She came to a halt, and the six soldiers pointed their rifles at the utility. Sorjana rotated the primitive crank handle that wound the driver's window up and down. The Terran law enforcement animal leaned forward with a cheerful smile and opened its mouth with a well practiced platitude.

'Good afternoon, Ma'am. May I see your license, plea-.' The officer's eyes widened as it took in Sorjana, her bandaged head and soiled appearance, and saw what looked like a Roswell Grey on the passenger's floor. It took a step back and went to reach for its *revolver* at its belt. But Sorjana was not only quicker, but anticipated this situation.

To the *Homo sapiens* in the groundcars behind, a sudden, abrupt flash was all they could see. None of them would have any clue what was going on, as anti-matter was never heard of in this time, let alone anti-matter *weapons* that were handheld. By the time the white hot flash dissipated about ten seconds later, and assuming the primitive Terrans were not temporary blinded, all that they would see was a Military groundtruck on fire, already charred to the core. The only soldier that was alive was only just getting to its feet now, and grabbing its primitive assault rifle. The officer was still alive, though unconscious, and likely now deaf.

What only mattered to Sorjana Hoolde the Pleiadian and Mishta the Grey was the fact that their faithful utility groundcar was now nearly half a kilometre away, and their escape was masked by the inferno and onslaught behind them. Once again, they were safe. For now.

35.

The refugees all scrambled to their Beamships, leaving their most trivial belongings behind; things such as eating utensils, plates, food, blankets and other items of little value. Marlon vam Rees was brief in his speech, and told them this was their one chance back to Modern times, back to their loved ones. He rallied them up in less than a minute, turning them from scared and demoralised to ambitious and militant. At least he was a good leader in that sense.

'Wait, everybody.' Called Pteru with his telepathy. He was the only one that had stayed behind, besides Magne, Skyler and Meerkah. 'Please consider the Chronophysical ramifications before we leave everything behind.' His telepathy trailed off as the other eighty-nine Sapients were already boarding and firing up *every* Beamship, including Pteru's.

'I am going to have to board my Beamship before we are left stranded here. You three, please gather up every item from the Modern age you can. Put it all in a pile or something. If any item is left behind and early man finds and uses them, it will change history, and probably for the worst.'

Magne said, 'Will you come back for us? We are unarmed, after all. What if primitives or dinosaurs attack us?'

'I am what you call a dinosaur,' retorted Meerkah cheerfully. 'I will talk to a dinosaur if it comes along and tell it not to eat us.' He looked pointedly at the adolescent Plieadian female, as if trying not to laugh. Skyler shifted awkwardly, as his female friend was making herself look foolish, and did not even know it. 'Don't worry, Magne, he will be back. He is responsible for us,' was all Skyler could say in her defense. Pteru was already trotting off and Skyler took this as a cue to begin rustling up Modern goods and ration packaging. The two others eventually followed Skyler's lead, but only after they saw that Pteru had indeed boarded a Beamship. Magne hesitated, dropped her litter and Modern belongings, and hurried after her former mentor, calling after him with her telepathy. She had managed to board his Beamship with only seconds to spare.

Skyler and Meerkah were left behind, and chose this time to talk, between totally different species of Sapients, separated by hundreds of millions of years of evolution. Within ten standard minutes, fifteen at most, they had mustered the belongings and litter into separate piles. Skyler and Meerkah tenderly laid a blanket over the pile of litter to stop any wind blowing Modern items away, into the brushes or to ride a zephyr, never to be seen again. They repeated the action for the belongings, only this time, piling them on the blanket and bundled the belongings into a kerchief.

Skyler and Meerkah presently strolled to a nearby natural windrow and sat together, contemplating how now to kill time. Occasionally, they heard the signature, telltale explosions of anti matter weaponry (and most likely, Amplifiers) being omitted from the south-east, from where the large freighter Beamships were landing some twenty standard minutes ago. Meerkah and Skyler had talked over these explosions, communicating via holotabs as usual, about the Oil Age and evolution on Terra, as if to desperately take their minds off the conflict in the distance, and the people and other Sapients being killed.

The conversation went from the evolution of the Alpha Draconians and Sirian bird dinosaur-like ancestors, and how this ancestor was the first sapient lifeform to have evolved on Terra, to the origin of Modern Humans. By this time, however, the distant thunder of an anti matter battle had ceased. Neither of them had even noticed. They both were stuck, sidetracked by a mutually interesting conversation, that they did not notice that faint rustle in the bushes, and a faint, humanoid and ape-like, figure that stirred the vegetation. Then there were two, and several. But neither of the Sapients still noticed. Still they were engrossed in their conversation.

The stirring ceased, and the ape-like figures had emerged from the brush, and were now skulking about the rear of the windrow. There were seven *Homo sapiens* in total. They wore animal skin cloaks to shield them from the dry, desert cold that was typical of the equatorial ice age. Five males and two females of the Paleolithic era were now metres away, and were loading their now state-of-the art arrows upon their bows, with the exception of a male and female, who both stalked forward with spears drawn. They were behind the two space and time faring Sapients, and still they were not noticed.

'Please do not be offended by the Draconians' taxonomy for your primitive ancestors. After all, even you, Skyler is still, technically an ape, and although Master Hoolde does not fully-'

The Alpha Draconian scientist broke off and spun, as if he felt someone, something was watching him. His bird-dinosaur eyes and head cocked and darted about the scenery. This prompted the *Miapiapithecus*, only three metres behind them, to halt. The savage Terrans knee locked and made an audible *click* with the still undiagnosed and mild case of osteoarthritis.

Meerkah spun around and locked gaze with the savage. It was a muscular male, well toned from years of fashioning stone tools and other hunter-gatherer duties. Its beard was surprisingly well trimmed, and a respectable standard of personal hygiene initially surprised Meerkah as his mind raced.

The savage *Miapiapithecus* made an obvious move, telegraphing its intent to strike with its spear. Meerkah's strong, taloned hand and arm grappled Skyler and tossed him unceremoniously, as the Ptahian boy sat doe-eyed, staring at the attacking Terran. The spear narrowly missed

Skyler. The *Miapiapithecus* went for the Pleiadian due to his comparitively fragile disposition, especially compared to the Reptillian. Skyler tumbled and rolled, but got to his feet instinctively. Growing up a different lad meant he got in his fair share of fights with other Pleiadian boys. Now it seems his pugnacious childhood had paid off. Skyler began to raise his arm as if to aim his Powers. He had not used them for over a month, and was not an exceptional psychic by any means, but had managed to snap a few arrows before the other savage Terrans had a chance to aim and release them. Only one was discharged, but Meerkah was already on his feet, his reptilian talons spread-eagled, inferno irises menacing. Not a big Draconian by any means, but he made up for it with superlative speed. Meerkah had never had a brawl since his juvenilehood, either, but he grabbed the first Terrans' spear in the blink of an eye. Meerkah stared down at the savage for a split second, nearly sixty centimetres taller than the Paleolithic people, and over two hundred kilogrammes of pure muscle; Alpha Draconians and their Sirian cousins were not genetically equipped to store fat.

Meerkah yanked with his one arm, downwards and circular. With the strength of about ten *Homo sapiens*, or at least now, with adrenaline pumped through his reptilian veins, the *Miapiapithecus* male was tossed to the ground like a ragdoll not yet invented.

Skyler was watching the Parapaleontologists' blind spot as the other primitives were either drawing a dagger-like flint sheath or another arrow. The female with a spear was coming up on Meerkah's flank, its spear raised. The

Pleiadian boys eyes narrowed and heart raced as his tele-kinetic powers were being more demanded of now; to lift a charging animal roughly fifty standard kilograms off its feet.

However, the Terran female was blown back in a psychokinetic concussion only a metre or so before she had stabbed Meerkah. The Alpha Draconian spun in time to see a "cave woman" faceplanted, spear out of reach. The *Miapiapithecus* female unhesitatingly grabbed the two-metre bird dinosaur with both arms around Meerkah's ankles, and hugged. Skyler knocked another primitive as it was dropping its bow set and unsheathing a flint knife, to the ground with his telekinesis, his heart rate increasing and breath becoming laboured.

'Do not kill any of them, Skyler. The one around my ankles could well be your ancestor.' Meerkah went on the offensive and swept a nearby Terran over with his scaled arm as it also drew a knife. He then bent over and plucked the female off his leg, with the faintest of effort, and tossed her into a Paleolithic Archer, as it was beginning to aim from what it thought was a safe distance.

Now, the remaining primitives began to clearly hesitate, their heads darting around for an escape route. Meekah chose this moment to skip towards the Pleiadian adolescent's side, and help him stare down the hunters. The Reptilian and the Nordic were now glowering at the savages, as if daring them to either make the next move, or preferably, yield.

36.

Sorjana began to use her telekinesis to destroy the trusty utility groundcar, but Mishta had a better idea. The prehistoric and dirty groundcar rocked and moaned on its suspension and its headlights flickered and exploded, when the Grey interrupted the powerful Nordic. Sorjana's breaths were laboured, even after only about half a minute of using her powers.

'What is it, Mishta?!' Sorjana demanded with her telepathy. The Grey could hear the adrenalin and other hormones being emitted.

'There must be a better way. You cannot destroy it with your powers. Why do you wish to destroy it, in the first place?'

'We need to get rid of the evidence. We cannot use this dirty old piece of shit forever. The *Homo sapien* law enforcement authorities will be looking for a groundcar with this description. And it's nearly out of fuel. I cannot stick a rag in its fuel reservoir and light it. We don't have a fire-making device. And the fuel tank with combustible liquid is empty. It doesn't work that way. It will not explode like in some idiotic film made in the time we are in, if that is what you are thinking?'

'The Terrans use metal plates with ciphers stamped on them, to identify groundcars, do they not? Why not just remove them? Can we do that?'

'Yes, but a groundcar without license plates will draw a lot of attention. That is the psychology of Oil Age Terrans. They are subliminally apathetic of vehicles *with* license plates. The people here will notice us before long, and give a description of this groundcar to the law enforcement caste instead. We will have a huge problem on our hands within fifteen standard minutes, or less.'

The Grey and the Nordic had pulled over on the verge and down an isolated dirt track within the outskirts of a small Commoncity, a Stone Age settlement made of wood and concrete. The landscape was still desert, and it was the time of the evening when it was not quite fully nighttime. The nearest star to this planet had long disappeared over the horizon, and the first stars could now be discerned in the night sky. The faithful F-Truck, about ten metres further down the track, away from the two extraterrestrials, was now about to have its loyalty repaid by abandonment and destruction. Sorjana said she would have to walk the rest of the way to town, and commandeer another groundcar under the cover of darkness, while Mishta waited here and remained out of sight.

As Sorjana left the dirt track and onto the main road of asphalt, she reflected latently that herself and Mishta needed new clothes, and bad. Sorjana thought she could tenderly appreciate a hot shower that these

Terrans indulged in (and not the bastardised version in her Beamship). She had no money, as of yet, and it was nighttime, or would be in five standard minutes or so. There might be a roadhouse in this parochial Common-town, where they would permit her a shower. But she could not, at least currently, communicate verbally with her ape-like ancestors. Her Holotab was confiscated and now, she realised, gone for good. Going back to the Terran internment centre for offworlders (or future Humans in her case) to retrieve it was out of the question.

It was nearly another standard hour to the Common-town. Sorjana had to duck in behind the vegetation or in the ditch whenever she saw a groundcar coming. At this time of the evening, however, they were few and far between; most travellers and groundtruck drivers had found accommodation for the night already. Darting between shadows, Sorjana found a public restroom where she could wash up and at least be halfway presentable. If she could steal a key to a Terran motel room somehow, and then a groundcar, she and Mishta might be able to get a few hours sleep; Sorjana was beginning to feel fatigued and hungry. And was she ever so thirsty!

She had managed to spirit away some clean, fresh clothes from a Terran's laundry hanging apparatus. Her clothes were ragged, soiled, and unsuitable, and would draw unwanted attention; her Pleiadian eyes, about twice as large as that of a *Homo sapien*, was bad enough. In the shadows, she changed, and bundled up her former rags and disposed of them. Sorjana had managed to find suitable garments for Mishta; the Grey would undoubtedly be starting to feel the harsh, dry, desert cold by now. She was running out of time, and now had to move with haste.

Darting in between even more shadows in the rustic, almost out of a prehistoric *Western* film, Commontown, Sorjana's luck had looked kindly upon her. Outside an ancient bar, a raven haired *Homo sapien* female had just parked in the shadows, and was oblivious to those around it, when it was exiting its *Chrysler*. Sorjana despatched the animal humanely but fatally from behind, barely making a sound at all. She took the female ape-like creature's groundcar keys and propped the *Homo sapien* in a recovery position, in a place where no one would find it until the morning. Or she hoped. Killing the animal was a necessary evil; it would cover her and Mishta's tracks until they got to her Beamship, with ease. If she had merely stunned the ape, it would report its groundcar stolen and complicate matters extremely. *This groundcar should do until we get to my Beamship. Unless we run into* another *roadblock. There is already a nationwide "man hunt" for someone of my description. And it will be released in prehistoric Terran television and radio first thing tomorrow morning. Maybe Mishta and myself should just push on all through the night on this planet*, she thought. *Forget about getting a hotel room. Just need water, food, and fuel for this slow, ugly and filthy groundcar. We might just make it by Star Rise. Maybe.*

Sorjana and Mishta did not have to deal with any more roadblocks, until their new prehistoric groundcar had reached the state border. This time, her ancient ancestors took even less chances. The traffic ahead was not so banked up, and it was indeed dark, with only the stars of the Milky Way galaxy, where Sorjana's home was orbiting the Star in the Pleiades cluster, on a planet that would not be Terraformed for another fifty thousand Terran years or so, and Terra's moon, providing the only illumination.

Despite of the relative darkness, Sorjana knew that the military presence here, at this roadblock, was at least *three* times as large as the previous one. *At least.* As she coasted forward in her newly spirited *Chrysler*, she thought to herself positively that this would chrbe the last roadblock herself and the Tall Grey beside her would have to face, and then another four or five Standard hours to the pre-historic farm where her Beamship lay dormant, sleeping.

This time, in the dark, the Terrans had set up portable floodlights, which gave Sorjana a clear view; four military groundtrucks, possibly up to fifty soldier caste *Homo sapiens*, and possibly air support with an ancient gunship helicopter or two.

Sorjana remembered the primitive but nevertheless menacing steel bird that chased her and Mishta yesterday afternoon. Bubble- shaped cockpit and rotary firearms on its sides that discharged Terra's weapon of choice; the full metal jacket bullet, at an impressive rate of fire.

Miniguns, Sorjana remembered they called them.

It was too late to turn back now, and would only make matters worse even if it wasn't. Besides, this was still the only way back to her bell-shaped Beamship. She could take the seldom used, more rural tracks once she got over the State border. But that meant getting past this formidable *Homo sapien* bastion.

'We have no Anti-Pistols left.' Mishta telepathised the obvious as Sorjana coasted forward another place. 'Your telekinetic abilities are relatively limited without the aid of an Amplifier. Do you think we can get past, Sorjana? Because in my opinion, it does not look good. Not good at all.' The Tall Grey's telepathy began to take on an almost childish, whining tone, though it was probably not intentional. Sorjana kept her Plieadian eyes locked forward, did not respond. She had not even bothered to take note of what her and The Grey were now wearing. Right now survival and getting back to the Beamship was all that mattered. Every other detail was laughably negligible, including the *Homo sapien* clothes they now wore. As long as they fit them. Sorjana crept another place forward in the cue.

Again she considered turning the ancient groundcar around and hoping for the best; even though the soldiers would indeed notice. Again, she told herself this was the only way off this hellish planet her ape-like ancestors called home. She had no choice but to push forward and hope. Hope she could come up with a plan that could work. Might work.

We are so close, Sorjana thought to herself, eschewing telepathy. *So close, and the only thing that is stopping us is a roadblock with fifty armed Terrans and an ancient military tank for good measure. As superior I am to to these Early Humans, I don't stand a chance. I am too exhausted and frightened to raise my hands now and howl in despair.*

Sorjana coasted the prehistoric *Chrysler* forward another pace. Only half a dozen or so groundcars in front. Sorjana was too close to the groundcars immediately in front and behind to pull out anyway. She found herself strumming on the groundcar's dash with her fingers nervously. She looked out the window futilely, at nothing but the pitch-black verdant landscape at night.

'Any ideas, Mishta?' Sorjana's telepathy was vaguely betraying her sarcasm. But the Tall Grey did not answer. Instead, it was fiddling inside the glove compartment almost childishly, when it faced Sorjana with its overlarge black eyes and neutral face on an overlarge head. Sorjana could barely see Mishta, the only illumination coming from the gauges inside the dash, and the small light inside the glove compartment. In the Grey's hand, was a small vial a sickly black liquid.

'My knowledge of Terran writing is limited. Can you confirm what it reads on this?' Mishta passed the vial to Sorjana, as she moved up another pace in the queue.

Sorjana reached behind her the instant the goundcar came to a halt again, and fumbled for the interior light in the rear of the groundcar's cabin.

'It says, "hair dye, raven black. Instant colouring with just one rinse, guaranteed."' Sorjana returned her Nordic eyes to the road once more, and assessed where they were in the queue. Five more groundcars. 'I can tell what you are thinking, Mishta. Even without telepathy. It might work, but there is one minor detail; the Terran law enforcement ahead would undoubtedly check for identification. Licences, for example. And I have nothing.

Plus there is you in the seat next to me. It simply will not work.'

'I can get out and sneak past on foot. My biological chemistry means I am practically invisible to infrared. As for identification,' Mishta reached inside the glove compartment again, and passed over a small object just as Sorjana coasted forward again. She scrutinised the object as she urged the *Chrysler* to a halt again. 'Texas driver's license. Belonging to a Ms. Maria Caterina Maccevelli.' She turned to Mishta. 'Well I can loose my blonde hair. And I managed find some eyeglasses. But there is still a matter of the fact that I still won't pass as a forty standard year old Italian-American female *Homo sapien*. My eyes are too big and blue.'

'Just try it Sorjana. You asked me if I had any ideas, as you humans put it. This is my idea. That, and plough through with this groundcar, and hope for the best.'

'Okay. Very well. Just get started on my hair, and get the hell out when you're done. We only have two standard minutes. Maybe three, at most.

As Sorjana hoped, Mishta had laid a blanket over her shoulders, to absorb the excess dye, and clambered over to the back seat. There he massaged the acrid Terran hair dye into Sorjana's scalp and hair as frantically as it could. Mishta achieved it in a little over two standard minutes, when Sorjana ordered, 'Okay, Mishta. That will have to do.' The law enforcement officer two groundcars ahead showed signs of summarising its scrutiny of the said groundcar. It would wave the occupants off in a few seconds. 'Grab the blanket, and any evidence you just dyed my hair, and slip out through the scrub. I will meet you exactly eight hundred metres past this roadblock. First, mop up any excess dye around my head and neck. No evidence. This is important. Leave the rest to me.' The Grey slipped the blanket from her shoulders and did as Sorjana instructed, including taking the empty vial, which Sorjana had prudently passed to Mishta over her shoulder. Ten seconds, later, and the groundcar ahead began to move off.

'Go now.' The Tall Grey slipped into the verge-side of the rear compartment, opened the door and slipped out like a sack full of offal, just as Sorjana began to urge the *Chrysler* forward. 'And good luck, Mishta.' Sorjana called over her shoulder with her telepathy, not caring if the Grey heard her or not.

Sorjana could not believe her luck, sitting there in the driver's seat of the prehistoric groundcar, as the *Homo sapien* State Trooper, flanked by a half dozen National Guard soldiers, armed with assault rifles just like the ones she and Mishta were using earlier that day. This time, they surrounded her *Chrysler* and had these assault rifles pointed directly at her. A military groundtruck blocked her path, She could tell it was parked across the road on idle, and would drive forward and back to permit ground-cars through, as if utilised as a makeshift "boomgate."

'Okay, Ms. Maccevelli. Please let the D.M.V. know next time you need to wear visual aids while driving.' The officer took in her hair and eyeglasses, her hair with greying streaks that looked almost blonde to it. Mishta did a rough and sloppy job of dyeing her hair, but it worked. That was all that mattered. 'The vehicle checks out. I have just received word that this *Chrysler* indeed belongs to a Ms. Maria Caterina Maccevelli. But you are still using an expired drivers license. On any other day or night I would give you a decent fine. But we are snowed under, and I don't have time. We have a serial killer on the loose. We have bigger concerns. Just consider it your lucky day. Or night.' The officer spent half a minute scrutinising the *Chrysler*, and had taken the keys off Sorjana to open the trunk, as well as make his and the soldiers' job easier. Now, the *Homo sapiens* officer, a mustached male of about thirty standard years, with sandy hair, handed the ignition keys back to the driver of the white *Chrysler*. As the driver he thought was a Ms. Maria Caterina Maccevelli placed the key in the ignition and turned it over, the officer took a few steps back and waved the driver on with an illuminated baton. The military groundtruck began to lurch forward again, and Sorjana drove off nonchalantly but inconvenienced, despite the fact that she was so nervous that she would do anything to throw up now.

As planned, Mishta entered the groundcar and sat in the passenger's seat half a mile past the roadblock with a terrifying military presence. The Grey was evidently covered in leaves and twigs and other vegetation, indicating that it indeed had went past the soldiers, as well as passing groundcars on the highway, undetected. Sorjana watched the Grey a moment, before looking over her shoulder and pulling the groundcar away from the verge. Fifteen seconds later, and they were travelling the speed limit once more.

'My Beamship is in Kansas. We have to make just one more border crossing, but don't worry. We will be taking an unsealed, private road. The Plieadians that are minding my Ship have a massive property that extends over the border of Oklahoma. No authorites will be minding it. We will be there in approximately four standard hours.' Sorjana reached over her seat and handed the Grey a blanket; it had left the one it was carrying on the ground behind when it saw Sorjana indicate and pull over. 'You might want to get some rest, in the meantime. Do you Serponian Greys sleep?' Sorjana inquired diplomatically.

'Of course. We are technically mammals incapable of reproduction, after all.' The Grey replied in an almost haughty tone. Mishta rolled over and draped the blanket over itself. It curled up and stared out the window, at the full moon of Terra, with rugged trees and cactuses occasionally blocking the moon. It was roughly a standard hour past the middle of the night, local time, on this planet. Mishta could tell by the fact Terra's moon was a half or so the way across the night sky. It drowned out the stars above, where its home planet Serpo was orbiting Zeta Reticuli.

Sorjana kept her eyes on the highway. The groundcar's headlights, the asphalt and markings of prehistoric acrylic paint was all she saw. She was not getting tired. At least not yet. It was not long before she heard the Grey sleeping in the seat next to her.

* * *

It was two standard hours before Sorjana indeed began to feel sleepy. She unwound the groundcar's window and put her arm out and up, catching the biting draught, keeping her alert, awake. She managed to rustle another half hour or so before even this had no effect on her drowsiness.

Sorjana pulled over at the next rest area. She parked behind a semi groundtruck there. The driver would hopefully not waken and investigate the occupants in the *Chrysler* parked behind it. That would be bad. For her, Mishta, and the *Homo sapien*. She had no way of waking, of setting an alarm. Her holotab confiscated by Bob Onslow, seemingly years ago. Mishta would unlikely have a Holotab on itself as well. It had been a long day indeed. Sorjana nestled back and closed her eyes. She slept awkwardly a few standard minutes later.

Sorjana woke, refreshed, only to find she had overslept. The groundtruck ahead made an audible noise with its prehistoric pneumatics, and lurched off. Sorjana opened her Plieadian eyes at the high-pitched whimper emitting from the groundtruck. The driver must have not looked at the occupants. Why would it? Sorjana watched sleepily as the groundtruck entered the highway again and slug-gishly gained speed. The star of Terra was unobstructed as the groundtruck left. It was early morning, dawn, and the star blinded her. She squinted, leaned forward, and sleepily fired up the *Chrysler's* combustion engine. Mishta stirred next to her. Sorjana rubbed her eyes. Her mouth was dry, and she swallowed saliva instinctively, as if trying to hydrate herself with her own fluids. The groundcar needed another standard minute or so to warm up. They waited in telepathic silence. Mishta was awake now.

'How much longer, Sorjana?'

'About another two Terran hours, and we will be at my Beamship.' Sorjana selected drive gear and pressed her foot on the accelerator gently. The Groundcar shuddered and protested but moved off anyway. They emerged onto the highway presently, and were at speed. They both sat in telepathic silence the rest of the trip, Mishta staring out the window at the blurring Terra landscape, Sorjana her eyes forward. She pulled onto a dirt road about one and a half standard hours later. Then, it was another twenty or so standard minutes down a bumpy, dusty dirt track, with verdant greenery bordering either side, when the white *Chrysler* came to a halt in front of the ancient, red barn that obscured Sorjana's Beamship from *Homo sapien* satellites high above, in the orbit of Terra.

37.

The two large Beamships, under the command of the Annunaki had recently landed near the Paleolithic *Homo sapien* settlement of mainly lean-to shelters of wood and leaves, with a communal bonfire in the centre. Rion Murphy had just begun to get the primitive humans' attention when nearly a dozen Beamships, only ten or so metres in diameter, appeared seemingly out of nowhere over the horizon. The fifty or so Annunaki had only just managed to disembark and form menacing, strategic formations around the primitive Terrans, when everyone's attention was caught as a fleet of Beamships approached over the crest of a hill, in an almost military formation.

It was too late for the Annunaki to scramble back to their now-standby ships; the enemy Beamships of standard size would land in a few seconds. Rion Murphy and the Annunaki only had time to prepare the weapons they were carrying for combat, and form defensive positions using their Beamships' ramps as cover. Indeed, the.......... Murphy counted them as they landed, or rather, came to a levitation about five metres above the ground..........nine enemy ships would be unburdening themselves of their load of Sapient passengers any second. Murphy called over his shoulder, his Holotab translating as usual, for some enforcers to go inside the Beamships and muster all the weapons they needed. There was, as far as Murphy remembered, one Anti Rifle for every two enforcers. The other half can hand the magazines of anti matter over, or fight with whatever was at their disposal.

The Annunaki were outnumbered two to one, but they had weapons to even the score. Even so, the refugees of the Commonwealth, stranded on prehistoric, Paleolithic Terra, kept a few Amplifiers in their Beamships. As they intercepted the Annunaki, prehistoric *Homo sapiens* could only watch in awestruck silence as god-like off-worlders, from both sides, landed in their unimaginably advanced chariots from deep space, and disembarked with their equally advanced small arms. Anti Rifle faced off against cybernetically enhanced telekinesis.

Rion Murphy, who also sported a captured Amplifier, was the only present Annunaki Enforcer with any Powers. The other three Modern humans in the band, preferred to fight the old fashioned way: with firearms and melee. The rest were Alpha Draconians with the strength of twelve *Homo sapiens*, or about twice the strength of Modern Humans. They could easily overpower the Refugees in a wrestling match.

Claudia vam Rees was bonded as a hostage with Anti Cuffs inside one of the large, captured Beamships. Murphy had decided to drag her out as the fighting intensified, as well as to ensure he would not get harmed or killed in the heat of battle. The Paleolithic Terrans had already scrambled and fled. As Murphy escorted the Commodore in a human shield fashion, with an Anti-Pistol at her head, already he could see that the Annunaki were indeed losing. Roughly two Enforcers fell for every one of their enemies. Murphy was yet to have identified exactly who The Annunaki's enemy was. Rion Murphy did not care, and he expected that the Enforcers were equally apathetic. All that mattered was that they were losing. Until now.

'That's my daughter!' A dark skinned Vegan, flanked and surrounded by Amp-armed Marines, barked with his telepathy. Murphy thought that he should recognise this dandy-clad man; obviously an authority figure, with a mustache and a head of hair the epitomised male pattern baldness. He wore a now-soiled robe of office.

A diplomat! Murphy sneered with renewed glee. *Perhaps we can test how strong a father's love is. That and win this skirmish after all. I was just about to give orders to retreat. But this is just too precious!*

'Father! Get away from here! Save yourself!'

'Shut up, whore!' Murphy struck vam Rees in the side of her neck with the Anti Pistol. 'Annunaki, Retreat!' His Holotab speaking on his behalf this time. Indeed, only a dozen, fifteen at most, reptilians scarpered up the ramp of the massive Cargo Beamship. They were waiting behind the ramp and popping out from the side to return fire; there was no other cover around; except a few shrubs and small trees.

Presently, only Murphy, the senior and junior vam

Rees, and about fifty Modern Humans, with their Anti Rifles or Amplifiers, were left in the open. Most of the Modern Humans lurked behind the cover of two of their landed Beamships, a few however, charged out in the open, either foolish or desperate to get home, to the Modern Age. Twenty or so citizens of the Commonwealth lay either Dead or wounded. The other seven Beamships were still airborne, but were the unarmed, civil variety, so could not provide air support. Fortunately for the Anunnaki.

Murphy crept forward, with Claudia as a human shield, certain that the commander of the other side gave the order to cease fire with his telepathy. *The father of this uppity Commodore of the Commonwealth*, Murphy corrected himself. *Well, what did I expect? An unarmed Draconian is no match for a Modern Human with Powers and an Amp. I should have given the order to retreat, and us find a different way to mine gold. No point in sympathy. An exchange for a Politician of the Commonwealth is even better.*

'Hold your fire! Cease fire!' Marlon ordered. 'That is my daughter in front of that beast of a human! Everyone, put your weapons down! That is an order in the name of Marlon vam Rees, Chancellor of the Vegan Chamber of Commerce!'

A second or so later, and nearly two dozen, heavy, black firearms that fired projectiles of depleted anti matter, and vaguely resembling and assault rifle of Oil Age Terra, could be seen and heard being placed gently on the ground. Indeed, the ramp of the Annunaki's Beamship that was used as a makeshift shield, was only made of titanium alloy, and was starting to show signs of losing its integrity. The two hundred or so projectiles it absorbed was starting to make it smoke and smolder, like an ancient plate of steel that had just been welded in the Oil Age.

Satisfied that the enemy Commonwealther would no longer pose as a threat, Murphy urged Claudia forward, and an agonising standard minute passed before the hostage and abductor were at halfway point.

'Now, Commonwealthers,' Murphy now knew of his adversaries affiliation by both their accents and their body language, and the fact that the senior Vegan trumpeted his job title in his own arrogance that rivaled even that of Rion Murphy, Lieutenant of the Annunaki. It was Murphy's telepathy speaking this time as he continued with and almost mandatory pause. 'We're gonna do us a little trade. Daughter for father-'

Murphy broke off as the sound of a heat-warped ramp could be heard, and out of shape, being retracted. Immediately, the unmistakable sound of anti matter propulsion engines, powerful enough to drive the three hundred metre Cargo beamship with thousands of tonnes of Sentinels into orbit, could be heard at the conclusion of the ramp being retracted.

Murphy, unhesitatingly, aborted his hostage and sprinted towards the ramp, but was a few seconds too slow. The ramp was retracted and the engines primed and ready by the time he got there. With insatiable rage, and as he stood there and seethed at the blatant mutiny, not ten seconds later and the massive, disc-shaped cargo freighter was airborne. Realising latently that he still held an Anti Pistol in his right hand, Rion Murphy instinctively and in a sociopathic fury of a tantrum, raised the anti matter weapon at the behemoth as it was ascending at an exponential rate of climb. The last thing Rion Murphy remembered as the concussion from his weapon knocked him off his feet, was that an Anti Pistol is laughably puny compared to the Draconium plating on his abandoning Beamship's hull.

About half a standard minute later, or it could be as much as two, for it seemed like Murphy's ears was ringing for an eternity (although he was still semi-conscious), Rion noticed that the Beamship was long gone. The second cargo Beamship, of roughly the same class and displacement, was out of reach, and most likely would be forever, even though Murphy was not significantly wounded, and even though it was less than half a kilometre away, visible above the shrubs and small trees. The Draconium plated workhorse was docked on four stout pods. Terran birds, Murphy saw as he looked over from where he lay, were now beginning to perch there. The star of Terra was setting, it was late afternoon, and the birds could be seen clearly, with the star at the optimal angle, despite the relatively small size of the Terran birds. Murphy had prudently given the order for his Enforcers to load the two cargo Beamships evenly, at approximately one hundred and fifty each, in case of the unlikely contingency of one being destroyed. *One hundred and fifty Sentinels*, Murphy thought. *Plus a decent Beamship to boot. No*

Modern Human had ever known such wealth, especially in a socialist galactic Commonwealth.

The main reason this wealth was so close and yet so far, however, was because the instant Rion Murphy had opened his eyes was the moment that, for the first time in his life, Murphy was looking straight at the receiving end of an anti matter firearm. Later, he realised there were several pointed at him. For the first time in his life, he was genuinely helpless. He thought there should be some hidden message or meaning to his current situation, but Rion could not think what.

All Murphy now presently knew was that he was now being roughly and unceremoniously hauled to his feet, with ten or so Commonwealthers surrounding him, his ears still ringing. Murphy looked up in time to see that Commodore facing him eyes of fury and defiance, as his arms were now being bound in the same Anti Cuffs that had previously bonded the junior vam Rees. The Commodore backhanded the Annunkaki in the face, almost the instant the Anti Cuffs were secured.

'Better, Commodore?' A telepathic voice with an Arcturian accent could be heard from behind Murphy, had his ears were not still ringing. He hardly felt the puny Vegan's dainty backhand amongst the pain already inside his head. 'Then lets get this animal aboard that freighter over there. We should be leaving tomorrow for Modern Times, first thing. But you are the new commanding officer here, and the choice is yours, Ma'am.'

'Are we all here? Everyone that went through Shrink-space, to this time, I mean?' Claudia looked around dartedly, as if trying to take a cursory mental roll call, even though she had no idea how many Commonwealthers there were in total, let alone who. Her father came over to embrace her, as Murphy was being roughly herded to the large Beamship.

'My Claudia! Are you hurt? Those Annunaki are going to hang without skin, every last one of them! As soon as we get back to Modern Times, we will hunt them down, and every last one of them, like the animals they are!'

'I am fine father, only got struck twice. Nothing I can't handle. I've been more badly beaten fixing a Biobrid. We should get out of here within the hour. Gather up every item, of course. Nothing will be left behind. Surely you know the basics of Chronophysics, father?'

'To hell with that! Let us just get a set of Sentinels prepared for Shrinkspace, and leave this hell hole the second we are ready!'

'That can be within twenty standard minutes, M'Lord Chancellor.' A Marine came to a halt in front of the diplomat and saluted. 'Already we have found a few sets of Sentinels on that Beamship over there. A few men over there have confirmed that there are at least a hundred more in the hold. They will need to be secured inside the Beamship, first, of course. The Pirates just dumped them in there and took off. They are about twenty standard tonnes each, and can do massive damage, both material and collateral, if that thing should lose control in Shrinkspace. They were lucky none of them got killed! Sir.'

Although only three metres across, and one metre high and one and a half deep, Sentinels, made mainly of

Draconium, required machinery to move. Presently, on prehistoric Terra, there was not even an android available, let alone something strong enough to move them. Thirty standard tonnes was a more conservative estimation of their weight.

'There are plenty of lashing field generators,' the Marine, one of the Arcturian bodyguards continued, referring to the high tech Arcturium "nets" that kept goods in check. 'In that freighter. We can have it set up in thirty minutes with ease, but if M'Lord wishes, we can push for twenty, and be airborne by then.'

'Take all the time you need, Sergeant. An hour would be more than fine. We are in no real hurry, now that we have Sentinels. But no more than three standard hours. The Annunaki will return to this time with reinforcements, and they can do it in as little time as four hours. Is that clear, Marine?' The rugged Marine Sergeant merely saluted in affirmation, and marched of to relay the Chancellor's orders.

'Father, you have not answered my question.' Claudia intruded. 'Is everyone here? We need to identify the dead, and tend to the wounded.' There were moans in the background, with Commonwealthers now assuming the role of makeshift soldiers to makeshift field nurses. Marlon looked around at the bloodshed. Most of his troops were tending to the injured, improvising a task in the absence of further directives.

'What about this lot, Chancellor?' Marlon darted his head to the other side of the battlefield, where a Lyran was casting his telepathy from. Two others were in the process of confiscating the fallen Enforcers' weapons. 'There are still Reptoids here that are still alive, about a dozen of them.' One Commonwealther had his Anti Rifle at the ready whilst the other kicked the myriad but lethal weapons out of their reach. The one that called out also had an Anti Rifle aimed fastidiously.

'Put them out of their misery, or let them suffer, I don't care. Just make sure they are no longer any threat.' Two more Commonwealthers rushed over instinctively with their weapons, aiming at the twitching and howling Sapient bird dinosaurs. Marlon adds, with malice uncharacteristic for Modern Humans, 'Just don't waste any medical science on them. And especially don't take them with us. Now, are there any of us missing? Speak now, citizens.'

A young Plieadian female took a few standard minutes to finally inform the Chancellor. She had been hiding in the safety of a levitating, dormant Beamship amidst the battle that raged only ten standard minutes or so ago. Marlon recognised her vaguely as she bowed to him. She had, unusual for a Plieadian, straight raven hair and purple irises. She was flanked by a boy of the same species and age, with spiky blonde hair. *She is with that troublesome, insolent Chronophysist and his Draconian lover. What do they want now?!*

'Speak up, Girl. What is the matter with the Chronophyicist now? Is he still too afraid to leave his Beamship?' Marlon did not bother to hide his smirk as he continued, with Xankyu glowering disapprovingly as usual. 'Did he have to send his..........niece, daughter?'

'Student, Sir, and a good friend and mentor.' Magne did not care if she was now treading on insubordination with her defensive and defiant telepathic tone. 'We heard your telepathic request broadcast over an Amp. The Chronophyicist and Parapaleontologist stayed behind, to pick up all Modern possesions and litter.'

Marlon rolled his eyes and cocked a sarcastic eyebrow. 'Well I suppose someone had best take a Beamship and get them, then.'

'Yes, Chancellor,' replied Magne evenly. 'We should take the very Beamship that was stolen from them as well, while we are at it.' Marlon could only shake his head, turn his back and give a contemptuous wave. 'Whatever. Just be back here in three standard hours. We will not wait for anyone. Not even a for a Parapaleontologist or Chronophyicist.'

38.

The primitives had drawn themselves true, and had long since fraternised with the offworlders. They were now sitting about the windrow, although at an awkward distance, as if one party, such as Meerkah and Skyler was made of water, the other party, oil. Meerkah did his best to communicate with them, stretching his science to its absolute limits. His Holotab was no longer of much help. Skyler interjected regularly, but was more a hindrance than a help. Thirty or so standard minutes had passed, and the offworlders got up to stretch their stiffness; the Terrans, being accustomed to squatting to make tools and fire, laughed audibly at Skylers' discomfort. 'Ask them if there are more like them, Master Meerkah.' Skyler put both hands on his hips and leaned back, followed by a myriad of arm and leg stretches. His hips *cricked* audibly.

'The dialect these *Miapiapithecus* speak is different to the generic one that is on a Parapaleontologist's Holotab. Their language is surprisingly complicated, with over four thousand different words. Nouns, verbs, even five hundred or so adjectives. My Holotab only recognises less than half of them.' Meerkah ordered his Holotab, fastened at his waist, back to the primitive's language, with a tweak on the screen with his taloned hand.

'Mayhr nook ahn geeh?' Meerkah asked via his Holotab, a silver thing designed for field use, rugged and hard to break.

'Ahn geeh telee nadhir.' The leader *Miapiapithecus* replied, pointing to where the massive Beamships were, and the ensuing, following battle. Meerkah's Holotab clearly laboured as it tried to translate desperatly with missing data. 'There more half day there.'

'Half a day?!' Skyler barked with his telepathy. 'Half a day's walk? I think they may need a lift back in Master Pteru's Beamship. When it gets here. *If* it gets here.'

'*Miapiapithecus* often travel for hours in pursuit of game. Typically, they weaken their prey with arrows, then chase it until it collapses with exhaustion. Sort of a strategic persistence hunting if you will. The arrows merely weaken it, like I said, or are only good for killing smaller game, such as rabbits and birds. It is the spear that actually *kills* the large animal, such as a gazelle or zebra or wooly mammoth or rhinoceros.' Meerkah's head tilted as if looking behind Skyler. Skyler spun around, and saw what Meerkah was troubled by. A Beamship was emerging over the horizon. It was doubling in size every few seconds, and was above them in twenty. At this distance, Skyler recognised Pteru's Beamship, distinctive by its square viewing window configuration. He waved his arms instinctively as the disc shaped spacecraft descended. It fell from its two hundred metre or so altitude in the blink of an eye and came to a hover five metres in the air. Seconds later, and Skyler found his new found adolescent love interest on the ground directly beneath Pteru's Beamship.

Magne strode forward confidently with feminine grace, like an ancient cheerleader alpha female from an Oil Age American high school. Despite her disheveled, antagonised attire from a hard day of indirectly fighting space-time pirates, she still looked shockingly exotic and irresistible to Skyler. Magne took in Skylers' recent exertion; soiled clothes and other evidence of a recent fight or struggle and was not mutually attracted to him in his current form. She had seen enough of the alpha type dominant males competing for her back at her academy on Erra. She found it a turnoff now.

'Master Pteru is on board. Chancellor vam Rees said we are leaving in-' Magne checked the time on her pink Holotab. '-two hours and fifty-two minutes. Have you gathered up all the stuff?' She looked behind Skyler at the primitive troop of *Miapiapithecus*. 'Who are *they*?'

'Just a few new friends we made. They're cavemen, don't you know, Magne?'

'I can see that, Skyler. What are they doing here?

'Could we not give them a ride and spend an hour or so at their cave? Be back with Chancellor vam Rees and the others in two hours. It would be kind of...educational to see our ancestors in the flesh, wouldn't you say?'

'Skyler! We cannot take any risks! You know that, as a junior Chronophysicist! What if we gave their tribe some disease they had no immunity to?'

Meerkah spoke up with his Holotab in bird-song

language. 'Pteru has medical masks in his Beamships' surgeon kit. And you needn't worry about me. Genus *Saurosapienia* and *Homo* have incompatible diseases. Whatever Dinosaur flu I am carrying wont affect any human of any kind.' Meerkah gave his best impression of a human's mischievous grin.

'What is taking so long?' An amplified voice of telepathy emitted from the Beamship. An electronic version of Pteru's telepathy, no doubt. *So, Master Hoolde's Beamship is armed with a built-in Amplifier?!* Skyler mused. *I thought those were forbidden on civilian Beamships?*

No doubt Magne was thinking the same, but Meerkah's Holotab could only detect *natural* telepathy. He wondered why the two adolescent Modern humans went quiet all of a sudden, and seemed to be listening to a voice inside their head.

'It's you and Meerkah's idea. You go tell him, Skyler.' Magne accused. Skyler trotted the ten or so metres over where the Beamship hovered and looked up. He shouted with his telepathy. Raw Telepathy. He turned his Holotab off long ago to conserve power. At least he could be proud of that right decision. Even though, with a battery of full power and integrity lasting over a month, Skyler had honestly though they could be stuck here, on prehistoric Terra.

Pteru heard him nonetheless.

'Give our primitive ancestors a ride in my Beamship? What do you think we are, Skyler? Friendly aliens from an Oil Age science fiction film? Who put you up to this? Don't tell me. Meerkah. That old dinosaur.' Pteru was uncharacteristically short tempered and sarcastic. Skyler guessed it was the desperation he had been facing today, and the stress. And that Chancellor and his attitude did not help, either. 'Very well. Just make sure you wear surgical masks. I have a carton or two up in here. Now, step back, will you?'

Pteru began to land his Beamship, not waiting for Skyler to get out of the way. Skyler practically yelped and dived out of the way. He had only just cleared the landing area by two seconds to spare when the Beamship touched down on its sturdy pods and powered its Arcturium engines down to idle, whisper quiet as usual. Skyler then decided to turn on his holotab, risk it for half an hour or so.

Seconds later, and Pteru emerged from a descending ramp with a disappointed yet amused look on his face. His clothes, the same burgundy-purple one-piece robe he wore the day before, was also soiled and had a tear at the upper left sleeve, though no one knew how it got there. Neither he, nor Magne were not amidst the fighting some fifteen or so standard minutes ago. In his hand, he held three fabric masks, not so unlike the ones an Oil Age surgeon would wear, and not significantly more advanced.

'Well, let's go. And put these on right away. You've probably contaminated these *Homo sapiens* already with offworld disease. You should know better than that, Skyler. It is one of the first lessons when interacting with ancestors with little or no access to adequate medical science. You could literally, or probably already have, wiped out millions of Modern Humans!'

'Master Hoolde, believe me, I...I mean Meerkah and me had no choice. These cavemen attacked us! They tried to kill us. Had it not been for Master Meerkah, I would be dead or dying. But we overpowered and subdued them. Now, they told us they only tried to kill me because...'

'They did not intend to kill you, or us from the start.' Meerkah continued on Skyler's behalf. Skyler forgot about the fact that Meerkah can now hear his thoughts via their Holotabs. 'The *Miapiapithecus* troop was only trying to subdue and interrogate Skyler, and thought initially that I was some kind of demon.' Meerkah let the rest of the story tell itself to Pteru and Magne.

Pteru and Meerkah did their best to coax the Paleolithic humans onto the Beamship, although Meerkah had made it quite clear, or at least thought he had, that the cavemen were being transported back to their village or temporary settlement. Pteru explained that he had all the Medical instruments on board for testing for diseases, and, when the Beamship was airborne again with all seven Paleolithic *Homo sapiens*, Meerkah did his best to pilot the flying saucer; Pteru's Beamship had minimal automata, and could not fly itself. Meerkah was no seasoned Pilot by any means; amateur at best, but he had managed to get them there, at the Paleolithic settlement, two kilometres or so further south of where the Annunaki's discus-shaped Beamships had landed.

'Hover the Beamship above the Common village.' Pteru ordered. 'We need another half an hour or so. We have only just managed to retrieve all the blood samples, one each, from these seven *Homo sapien*. You got there fast, my friend.' Pteru held the syringe in his hands carefully, while Magne and Skyler assisted. All seven Paleolithic men were sedated, with the one they were working on now, the female with a spear, on a fold out stainless steel gurney. Magne had her sterile gloved hand, (all three wore masks, gloves and hairnets, of course) hovering over the instruments, particularly the gizmo-looking one that tested blood samples for genetic defects and pathogens, in under a standard minute. She then handed the instrument over to Pteru solemnly and silently. The instrument resembled an ugly, overgrown and ancient ice-cream scoop. Pteru had recently called it a "Haemometer."

Illumination inside the Beamship was set from a pleasant fluorescent purple-blue, to a clinical, bright white. Pteru said it keeps him in a scientific, examining mood. Most set their Beamships to this mode of lighting whenever doing chores like this; Alien Abduction, their victims have been reported to call it. His cousin, Sorjana, who was almost more like a sister, told him this once, when he visited her in the Oil Age about two standard years ago, his time. Pteru wondered for a split second how Sorjana was doing, before frowning and concentrating on the job.

An audible, simultaneous *buzz-beep* that was unpleasant to the ears of any species of human, emitted from the device that Magne had recently passed her mentor.

'This specimen has not been contaminated with Pleiadian Human diseases. Six more to go. It seems that you are lucky so far, Skyler. But let it be a lesson to you.' The

Plieadian adolescent shifted on his feet awkwardly, and humbled. The Paleolithic men and women's hunting tools were piled in a corner, where they were secured. Magne and Skyler lifted the next subject up on the bench, next to the first. The animal of Prehistoric Terra was surprisingly light, despite being fully grown. The sedated animal was under fifty standard kilograms, and the two Plieadian teenagers lifted the thing as if it were a small child. Pteru prepared to extract the next blood sample as they lifted, and took its blood as soon as the two had stepped back. The syringe, also marginally more hi-tech than an Oil Age predecessor, filled with *Homo sapien* blood, more than enough for a sample, nowhere near enough to make the creature anaemic.

'May I have the Haemometer, when you are finished refreshing it, Magne?'

'Yes, of course, Master Hoolde.'

'Call me Pteru, Magne. This isn't the time or place for formalities.' Magne darted forward as if humbled and embarrassed for forgetting to prepare the Haemometer. She sterilised the contraption frantically with an alcoholic wipe, passing it to Pteru while still cleaning it. Pteru repeated the process he performed on the first specimen's blood. The three Modern Humans stood in silence for half a minute while Meerkah, in the pilot's seat, ensured the Beamship remained in a hover. Eventually, the same simultaneous *buzz-beep* emitted.

'This one has passed quarantine, as well. Five more to go. Give us another five or so standard minutes, Meerkah. How is this Beamship doing for anti matter?' Pteru's

Holotab shouted on his behalf as he worked quickly and efficiently.

'A little over three quarters,' came the reptilian reply from the other end of the Beamship. 'That is what, good for six standard months? Just worry about your testing, my friend.'

In the meantime, Skyler and Magne took the initiative to clear the bench and replace it with two fresh subjects. Pteru did not acknowledge the teens' extra effort, did not have time to. He simply took another blood sample while Magne prepared the Haemometer.

'This subject has hereditary osteoporosis in it's genes, which will manifest itself in twenty or so standard years.' Pteru announced, more to Meerkah, when the *buzz-beep* chimed. 'These hominids seldom live past forty anyway?'

'Thirty standard years is the average life span of *Miapi-apithecus* in the wild. The record, I believe, is forty seven.' Meerkah responded while piloting the ship, and glad for the distraction.

'No pathogens though?' Skyler asked.

'No pathogens. Remember, these hominids have no resistance to diseases that our immune systems would find mundane. Now, you may clean the Haemometer again, Magne.'

The last four also showed no traces of Modern diseases such as Arcturian meningitis or the Lyran influenza. Pteru relaxed significantly now. He turned to Meerkah. 'Okay, my friend, you may set the Beamship down at the settlement. We will finish up here.'

Magne steralised the medical instruments while Skyler

and Pteru grabbed an end each of each Paleolithic man, in turn. They did not bother with lowering down the high tech way; the old fashioned way would do; carried down the ramp and outside, into the recovery position. Anti matter was still relatively expensive, and Pteru's beamship was privately owned, fueled by his own funds. There was no way Pteru was going to waste anti matter by lowering them down with expensive anti gravity like he lowered Magne.

All the while, the Paleolithic men and women stood there, staring at the hovering flying saucer and watching their hunting party being carried off board. Pteru told Meerkah to fire up the anti matter engines and have them on standby. Skyler and Pteru hurried back on board after the last *Homo sapien* was being dumped gently on the ground, next to the other six sedated animals. The ramp to the Beamship closed promptly and they were airborne in seconds, before the ancient Terrans decided to attack in revenge.

Skyler asked his mentor, as they were taking off their masks and gloves, while Magne packed up the instruments and put them away in a designated place that Pteru directed her. 'Well I am so relieved we didn't make any of those cavemen sick. Now, can we go back down and meet their tribe we still have a standard hour, easy. Is that okay, Master Hoolde?'

Magne discreetly shook her head while Pteru shot Skyler his most disappointed, unamused expression. Meerkah, being learned in Modern and ancient human behaviour, though it was best to simply ignore that, pretend he did not know that the awkward *faux pas* was said. He simply kept facing forward, and piloted his friend and fellow scientist's Beamship back the where the Commonwealthers had mustered, and back to the only way back to Modern civilisation.

39.

Dr. Nero Suzuki was an unremarkable elderly gentleman, who owned a hectare sized cybernetics factory in the industrial district, which Darius had no trouble finding, and not just because of an enormous but entropied sign that read, *"Suzuki and Sons, Cybersmiths Ltd"*. Dr. Nero Suzuki stooped hunched over at a drawing desk up in his mezzanine office, conferring with a magnifying glass, over some blueprints an apprentice had produced the day before. When Darius knocked, waited, entered, and handed him the Bonds and showed him the letter, he frowned across at the war veteran from over his spectacles. Obviously the type to shun away from laser eye surgery, which was available since the Mid Oil Age.

'Oh yes. You are that war veteran whose parents make fairly decent wine. Well, now. There is some good news. We may have an artificial leg, already made, that just might fit you. Do you mind?'

'Eh?' Darius wondered what the old man was referring to. Nero Suzuki turned back to his desk and produced a length of measuring tape, the same kind that a tailor would use. 'Oh, you mean measure my leg.' Darius took a seat and stretched out his one remaining leg. 'Not at all. Ready when you are.'

Suzuki took the length, and girth of Darius's good leg, at the shins, ankles, thigh and foot. He recorded them on a notepad that seemed to compliment the measuring tape. Suzuki measured them again, and noted them, obviously drawing differences in the rounds of measuring data. *A good old-fashioned perfectionist*, Darius thought. *Maybe that's what makes him the best Cybersmith on Tsorra.* Dr. Suzuki then took recorded measurements of what remained of his amputated leg, and then repeated, of course.

'This is so I know whereabouts to cut your new leg, exactly.' He explained with his telepathy. 'Please, wait here a moment. Good news is, you are a mesomorph with average bodily proportions. We will have plenty of cybernetic legs in your size.' He walked off, but paused and turned after a few steps, then added, 'That is if my apprentices have done a decent job of monitoring stock, Sir.' Nero Suzuki's tone betrayed signs of past incompetence from apprentices that had humiliated him. But he was already halfway down the mezzanine stairs by the time Darius had processed this.

Darius kept himself entertained by looking over Nero Suzuki's office. Various artworks from, grandchildren? lined the wall adjacent to the wall. They were fingerpaintings not unlike what a *Homo sapien* child would produce, their name, age and grade written neatly at the bottom in Common by what obviously was their teachers. Darius was drawn to a roughly drawn cat, for some reason. He stared at it for several standard seconds, then leaned back on his chair when he realised why. The cat resembled the domestic type of prehistoric Terra where he was stationed. Modern cats, of today, like their canine rivals, had evolved bodily proportions due to a millennia-long diet of processed meats.

Darius looked about the room again, and came to the wall opposite; the wall behind the desk was a transparent window that enabled Dr. Nero to look out on his factory from his office, for whatever reason behind it. The wall opposite had various framed licences, certificates acknowledging Suzuki And Sons, Ltd's acts of philanthropy, and finally, sepia photographic portraits. Darius squinted at the inscriptions underneath each portrait, even though the office was brightly lit with florescent, clinical lighting. He came to Nero's portrait, one of the few that was smiling, and stared.

So, a ninth generation Cybersmith. He thought. The portrait was placed directly beneath what looked like a father, until Darius squinted at the date, and realised it must either be a cousin or elder brother. His deep thought was startled out of reality when he heard footsteps up the metal mezzanine stairs again. Nero Suzuki opened the simple, hinged door again a moment or two later.

'We have plenty of legs your size, in stock, Mr. Ferrari. A senior worker, one with nearly as much experience in Cybersmithy as I, will cut it to length shortly. In the meantime, may I offer you herbal tea?'

'Sure. Yes please.' Darius had not had a cup of herbal tea

since his bout of binge-drinking his parents, raw, distilled wine. Nero walked over to an automated percolator that Darius had not noticed before, and distilled two cups, without saying a word. He handed a cup to Darius with a vaguely arthritic hand. Old Nero Suzuki struggled to pull up a comfy office chair and sat opposite Darius, with is cup. He blew and sipped at his tea, as if contemplating.

'The Commonwealth is getting ever closer to perfecting is biological replacement limbs, Mr. Ferrari. There is talk, though not publicly official, that a new arm or leg can be grown and surgically attached in as little as ten standard weeks, so I hear. Do you know what that means Mr. Ferrari?' Darius shook his head silently and sipped at his tea. Nero continued, 'It means, a new leg can be grown faster than cybernetics can fabricate them. Even cheap knock-off arms, mass produced in fully automated factories struggle to achieve that. What hope would the custom built, hand made variety, built in a relatively small factory like this one have? I ask you, Mr. Ferrari?' Darius could only look down at his tea and take another sip. 'I'm sorry to hear that, Dr. Suzuki. I hope my business helps. Please, call me Darius.'

'Very well Darius. I appreciate your business, although it is only delaying the inevitable. Last month, for the first time in nine generations, I had to turn down a new apprentice. And not because of financial difficulties. Because I am an honest man, Darius. I told the hopeful young lad, still at the academy, he would be wise to seek a different career, a different trade, like a Biobrid panelbeater. You will always have a job as a panelbeater, no matter how smart automata gets, or what Biobrids run off. You will always have a job, because humans of all species and both sexes, across the entire Commonwealth, will always crash vehicles, get careless and have accidents. The lad merely nodded in reluctant agreement.'

Darius blew on his herbal tea and took a significant sip. 'Because Cybersmithy is becoming an obsolete trade,' Darius stated.

Nero changed the subject. 'I was in the Navy once. Before you were born, I would say. I was stationed in what they called the Iron Age, back in the Days of ancient Rome. Us Tau Cetans fit right in there, don't you know? We can pass for a large statured Roman, especially at a distance. I once saw the Emperor there, on prehistoric Terra, who shared my name. A tyrant of a *Homo sapien*, he was, but not a Draconian Agent by any means. Just a nasty piece of work. A real bad apple. Epitomised the violent, barbaric behaviour of our ape-like ancestors on Terra.'

'Emperor Nero. I have heard of him.' Darius replied. 'What was Rome like? I was stationed about two thousand Sy's later, in the Oil Age of Terra.'

'Sy's?' Nero Suzuki looked perplexed. 'What are Sy's?'

'Standard Years. A colloquial abbreviation. Surely you've heard apprentices speak of them?'

Presently, before old Nero could telepathically reply, however, his Holotab sounded, and a message displayed itself in Common, projected from Nero's desk where the Holotab lay. The message was a hologram, three dimensional in fluorescent pink, and both men could read it.

"Marcelles here, Mr. Suzuki. The job for a Darius Ferrari is completed. Ready for collection at his convenience."

'Well, why don't you just quickly finish that beverage, and try out your new leg?' Nero exclaimed in an almost childish telepathic tone.

The cybernetic leg was not finished in the same colour as Darius's skin tone, a matte-finish gunmetal grey, but still it fit Darius perfectly, where his leg was amputated. It was as though he never lost a leg in the first place. 'How does it attach?' Darius asked.

'We will put a realistic looking sleeve over your new leg. The sleeve extends to your groin, and we will fasten the cybernetic skin with a strong but low irritant resin. The sleeve is high tech, and so advanced that it makes up for a third of the entire cost. It feels like real skin, its very hard to tell the difference, and it breathes.'

Darius got up with his new cybernetic leg. It was fastened temporarily with suspenders. He walked around the office, without being asked to do so. The new leg was not only incredibly powerful, it seemed to have a mind of its own.

'It moves just like my other leg.' Darius commented feebly.

'Microprocessor controlled. The best commercially available. Algorithm perfectly emulates walking.' Nero replied.

'I'll take it.' Darius proclaimed. 'And to hell with a new, grown leg. I want this one! So what if women folk would prefer an organic replacement. I have no interest in womanising anymore. I, myself am getting a little too... mature for that, Dr. Suzuki.'

'You are a rare breed, Darius. A man of ambition. To become immortalised as a mover and a shaker, not as a mere mortal who wishes to pass on his genes to the next generation. What is it you wish to do with this new found power?'

Darius turned and glowered at a child's painting of a Ciakar, and narrowed his eyes. A moment later, and the painting began to rustle and scrunch with telekinetic molestation.

'Enough, Darius!' Old Nero's telepathy intruded. The voice seemed distant as the part of Darius's brain that produced telekinesis seemed to entrance him in a state a nirvana. 'Your point is clearly made. Is it revenge against the Empire you seek?'

Darius terminated his telekinesis, and snapped back into reality like an ancient hypnotised patient. 'Not revenge, but...' His telepathy trailed off.

'You want to be useful again, in the Cold War against the Empire.' Nero seemed to be putting words into his mind, speaking for him. Darius remembered something, and immediately humbled. He faced the old Cybersmith with sycophantic, almost humiliated, dark eyes.

'There is one minor problem. I have no money for A Biocab to get to the spaceport. I was hoping for a ride?'

'Why don't you go there on foot? It is only about ten kilometres or so away. Try out your new legs.'

Darius finished his tea, while an apprentice fitted on the synthetic skin. He waited ten or so standard minutes for the resin to set, as Nero had advised. Darius felt ashamed about paying seven hundred standard kilograms or so worth of titanium, just for a ten kilometre ride. He thanked everybody in the factory within telepathyshot, including the apprentice that fitted him, and clambered down the stairs with his new leg. As soon as he left the gates of the cybernetics factory, he swung his duffel bag over his shoulder in a backpack fashion, and ran for the first time in a while. It felt invigorating. He ran the whole way to the spaceport, with the exception of crossing roads, and walking the occasional kilometre to catch his breath. His duffle bag bounced on his back uncomfortably, but still he ran, heedless of the children in passing Biobrids jeering telepathically as a jogged.

He reached the spaceport (an exact duplicate to the one on his continent), all red and flustered, in a little over one standard hour. There was no way he could have got lost; large beamships, five hundred metres in diameter, descended from the sky every ten to fifteen minutes in the distance. He just had to follow where they were descending. The skyscrapers in the distance were so tall, they capitalised the background scenery above the industrial area's single or double-storey workshops, warehouses or factories. It was the middle of the day, or early afternoon at latest, when he left Dr. Suzuki's cybernetics' factory, but already, the star Tau Ceta was beginning to disappear behind these mountainous skyscrapers where most of the citizens on this continent lived.

Darius walked straight to the spaceport's ablutions

and took one of the communal shower booths, with soap in liquid dispensers. He undressed and refreshed in a luke-warm shower, taking for granted the fact he could stand on two legs while he washed. Darius felt a sudden sadness in his heart when he realised this.

He grabbed the towel out of his duffel bag, and a spare change of clothes. He emerged from the shower booth a new man. He went to the same, familiar queue at the check-in booths. Only this time at a different spaceport, and only this time, no one let him jump the queue. Not that he cared. He likely had hours to kill here.

When it was finally his turn to confer with the android inside the booth, for the next passage to his continent, Darius had a change of heart, an epiphany. His war pension should have been transferred into his left eye by about now. It was payday, and Darius got paid monthly.

'When is the next Beamship offworld?' He asked the Artificial.

'Tomorrow evening, Sir.' The android, a male-form this time.

'Perfect. Can you please check my retina for available credits?'

'Certainly, Sir. Please face forward at this scanner to your side.' Darius side stepped at a retinal scanning console and willed his left eye to stay open. A moment later, and an audible sound emitted from somewhere. He sidestepped back in front of the android. 'Five hundred kilograms of Draconium, or three thousand, three hundred standard tonnes of titanium, Sir.' The android summarised.

'Excellent.' *My pension went through.* 'How much for a passage to the Oil Age on the next Timeliner? I only need a one-way passage.' Darius asked, his heart rate increasing hopefully.

'Also tomorrow evening, Sir. It is the same Timeliner.'

'Hurry up, Arcturian-loyal!' Someone behind Darius telepathically grizzled.

'Do I have enough Bonds of commodities for a passage?' Darius asked.

'You are seven hundred standard kilogrammes of titanium, or about one hundred of Draconium short, Sir.'

'Is my return passage redeemable?' Darius asked quickly, hopefully.

'You lose ten percent, as an honour fee.' The android replied robotically, and not because it was a machine. It was actually getting irritated. Darius made his move.

'Yes. Yes. That still means I get about fifteen hundred kilo's of titanium in refund, eh? Yes, fine. That's fine. Just do it then, please. Refund my return.'

'Then, in that case, your six hundred and fifty kilograms of titanium, the balance after you purchase your time-faring passage, will be refunded to your credit account. Please face the Retinal Teller again.' Darius sidestepped to the console again and forced his eye open. At an audible cue, he returned to the android. The artificial handed him his new, advanced passage, and wished Darius a good day. When Darius returned the platitude, and walked off, the Tsorran behind him (the sex or age, Darius did not care about) marched up to the booth impatiently. Another even cheered venomously, sarcastically.

Darius had more than enough credits for a couple of decent meals and some cheap, spartan accommodation. Not that he cared about staying in a luxury hotel. He would rather save his credits. When tomorrow evening finally came, after a good night's rest and some sightseeing, Darius arrived at the spaceport three standard hours early, and was the first to board the Beamship that would shuttle him, his new leg, and hundreds, if not thousands of other passengers, into orbit and onto a nearby, waiting, ivory-coloured Timeliner.

Darius Ferrari nestled back in his seat, and surfed the various entertainment programmes on his Holotab while he waited for the other passengers to board, and the Beamship to cast off into orbit. It was nearly a Standard hour before the Arcturium anti matter engines finally roared to life. It was a familiar, mundane sound. Especially to a veteran who once upon a time had his own scout Beamship, that hulking, bell-shaped monstrosity with three half-spheres under its fuselage. That flying tank, made largely of Draconium. Slow and clumsy, compared to others, but it was tough. Darius missed it, but once he boarded that Timeliner and emerged from Shrinkspace, and liaised with *The Athena*, he could be flying one again. The Admiral would surely let him re-enlist prematurely, providing he passed a medical.

His thoughts were cut off when the large Beamship began to ascend, slowly, whilst his seat, and the seats of the other passengers oscillated upwards. Darius found himself staring forward but facing the ceiling. He knew why, as did the others. *The only way a human could be shot into orbit, and still withstand the gravitational forces.*

It was not long before stars could be seen outside the Beamship, and the seats oscillated back to their original position once again. Darius looked out the nearest window. Planet Tsorra could be seen below, a tropical paradise of a terraformed world, and it was shrinking. Out of an adjacent window, Darius saw the massive but angelic Timeliner increase in size, as it waited patiently for the Beamship.

Darius, on an unexplained impulse, decided to take one last look at his homeworld, despite not being particularly fond of the place. The blue, clean oceans with white sands and beaches, and the pastoral continents. Darius stared at his homeworld one last time. He stared as it shrank, and-!

It's not possible! He rubbed his dark, infrared eyes, and looked again. But the image was the same. *No! What is happening to Tsorra? It's dying?* Like a massive Chronophysical tidal wave, an unseen barrier seemed to *unterraform* Planet Tsorra. It travelled hundreds of times the speed of sound, but the tidal wave turned ocean and civilisation and farmland, into pure, unadulterated, lifeless rock. Planet Tsorra, in less than half a standard minute, was a dead, atmosphereless sphere. *What is happening? Tsorra seems to be reverting back to the way it was?! How is this possible? Am I dreaming?*

Darius Ferrari, a former Chronophysical Intelligence agent of the Commonwealth, hoping to re-enlist, became breathless. For how long, he did not know. Then, like the unseen tidal wave that destroyed Tsorra, a wave of real-isation crashed through his consciousness. His eyes and mouth widened in shock.

'The Draconians have one the Cold War!' He telepath-ically shouted inside the Beamship. He was shocked, far too shocked, to notice the other passengers stare at him, humiliatingly.

EIPLOGUE

Pteru was still not satisfied with the blood tests he took, with the help of his two adolescent protégées. Although all seven *Homo sapiens* or *Miapiapithecus* passed an initial clean bill of health, with only a couple showing genetic defects in their blood, he insisted he quarantine them for another forty-eight standard hours, preferably more.

'Master Pteru,' Magne pressed. 'You do realise Chancellor vam Rees and the other survivors will be leaving in a little over two standard hours?'

'Whatever it takes, Magne. It is better if I am marooned here, on Paleolithic Terra, for the rest of my life, than to let a terrible disease, one that these early humans have little or no immunity to...' Pteru's telepathy trailed off. He let the unspoken continuation tell itself for a few moments, and then continued by saying, via his Holotab for Meerkah, 'There was one time, my cousin Sorjana once told me, on Terra, where an outbreak of Arcturian Influenza occurred. Early Oil Age, if I remember correctly. Killed over five million, she said. Now five million might not sound like much compared to the Entire Commonwealth's population, but that resulted, nearly a quarter of an eon later, in over one billion deaths in Natural Time. One billion. About as much as one of the smaller planets in our beloved Commonwealth. No planets were *unterraformed*, fortunately.'

Meerkah interjected, over from the pilot's seat. 'As a Parapaleontologist, I can confirm the population of *Miapiapithecus* is currently a little over ten million. If an outbreak occurs, here, it will fortunately only likely wipe out the tribe, and not spread.' Meerkah almost blanched, despite his green scaly skin. 'This is, unless they decide to trade with other tribes before the virus dissipates.'

The Beamship was almost at the muster point now, where the largest one perched, with its booty of precious Sentinels.

'In any case, I cannot take that risk,' Pteru continued. 'We, as Modern humans, have learned from our mistakes. All Agents, such as the likes of my cousin Sorjana, are regularly screened for any new pathogens that may mutate in their bodies. In addition, about one in every ten thousand *Homo sapiens* is randomly sedated, before being taken aboard a Beamship. There, someone, anyone who has joined the Commonwealth armed forces is qualified to do it, takes a blood sample, and tests it with a Haemometer. Rather like what we just did with our seven little savage friends down there.' Pteru nodded pointedly at the still-unconscious Paleolithic men and women.

'We are about to land, Pteru. We are here.' Meerkah tweaked the Beamship's controls and bought the craft to a hover, and finally a descent.

'I highly doubt that nimrod of a politician will spare us a set of Sentinels, to leave them behind for us. My Beamship is too small to travel through Shrinkspace, regardless. That would mean trading this one for a larger one, at least twice the size, one that is capable of discharging Sentinels. I would assume that is out of the question. So I leave you three with an ultimatum. You can go back, to Modern times with the others, or, if you want to stay here with me, you're more than welcome. We have six months worth of rations, maybe nine, if one would wish to lose a bit of weight. But that is only six months for one person. Do not worry.' Pteru grinned theatrically. 'We can always hunt more.'

The Beamship touched down, and Meerkah powered down the engines. 'I am staying, my friend. The Empire has likely deemed me deceased, and replaced me. That leaves Magne and Skyler.'

'I will go, Master Pteru. Even though it is partly my fault we are in this predicament, I have still yet to have graduated from the academy.' Skyler said solemnly. 'I will, however, come back. If it bankrupts me for the rest of my life. Mark my words, we are coming back for you.'

'*We?* Inquired Magne flirtatiously. She looked in Skyler's eyes raunchily, yet clandestinely, so her mentor would not notice. 'Oh, yes. We. Someone has to guide you through Shrinkspace!' Magne pushed Skyler playfully. Meerkah opened the Beamship's doors, while Pteru, Skyler and Magne embraced each other farewell. Meerkah stood up to meet the two adolescent Plieadians, and shook both of their hands proudly in an incredibly strong, taloned grip.

'Time to go.' Pteru said. It would surprise me if that bureaucrat does not leave early. Magne and Skyler nodded curtly, together, turned and started off down the ramp, Magne first, Skyler immediately behind.

At the foot of the ramp, they both turned and waved at Pteru and Meerkah, as the ramp doors folded up again on hydraulic actuators. When the door was fully closed, they took a few steps back, while the Beamship's Arcturium engines fired up again. Less than fifteen seconds standard later, Pteru and Meerkah and their Beamship were already gone, out of sight.

Magne took Skyler's hand, and squeezed. He turned to face her, and saw her purple eyes full of teenage innocence and lust. Magne leaned forward slowly. Skyler took her cue to follow. It seemed like an eternity before their lips met, and they both, deep in the back of their minds, while they kissed, thought they might miss the giant Beamship back to Modern times.

For a long moment, however, neither of them cared.

Back on the *Athena*, Sorjana was too fatigued to take any criticism from her superiors, particularly The Admiral. Not simply for bringing a reviled Grey aboard. But because a Chronophysical disaster, to put it mildly, occurred about six or seven standard decades from the present, which not only marked the end of the Oil Age, but also consumed the lives of over two-thirds of the *Homo sapiens* living on Terra then. Sorjana did not hear any significant details, but a Timeliner had just emerged from Shrinkspace not one standard hour ago, bringing with it the dire news.

'Director, do you realise what has, or more importantly, what will happen, two hundred or so thousand Terran years from now?!'

'Sir, I have just escaped the confines of a Terran prison, trekked in an ancient, Oil Age groundcar for over ten standard hours. I have recently arrived on my Beamship. All with absolutely no help from anyone but Mishta. He is the Grey I bought with me. I said he could use my Beamship and some Sentinels. But now there is a Timeliner here, all the better. So if you would kindly fill me in, what has happened, or will happen, I would appreciate it. But not until I have had some ablutions. Sir.'

The Admiral and Gunnery Sergeant Klaan O'Brien had insisted on meeting Sorjana directly when they heard a request for a Commonwealth Beamship to board, the one piloted by Sorjana Hoolde, Director of Chrono-physical Intelligence aboard the *Athena*. The two aging Arcturian humans confronted the Plieadian human of another species as she disembarked her Beamship. Mishta the Grey was already being escorted away under armed guards. Sorjana tried to reassure the Tall Grey that it will not be harmed upon a military asset of The Commonwealth. That she could guarantee, at least.

'I will inform you now, Director.' The Admiral ordered unquestionably. 'Your damned shower can wait. Right now, you might want to get comfortable, because this is going to be a long story.' Sorjana took two steps back, looked down and behind her, and sat on the makeshift seat that was the stair-ramp of her Beamship.

Planet Tsorra has returned to its unterraformed state. Every Tau Cetan living there, in an unfathomable twist of Chronophysics, disappeared with its civilisation. Planet Ptah in the Plieades system, also suffered the same fate. A similar fate had happened to the Lyrans, millennia ago. Now it seems, that what is left of the Commonwealth would be housing dispossessed refugees that were lucky enough not to be in Natural Time when their respective planets became, effectively, sterilised.

'We have lost an estimated fifteen percent of the Commonwealth.' The Admiral lectured. 'Two thirds of our ancestors exterminated, for just over a tenth of ours. Funny how time travel works, eh, Director?' The Admiral was sarcastic, almost venomous. He clearly held Sorjana partly accountable, as head of what was dubbed in Commonwealth media, in Modern Times as *Time Wars*. Obviously, humans are losing their originality.

'Please fill me in, Sir. How am I accountable? It happened sixty Sy's from now. Our post is at the height of what our ancestors called "The Cold War Between Capitalism and Communism.'

'This so called Cold War was just a decoy from our friends in the Empire!' The Admiral barked with his telepathy. 'A war on ancient Terra has already happened, sixty standard years from the present. And it was, or will be, however this shit works, a Nuclear war. We are talking a fifth of the primitive atom and hydrogen bombs and warheads these animals on Terra own, used. Just... used. And used carelessly. We don't have the details yet on who, or which, of these ape-like hominids is directly responsible, but we know. Terra will be a smoldering pile of rubble, of scorched forests and black, perpetually ashen skies. It will be a place where crops will not grow on most of the land. And Director, I must stress, that two thirds of our ancestors *initially* have died in the nuclear holocaust. I have been told that the death toll could reach as much as *nine tenths* from other factors such as radiation burns, poisoning and famine.'

The Admiral turned, walked a few paces from Sorjana's Beamship and paused to call over his shoulder with his telepathy. 'We've failed, Director. I've failed. You've failed.' and he marched off again in the same direction. Gunnery Sergeant Klaan O'Brien could only give Sorjana a disapproving glance, *en passing*, as he strode off to hurry after his superior officer.

Like the lapdog with no opinion that he is. Sorjana thought in her exhaustion, then slumped on the stairs that doubled as a door on her faithful Beamship, only now remembering the fact he rib was still broken and she had neglected seeking medial attention.

Appendix i:
Evolution of the Alpha Draconians

Saurosapiena Draconis

Terra, 75,000,000 B.C.

An unknown species of theropod dinosaur discovers, approx 75,000,000 B.C. how to control and maintain fire. Later, by vigorous friction of late cretaceous wood, they learn to make fire. In turn this leads to the fact that this same unknown theropod found the meat was more palatable cooked. Cooked meat is rich in protein and much easier to digest, using less energy. This saved energy enabled their brains to grow geometrically larger over time. They also evolved to walk erect, so as to enable the brain to grow without compromising biomechanical integrity. Because animals that have horizontal parallel gaits are limited to the size of their brain, lest they become too front heavy and would have difficulty maintaining balance, as well as be severely handicapped in agility, making it very difficult to catch prey, if not impossible.

By this process they eventually evolve into intelligent, sentient beings. They were the first lifeforms to create civillisation, roughly 66 million years before mankind. This civilisation evidently led to space exploration, spacefaring, and trade networks. It is for this reason, a 66 million year head-start over humanity, that their civilisation centred on Alpha Draconis system (about 300 light years from Terra) is so radically advanced. On their planets they have terraformed during the late cretaceous period of earth, complete with contemporary flora and fauna. This enabled them to survive the infamous late cretaceous meteor.

Modern Reptoids come in two forms;

The "worker" caste. These are the most commonly encountered, approx 2 metres tall. Scaly tough skin, claws, brute strength, no supernatural powers, however, still terrifying. Communicated from a bird-like song language, only about 3000 words, though still communicate efficiently, (one word per noun/verb/adjective)

The "ruling" caste. Or Ciakars; average about 1-2 m taller than worker caste. Reports from 10 to 14 feet tall, according to witnesses. Though rarely seen. Skin and claws similar, aside from being taller, have bat-shaped wings, an iguana-like wattle on chin, communicates both through bird language to worker-caste, and telepathy universally, and, combined with unparalleled pyrokinetic abilities, (produced by accelerating hydrogen and/or helium atoms into nuclear fission, thus combusting the air that surrounds them) it is easy to see where the idea for medieval fire-breathing dragon came from............

Both castes have three fingers and one opposable thumb, feet being chicken-like with three spread out on ground, and one vestigial on upper ankle, not touching ground.

Females tend to be larger than males, translating to a matriarchal gender hierarchy. It is also the females who have a crest of brightly coloured long feathers, for display, originating from back of neck. Juveniles of both sexes are covered with a dull feathery down, which they lose around puberty.

They have a star system devoted to being a "time zoo", with practically every animal that had ever lived on Terra, with contemporary flora. One Planet being devoted to each geological epoch, from the Cambrian seas enriched with trilobites and other enigmatic clumsy attempts at evolution creating complex life, to the grasslands of the Cenozoic era with prehistoric mammals capitalising on the absence of large prehistoric reptiles. They even have, in a cultured laboratory-museum, complete with micro-scopes for visitors to view, the single celled organisms that hailed from the dawn of life. This was benevolently commissioned so generations upon generations could have intimate knowledge of Terran paleontology.

They all see Homo sapiens as cattle, in fact the Homo sapiens are abducted and taken to A.draconis to add to the "human-farms'" gene pool, as humans are put through their selective breeding process to produce more productive human cattle. It is for this reason they may be vilified and labelled as "evil", But this is not accurate, such a comment is the epitome of human ignorance, arrogance and hypocrisy, based on the assumption that *Homo sapiens* is the pinnacle species and no other lifeform shall thus predate on them.

They have evolved differently from a different ancestor, so it's not surprising they lack many emotions, such as empathy, so how they treat humans is out of sheer apathy rather than cruelty and malevolence. See themselves as a superior race, and all other life forms exits for their servitude and convenience, much like humans see other animals on earth. In other words, they can appear sociopathic, but this does not make them by any means evil.

In fact, ironically, their personality is more like Homo sapiens than their Pleiadian, Arcturian, etc. descendants.

Their society is the above two-caste system, can be loosely coined cutthroat capitalist, vehemently right-winged, as empathy and tolerance to lower life forms and to change is beyond their comprehension.

Sirian Reptilians

Saurosapiena Sirius

A benign species that dwell in the Sirius star system. The closest living relative of Draconians.

Have more streamlined, amphibian-like body and sport the trademark cone head, and average roughly the same height as their worker caste genetic cousins. Share approximately the same amount of DNA as Homo sapiens vs. Lemurs.

Staple diet of aquatic life and seaweed. Their Planet is Terraformed as swampy and humid, however have an advanced civilization that has unparalleled technology, though none devoted to warfare.

Appendix II:
The Pleiadians

Homo Cras Pleiades

Two hundred-thousand or so years of evolution means they look very similar to their primitive oil age Homo sapien ancestors, but with notable differences. Larger earlobes evolved to incorporate higher frequency sound on humanity's new homeworld, Erra, (orbiting Taygeta star, about 450 light years from Terra) and also because they have not used verbal communication in millennia, telepathy instead. Lack rear molars because of 200,000 years of processed, easy to digest food eliminated the need for chewing. Consequently their stomachs are also smaller, unable to digest raw food such as carrots.

Can teach each other telekinesis just like today's humans learn martial arts, though they must be taught and are not born with the knowledge on how to use it.

Hence their Nordic nickname, they have Scandinavian features, most elementary characteristic is the blonde, long flowing hair, eyes are noticeably larger, able to see ultraviolet light spectrum, thus seven more colours than Homo sapiens. These eyes are almost always blue, as the hair is almost always blonde. High, larger cheekbones are also noticeable, partly to accommodate the larger eyes, and partly because, though millennia of telepathy, speech muscles are now vestigial, as are the vocal chords. Needless to say they average 40 cm taller than their oil-age ancestors males averaging 2 metres, females 1.8 metres. Through a combination of eugenics and the heavier gravity on Erra, males are very muscular, females are well toned. Their ribcage is more thicker and robust to accommodate the larger, more powerful heart and lungs needed to support the powerful brain, now range between 2500 and 3000cc in capacity (Homo sapiens being about 1300cc). Larger lungs mean that their heart is now where Homo sapiens' liver is. Because generations of eating processed liquefied yet highly digestible foods, their digestive system is about as powerful and efficient as a two-year-old *Homo sapiens'*. This means their torso stays in proportion to their body, as their stomach has become smaller thus compensating for the larger lungs. Heartrate averages 240 BPM and pressure 80/40, is required to maintain a brain roughly 5 times more powerful than the average Homo sapien. To protect their heart, the sternum has extended 35mm downwards, meaning the solar plexus has also moved down where Homo sapiens' upper abdominals once were. They are now incapable of eating raw vegetables. The absence of rear molars, used for grinding vegetation reflects this. They have twenty-eight teeth in total. Their diet consist of mashed vegetables, fruits and cooked fish, though the fish are bought over from ancient Terra, and because of oil age overfishing and a drastically diminished fish population, Terran fish are now inbred, meaning the meat is poor quality.

Interbreeding of oil age races meant humans were all coffee coloured, but the final ice age forced humanity's skin to go pale in order to efficiently absorb vitamin-D. Although not all Plieadians look like their almost derogatory "Nordic Alien" nickname that their ancestors gave them during brief and seldom chrononautical expeditions, as the Vegan race have brown skin, because their planet New Venus, second planet orbiting Vega, hot and semi Arid, has roughly 10% more gravity than Erra, (Erra, 14.6 N/kg, New Venus, 16.2 N/kg) meaning time passes 10% slower, so Pleiadians and Vegans age at the different rates (see: theory of relativity).

As for The Hyadeans, their tropical environment on New Titan, (gravity 13.9 N/kg) nine tenths the size of Erra, gives them their exotic look, olive skin, vaguely oriental features, shiny raven hair and an iris colour range varied like that of the Vegans. The three races mentioned all have the common ancestor that was the higher caste in the evolution of man that fled the last Terran Ice Age. Of course, Erra has a temperate, colder climate, though the tropical equator averages 25 degrees, desirable for an optional tan.

Their psionic powers originated from a gene discovered by their ancestors, that promotes the part of the brain that produces brain waves to develop freely.

A eugenics programme was introduced in an attempt to help humanity evolve telepathy and even telekinesis through powerful enough brainwaves to penetrate the human skull.

Telepathy works in a similar principle to analogue radio. Phonetic sounds are produced by distinctive brain wave frequencies. For example "sh" is manifested in the human brain as a low frequency alpha wave, "ee" a high frequency gamma wave, "p" a low frequency Beta wave. So if you thought of the word, "sheep" it would manifest itself as a low alpha, high gamma, low beta. Those with telepathic abilities send the corresponding phonetics as assorted corresponding brainwaves to another midbrain recipient that is another person or being. The recipient processeses this data in the form of the phonetics and thus the original word. Oil-age terrans seldom have this ability because the gene is highly recessive and thus the gene has not manifested itself into the genepool, eluding oil-age science, so the midbrain stays relatively underdeveloped, producing weak brainwaves.

Telekinesis is much more mentally stressful, however pleiadians communicate constantly telepathically so they can use the same "muscle" for a different task (this case being telekinesis) much more fluently than the oil age primitives.

Telekinesis is produced from ULF Alpha brainwaves so powerful as to distort the fabric of space/time and therefore overpower gravity and material state to move or distort solid objects with the mind.

Also through millennia-wide eugenics only specimens showing benevolence, altruism and intelligence can pass on genes. Another gene was found that produced people to cry joyfully while experiencing benevolent and or happy phenomena, such as cherry tree flowers dropping their pink petals in an oriental fall, or the look of gratitude in another human when bestowed needed charity. This gene was one of many incorporated into a breeding programme projected for centuries with a goal of an ascended race that is spiritually tamed.

Eventually traits in Oil-Age Homo sapiens such as greed, vindictiveness, hate, belligerence and even anger disappear completely. This model was how early man domesticated wild dogs into the tame, loyal companion that is man's best friend. Humans lacking these traits were passively and actively culled, denied the right to procreate and contribute to the human gene pool. The result was a race that appears benevolent, joyful, protective, generally angelic traits. The unfavorable specimens branched off as a lower caste sub-species, were left at the mercy of the final Terran Ice age roughly 100 000 AD, the higher case escaped to various star systems, while the survivors were left to endure.

Because they raped the gas giant Jupiter of all her gases, (the gravity produced by Jupiter deflects the lion's share of meteors, asteroids, etc from the inner asteroid belt, while the outer gas giants' gravity keeps the Kuiper belt in check), and without technology and lacking the intelligence to constuct counter-measures against a 200 kilometre-wide behemoth of a meteor from crashing into Terra. Today (about 230,000 AD- The Gregorian calender is obsolete, with the absence of organised religion) Terra is now an extinct spherical rock, as nuclear weapons cleansed whatever remained of life on Terra, with the exception of prokaryotic life. The meteorite penetrated earth's crust and ripped a huge cavity in the atmosphere. Magma that escaped the dying atmosphere has hardened into rock, which formed an orbiting ring around the rock, similar to Saturn's.

See also;
Arcturian Humans . . . . . *Homo cras arcturius*
Hyadean Humans . . . . . . *H.cras hyadea*
Lyran Humans. . . . . *H.cras lyria*
Tau Cetan Humans. . . . . *H.cras taucetaus*
Vegan Humans . . . . *H.cras vegas*

Appendix III:
The Zetas and the Bellatrix

NB: exempt from taxonomy as does not, strictly speaking, naturally reproduce and therefore does not constitute a lifeform.

These are the manifestation of an Oil-Age Terran stereotype of an extraterrestrial being; manifested by the famous grey skinned eunuchs with a head to body proportion three times more of a human. Large black tear shaped eyes, small nostrils and a mouth vestigial, also has telepathy is now the form of communication, and the fact that their digestive system is equally vestigial. They obtain nutrition through absorbing protein matter through their skin, aided by a high pH solution to help break down the matter.

Like the Draconians who engineered them by an unknown prehistoric Terran Cetaceans (whales and dolphins) due to being undiscovered as yet by human science, and a "Frankenstein-like" composite of purely indigenous extraterrestrial lifeforms, they lack many emotions, though have more than the Draconians because of the human DNA in them. They still however regard *Homo sapiens* as a farmer-to-cattle relationship, using them not only for nutrients but as raw materials for reproduction, reproducing by cloning, with the needed human DNA to keep their gene pool multifarious. Hence they reproduce asexually with biotechnology. Projections estimate that in 3 million years they would have incorporated so much human DNA that they would become 98% human, about as close as a chimpanzee as to a human.

They come from Zeta Reticuli (39 light years from Terra) and Bellatrix star systems. They colonised planets that were formerly inhabited by Alpha Draconians, who did not bother naming the planets. Since they were discovered and colonised before humanity, Acturia and her Socialist Commonwealth, did not think it right to name a planet found first by another sentient lifeform. These were hence given numbers that corresponds to which order they orbit the star.

Their ultimate goal is, through biotechnology, "evolve" reproductive organs and reproduce naturally. They detest the way they are forced to reproduce, travelling through space and time to gather genetic raw materials, to prevent inbreeding. As they were originally created as mules they have thus lost their reproductive organs. Although sexless on the outside, they do have trace amounts of hormones so they still behave as if they were either male or female in respect to things such as pastimes, hobbies, manner-isms, personality, etc. They do not however, form male/female partnerships for companionship's sake as, quite tragically, they have become to terms with what they are have become. They have long lost their desire for boy-meets-girl romances.

They have no commodity and are forced to trade their services, as their Draconian masters are only interested in that sort of currency, and The Arcturians see them as having even less commercial merit to their interests. They trade servants for Draconium bonds, Draconium measured by metric Standard tonnes (1000 kilograms@10 Newtons per kilogram).

The Draconian Empire denies them the right to breed sexually so as to control their numbers by making their breeding process inefficient and laboured. Arcturians and The Commonwealth deny them because something created, not evolved, is an abomination and thus should not make more abominations.

Zeta Reticuli Greys- are the lower caste and do the menial tasks, like laboratory assistants, they are naked and average 1.0-1.2 metres tall. They are the least intelli-gent but far more than *Homo sapiens.*

Bellatrix Greys- Are the taller greys, are lanky and wear black jump suits, and seem to partake in the roll of su-pervisor, or scientist as they are the higher caste and complete the more technical tasks, such as cloning and gene splicing. They exceed 1.5 metres regularly, often up to two.

Appendix iv: Arcturians

The Commonwealth Of Arcturian Socialist Federations-CASF (usually shortened to the United Commonwealth) is the governing entity that oversees all the planets colonised by humanity's higher castes. They are also descended from the higher castes that left Terra circa 100,000 AD to escape the final ice age. They are a galactic superpower, but far from rivalling the Draconian Empire. They look different from the other Citizens of the Commonwealth satellites, mainly due to the fact New Terra was the first planet to be colonised, and party through millennia of interbreeding with the other races, means they have light brown skin and with more defined, chiseled features, with black eyes and an upturned pig-like nose.

New Terra; one of the largest known rocky planets, over two times the mass of the planet it was named after, with gravity of 21.1N/kg. Environment and climate is pastoral grassland with wet seasons.

Although humanity has lost its penchant for aggression, they have a powerful military, especially after diplomatic relationships soured in the past 5 standard millennia with the Draconian Empire. Psionic-cybernetic weaponry in the form off an advanced EEG headrest console that amplifies alpha waves so telekinesis has military applications. See; Acturi Psionic Marine Corps-APMC. They follow an ancient tradition to name planets and battle spacecraft after ancient Greek and Roman gods/goddesses (hence CASFSS Athena stationed near Oil-Age Jupiter. CASFSS Persephone and Agrapoena are a few Sisterships in the Acturi Navy)

Appendix v:
The Andromedan
Hyper-Sentients

These are sentient far beyond even the above life forms, who exist in the atomically turbulent Andromeda Galaxy, which is simply a c.250,000 x 250,000 light-year, disc-shaped natural particle accelerator, destined to assimilate with the Milky Way in 3.5 billion Standard years.

They manifest themselves as human shaped light energy, for reasons not certain but theories range from the hyper-active atoms that are thousands of times more active than they would be in the Milky Way. They glow as manifested energy, because space/time fabric is being bent convex/concave millions of times a second. Space-time fabric therefore struggles to maintain its integrity under this atomic energy, and with quick movements these hyper-sentients can tear holes in the fabric of space-time. For this reason, the organic matter that makes up their body is plasma-based, rather than with amino acids, which could not maintain their atomic integrity in the Andromedan galaxy.

They generally regard even the most advanced civilisations and lifeforms in the Milky Way with the contempt that these condescended life forms would otherwise give *Homo sapiens*.

This is the limits to what scientific knowledge we have on Andromedan Hyper-Sentients.

Appendix vi:
the Terranova SemiSynthetics

Descended from the lower caste of humanity, these sentient beings were once human. Their thirst for immortality consumes them so much that they even willingly turn themselves to mechanical abominations. As each organ deteriorates through age, they are cybernetically replaced. Eventually, when even their brain succumbs to the inevitability of its demise, they first synchronise their thoughts and memories to a computer and then install it in their new android bodies. As a result each specimen is extremely ancient, many being over ten thousand standard years.

They lack Shrinkspace technology and must spacefare by primitive anti-matter propulsion craft, so they cannot exceed speeds more than one-tenth of an astronomical unit-per hour.

This ensures they are marooned in the Terran Solar System, as long distance space travel would be horribly slow, which is good news for the Arcturian common-wealth, who want nothing to do with the Semi-Synthetics.

They still manifest human behaviour, in respect to their gender. The masculine entities still pursue masculine pastimes, and feminine female pastimes. They are even rumoured to still partake in human courtship and forming romantic partnerships.

Appendix vii:
Atomic Mining

Draconium- Dr, number 248 on Periodic Table. Atomic mass: 1571

Produced when Hydrogen and Helium atoms from a star become assimilated into a black hole. The dense gravity from the black hole combined with the nuclear fission of hydrogen and helium atoms, produces hyper-heavy metals. Draconium is silvery-dark grey in colour. One cubic metre weighs over 50 standard tonnes. Commercial applications: General super heavy-duty metallurgy.

Acturium- At, number 249 on Periodic Table. Atomic mass: 1614

Produced also by black holes, but this time from the Helium of a dying white dwarf star as it is sucked into the immense gravity of a black hole. Comes in a form of a lime green dense radioactive powder, although not as heavy as Draconium. Commercial applications; used in Shrink-space (see appendix viii) to produce, through nuclear fusion, the necessary super heavy anti-matter particles. By charging the Shrinkspace with the anti-matter produced from this element, the polarity of space/time is reversed, thus enabling time travel backwards.

METHODS: A mining vessel approaches black hole at a safe distance. As the hydrogen and helium atoms are still acting in nuclear fission, at the moment they are compressed in the black holes' gravity, Draconium and Acturium atoms are ripe. The atoms are then focused on with a particle accelerator beam from the mining vessel, essentially teleporting from the face of the black hole to the cargo hold of the mining vessel. The ore then accumulates in the cargo area as the particle accelerator delivers to mining vessel. Because when a star's matter enters a black hole in the form of a vortex, atomic mining can take years to harvest a single star.

Appendix viii; the Terran Simians and Neo-Terriers

Both these creatures are kept as pets in the entire Arcturian Commonwealth.

Neo Terriers- Descended from ancient Terran dogs. Cranial capacity has doubled and is now learning to communicate with speech, with a vocabulary of approximately 1000 words. Their front paws have become semi-dexterous, about the same dexterity as a lemur's, enabling them to hold simple tools and climb trees.

Terran Simians- are descended from Homo sapiens' closest relative, the chimpanzee and bonobo. Sometime during ancient Terra an underground, unofficial experiment was conducted to put a stock of approximately 1000 male and 1000 female Chimps through the same evolutionary conditions as Australopithecines faced. After thousands of generations, they now walk upright and their cranial capacity 1000cc. They have also evolved speech and can communicate with Neo Terriers fluently.

Appendix xi:
Shrinkspace

Faster than light travel cannot be achieved by brute force alone. This is because an object with any mass would require infinite energy. The fastest speed a solid object could theoretically travel at is just a fraction of the speed of light. To make travel to neighboring star systems feasible, space itself therefore must be shrunk and then traveled through. In the distant future Sentinels will be deployed one astronomical unit ahead of the space and/ or time faring craft.

Sentinels must be made out of Draconium, because it is the only known element robust enough to withstand the extremely high (many times hotter than a star) temperatures produced from the energy of shrinking space. Because space and time are synonymous, for every lightyear travelled through Shrinkspace, one standard year would elapse. The Sentinals therefore also nullify time in Shrinkspace, so the journey is completed in real-time.

9.46 trillion kilometres (one lightyear) are compressed into an area of space measuring only approximately 1.5 million kilometres. At 25,000 kilometres-per-second which is what most spacefaring craft cruise at (almost the maximum theoretical speed of a solid object), one lightyear now takes only about one minute to travel through.

Chronolgical-Reversal Sentinels (CRS) are equipped with Acturium-powered anti-matter fields that are powerful enough to reverse the polarity of space/time. Like the conventional (Chrono-retardant) Sentinels they are also deployed one AU ahead of the space/time faring craft. Not being made of the heavy Draconium alloys, most space-faring craft would simply melt if they were too close to Shrinkspace.

If one would endeavor to travel, for example,1000 years ago on the planet one was living on, A vessel must travel 1000 light years away, then turn around to face the destination, deploy the Sentinels, and when the vessel emerges from Shrinkspace, it will be in a place and in a time 1000 years ago.

Even at Shrinkspace speeds, it takes approximately one standard year, with the above method, to travel back 250,000 years in time. Therefore to travel back, say to the age of the dinosaurs, would take centuries. This is why the Draconians have the strategic advantage in regards to Chronophysical Warfare.

The only solution is at yet only a theory to Arcturian and Draconian science, which has created a "Chronophysical arms race" to find this solution. The theory goes that if Draconium is exposed to very cold temperatures, i.e. the temperature created when space is *expanded*, the atoms in Draconium, snap-frozen at temperatures thousands of times below Absolute Zero, then an extremely atomically volatile element is created. Made of sub-atomic particles that are thousands of times more vigorous than any matter known to science, it would theoretically be violent enough to cut the very fabric of time and space, allowing the formation of wormholes, and boundless access to time and space. Whichever side of the arms race found this substance would virtually secure their victory in a Chronophysical method of warfare. This substance has been coined **Andromedium**, because it would resemble the matter found inside Andromedan Hyper-Sentients.

Appendix x:
Yngkazhian Indigenous life

Yngkazh is the only known planet in the galaxy with completely indigenous extraterrestial life. No Terran origins whatsover. Is the holy grail of Parapaleontologists everywhere.

Yngkazh is a large siamese planet, two planets having collided slowly and semi-assimilated billions of years ago whilst still hot. Resembles an inverted figure eight. This causes dynamic forces of gravity (varies from 8.0N/kg to 11.7 N/kg) as it rotates and orbits around its star.

Has an acidic climate with an atmosphere of mostly nitrogen, hydrogen and sulphur, with very little oxygen. Smooth rocky, surface, almost as consistent as man-made asphalt. Constant sulphuric acid rainfall. Over 700 seasons per year (1.18 Terran years) due to its wobbly orbit.

Water is sulphurous and has about the same pH as battery acid. Most water accumulates in the equatorial cavity between the two planets. The water is highly conductive and stores vast amounts of electricity for months without needing to be charged by electrical monsoons.

Hence, calcium is non-existent there.

All microscopic life anaerobic and thus complicated life comprised of cells with no nucleus. The ocean formed in the equatorial cavity is home to relatively giant (about 20mm) amoeba--like plankton and the giant slug-like animals that form a similar niche to whales.

The land is two large deserts with only complex life forms, with a non-linear food chain, similar to rock/paper/scissors.

Umbrella Fungi – Channel acid rain into its roots and harvests water, sulphur, electricity. Preyed on by Mastodons, but incubates and gestates its offspring inside a Maglev, eventually killing it. Around fifteen feet tall. Green and beige coloured.

Wheeled Mastodons – are the only lifeforms, known to all science, to evolve a rotating foot or leg, thus making a functioning wheel. Enables it to travel long distances on flat ground energy- efficiently. However, two legs provide locomotion. Elephant sized and dome shaped, slow moving. Beige and orange coloured.

Maglev Slugs – Prey upon Mastodons and glide using stored electricity, its bottom made of high concentration of iron, that repels against the planets' magnetic field once electrified, and protects the iron with a slimy, acid proof top. Moves over ten times faster than a mastodon.

Crocodile sized. Purple-pink coloured, and resembles a flying rug or blanket.

NB: all complex life have no sense of sight, smell, or hearing, and rely on magnetic displacement in which to feel. Camouflage is essentially redundant.